Advance]

"The best hard SF I've read in years!"—Laurell K. Hamilton, author of the NYT bestselling Anita Blake vampire hunter series

"Big ideas, politics, aliens and ethical dilemmas—in the third volume of his SECANTIS SEQUENCE, Mark Tiedemann continues to build meticulously working worlds and populate them with interesting, complex people."—Nicola Griffith, author of *Slow River*

"Mark Tiedemann's The Secantis Sequence takes place in a richly complex, somewhat Asimovian elsewhen, illuminated by the occasional gem of image and concept reminiscent of Delany's space opera days. Peace and Memory demonstrates why visits to the Secant will be on a lot of to-do lists over the coming years. Mark has an eye for the telling detail and manages to infuse his work with a resonant and distinctive voice. My suggestion is to try his work sooner rather than later."— Steve Miller, co-author of the award-winning Liaden Universe® series

"The Secantis Sequence is broad-reaching future history, complete with politics and pop culture, conflict and cooperation, and the kind of cultural stew that convinces the reader that humans were here. But Mark Tiedemann never forgets that history is made from choice and consequence—from the desires, mistakes, fear and courage of individual people. The Secantis stories are full of real people making compelling history"—Kelley Eskridge, author of *Solitaire*

"The galactic empire is a cornerstone of SF, and Mark Tiedemann's SECANTIS SEQUENCE boldly opens a new chapter in that grand tradition, his Pan Humana Empire every bit as complex and multifaceted as the characters populating it.

"Like a statue being revealed bit by bit with each blow of the chisel, every new world explored and character introduced reveals more of the rich tapestry of Secantis, answering the old questions, but always uncovering new mysteries. *Peace and Memory* continues the tale, asking the questions 'how can a fragmented empire and a fragmented memory be healed, or should they?' In the tradition of Asimov's *Foundation*, and echoing with the complexity and intrigue Herbert's *Dune*, *Peace and Memory* is not to be missed."—Robert A. Metzger, author of *Picoverse*

Praise for the prior titles in
Mark W. Tiedemann's
The Secantis Sequence

For the Philip K. Dick Award nominee
Compass Reach

"*Compass Reach* is space opera for those who've outgrown starship battles and phoney heroics. Complex, mysterious and engaging, it's reminiscent of the early work of Samuel R. Delany. Mark Tiedemann is a fine writer, and this novel proves that he's of the best new SF authors on the scene today."
—Allen Steele

"*Compass Reach* is a rousing, inventive, far-future adventure by one of the most distinctive new voices in the field."
—Jack McDevitt

"A vivid and unexpected view of the underbelly of interstellar society.Mark Tiedemann writes with an engaging energy, gritty realism, and a genuineconcern for his characters. Here's a new writer worth watching!"—Jeffrey Carver

Metal of Night

"Mark Tiedemann's first two "Secantis Sequence" novels—*Compass Reach* and *Metal of Night*—are enjoyable reads for a number of reasons. For one, they are related novels that stand completely on their own: you don't have to read one to enjoy the other, though certainly they enrich one another. More important, however, they are novels that focus on character. They contain all the tropes of space opera—the far future, intragalactic human civilization, military expeditions, alien cultures, FTL space travel—and all the of the excitement and entertainment that those things provide. But what really makes the books connect with the reader is that, at the core, the books are about people, and about the real impacts that war and politics and social/cultural/economic clashes have on individuals. Ordinary people—caught up in extraordinary events, perhaps, but people we can relate to. That's what makes these books work, and I eagerly anticipate the next book in the sequence...and the next...and other books Mark Tiedemann will write inthefuture."—Richard Russo

"The second novel in Tiedemann's Secantis Sequence series is convincing military science fiction with an emphasis on the human costs of war.

"Although this is a standalone novel, Tiedemann builds successfully on the background established in his first Secantis novel, *Compass Reach* (a Philip K. Dick Award nominee), to create a highly believable historical background and political system, weaving the experiences of various characters together in a fast-paced story that never loses its emotional focus on the effects of war on the people involved." —Amazon.com

"In *Metal of Night*, Mark Tiedemann returns to the universe he created in the first volume of the Secantis Sequence—his PKD-nominated novel *Compass Reach*. *Metal of Night* starts out as straightforward military SF, but quickly expands into a complex, intelligent and engaging epic involving journalists, spies, soldiers, and capitalists—with the enigmatic "setis" lurking in the background. The term "space opera" is appropriate, but a bit deceptive. Tiedemann's Secantis Sequence continues in the tradition of science fiction's great literary epics, with a scope and scale reminiscent of the TV triumph "Babylon 5". Tiedemann explores the Big Picture, but he also gives us a solid look at how individual players react when their worlds and beliefs are turned upside down.

"*Compass Reach* and *Metal of Night* only scratch the surface of the richly imagined universe of the Pan Humana. Mark Tiedemann is well on his way to solidifying a reputation as one of science fiction's great world-builders."—John Snider, www.scifidimensions.com

"Mark Tiedemann is to be congratulated for choosing a mosaic approach to his future history, rather than endlessly milking the same cast of characters and situations.

"It's a very lived-in future, full of battered, obsolete ships and colonial towns that never quite succeeded and family farms where tradition rules and abandoned alien monuments. Tiedemann succeeds in making us believe that this show has been up and running for generations, not just some stage set constructed minutes ago. And his characters inhabit this landscape authentically. Cira's conflicts about the clash between her family's expectations and her own desires is a genuine result of all the factors Tiedemann establishes. Maxwell Cambion's ambitions for himself and his real son, Nicolan, also spring from the soil of Finders in organic fashion.

"Tiedemann also deserves credit for his unconventional attitude toward space war. As introducer Jack McDevitt mentions, the author is not one to glorify or dwell on crashing space battles. The initial assault on Finders lasts five minutes and ends ingloriously for the Armada. On the planet, the civilian social turbulence and firefights are presented as brutal, confusing incidents where all Cira and her new friends can do is scramble to stay alive. (A graduate of Clarion, having studied under Chip Delany, among others, Tiedemann's portrayal of civilization's breakdown resembles early Delany work such as *The Fall of the Towers* [originally 1963-65].) All in all, Tiedemann captures the futility and wastefulness of war more in the manner of Joseph Heller than of David Drake and others. Given this, there are still affinities with the work of, say, C.J. Cherryh and William Barton."—Paul Di Fillipo

"Mark Tiedemann's *Metal of Night* opens with a major space battle, but quickly settles down into a story of refugees and rebels, perhaps. Nothing in *Metal of Night* is as clear-cut as Tiedemann initially posits, and the reader can't be sure of where any of the characters stand or even what the situation is. He is careful about only revealing a certain amount, but even that, the reader quickly learns, should be read with suspicion.

"Each of the characters in *Metal of Night* share an Heinleinian competence with each other. This increases the satisfaction of the novel because when they act in opposition to each other, as often happens, all the characters act with intelligence. Furthermore, each has a multitude of motives for their actions which helps flesh them out. In his introduction to the novel, Jack McDevitt laments the two-dimensionality of too many space opera villains, but he is correct in stating that Tiedemann's villains do not suffer from that problem. Even the psychopath McDevitt mentions is given his complexities, which are many, given his initial state as a self-declared quadruple agent.

"The complexity of Tiedemann's situation is such that the reader does not continue to turn the pages in order to find out what will happen, but rather in hopes of finding an explanation for what has happened. Characters are recovering from wounds or trying to figure out what to do with their lives after they have become uprooted from their understanding of the world.

"Despite all the complexities of plot and character, Tiedemann manages to weave his story without sowing confusion among his readers. Information is revealed at a pace which allows the reader to process it and form a more complete picture of what the situation may actually be, while acknowledging that what the situation is may be based on point of view. Even if Tiedemann doesn't provide all the answers in the end, he provides enough to sate the reader's curiosity while still leaving the reader wanting to follow possible future events in this multifaceted universe.

"*Metal of Night* is a fast-paced story with heroes and villains as flexible as the situation in which they find themselves. While nobody, not even the viewpoint characters, are what they seem, the slow revelation of their real personalities and objectives keeps the reader's interest as Tiedemann continues to peel back layers until he reveals the core of the story."
—Steven H. Silver, www.sfsite.com

PEACE AND MEMORY

VOLUME THREE OF THE
SECANTIS SEQUENCE

BY

MARK W. TIEDEMANN

Meisha Merlin Publishing, Inc.
Atlanta, GA

PEACE AND MEMORY

Published by Meisha Merlin Publishing, Inc.
PO Box 7
Decatur, GA 30031

Editing & interior layout by Stephen Pagel
Copyediting & proofreading by Teddi Stransky
Cover art by O. B. Solinsky
Cover design by Kevin Murphy

ISBN: Soft Cover   1-890065-96-7

http//www.MeishaMerlin.com

First MM Publishing edition: June 2003

Printed in the United States of America
0 9 8 7 6 5 4 3 2 1

Dedication:

This novel about friendship is dedicated to three of the
best and longest of my life
Jim, Tom, and Greg.

And to the truest friend I've ever found
Donna.

Introduction to *PEACE AND MEMORY*
by
James Morrow

Every epoch has its courtiers and sycophants, always standing ready to assure the naked emperor that he is stunningly arrayed. In the present day, these blandishments sometimes entail a critique of reason per se: rest assured, my Lord, that Western rationality is a dead end. The argument takes many forms, from the New Age fantasies of middle-class mystics, to the hot-eyed hatred of Charles Darwin fomented by religious conservatives, to the cavalier dismissal of the 18th-century Enlightenment perpetrated by postmodernism's prolix apostles. At their best, the naked emperor's courtiers are highly articulate and persuasive—so articulate and persuasive, in fact, that they can occasionally make a scientific humanist like myself begin to doubt his sanity.

In May of 2001 the admirable mind of Mark Tiedemann rescued my sanity from a particularly aggressive onslaught of postmodern hyper-relativism. The setting was the Kansas City SF Convention known as ConQuest, at which I was the Guest of Honor. During a Friday night party I ended up in conversation with a passionate philosophy student whose worldview managed to embrace all three assaults on the Enlightenment—the mystical, the theistic, and the deconstructionist—simultaneously: once you open your heart to God and Derrida, this earnest young man seemed to be saying, you will see that science is at base an ideology, a faith system, a "narrative," and not a very nourishing one at that. But then suddenly this guy named Mark Tiedemann, whom I'd never met before, appeared at my side and began arguing persuasively that science and reason in fact have far more going for them than is dreamt in either revealed religion or postmodern nihilism.

Throughout this performance Tiedemann displayed great aplomb, considerable wit, and an enviable armchair knowledge of Western philosophy. He listened to the student's arguments with patience and politeness. I don't think Tiedemann turned the young man's thinking around that night—why should you heed a mere science-fiction writer when you're paying thousands of dollars in tuition money to be miseducated by college professors?—but I, for one, came away certain that any future conversations I might have with Tiedemann would be valuable encounters indeed. Here was a fellow who loved talking about ideas as much as I did, and who also had the sort of vulnerability that separates the true thinker from the intellectual bully. I wanted to hear more of what he had to say—and to read what he'd put on paper in the form of fiction.

It is perhaps no accident that the book most commonly cited as the greatest work of philosophy ever written, Plato's Republic, draws its energy as much from political speculation as from its rarefied and exquisite considerations of the Good. The joys of abstraction are palpable, but at some point we want to know how any philosophical system will play out in the arena of actuality—the real world of mutually incompatible human ambitions.

Given this natural reciprocity between philosophy and politics, I was not surprised to find in Tiedemann's Secantis Sequence an idea-driven epic centered around the question that Phil Klass—the "William Tenn" who wrote so many 1950's classics of satiric short sf—regards as central to our genre: How, then, shall we live? You hold in your hands the third Secantis book, *Peace and Memory*, a novel that treats the problem of meaningful and purposeful living with a seriousness not normally on display in this variety of sweeping, fast-paced space opera. Upon finishing *Peace and Memory*, which can be enjoyed quite independently of *Compass Reach* and *Metal of Night*, I found myself pondering an earlier tour de force of world-building, Frank Herbert's *Dune*—a novel that, for all its narrative drive, vivid vistas, and magisterial sense of wonder, offers only the most retrograde response to the Klass conundrum. How, then, shall we live? As cheerful cogs in a caste system retrofitted to a demented neo-feudalism, the whole thing made marginally palatable via eschatology and hallucinogenic worm-dung? Such is the only answer I can glean from Herbert's swollen opus—an answer for which, I surmise, Tiedemann would never settle.

Where Dune gives us vacuous boy messiahs, demonic barons, off-the-shelf storm troopers, and eros-forsaken Wiccan nuns, *Peace and Memory* offers up characters whose most salient trait is their utter humanness. To be sure, Tamyn Glass, Benajim Cyanus, Sean Merrick's persona, and the rest of the cast boast remarkable natural gifts (and in some cases technological augmentation), but we never cease to recognize our own inner turmoil in theirs. Even the aliens—Tiedemann's "seti"—register as wholly sentient creatures with fully developed psyches.

Although the escapades of Tamyn and Benajim are ultimately informed by political idealism, Tiedemann does not presume to offer us a blueprint for a perfect society. To be sure, there is a utopian concept at the center of the novel—the idea that a corporation should never outlive its founder—but the author's agenda remains fundamentally humanistic. All during my reading, I kept thinking of Lewis Mumford's *The Pentagon of Power*, in which he offers a cogent and devastating critique of the utopian impulse, whether it takes the form of Plato's benign monarchy, Augustine's *City of God*, More's collectivist paradise, or Marx's dictatorship of the proletariat. "On the surface," writes Mumford in his chapter on science-fiction literature, "the concept of utopia implied just the opposite of progress: once perfection was achieved, utopian authors saw no need of further change ... Thus the ideal society would operate like a well-oiled machine, under the guidance of a collective dictatorship. The behavioral adaptations of the social ants and bees have demonstrated that such a mechanized collective is actually within the realm of organic possibility."

Well aware of this pitfall, Tiedemann has elected to present not a static utopia of human insects but a benign and dynamic civilization called the Commonwealth Republic—I suspect the echo of Plato is deliberate—recently split off from a calcified and decadent Pan Humana, a schism foreshadowed in *Compass Reach* and actualized in *Metal of Night*. In *Peace and Memory* you will experience these two compelling and complementary worlds via a grand interstellar adventure evocative of Cordwainer Smith, reminiscent of Leigh Brackett, and worthy of Robert Heinlein. It is a journey you are certain to enjoy, and I shall delay your embarkation no longer.

James Morrow
State College PA
March 2003

Why "Sequence"?
by
Mark W. Tiedemann

Labels are two-edged instruments—useful and deceptive simultaneously. We live by categories but reject their implied limitations,
and rightly so. Labels might provide a useful starting point in understanding something—or someone—but it's all too easy to forget (or
never know) that a label doesn't come close to exhausting the content of what it describes, nor does it set any kind of natural limit on
where something—or someone—can go.

As long as labels are descriptive rather than proscriptive, they're
useful. But they tend to become a shortcut in aid of taste, a cheat, a
passive—but powerful—arbiter of aesthetic choice. They begin
doing what titles ought rightly to do—suggest actual content.

Content itself is a tricky concept. What does the work contain? Will one reader actually recognize the same contents as another? The title is there to give entry to the aesthetic potential of the
story, maybe suggest something about the concerns of the story, but
it's not possible for the words on the cover to tell us what is actually
in the story. What does *Gone With the Wind* actually say about what is
in the book? Or *Wuthering Heights?* Or *The Stars My Destination?* At
best, a title becomes, after reading the work, a handy mnemonic by
which memories of the reading experience trigger.

But a category label?

Science Fiction Contained Here.

And what does that actually mean? That any ten, five, or even
two SF novels are so much the same that you know by virtue of the
label that the reading experience will be the same (and therefore
don't waste your time...)?

Does *The Left Hand of Darkness* actually share anything remotely
in common with *Ringworld?* Or *The Demolished Man* with *Triplanetary?*
Would you expect an identical experience with *The Female Man* after
having read *The Space Merchants?* Are the Galaxies of Asimov's *Foundation* stories and Banks' *Culture* stories the same place?

Likewise the more general labels you run into with large works.
Trilogies, Dekologies, Series, Sequels, Prequels, Spin-offs, and the

like. Some, when precisely used, do describe something distinct.
"Trilogy" goes back to the ancient Greek and describes three trag-
edies on a connected subject. It has come down to us fairly intact—
any group of three works about more or less the same subject. Of
course, very often now we have trilogies about the same people but
dealing with distinct themes in each book, so the drama is not so
much connected as the *dramatis personae*. A series is a group of works
featuring the same characters or set in the same locations. Trilogies
and quartets are specific kinds of series. (A series can also be a
publishing format—books on mathematics, say, by different authors, but done in uniform volumes.)

What about a Sequence?

Well, generally the term is used to describe poetry united by a
single theme, containing similar or related elements.

I've chosen to call these stories, beginning with *Compass Reach*
and *Metal of Night* now continuing with *Peace and Memory*, a sequence.
The background is similar, the politics connected, but I intend each
work to be readable in isolation from the rest. Nevertheless, they
are related by a set of common themes, questions, interests. So far
only one character appears twice, the settings of the stories are different, and the point of departure in each is unique. Over time, they
will construct a common tapestry.

But I most specifically wanted to write them in such a way that
no one will be forced to buy and read the rest in order to understand any given volume. Or short story. (Yes, there are a number
of short stories in the Sequence; eventually they will be collected.) I
wanted to be able to present a richer examination of this universe
with each additional volume.

I didn't want anyone trapped—or locked out—by a label that
obligated them to do more than what they wanted or kept them
from reading any of it at all for fear of being required to commit to
other books. It is not a trilogy—you don't have to read three books.
There are no direct sequels or prequels—you don't have to hunt the
previous volume down or wait impatiently for the next in order to
get the entire story.

Unless the entire story you become interested in is the overall
universe in which these tales take place.

The Secantis Sequence is a history. It has a shape and a backstory
and a direction—several, in fact. But like real history, the stories

about the people—or the aliens—do not require that you know all of history to understand.

So it is both a title and a label, but only in the most limited sense—a name to remember, a point on a map, a destination. It doesn't describe what is within the story, only a placemarker where you can find a story, in this case a particular kind.

But what kind? I leave that for the reader to decide.

PEACE AND MEMORY

VOLUME THREE OF THE
SECANTIS SEQUENCE

BY

MARK W. TIEDEMANN

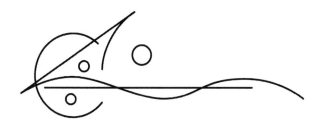

Prologue

The thief stepped off the shuttle and joined the flow of traffic surging within the body of the station. Human, seti, robot-motile, all pushed through the circuits like blood, the station's anima. The thief felt anxious in the presence of so much life, as if he could sense the latent death in all of it.

He walked along a main circuit, his attention shifting from person to person, human to seti, arcade to shop. He avoided the touchpads spaced evenly along the walls between facilities; people brushed them with fingertips, drawing information directly from the station's dataflow through the interface gates. The station knew them all, and gave freely of itself. He felt like an imposter among them, a mimic who had the act down pat and could even fool himself most of the time.

Not long now, he thought, *I should be out of here and I won't have to worry about it. At least, not until I encounter more of you...*

Nervously, he stopped in a shop near a shunt terminus to buy clothes, toiletries, and an assortment of book and vid disks. He did not need any of it, but he decided to test his identity once more, before he reached his target. He touched the milky surface of the shop's interface with his fingertips. The unsheathed polyceramo caps clicked lightly. The gate read his code, charged the purchases to the account indicated—

—and he waited for an alarm, a warning, an indication that he was being sought. He looked up at the shopkeeper and smiled. Nothing happened. The transaction concluded and he was still free.

He placed the purchases in his bindle and headed for a shunt. He felt relief, certainly, but it was troubling, too. The authorities should know by now; the death discovered, the data spread throughout the Flow. The thief must be found and detained. After all, he had stolen a life.

He boarded a single-passenger shunt and pressed his fingers against the interface gate. He issued commands, waited, his consciousness half-immersed in the data continuum. Surely his next destination would trip an alarm.

The shunt began to move.

He settled back for the ride, pulse coming quicker. Joss should be used when available, no point questioning good fortune. Time for assessments later, if all went as planned. He concentrated on his task, on thinking about what was necessary, blocking everything else.

It bothered him a little that he could not quite remember his name...

The shunt wound a path through the enormous meandering volume of the station. It slowed, stopped, and the door unsealed.

At the end of a short corridor, the walls stretched up into a high, pointed arch. An inscription on the polished floor read SEAN MERRICK HERITAGE MUSEUM. A plaque set in the wall by the entrance said "Maintained by the Merrick Historical Foundation in cooperation with the Board of Regents of the Commonwealth Republic." The thief stepped over the letters in the floor, into the softly-lit apse.

It was nightcycle in this section. Only one person tended the information desk, and he was absorbed in something on a monitor the thief could not see. The thief walked up and waited.

"Oh," the attendant was startled. "I didn't..." he began, then stopped and frowned. "Ah, we aren't open at the moment..."

The thief pressed his fingers to the gate on the desk. The attendant glanced at a screen, frowned deeper, then shrugged.

"Oh. Very good, co. Go right ahead." He pressed a contact and the main access to the galleries opened to the thief's left.

"Thanks, co."

The attendant forced a smile. "We don't get many visitors from the board of directors..."

"And you didn't this time," the thief said. "This is a private visit."

"Ah. Of course, co. Sorry." The attendant touched his own gate, then smiled at the thief. "Filed confidential, restricted access."

"Thanks."

Good enough, the thief thought as he strode through the access, amazed he had gotten this far. By the time anyone with the proper authority dug the record out, events would be too far along to stop.

He had left behind a body. A corpse. An old, horribly rich invalid whose existence persisted only through the use of the vampiric technologies of life support—and the thief had switched it all off. Well, not quite that simple, but...

On either side of the aisle, display cases stood, filled with memorabilia, objects that had something to do with the early days of the Republic and the part played in them by Sean Merrick. The thief wondered at the need to gaze on the discards of a life once its owner became famous. Or infamous, depending who you asked. Old clothes, journals, the tableware once used, odd artifacts from strange places. He walked through the section housing all the bits and bobbles from the seti realms, the nonhuman spaces, that the man had brought back from his explorations. This was more interesting, something that indicated the flavor of the Republic, what had separated it from the staid, tired, xenophobic first empire of humanity.

He wondered what that first empire was like now. Maybe he would find out.

At the end of the long winding path through the various rooms, displays, library booths, and detritus he came to a circular chamber. In the center hovered a model of a ship.

The thief studied it: curiously aquatic, smooth surfaced, swept-back lines from a central spine, a dark hull that nevertheless caught light, shattered it into a hundred fragments, jeweling the ship.

Below the model was a hatch in the floor.

The thief dropped his bindle beside it and stretched his hand toward the gate set in the center of the hatch. He licked his dry lips. If an alarm was ever going to sound, this would do it. But he was not afraid of that. He was afraid the hatch would simply refuse to recognize him, and remain closed.

He touched it.

The hatch hesitated. Perhaps it had been so long since anyone had activated it that it could not quite believe it. Perhaps the ID code it scanned was—

It unsealed and slid open. The thief laughed sharply, once. He dropped the bindle down the shaft and followed.

He lowered himself into the lock of the ship and stood there. Lights had come on when he entered. The sepulchral stillness embraced him, made him tingle with the awareness that he was an intruder here. The ship waited. The thief felt its attention, ready to judge him by his next actions.

He had been briefed, he knew what to look for, what to expect. Still, it was unreal to him that he actually stood here, where no one was ever intended to stand again.

The air smelled freshly recycled...

"Hello," he said quietly. "I'm here to free you."

The opposite hatch opened. The thief started, then laughed. He grabbed his bindle and walked through.

He made his way to the end of the passage, into the huge common room. Aft, he knew, were individual cabins, the engine room, access to a lower deck. He headed forward.

The deck angled up through the arched connecting corridor. As he reached the top he stood just within the bridge. Equipment jammed the bulkheads. Couches faced collections of components, ready lights shining steadily indicating systems already coming on-line.

Opposite the entryway, two command couches faced a hulking array of monitors and control panels.

He went to a small booth to starboard and sat down. It was a simple station-gate set in the arms of the couch, a flat surface like a desk top in front of him, readouts above, and a slot in the base of the panel. From within his jacket he pulled out a hard case containing two shiny gold disks, very old-style encoding medium. He lifted one disk from the case. The other was for delivery to...someone...he could not quite remember just now...

He slid the disk into the slot.

The air above the flat surface roiled momentarily, wisps of color that tried and failed to coalesce.

"Please link," a voice requested.

The thief set his fingertips—both hands—on the gates in the couch arms.

Only a second. Less. He felt a shift of perspective, a brief vertigo, and then he was out of the link, staring around him.

The occlusive persona overlay was gone.

Amnesia dissipated and memory returned.

He remembered.

Everything.

His eyes burned. He rubbed at them, at the sudden tears.

"Welcome aboard, Benajim Cyanus," the voice said. It sounded much more human now, and familiar.

"Sean...?"

"Instead of wondering about it, let's get us the hell out of here, shall we?"

Benajim—so good to know his name again, to feel it's truth—laughed, wiped at his eyes, and went to the command couch. He sat down and rubbed his hands along the arms, touched the console before him.

"You can stroke things later," the ship said.

Benajim looked up. "You are—"

"I'm *Solo*. And it's been too damn long. Shall we?"

More monitors came up, the bridge suddenly alive with activity.

"We shall," Benajim said.

"Somebody is going to be really pissed off about this," *Solo* said.

Just before Benajim placed his fingertips on the command gates, he quickly inventoried his memory. He knew who he was, where he was going, and why he was doing it. He remembered the last five years and everything that had led to this moment. He remembered many things with marvelous clarity; other things remained murky, but it seemed he had recovered satisfactorily from the persona occlusion that had masked his true identity for the last few days, since he had switched off the life support and watched the old man fade into grateful death...

Time to leave.

He touched the gates and became one with the ship.

Chapter One

Tamyn Glass felt her dreams fade, like old memories. Eyes still closed, she tried to hold the fragmenting images, fix them in place a few moments more. The familiar parts lingered longest—images of her ship and crew—but mutated as she recognized bits of other ships, faces of crew members long gone. She slitted open her eyes. Silvery light patterned the darkness with a shifting graininess. The dreams vanished. Tamyn sat up in the austere space, blinking at the morning light filling the curtained doorway.

A small statue stood against the opposite wall, watching her from oversized, blind eyes. Neckless, constantly vigilant, the wide head sat on a featureless column of grey-white stone, a gift from her Pronan hosts.

Tamyn stretched slowly, working her muscles. She stood and extended her arms upward, reaching, pushing herself up onto her toes. She drew a lung full of air—it smelled slightly burnt, but sweet—and let it out slowly. The odd aroma made her wonder if her bioaug was working properly. She opened a portable toilet and went through her ablutions, then did a blood chemistry. She dressed while she waited for the numbers to come up. The small device gave her all positives.

Relieved, Tamyn switched on her multilink and touched one finger to the gate, a small square panel in the center of the pad. The link ran through the polyceramo cap on her fingertip, up the trail of fibers into the mesh permeating her cortex. The imaged space in her mind occluded the room around her. She perceived a honeycomb of data points, each one a path to a different source of information. Several glowed warmly. She accessed the nearest.

Good morning, cohabitants, friends, fellow sojourners.

Good morning, Tam. I thought you were going to sleep the day away.

Clif? Where's Joclen? Stoan?

Off with Co Dover's research team. They left me tending all the details.

Well, tell them I checked in and tell them I expect an answer from Hrer M'San today, maybe this morning.

About time.

Developing an itch?

Laughter colored the link with bright splashes of yellow and blue. Tamyn signed off and took her finger away. The honeycomb winked out of existence.

Tamyn zipped her utilities and pulled on her boots. She washed a nutritab down with a cup of water from her canteen, enduring the bitter aftertaste. It would be good to have a real meal again. Few native foods were human-digestible, and of those that were, both taste and nutrition differed from human requirements. She had spent several days among the Pronans, living on local diet and supplements.

She pushed through the gauzy curtain covering the arched entry and stepped outside.

Morning sunlight fired streaks of clouds orange against the pale violet sky. Her hut was one of thirty of various sizes, centered on a large central pavilion, clustered together within a low wall. Tamyn wound her way between the truncated structures to the perimeter of the compound.

Beyond the wall, the paved walkway led down a gentle slope and forked sharply right and left, bordering the vast fields filled with rippling stands of silvery stalks. Light chased through the plants in shifting waves. Far to the east, foothills huddled against dark cliffs that rose up to meet the clouds gathered along the crest. Light reflecting from the fields danced across the rock.

Pron's beauty worked on her; the light especially, almost liquid in the way it flowed across the landscape. Surrounded by the barrier cliffs, it seemed at once so vast and self-contained. She would miss it.

Tamyn barely heard the stalks singing, a gentle whispering that teased at her awareness. She sometimes found herself listening for hours at a stretch, transfixed by the slowly changing patterns of tones. The sound altered gradually over the course of the day; Co Dover's people speculated that it had to do with temperature and humidity, but the process remained unknown.

Tamyn leaned her elbows on the outer wall and watched the Pronans scattered through the fields. They began harvest before sunrise, every day, and worked till a few hours before sunset. No machines, no tools, the stalk picked by hand over the two month harvest season. They moved slowly, methodically.

Even while she enjoyed the scene, the beauty, the peace, she felt restless. She glanced skyward often, watching for other ships. The legality of this visit was questionable and the possibility of discovery kept her from surrendering to the idyllic tranquility of Pron.

She began to straighten when something off to her left snagged her attention. A Pronan sat against the outside of the wall, gazing at the fields. She had never seen a Pronan unoccupied this early in the day.

A shuffling sound caught her ear, and she turned to see another Pronan approaching her, moving with its characteristic wobble.

"You see now," Hrer M'San greeted her, speaking a lilting form of Rahalen, one of the common languages of the Reaches. The lattice at Hrer's throat vibrated. Moist eyes reflected the light in sweeping arcs. Its honey-colored skin possessed the texture of fine linen.

"And hear as well," Tamyn returned in the same tongue, aware of her harsher enunciation. She stepped toward the Pronan, away from the wall.

"Was your interlude productive?"

"My mind worked on many things, Co M'San." Pronans did not seem to grasp that humans simply slept to compensate for accrued weariness. They meditated, letting their minds play with what Tamyn thought of as philosophy. They had been slightly dismayed at the length of sleep time humans required. Finally, they had decided that dreams counted as a form of meditation—which raised Tamyn in their estimation as a profound thinker. "And your own?" she asked.

Hrer M'San moved closer. "I have come to a conclusion. You will be interested."

Tamyn felt a surge of excitement. "Regarding what I have discussed with you these past days?"

"Yes. I have concluded that you, Tamyn Glass, grasp details of our nature. So I can say to you with some certainty that you will understand that I do not share your concept of trade."

"But—"

"But I do have *a* concept of trade. Perhaps it will suffice. It will not make a perfect whole with yours."

Tamyn nodded slowly, controlling herself. "What do you propose?"

"I propose you give us nothing except who you are."

Tamyn waited. When HRer remained silent, she said, "I'm not sure I understand, Co M'San."

"It is doubtful you have any object which we will find useful. But I have informed others of your eclectic nature, shown companions your language, and they see how interesting you are."

"Me personally or humans as a whole?"

Hrer M'San's eyes shimmered, a sign, Tamyn had learned, of amusement. "Are humans a whole? You are of many parts, but the cumulative may be more, don't you think?"

"Or less, depending on who you ask."

"As with us, certainly. But I did mean humans as a species. Tamyn Glass has other places to go. It would not be reasonable to expect her to stay."

"Not that I wouldn't like to. I have discovered much of value here."

"What?"

"Friendship."

Hrer M'San looked out over the fields and was silent for a long time. Then: "I am honored." The Pronan turned toward her again, eyes dancing, and added, "That is trade we understand. My home will always welcome you, even after my dissolution."

"I hope that will be a long time off."

"I have no sign that I will be rejected soon. You may hope in certainty."

When Hrer M'San said no more, she drew a breath and said, "So how may we proceed? I've explained to you what we wish."

A limb snaked out from a slit in the robe and pointed at the field. "I have instructed Nesh K'San to deliver this day's pick for you. In return, I wish a representative left behind. Perhaps a pair. That is the nature of your people. Representatives and the resources for them to explain your culture."

Ah, Tamyn thought, that's more tangible...

Tamyn figured quickly how much distillate could be derived from one day's pick of the stalks. Its therapeutic effects on aging were priceless and till now the sources had always been through seti intermediaries. That much would make all the risks worthwhile, underwrite the entire expedition, more. It had been a long time since Tamyn had gambled at this level—a long time undoing the consequences of a less cautious youth.

Leaving someone behind, though...

"I would have to ask for volunteers," she said carefully. "No one may wish to. As beautiful as Pron is, none of us may be willing to part from the rest."

"If not now then another time. You will be back."

Tamyn did not want to disappoint Hrer M'San, but she could not promise another visit. There's a way to work it, she thought. Take what you have and be glad.

"I'll see what I can do," she said.

"Then we have concluded business?" Hrer M'San asked.

"I believe so."

"Good. Then the balance of your stay will be undisturbed by outside considerations. You will enjoy."

"Yes," Tamyn said. "Yes, I will enjoy."

Hrer M'San moved away. Tamyn watched the Pronan reenter the compound. Then she turned back to the fields, letting her enthusiasm take her. One day's pick! Automatically, she scanned the sky. Empty. Time to get ready to leave before reality had a chance to tangle her up.

The other Pronan still sat by the wall, watching the fields.

Curious, Tamyn moved closer. Still several steps away she recognized this one. Rith M'San. For some reason, Tamyn identified Rith as female. Rith was stouter than most of the others—and old. There was a delicate desiccation to her skin that few of the others possessed and she moved more slowly, carefully.

Rith seemed rapt, gazing out over the fields. She was so intent that Tamyn felt reluctant to intrude. Rith's large eyes were moist and filled with light. Tamyn shuddered for a moment. She had seen that look before. Silly, she thought, I must be projecting—this is a different race. How could death look the same?

She gunned the hover down the earthen track at a fast clip, toward the foothills. Tamyn felt exhilarated. So far this had been *Wicca's* most profitable venture. Not halfway through the itinerary of worlds planned for this sojourn and Tamyn was well into the black. All they had to do now was collect their cargo and leave before their luck changed.

The road rose into the hills. Out here, the wild flora had more copper and bronze hues, but there were dozens of colors in thick pockets. Deep blue, periwinkle, amber, scarlet. Pron was a world of bright splashes amid stretches of sameness. The orange sun headed toward midday and the temperature was rising. Tamyn looked forward to the cooler heights of the breastworks. Just before the hills met the base of the cliffs the road began to turn right, back toward the compound. Tamyn engaged the remaining agravs and took the craft straight up the wall of rock. As she entered the lower clouds the temperature began to fall perceptibly. Tamyn closed the canopy. Sunlight strobed as she flew in and out of denser and denser patches of cloud. Her sensors told her when she crested the rock. She leveled out and followed the path of stone. Finally, she broke out of the clouds. Ahead stretched the wide ridge, jagged with age and shifting stresses. She flew north. On her right lay the island-continent, on her left the ocean.

Three hundred days into this sojourn and she had seen four new worlds. Each had been a puzzle, a unique configuration of possibilities, impossible to comprehend in a lifetime let alone a short mercantile visit. But the impressions each left on Tamyn were profound and permanent. Two of them had never before been visited by humans. Pron was one, a world existing in the cracks between civilizations...

Soon she saw the beacons that marked the landing site. Then, as wisps of cloud moved away, the squat shape of the shuttle appeared, perched on the ridge, the clutter of the research camp scattered around it. Tamyn slowed, then began cutting out the agravs one by one, letting the craft settle gently.

The hover touched down and Tamyn shut off the power and stepped out.

She crossed the ground in long, energetic strides. Two people left the huddle gathered around one of the big field consoles and came toward her.

Stoan, her exec, was an Alcyoni Transmorph, short and stocky, his head entirely hairless, and his eyes the color of lead. Joclen, her chief pilot, was a few centimeters taller and a couple of kilos heavier than Tamyn, hair mahogany and thick. Human.

"Shipmaster," Stoan greeted her cheerfully. "Fine mist on a bright air, wet as hell." His head jerked around sharply and he grinned out at the ocean. Then he snapped his attention back to Tamyn.

"Stoan. Joclen." She kept walking toward the shuttle ramp. Stoan and Joclen fell into step on either side. Tamyn glanced toward the huddle. "Anything important?"

"Co Dover thinks he's discovered proof that the Pron once had an industrial culture," Joclen said. "He's been a pain in the ass since yesterday."

Tamyn grunted. "This is different in what way?"

Joclen chuckled. "Intensity."

"Good. Then he'll be occupied for a while. We need to talk uninterrupted." They reached the ramp. "We've got an arrangement with the Pronans."

"So fast," Joclen said wryly. Their stay was already days longer than expected.

"The Pronans move at their own pace," Tamyn said, "according to their own priorities. Whatever those may be."

She led them into the shuttle's cargo bay and forward. Tamyn climbed the ladder to the next level and went through the hatch into the cockpit. The door sealed and she turned to her officers.

"We have a deal," she said. "Not a bad one, but there might be a problem."

Stoan cocked his head to one side. "Conditions?"

"In exchange for today's pick from Hrer M'San's fields, we leave two 'volunteers' to serve as cultural representatives."

Joclen frowned. "That could be...I mean, what if they're found? We don't know how the Cursians will react."

"Or anybody else," Tamyn said. She sat in one of the rear couches. "Truth is, I didn't really expect the Coro data to be accurate. Close, maybe; the Coro won't ever outright lie; but I expected to have to do some trolling out here before we found Pron. Instead..." She waved a hand toward the canopy and the landscape beyond. Not only the correct coordinates, she mused, but the right time of their year as well.

"The Cursians have been our source for Pronan antiagathic compound for—"

"Forever," Tamyn finished, nodding. "And charging monopoly prices. But as far as we've known—as far as I've been able to find out—there's no treaty anywhere guaranteeing them sole right. And it's fairly obvious that Pron has been visited by more than just Cursians. They speak Rahalen and seem familiar with Menkan mysticism. They aren't spacefarers, so we have to assume they get regular guests. Maybe having visitors stay for a time is the way they do their exploring. Maybe it won't cause an incident." She looked up. "What would actually happen if a Cursian ship stopped here and found a couple of humans keeping company with the Pronans?"

"Ponderous fuming," Stoan said, "brittle words and indecorous pouting. Cursian reputation requires less action."

"But the Board of Regents and our judiciary might decide we've committed a crime," Joclen said.

Tamyn stared out the transparency, tapping an index finger anxiously against her chin.

"One day's pick," Joclen prompted. "That's a lot of Q."

"It would pay for the entire sojourn, even if we make nothing on the rest of our contracts," Tamyn said. "We've got what, two more university research teams on board?"

Stoan opened a handslate and swiftly entered a series of figures. After a moment he nodded and laughed sharply. "Yes. Among them, we have eight potential representatives on board. Shall I ask for volunteers?"

Tamyn drew a deep breath. "I'm thinking that if we get this load back and establish the route, the Q will dampen any awkward questions. What's done is done, no one will care."

"They'll only censure us if we fail," Joclen said. "Is that what you mean?"

Tamyn laughed.

"Volunteers?" Stoan asked.

"Soon as convenient. I want to be gone before anyone else shows up to ask us what we're doing."

Stoan nodded, turned, and left the cockpit.

"How do you get used to him?" Joclen asked, grinning.

"Stoan? You don't. You learn to like him or stay away. As Alcyoni go, he's not bad."

"What did he look like when you met him?"

"The same. He hasn't confided why he chose to look human." She shrugged. "His business." She got up and moved to the front of the cockpit, gazing out. In patches through the clouds she could see the quiltwork landscape of neighboring farms. Here and there at odd intervals rose towers that had something to do with the way the Pronans governed themselves—at least, on this island. The world was mostly ocean and the dozen big islands and most of the smaller ones were inhabited. Tamyn had not discovered if they possessed a unified governing body. Somewhere in the center of this island, too distant to see from here, was the one large city. She had not been there, either.

"I'll be glad to move on," Tamyn said.

"I don't know," Joclen said. "I like it here. They're gentle people. It's been pleasant."

"That's why I want to wrap it up and leave." She saw Joclen's puzzled expression. "I don't let any world hold me. I might come back—often—but I'll never stay."

Joclen shook her head. "And when you're too old for spacing?"

"Never." Tamyn straightened. "Let's get things started for departure. I want everything ready."

The comm chimed. Tamyn touched the contact. "Glass here."

"Sorry to disturb you, Shipmaster," a man said, "but I'd appreciate some time."

Tamyn glanced at Joclen, who whispered, "Dover."

"I'll be right out, Co Dover," Tamyn said, cutting the link. "I want you to start preparations for receiving the stalk."

"Already on it," Joclen said.

Tamyn went back outside. Colum Dover, head of one of the planetary survey teams chartered on *Wicca*, waited at the foot of the ramp, his slate tucked under his arm. He smiled at Joclen.

"I'll see you later," Joclen said and headed to the rear of the cargo bay.

Tamyn descended the ramp. "You have something, Co Dover?"

"Yes, I do," he said. He grasped his slate and glanced at it quickly. "A couple of things. My geologists have confirmed that these, uh, cliffs are, as I expected, constructs. Artifacts. We've found clear traces of thermal reformation, and this morning we found a reinforcing rod of some kind of aggregate material descending a good three hundred meters. I'm setting up a survey to find more of them, now that we know what to look for."

Tamyn looked north along the ridge line. The nearly sheer walls encircled the island, and it was easy to imagine that they formed a breastwork built to defend the interior. Certainly they had found old structures here and there that had been built, but most of it seemed natural. But Dover had argued that natural mountain building would not have resulted in such an even distribution over such a length. Tamyn had been reluctant to believe they were artificial, was even now.

"They built this thing?"

"Well, someone did. When I asked Yras T'Lor if anyone knew when they had been built I was asked why it mattered. Yras said, 'They have always been there that I can remember.' Cramer, my anthropologist, puts it down as another example of Pronan solipsism."

"Hmm. I wonder. Solipsism or indifference?"

Dover shrugged. "Rough dating suggests the wall was built about ten thousand years ago. I doubt anyone is alive now who remembers the event."

"They don't talk about their history very much, either. Only about what they personally remember."

"Very like you Akaren in that respect, I should say."

Tamyn looked at him silently and Dover reddened and studied his slate. Tamyn looked toward one of the towers on the plain below.

"Not a bad point," she said finally. "Depends what you think the Akaren do." When she looked at Dover again he tried to hide his confusion with a nod. "That's fascinating," she said. "What do you need?"

"I need to know how much longer we're staying. This could take some time to study thoroughly."

"Our business is almost concluded," Tamyn said. "How much time do you want?"

"Um...I'm not...a few more days? I think..."

Tamyn had told none of the survey teams about the questionable legality of *Wicca's* visit here, and she had continued to be careful how she talked to them. If Stoan came up with volunteers from Dover's group, all problems would be solved—at least, in Dover's mind.

"Let me see what I can arrange, Co Dover. I might be able to get you more than that."

"I'd appreciate that. Thank you." He hurried back to his people waiting by the console.

Tamyn shivered briefly in a chill wind. It was continually wet up here. Tamyn could tolerate, even enjoy, the surfaces of worlds, but it was always a relief to return to her ship. She strode up the ramp and entered the shuttle.

Tamyn looked up from the manifest report on her screen. The knock came again.

"Come."

The door slid open and Joclen stepped in. "I just got off the link with *Wicca*. Ratha says we're being hailed by an incoming ship."

"Damn!" Tamyn closed her eyes briefly. "Who?"

"Never heard of the *Solo* before, have you?"

Tamyn started. "Did Ratha confirm that?"

"N-no...I see you have heard of it before."

Tamyn turned back to the console and touched her fingertips to the gate. The tips clicked delicately against the surface. A moment later her awareness entered the bridge of her ship.

Ratha.

Shipmaster?

Transmission from Solo. Feed it through.

Signal shunted through her link. Code numbers scrolled by— M688.2CR.

Ratha, ETA?

Tomorrow, eighteen hours from now.

Tamyn withdrew from the link and stared unseeing at the screen. "What the hell."

"Tam...?"

Tamyn drew a breath. "It's just—the *Solo* hasn't seen the outside of a dock in twenty years. It belongs to Merrick."

"Sean Merrick? Merrick Enterprises and Mirak Corporation Merrick?"

"The same. What in hell is it doing out here? Sean hasn't left Mirak in almost as long. Last time I tried to see him I couldn't get through his staff."

"You went to see Sean Merrick?"

"We're old friends."

"I'm impressed," Joclen said snidely. "How did that happen?"

"I've known him for almost forty years. He was rich then, too, but nobody considered him a threat to civilization."

"Sorry. I didn't mean—"

"I know, you didn't mean to sound critical. That just makes it worse. It's become fashionable to ridicule him." She tapped a fingertip against her chin. "I don't care much for fashion."

"I didn't know you knew him, that's all." She moved toward the door.

"You don't have to leave."

Joclen hesitated, then sat on the edge of the bunk. Tamyn watched her and thought, she's so damn young. She considered explaining Merrick to her, rejected that idea, then considered apologizing. She valued Joclen's friendship, which had come as a surprise. Tamyn had hired her less than five hundred days ago as a standby pilot, then quickly promoted her to primary when Whitson had quit to stay on Tiaj. Joclen had more than proven her ability, but ability explained nothing about the bond Tamyn found growing between them.

"I'm sorry," Joclen said. "I should know better than to listen to popular venom."

Tamyn felt herself soften slightly.

"Sometimes," she said, "venom has some truth in it. Merrick's people have done a lot that I don't think Sean would ever allow if he were in control. It's hard to keep in mind that the man is not the company all the time."

Joclen nodded but kept silent.

Tamyn looked back at her terminal screen. "What the hell is he doing out here?"

"Maybe he sold the ship."

Tamyn laughed sharply. "Not very likely. It's in a museum. Or was." Tamyn shook her head. "Speculation. We'll wait and see who's on board when it gets here. Meantime, what about our next destination?"

"Already plotted. I worked it out last night, just on the off chance."

"Off chance of what?"

Joclen grinned. "That you'd mess up and we'd have to leave in hurry."

"Angry natives at our backs?"

"Something like that. But it seems I underestimated the Pronans."

Tamyn pointed a finger at Joclen. "You—"

A chime sounded from Tamyn's console.

"Yes?"

"Shipmaster," Stoan said, "*Wicca* has informed us that another ship is approaching."

"I've already been informed about the *Solo*—"

"Another one, Shipmaster."

"What the—? Identified?"

"It's a Regent ship, the *Jarom.*"

Tamyn uplinked to *Wicca*.

Ratha...

Regent Judiciary Force Vessel Jarom, *code* 2RJF39.CR, *A. Vollander commanding.*

Warrant?

Not transmitting.

Request link earliest opportunity.

She closed her hands and gnawed her lower lip for a moment. "More than likely this is a coincidence."

Joclen snorted derisively. "You're joking, right?" Then she frowned. "You don't think someone stole Merrick's ship, do you?"

"It would be a neat trick. Someone with that kind of talent, it would be a shame to arrest them." Tamyn stared at nothing for several seconds, her thoughts careening. "Unless that Coro bastard told the Board about our itinerary..."

"We're independents," Joclen said. "Our data's in order, we haven't done anything illegal—"

"That we know of. That's the problem with less than above board data, you don't know."

"You checked it, though," Joclen said. "Didn't you?"

Tamyn snorted. "How, without giving away our entire transit schedule? No, we made this run entirely on spec. Which means there are no safeguards. Maybe our source sold the same information to a competitor. Maybe—oh, hell, this is pointless." She shrugged, abruptly calm. "We're well outside C.R. jurisdiction. If I have to I'll sell my cargo in the Reaches and come home with an empty hold." She steepled her fingers and rested her chin on the tips; the caps felt cool, pleasantly smooth. "Then again maybe this does have something to do with the *Solo*. It would be just like that son-of-a-bitch to come foul me up—"

She realized then that she was thinking out loud and she glanced at Joclen self-consciously. She straightened.

"I have to spend one more night in Hrer M'San's compound. Probably by tomorrow mid-morning we can start lifting the stalks offplanet and prepare to leave. The *Solo* will probably be here before we finish. Let's see if we can keep out of trouble until then."

"Anything else?"

Tamyn shook her head. "I need to think."

Joclen left. The small cabin suddenly seemed smaller.

The orange sun was beginning its descent into the sea as Tamyn headed back toward the compound. The gray-green waters sparkled with copper and rust. The land below was in shadow; bright clouds, fired by the waning sun, obscured the view below. She turned off, engaging more agravs, and fell toward the foothills.

She descended into shadow.

She would be glad to leave and return to *Wicca*. Sometimes...sometimes Tamyn wished she could just keep going. She did not know if this was an urge to run or an urge to find. She did not examine it too closely; she was afraid understanding would eliminate the impulse and she would stay trapped in one place till she died, a possibility she feared more than anything else.

The foothills rose up around her. Soon she was back on the road surrounding the compound. She switched on the forward beams and the road jumped into bold relief. In the distance she could see the compound as a collection of dark shapes around a faintly glowing center. The sky was reddish purple; a few bright gold clouds streaked the horizon.

Something moved in the field to her right. Tamyn began braking before she was fully aware of what she had seen. Just stalks, she thought, then keyed her infrared scan. A vaguely humanoid shape appeared on the screen and Tamyn looked out over the field.

She saw the movement again.

Pronans did not go out of the compound at night.

Tamyn shut down the hover and sat in the darkness for a time. It's wrong to pry, she told herself. But she knew so little about the Pronans.

Curiosity won.

Quietly, she got out of the hover and, with a handscan and lamp, entered the field. All around her the stalks hummed their near inaudible songs, much quieter at night.

The Pronan was deep into the field. Tamyn hurried as quickly and quietly as she could. The Pronan was not moving very fast. Whoever it was took many pauses.

Tamyn slowed, listening. The stalks' song was different now, discordant and oddly despondent. Tamyn shuddered and pushed on. As she neared the Pronan the sound deteriorated further into a bleak cacophony.

"Mres c'osa nem savro...Mres c'osa...nnnnnn!"

She found the Pronan, a huddled lump amid the stalks. In the waning light Tamyn thought for moment that its body was erupting, the way shadow shifted over the robes that hung on it so loosely. Automatically, Tamyn reached out to help.

The Pronan's head came up and Tamyn stopped. The eyes were hard, glassy, unkind. A hiss escaped from its throat. For an instant Tamyn thought the Pronan would attack her. But then the head fell with a groan.

"Mres c'osa nem savro..."

"Can I help?" Tamyn asked.

The Pronan heaved upright. With a start Tamyn recognized Rith. The Pronan looked toward the breastworks and a thin appendage came from the folds of her soiled robe and pointed.

"I must be there, at their feet..."

"Let me help."

Tamyn half hoped Rith would refuse. But the Pronan came forward and stumbled into Tamyn's arms. Her body seemed insubstantial, light. Something shifted under Tamyn's hands and she nearly let go. Rith leaned against her, though, as Tamyn led her back to the hover.

She managed to get Rith into the craft. Behind her the moaning stalks quietened. Tamyn's nerves felt raw; it was a relief to close the canopy and raise the craft.

"Shall I take you back to the compound?" she asked.

"No!" The appendage wrapped around Tamyn's wrist. "The hills. Please." Rith groaned again and release her grip.

Tamyn turned back the way she had come and sped toward the foothills.

"Mres c'osa nem savro..." Rith breathed. There was silence. Then: "Almost too late. I am grateful. You see well." She peered out at the passing fields. "I could not bring myself to leave it all."

She was silent then. How much custom have I just walked all over? Tamyn wondered. It was too late to worry about it now. Rith muttered something and Tamyn glanced at her. The robe shifted again. Tamyn felt cold and forced herself to look ahead. She reached the foothills.

"Rith...where now?"

The Pronan managed to straighten and look. She pointed to the left, toward a hill that jutted out from the others. Tamyn drove to the crest and set the hover down. Rith cried out as Tamyn helped her from the craft. Rith took a few steps away toward the center, then sat down. She raised herself and looked back toward the compound.

"I will continue in my parts," she said. She looked at Tamyn. "Thank you."

"Is there anything else—?"

"No. Leave. I wish solitude."

Tamyn backed away, then, with both reluctance and relief, she turned to the hover.

"Human. It has been a joy to know you."

Tamyn looked back at Rith and saw her watching. Tamyn started to say something, but Rith winced and shuddered all over. She slumped to the ground. Tamyn stood frozen, unable to look away.

The robe writhed; it was no longer possible to believe it an illusion of shadow. Rith became lost in the changes working beneath the fabric. Her face was pressed into the grass; a deep vibrato sounded from her.

From the hem of the robe a shape emerged. It was small, dark, and wet. It crawled away a meter or so, to be followed by another. Then another. Tamyn reached into the hover and pulled out a handlamp. Holding her breath, she flipped the beam on and shined it at the growing group of viscous lumps.

They were all grayish red. Each was slightly different. There was something that could be called a head, with two large blind patches where eyes ought to be. They pulsated and shifted. Appendages grew from odd places on their small bodies, all of which were different.

The robe flattened out as these organic masses emerged. One last mass left it and this one, when Tamyn aimed her light at it, looked at her. The eyes were fully formed and it was most clearly Pronan in every other respect.

By now some of the other forms had ceased moving. The color was leaving them and they seemed to be drying out. The miniature Pronan broke its gaze from Tamyn and moved toward each of the other objects. From each it extracted something, a piece of their substance, and carefully placed it somewhere on its own diminutive body.

Tamyn shifted the light to Rith's head. The robe was completely flat. Her head had rolled over so Tamyn could see it clearly. The eye holes were empty.

Tamyn snapped off the light. She drew in three careful lungfuls of air and got back into the hover. A minute later she was driving toward the compound, trying to sort everything out that she had seen.

The fields sang a peaceful whispering song.

Chapter Two

A trio of tugs fell out of the sky like drops of silver, each carrying
an empty cargo nacelle. Tamyn oversaw their landings, arranging
them on the wide ridge with ample room for loading. Agrav haulers had been bringing the harvested stalk all morning. With the
arrival of the tugs, the stalks could now be transferred to the *Wicca,*
into a cargo supplemental modified for stasis. Tamyn worked constantly, keeping her anxiety at bay.

No one among the members of the M'San compound had
mentioned Rith the previous night, or seemed at all concerned by
her absence. Tamyn had walked through the formalities of her final
hours among the Pronan in a state of hyperawareness; she was among
beings she could speak with but probably never understand. If
Hrer M'San had noticed her stiffness, it was not mentioned. After
formal farewells early in the morning, Hrer helped her load the guard-
ian that had watched over her stay into the transport, leaning it back
in the passenger seat, eyes skyward. Tamyn then introduced the
volunteers who would stay to represent humans and the C.R.—
Colum Dover and three members of his survey team. No one
from the other teams had come forward and this left five of Dover's
original group to carry their research back. She hoped the Pronan
would not mind two more than they had suggested. No objections
came. She left, then, driving down the same road she had used since
arrival. She did not look toward the hill where she had witnessed
Rith's dissolution.

Biology, she told herself, it was all a matter of biology. Not
biology as destiny, no, but biology as history. Things done to
meet the demands of evolution long before reason came along
to mediate.

One by one the haulers emptied their smaller holds into the
nacelles, for transport by tug upwell to the ship, then headed back to
the M'San compound for another load. Two more trips by each of
the haulers and they could leave the surface.

She crossed the ground between her tugs. Clif worked in the
large bay of the survey shuttle overseeing stowage of gear for

transhipping upwell to *Wicca*. The bay was a maze of squat motiles, their articulated arms extended and waving like insects, moving about and shifting bundles, crates, and equipment. Clif nodded to her as she mounted the ramp.

"Don't get stowed yourself," she said.

"Never happen," he said, gesturing at the motiles. "I've got them trained."

Tamyn climbed up to the next deck. Polycoms, multilinks, small material analysis equipment, and data reservoirs crowded the forward section of the bay. She climbed through a hatch onto the lab deck. Two of Dover's team, from those remaining with *Wicca*, were busily feeding the accrued information of the last five days into the data reservoirs and organizing whatever material and equipment were no longer needed, making arrangements to leave behind what Dover's volunteers would need. Dover's team had bought a hover and three portable domiciles, plus a portable biomonitor and field medical unit. They were leasing a TEGlink satellite as well.

A central gangway connected the lab to the cockpit. Port and starboard off the narrow aisle were two small berths for passengers.

Stoan occupied the copilot's couch, running through preliminary checks, his face a constantly-shifting display of smiles, grimaces, and winces. Tamyn settled herself in the pilot's couch and began to feel at ease. She drew in the scent of metal and plastic, the spiciness of the recycling compounds, and the thought came so naturally, precluding any question, any doubt: I'm going home.

"Updates?" she asked.

"No. Ratha reports both ships on their original vectors, the *Solo* is still broadcasting a standard hail and the *Jarom* is still broadcasting its ID."

"Have we acknowledged either of them?"

"Not since the initial contact."

"Good. All systems check?"

Stoan nodded. "Statically in detail, ripe for use and whatever else you have in mind. Hah! Do you wish to duplicate?"

"No," Tamyn said. "Where's Joclen?"

"In the engineering compartment." He glanced at her with a puzzled expression, then shrugged and continued his work.

On one of the monitors she saw a hauler lifting lightly from the ground to go for another load.

Joclen stepped into the cockpit and went to the engineering panel. "We'll have Dover's requisitions ready in half an hour," she announced. "Any update on our visitors?"

"Nothing new," Tamyn said. "I want to be on *Wicca* when they arrive."

"Shouldn't be a problem." Joclen leaned over the back of Stoan's couch. "Everything check out?"

Stoan nodded again, energetically. "We can lift anytime. I said and it is and that's all."

Tamyn watched Joclen go through launch procedures, sealing up the shuttle, alerting the remaining ground crew—mainly Dover's people—and when she was satisfied, powering up. Through the couch, the deck, the air, Tamyn felt the vital thrum of the engines. Joclen laid her hands on the interface panel, her eyes fluttered closed.

Tamyn glanced around the cabin quickly. The last of the tugs had lifted twenty minutes before. The remainder of Dover's gear had been loaded on the hovercraft that now sped down the spine of the mountain, away from the landing site. Satisfied, Tamyn touched her fingertips to her own gate.

Almost at once—as quickly as she could absorb the information—she was viscerally aware of the shuttle. Dataflow ran through her mind, any wavelength of the spectrum was available for her inspection, she felt the strength of the engines as though they were part of her body. The Flow, the cybernetic envelope that permeated the ship, the crew, connected an individual's consciousness to a vast ocean of information, sensory experience, and all other operators. Tamyn was the ship now. She turned her attention skyward. Joclen engaged the agravs.

The ship rose straight up. Tamyn felt it as though she was naked to the environment. Wind jostled her. Temperature dropped as she entered the mesosphere. Below, the island continent slid behind her. Joclen kicked in the engines and shot up out of the atmosphere.

Pron became a gold-green dome below. The few big islands that comprised the major landmasses of the planet stretched from pole to pole, all the thousands of smaller islands scattered between them. Beautiful, Tamyn thought. But she was not unhappy to leave it.

Wicca was a faint speck over the horizon. Joclen locked with its telemetry and pushed toward her. The ship grew quickly.

Wicca's cowled mantle swept back into four paired arms that curled down and around the thick shaft of the supplemental assembly. The spine extended from the bridge structure, tapering past the end of the collection of cargo nacelles, laboratories, and passenger creches. Blue-white, violet, and yellow lights jeweled the smooth skin.

Tamyn "saw" the thread of microwave that shot out to guide them in. She followed it to the bay on the underside of the mantle, forward of the ring lock connecting the supplementals to *Wicca*. The docking cradle seized the shuttle and drew it inside, through the containment blister that maintained internal atmosphere, and pulled it up against a platform.

She withdrew from the Flow, stretched, and glanced over at Joclen, who was still linked, busy shutting down the shuttle and running the preset decontamination sequence established since the first few days of exposure to Pron's biosphere. Atmosphere was exchanged and by the time Tamyn got to the lock she was breathing a cocktail of prophylactic antigens. Tamyn cycled through to the ramp joining the shuttle to the upper platform. Below, the shuttle's stowage doors stood open and equipment was being hustled out by motiles.

Three people waited on the platform. Tamyn crossed the ramp.

The cooler air, though bland compared to the organic complexity of Pron's, was pleasantly welcome. Scores of sounds formed an aural ecology, and for a moment seemed the articulated components of a symphony. The basso thrum of the engines that never shut down, faint and powerful, provided a foundation for the myriad clicks and chimes, whirs and theramin trills of machines—stationary and mobile—and the familiar echoing eruptions of living voices. In other parts of the ship the walls absorbed most sound; here in the shuttle bays and aft in the permanent cargo sections there was no such attempt to muffle.

Thijs, Traville, and Kryder waited expectantly.

"Welcome home, Shipmaster," Thijs said and immediately pushed up Tamyn's sleeve and extracted a blood sample. His slender fingers held her forearm firmly, his touch warm and dry.

"Couldn't you wait?"

"The sooner the better," Thijs said, scraping a patch of skin. He deposited his samples in his kit, then extracted a face mask and placed it on her. "Exhale hard."

Tamyn obliged, trying not to laugh at the serious expression on his round face.

"You were around the Pronans most," Thijs explained, turning away. "You ate their food, touched them, I presume. Our global decontamination works very well, but—"

"No, it's fine. Thanks."

Thijs hurried off. Traville grinned. The expression created a series of creases in his long, thin face.

"Are we ready to move?" Tamyn asked, pulling her sleeve back down.

"Absolutely," he said. "The stalks are taking to stasis perfectly. Shreve just finished a deep-system diagnostic. Everything checks. Uh, Co Yaris is complaining about the extra layover. He stresses," Traville bobbed once on his toes in mock emphasis, "that he must get to Verax in the time contracted for."

"I'll talk to him. I want you to put Innes on full service to Co Dover till we leave. I want a TEGlink satellite left in orbit at his disposal. Make sure he's got everything he needs before we're gone."

Traville nodded.

Kryder stood waiting, exuding a coiled preparedness, both annoying and reassuring. Tamyn enjoyed being away from him from time to time—she no longer felt the need for a personal prophylactic, but she could not bring herself to dismiss him. He acted now as the ship's prophylactic. His assistant, Haranson, acted as personal prophylactic to any guests that might require it.

Kryder stood two-and-a-half meters tall, a slab of hard flesh that contradicted the gentle impression of his voice.

"It's good to have you back on board, Shipmaster," he said.

"Thank you, Kryder. It's good to be back. I'm going to the bridge. I—"

Stoan stepped out of the shuttle. His head swiveled quickly as he inspected the bay. "A mess is a potential curve that's steeper when we don't plot the line." He sighed heavily and laughed. "It's good to be back." He stamped his foot lightly on the deck.

"Stoan," Tamyn said, "go over stowage. Work with Crej. I want to be ready to move in a hurry."

"Absolutely!" Stoan nodded and walked away, toward the long control blister that oversaw the bay.

Crej'Nevan worked alone there, her several appendages waving about, touching the broad console. She looked like a saffron-colored tree whose limbs possessed no rigidity, capped by an expanding mantle which could enfold the entire body. Crej'Nevan "created" limbs as needed; no one knew the number of appendages a Stralith could manage at one time, perhaps not even the Stralith. Crej managed every detail of lading, controlled all docking procedures, and never seemed to sleep. She noticed Tamyn now and four appendages waved in unison.

Stoan climbed up into the blister and immediately began pointing at things and talking animatedly. Crej'Nevan retracted a number of limbs, the mantle folding down slightly

Tamyn paused, watching the Stralith. "Have Crej see me when she's off-duty."

Traville raised his eyebrows. "When is Crej ever off duty?"

Tamyn looked at him.

"I'll see to it," he said.

Kryder and Traville fell into step beside her.

"Tell me about *Solo,*" she said.

"The *Solo* is still coming toward us," Traville said, "broadcasting a request for recognition. The *Jarom* has ceased communication. They've provided no clarification or authorization for their mission. We still don't know why they're here."

"I presume to take the *Solo* back," Tamyn said. "Whoever's flying her can't very well have permission."

"As far as our scans show, Solo has not armed itself."

They reached the shunt and she touched the panel. The door opened and they stepped into the small cubicle.

"And the *Jarom* won't be scannable," Tamyn said. "Who will reach us first?"

"Presently the *Solo.*"

"Still no ID on who's piloting her?"

"No."

The door opened and Tamyn stepped onto her bridge.

Traville went directly to his station beside Ratha's, one of nine couches ranged in a circle. The round chamber surrounded a large holographic display in the center. Within the four-meter-diameter field the dark manta-shape of the Solo was visible against the spatter of stars. As Tamyn walked around the display the perspective shifted; when she reached the opposite side she saw the sun of Pron, orange-white, and the green-gold dot of Pron.

"Show me the *Jarom*," she requested.

Traville nodded, laying fingers against the gate on his board.

The scene in the display changed. Tamyn stared into the rear of a long, chunky ship, most of the details drawn from ship's records. The computer, anticipating, provided flashing markers to show the location of Pron and the *Solo*. Tamyn continued around the holo. The *Jarom* was an old, old ship and the skin showed it in the multicolored scoring; lovely in a stately sort of way. At one time it had been a merchanter. Now, a collection of supplementals permanently attached around its spine, it was a warship.

Tamyn did another circuit. Including Traville, only three couches were occupied. Shreve was immersed in the Flow through the gates on the arms of his couch. Around him the cluster of monitors flickered with data as he worked. Ratha sat at communications, next to Traville's telemetry and sensor station. He looked at her with dark brown eyes and a quizzical arch of his thick black eyebrows.

"Still no clarification from either ship?" she asked.

Ratha shook his head. He turned his couch half toward the console behind him and indicated a screen. "Those are the codes both issued when they entered the system. *Jarom* is still transmitting a carrier wave, but it no longer contains any interrogatives. They expect us to bow and scrape, no doubt. We have not identified ourselves to either vessel."

"We'll have to eventually. But...the Regents have no authority out here," Tamyn said, leaning close to the screen and reading the codes. She sighed. "Link me through to the *Solo*, Ratha."

She went to her couch, next to his, and sat down. She set fingers onto her gate.

Bright lines traced against a mother-of-pearl background; darker nodes—violet, red, dull blue—indicated nexi of data lines; a glowing sapphire spark was Ratha. She moved into it. The spark peeled apart and closed around her again. The background was darker, grey-green, and Ratha provided a sapphire line for her to follow into a communications nexus.

This is Shipmaster Tamyn Glass of Wicca, she transmitted through the Flow. *Respond please.*

This is Solo.

Who is commanding?

Personal contact is preferred. I suspect monitoring by the Regents vessel.

Are you in command with the knowledge and permission of the owner?

Yes and no. I will explain in person. Will you provide assistance?

Conditionally.

Thank you, Shipmaster Glass.

The link severed. She was about to withdraw when another link was forced, borne on a powerful carrier wave.

Shipmaster, this is Trace Alek of the Board of Regents.

Tamyn felt a flash of resentment at the abrupt intrusion. Silent all this time, ignoring her requests for a link, now the *Jarom* forced an exchange. Tamyn set her annoyance aside.

Greetings, Regent Alek. How may we assist?

Courtesy, Shipmaster. Please identify yourself.

This is Shipmaster Tamyn Glass of the clipper Wicca. *I ask again, how may we assist?*

You've been in contact with the stolen vessel now approaching you. We ask that you lend assistance in apprehending and securing it.

Your pardon, Regent Alek, but we're not equipped to engage in police actions. Did you say "stolen"?

Yes I did. That ship was unlawfully removed from its station berth.

Unusual that a member of the Board would take personal action in the investigation of a possible theft.

Not possible—definite. If you cannot actively assist in its recovery, I must insist that you do nothing in this situation. Stand down and leave this to us. Your interference will be considered only in an unfavorable light.

A threat, Regent?

A statement of fact, Shipmaster. We both seem to be a bit far out of our ways. I'm unaware of this system being on any of the treaty sanctioned routes.

Nothing in the treaties forbids exploratory or courtesy visits.

Of course not. And I'm sure your being here is entirely a matter of intellectual interest and has no commercial intent.

Tamyn felt her temper flare. Caution gave way briefly. Arrogant son-of-a-bitch, she thought. She paused before responding. Then:
That ship has identified itself as the Solo.
It is.
Sean Merrick is a friend of mine.
Yes?
It is unlikely anyone could have stolen his personal ship.
Nevertheless—
Considering how unlikely it is, whoever is now commanding her deserves a hearing.
Shipmaster—
You are aware, Regent Alek, that I am a registered jurist of the Commonwealth.
Do you intend to invoke such authority now?
I have the privilege.
This may not be a situation where you will wish to squander such privilege. I caution against it.
The more you protest the more I am forced to insist. That is, after all, the purpose of the Independent Judiciary.

The link ended. Tamyn waited a moment, then withdrew. She blinked at the display. The *Jarom* loomed. She glanced at Ratha.

"Provide the *Solo* with a directional beacon," she said. "Bring him in."

Ratha nodded and linked.

What am I doing? she wondered. It had been years since she had invoked judicial privilege, and then only in a private dispute over a contract issue. Certainly she had the privilege and authority, but...

"Solo has locked on," Ratha said. "ETA two hours twenty-three minutes."

Tamyn nodded and stood. "I'll be in my quarters." Thinking, she added to herself. Trying to figure out just what I'm doing.

Tamyn went down a short, private hallway to her cabin, just aft and to starboard of the bridge. A panorama of the Great Nebula in Orion dominated the wall of the main chamber, opposite her polycom. The next room contained her sleeping field, shower, and toilet. Between them, a spiral stair descended to lower chambers.

Tamyn stripped and showered. Warm water sluiced down her body, relaxing her.

You can't keep your hands out of it, can you? she thought, toweling her hair. No, she answered herself. Never.

It was like a curse that followed her from place to place. She had studiously attempted over twenty-nine years as a shipmaster to avoid political involvements and meddling in things that were none of her business. Her business, she had told herself and others, was business. Leave politics to those who enjoy such things and let them all leave her alone.

But she had voluntarily—almost eagerly—become an independent jurist. To better defend her business interests, she remembered saying, and she had used it for that only seldom. Usually just the fact that she could wield court authority proved sufficient to keep everyone honest in a negotiation.

But you're not so honest yourself, are you?

Pron was over a hundred light years from the muzzy border of the Commonwealth Republic. Sometimes her curse went to great lengths to follow along.

She padded back to the main room and sat down before her polycom. Just inside the cabin door, the Pronan statue now stood vigil, watching her. She touched the gate with one finger and called up a file. The screen cleared, turned blank green; an interrogative coursed back up the link, identified her; the screen turned white.

Tamyn cleared her throat.

"I do not understand what I witnessed among the Pronan," she said. The words appeared in elegant langish script across the screen. "Rith, whom I thought of as female and elderly, a matron among the other members of the M'San Stead, died. Rith no longer participated in the day to day activities of the compound. I witnessed her death. If I had not found her accidentally she would have perished alone and, judging by the fact that no one else among her family mentioned her or seemed in the least changed by her absence, forgotten. Her death was one of the strangest deaths I have seen. In fact, I am not even certain that she did die. Her body, beneath robes every Pronan wears all the time, came apart. In the time since, I have thought about it and I've concluded that Pronan's carry their organs arrayed on the outside of their bodies. These organs, at the time of death, seem to be acquire some autonomy. They leave the body, dragging themselves away. Rith...discorporated... abandoned by her own components."

Tamyn licked her lips and reread the last line. It gave her an odd, uncomfortable feeling, but she decided to leave it.

"In a way, perhaps, Rith is not dead. The last component that left her had the appearance of a Pronan—head, eyes, and some capacity to sense. I'm sure it responded to my presence. Perhaps what I witnessed was not a death so much as a rebirth. The small Pronan went from organ to organ and took a piece of each and placed it on its own body, as if rebuilding what Rith had lost. I'm not sure. For now, I do not know what it meant, what I witnessed. Perhaps someday I—or others—will come back and learn more."

For now, I do not know what it meant...

She closed the file, went into her bedroom and pulled a robe from her locker. She had consigned the memory to her records. Later she could deliver it to a lodge, share it with others of the Akaren. For now, she could stop worrying over it. In theory, anyway.

Her door chimed.

"Enter."

Crej'Nevan waddled in.

"You asked to see me, Tam?" Crej Nevan's voice sounded like three or more woven together in a mellifluous harmony, an imitation, Tamyn knew, of the pleasant voices of Ranonan. She brought with her a sweet aroma that quickly filled the room.

"I need to sort things. My mind..." Tamyn swallowed. "My mind feels cluttered."

"Do you wish to forget?"

"No!" Tamyn looked away, struggling with her discomfort and her...fear? "No," she repeated, more gently. "I just need the tangles straightened."

The Stralith moved closer, mantle opening and limbs forming a bizarre parody of a welcoming hug. Tamyn's heart raced. She closed her eyes, drew short breaths. She forced herself to relax, knowing she would when Crej finished anyway, but—

The interface net that gave her access to the Flow also allowed Crej a way in to do...whatever it was the Stralith did that brought her a short span of calm. The neural mesh that permeated Tamyn's brain, lying alongside her own synaptic pathways, intersecting with them, complementing and augmenting them, enabling her to think and feel when in the Flow, provided an avenue, a quasi-telepathic doorway. The sweet odor smothered her as the Stralith took her in a warm, intimate embrace. Almost at once Tamyn began to feel at peace, calmer. The tendrils of mental probes, seeking the knots, touching the places of tension and confusion, worked through her. Everything began to come clear...

Tamyn opened her eyes to the chime. She blinked, stretched briefly, and rolled off the suspensor field. She had napped for almost an hour. She pulled on her robe and went into the living room.

"Come."

Stoan entered.

"Excuse me," he said. "The *Solo* is twenty-five minutes away now."

"Anything further from the *Jarom*?"

"Nothing."

"Your recommendation...?"

"Hah! Mine?" He shrugged elaborately and shook his head, then laughed again. "We should leave enough alone. Well alone, as healthy as we can. We have four more ports of call on this sojourn, plus contracts with two more academic teams on board. Our profit margin is likely to be greater than any we've yet had."

"Unless I break off now to get involved in some petty non-sense with the Regents and Merrick Enterprises?"

Stoan gave the quick dip of his head. Tamyn suppressed a smile. She sat on the end of the sofa and glanced at the panorama. She wanted to go there someday, beyond the Rahalen Coingulate, beyond the *Sev N'Raicha*, the Seven Reaches as most humans called them. "So you caution business as usual?"

"Caution is relative, but to me it is as usual."

"Sean Merrick is a friend of mine," she said slowly.

"So if this is an emissary from Merrick?"

If indeed, Tamyn thought. It would simplify her life considerably to just pack up and run now. If the *Jarom* was here for the *Solo*, they might just ignore *Wicca's* questionable presence. Profits would be higher, risk lower. She did not, however, feel especially disposed to assist the Board of Regents, and if someone had managed to steal the *Solo* from right under their noses, she was tempted to applaud and at least slow them up. But tangling herself in this affair might draw too much attention to her own venture...

Too many questions, she thought, the most worrisome being how this alleged thief had known where to find her. And that was a question she could not ignore.

Damn.

"Let him dock," she said, "but keep a security bottle on him."

"I agree. Food, wine, comfort, probing interrogation?"

"I'll be on the bridge in fifteen minutes. Do it."

Stoan bowed slightly and left.

Tamyn pulled on clean utilities and downed a stim dispensed from her personal pharmacopeia. She stood very still, enjoying for a moment the clarity of her thoughts, the focus of an uncluttered mind. Already she felt the first intrusions of chaos and ambiguity, the undoing of the peace Crej'Nevan had left her.

The *Solo* moved gracefully toward dock with *Wicca*. Tamyn watched the display with growing anxiety. The *Jarom* had closed steadily, and now both ships were near.

"*Jarom* is locking weapons onto the *Solo*," Stoan said.

Anxiety blossomed coldly in Tamyn's chest. She dropped into her couch and linked.

This is Shipmaster Tamyn Glass, Jarom. *We have monitored your weapons lock. Any assault against my people will be brought before the full Council and judicial action will be taken.*

Our action is directed against the Solo.

Which is within a thousand meters of me. Any attack on the Solo is a threat to my ship.

This is obstruction, Shipmaster.

I repeat, any assault now will result in judicial action at the very least.

Tamyn withdrew and fixed her attention on the two shapes in the holographic field. She had never been threatened by the Board of Regents before, not like this.

"Bring our defenses to full readiness," she said. "How many unassigned supplementals do we have?"

Traville linked briefly. "Eighteen," he reported.

"Prepare to disengage them. Plot for interference dispersion."

"*Jarom* has canceled its lock," Stoan said. "Hah! Good, good."

"Maintain defense readiness," Tamyn said.

"The *Jarom* is coming about," Joclen announced.

In the display the big ship turned. Tamyn relaxed a little.

"Taking up a position to intercept us should we run," Stoan added.

The *Solo* closed the gap.

"Joclen," Tamyn said, "I want a shuttle downwell running independent telemetry. Back-up in case we need it, and an escape hatch for Dover's people if we have to pull everything out. Take Clif and someone from cargo security, in case you need to be insistent."

Joclen frowned, but nodded.

"I'm going down to the docks," Tamyn said, standing. "Whoever is piloting *Solo* better have a good story to tell or I'll personally hand him over to Alek trussed and gagged."

Tamyn waited for the locks to seal, watching Crej'Nevan work. The Stralith worked quickly, tentacles operating the controls deftly.

Kryder arrived with two dockhands, both wearing sidearms. He gestured for them to take positions on opposite sides of the lock.

The lock cycled opened.

A man stepped through. Young, thick hair, almost blond. His face was rounded, the sharp line of his jaw mitigating the suggestion of plumpness. He wore sleeveless utilities; his arms were long and well-muscled. He stood with an easy athletic grace in spite of his thick torso. He smiled at Kryder and for an instant Tamyn thought it was a smile of recognition, of familiarity. She felt the brief displacement of *déjà vu*.

"Crej," she said, "have a probe explore the *Solo* and make sure no one else is on board."

"Yes, Shipmaster."

The man frowned slightly, studying the Stralith, then turned his attention to Tamyn.

"Greetings, Shipmaster Glass," he said. His voice was a gentle tenor, soft and easy to listen to, with a faint lilt she could not place. "I am Benajim Cyanus, out of Miron." He jerked a thumb back toward the lock. "A probe won't work. *Solo* won't permit it. You'll have to take my word that I'm alone."

Tamyn nodded politely, glanced at Kryder. He came around Cyanus, the dockhands moving to the opposite side.

"He's unarmed," Kryder said.

Benajim shot him a startled glance, then looked at Tamyn. "Of course, I'm unarmed." He pulled a wallet from his breast pocket and extended it to Tamyn. "I brought this for you."

Tamyn accepted it. The disk case bore the star and stylized "M" of Merrick Enterprises emblazoned on its black surface.

"A communication from a friend," Benajim Cyanus said.

"How did you get your hands on the *Solo*, Co Cyanus?" Tamyn asked.

He shrugged. "Wasn't easy."

"No witticism, please, I have a pissed off member of the Board of Regents out there and a damned expensive litigation ahead of me if you don't say something to make it worth my while not to just hand you over."

Cyanus gave her a look of mock dismay. "After that lovely bluff you played to keep the *Jarom* from burning me down? I don't really think you want to hand me over."

"What makes you think I was bluffing?"

He blinked at her, dismayed, then shrugged again. He glanced uneasily at the dockhands.

Tamyn tapped the case against her hand and waited, staring at him. He had the beginnings of deep laughlines. This close she could see that the shipsuit hugged his figure tightly: he was solid, powerful-looking.

He sighed. "I have Sean Merrick's permission. It's all on the message. Things have gotten...complicated...around him lately. No one else would take my word for it. I had other proofs, but it didn't matter anymore. The *Solo* is considered a state treasure. Pity. It really should be sailed."

"You stole the *Solo*?"

"They didn't leave me much choice. I choose to say that I liberated her. Wasn't the first time I had to do something like that. It won't be the last."

Something nagged at Tamyn about this man. It had no shape, no name, just a persistent feeling.

"All right. Kryder, escort Co Cyanus to the diplomatic quarters. I'll view your message and make my decision based on that."

"That's all I ask," Cyanus said. He bowed slightly from the waist, turned, and let Kryder and the dockhands take him away.

In her cabin, Tamyn opened the case and slid the disk into her hand. She was mildly surprised to find that it was an old type. It shone dully in the subdued light. There was no problem reading it—there were millions like it from before the War—but she wondered why Sean had used something so archaic.

She slid the disk into the reader of her polycom.

Above the projection plate the air shimmered.

"Identify," commanded a neutral voice.

"Shipmaster Tamyn Fitzgerald Glass of the *Wicca.*"

The wavering air coalesced into a head with a face she knew. The shock of recognition was made sharper by the condition of the face. She did not recall Sean Merrick being so obviously old. He looked dried out, leathery skin tight and cracking around a skull too large. But the eyes sparkled, still blue, still intense with life.

"Sean?"

The face smiled. "This interactive stuff never ceases to amaze me," the head replied, a hint of an old, affected accent still clear. Pre War, Pre Secession, old Pan. "I'm only a program, but it feels like I'm alive. There are probably limits, but I'm damned if I can feel them. You look good, Tam. Do you still have the *Wicca?*"

"Of course."

"Good, good. I have no idea how long you've been gone. I wasn't updated after encoding. You'd been away from Miron sixty eight days when I made this."

"We've been out three hundred and seven days."

"Oh." He sighed and seemed to swallow. His eyes drifted right to left, then centered on her again. "There's no easy way to say this, Tam. I'm dead. If we're talking, Sean Merrick has been dead for some time. I made this when I knew it was unavoidable. No doubt my physicians thought different, and no doubt they tried to keep me alive, but I'm tired. So, the face you see no longer lives except on this disk."

Tamyn's fingers tightened on the armrests of the couch. The face waited for a response. After awhile Tamyn relaxed and nodded.

"So Sean Merrick is dead."

"That's right. I left instructions that you were to receive this as soon as possible. If necessary, you were to be tracked down. You alone in the C.R. can access this encoding. Anyone else tried, it would've wiped the program and all kinds of nasty shit would have happened then. It was in my will, which is the point of this whole macabre exercise. Are we in Miron System or not?"

"Not. Apparently it was necessary to come looking for me. Someone named Benajim Cyanus stole the *Solo* and came out here. We're not within C.R. jurisdiction at all."

"Ben actually did steal *Solo?* He pulled it off, I'm impressed! That boy has potential, Tam, you watch him."

"Did he steal it outright or did he have your permission?"

"Oh, he had permission. *Solo* herself would never have let him take her unless he did. No doubt, though, some other people didn't agree."

"I've got a Regents police cruiser sitting nearby that would dearly love to take your ship and Cyanus back."

"Hm. Bastards. It's my will and they can't accept it. You can also bet on it Ben wouldn't have been able to do it without help. Some pretty powerful concerns have a profound interest in seeing that you didn't get this encoding. And some others, just as powerful, who do. Everything hinges on it."

Tamyn felt a chill. "What are you talking about, Sean?"

"I have a run for you, Tam. A last commission from Merrick Enterprises, far as I know. What happens afterward—to you, to the corporation, to Miron—I don't know. I could make a couple of guesses..." He chuckled, a harsh sound, and the cracked face seemed on the verge of splitting. "Idle speculation. Let me give you a little background first."

The image cleared its nonexistent throat dramatically and assumed a mock lecture tone. "I finally got hit with monosclerotic dysphasia, which is a fancy way of saying that I was losing control of my body and internal organs little by little, and nobody knew what to do about it."

Tamyn envisioned Rith M'San for an instant, her body components abandoning her. She shuddered and concentrated on Sean's recording.

"Doesn't matter. I haven't been allowed outside the corporate matrix in fifteen years. Too many competitors would like to kill me, too many of my own people are afraid I might declare a new company and dissolve Merrick Enterprises, too many people afraid I'll die somewhere, murdered or otherwise, without final brain imprinting for my will. Paranoia. Paranoia for my health and well-being. Ironic, eh? I'm goddamned stifled! Maybe I got terminally ill just to spit in their collective eye!" He laughed deeply.

"Anyway," he went on, "I got tired of it. I didn't come out here to the Distals, the fringe colonies, fight in the damned Distal Wars, work my ass off to found the C.R. just to be cooped up on one world, and certainly not in one damned city. I tried making do with something like you Akaren do with your storytelling traditions. I sent teams out to make full-sensory encodings of the worlds they visited. Not the official side of their visits, but the off-duty side, the interesting stuff, if you take my meaning. Bad idea. Just whetted my appetite for the real thing. I couldn't control the recordings to the same degree I could in reality—or maybe it was too controlled, I don't know—anyway, it wasn't real, and I knew it. So I tried to arrange a tour. A grand tour with a full entourage, prophylactics up the ass—I'm the richest man in the C.R., I can afford the most pro-phylactic expedition you ever saw! Well, in fact, I couldn't. My own people loused it up. Delays, obfuscations, obstructions, they de-layed, detained, and dithered...I never got past the planning stage. Couldn't get through my own goddamned bureaucracy."

He looked compressed with bitterness, defeat and rage blend-ing to form an acrid emotion that had no name. Tamyn resisted an urge to reach for the hand that was not there.

"But now I've done it to them," he said quietly. A half-smile, cocky and stubborn, returned. "It'll be some time before they real-ize it, but I've got them. Here's the part where you come in."

"You know I never wanted a business involvement—"

He shook his head impatiently. "Listen! Please, Tam! I know how you feel and I respect that. It's not what I want, not what I'm offering. This comes off you'll be well-paid—in fact, you may never have to work again—but you won't be stuck. Believe me, I under-stand being stuck! I won't do that to you. I just want you to make one run, Tam. Just one."

"One run to where?"

"Earth."

Chapter Three

Benajim sat on the deck, arms resting on his knees, practicing patience. The closet walls smelled faintly of solvent. Unlabeled canisters filled one damp looking corner. A locker filled another corner, facing him, and to his right hung an offline motile, limbs dangling loosely.

The door opened and Tamyn Glass stepped in. The large man named Kryder—Tamyn's prophylactic—loomed just outside in the corridor. Benajim pushed himself up to his feet.

Tamyn Glass exuded authority, something the images Sean had shown him only hinted. She was, he now saw, the kind of person who walks into a room and is immediately felt by everyone present. Tall; thick, almost black hair; dark eyes beneath sharp brows, nose slightly crooked; a wide mouth. He felt anxious around her, inexperienced and uncertain.

"These are not the best circumstances in which to become acquainted, Co Cyanus," she said.

"I'm sorry—"

"I have obligations," Tamyn said. "I expect that any involvement with you and whatever situation you've brought with you will make fulfilling them extremely difficult."

Benajim stared at her. Sean had told him to trust Tamyn Glass. Shipmaster, Akaren...friend. Sean had never used that word lightly, it always meant something profound. Naïvely, Benajim had expected a welcome, one friend of Sean's to another. He should have known better.

"I'm supposed to trust you," she said.

Benajim blinked, dismayed. Her face was drawn—controlled, but the ill-ease showed clearly.

"Do you know what was on the disk you brought me?" she asked.

"It was keyed for you."

She pursed her lips and her right hand tapped her thigh. "Basically, Sean Merrick asked me to take a commission. You're supposed to know what that entails."

"Ah."

"I don't know you, Co Cyanus. Sean didn't keep many confidences, but those he did keep tended to be total."

"And he kept your confidence."

Tamyn nodded.

"How long has it been since you've seen him?" Benajim asked. "I don't remember you—"

"It's been a long time. What about you?"

"I only knew him for the last five years," Benajim said.

"How did he die?"

Benajim opened his mouth, then snapped it closed. Tell her the truth, he thought, otherwise there can be no trust.

But how can she trust a murderer...?

Tamyn stepped closer. "Sean asked that I trust you, Co Cyanus. I'm not likely to do that if you don't return it."

Tamyn's exec, Stoan, leaned into the cabin.

"Excuse me," he said quietly. "Shipmaster, we have a problem. Regent Alek..."

Tamyn continued to stare at Benajim. He felt her demand for an answer as if it were a physical thing—hands, arms, muscle, pulling him.

"Co Cyanus," she said, "come with me. You're probably the subject of this anyway."

When she turned away Benajim let out a breath. He felt released. He glanced at Stoan—bald, hairless—and smiled tentatively. Stoan shook his head sadly, and followed Tamyn.

"You insist on verbal communications?"

Tamyn sat in her couch, and smiled at the face on the flatscreen. Benajim stood off to her left, out of range of the polycom pickup. He could see the man on the screen, though, and he recognized him—Regent Trace Alek.

"Yes, I do, Co Alek," Tamyn said. "I see no reason to link with you under present circumstances."

"You see no reason..." Alek said. "What are you worried about, Shipmaster? We're on the same side."

"I'm not worried in the least. As for being on the same side, that remains to be seen. What do you want, Co Alek? I have work to do. I run a busy ship on a tight schedule."

"Not tight enough that you don't have time to help a thief. All right, to the point. I want Benajim Cyanus and the return of Commonwealth property, specifically the *Solo.* "

"Do you have the proper warrants for Co Cyanus's arrest?"

"I have the authority—"

"I'm well versed in the authority members of the Board of Regents carry and how much they do not. Proper warrants must be issued by a member of the court and made public before action. I require proof that these points have been covered."

"You're overstepping yourself, Shipmaster Glass."

Tamyn looked up at Benajim, then back at the flatscreen. Benajim wanted to jump into the confrontation, call Alek a liar. Benajim's fingers flexed on the edge of the console.

"Arrogant son-of-a-bitch," someone whispered. Benajim looked around at Tamyn's crew. All of them wore expressions of strained tolerance. Except Stoan, who grinned. Alek had made no allies here.

"Am I? Do you have warrants with you or not? If not, the question of 'overstepping' is problematic."

Alek sighed audibly. "There is no need for us to be antagonists over this. Cyanus has given us a good chase for the last twenty-nine days. We're all stressed. I'm sure there's a way we can work together to come to a solution."

Tamyn did not react. "What are the specific charges against Co Cyanus?"

"Benajim Cyanus removed Commonwealth property and fled a lawful order to stand down when challenged by police cruisers. The charge is theft and abrogation of transit authority, refusing inspection."

Tamyn's eyebrows rose a bit, but Benajim had no idea what that might suggest. Others around the bridge smiled.

"For that you commandeered a Regents warship to pursue?" Tamyn asked. "Which of us is overstepping, Regent?" The fingers of her right hand began drumming idly on the arm of her couch.

"As representative of the Board in this matter, I demand compliance, Shipmaster."

"Warrants, Co Alek," Tamyn said. "If you have no respect for the juridical process, I have enough for both of us. I'll be more than happy to cooperate with you once you've demonstrated that you're operating in the best interests of the Commonwealth."

"Cyanus did not allow us the time to collect all the appropriate formalities. The process was begun, however. I assure you that once we've returned to Mirak all the niceties will be in order."

"It's C.R. custom to tend to the 'niceties' before you incarcerate anyone, Co Alek. In fact, it's required under the Charter."

Trace Alek drew himself up, looking a bit redder and frustrated. He closed his eyes briefly, then nodded.

"Of course you're correct, Shipmaster. Nevertheless, Co Cyanus is still in possession of Commonwealth property. May I suggest that you return the *Solo* to us? We can allow you to keep Co Cyanus aboard your ship under the condition that you bring him back to answer allegations of misconduct—"

Tamyn's mouth flexed briefly. "I'm not aware that you are allowing me to do anything, Co Alek. I don't require your permission to hold Co Cyanus and I am not required to bargain with you. So far you've shown damn little evidence of just cause. Until I am better satisfied, both Co Cyanus and the *Solo* remain in my care as long as I see fit." She cocked her head to one side. "Unless, of course, you're prepared to bring charges against me."

"The *Solo* is Commonwealth property—"

Tamyn frowned. "You keep claiming that. I understood that the Solo belonged to Sean Merrick."

"That's true."

"I understand Sean Merrick has died."

Trace Alek hesitated several seconds. Tamyn glanced curiously at Benajim. He nodded to reassure her.

"That is," Trace Alek said finally, "unfortunately true. However—"

"Ah. Then I assume Merrick Enterprises and Mirak Corporation have dissolved. So ownership of the Solo is to whomever Merrick named in his primary designation."

Another pause. Then: "Merrick Enterprises and Mirak Corporation have been taken under Regents control."

Tamyn ran the tip of a finger across her lower lip. "The Board of Regents has assumed control of a private institution? How does that work in the absence of criminal charges or—"

"Circumstances," Alek snapped, "are...extraordinary." Alek scowled. "I would rather discuss this over a secured channel or in person, Co Glass. Aspects of this affair are not public knowledge."

"Obviously. I'll take that suggestion under advisement and get back to you, Co Alek. Thank you."

She touched a contact on the console and cut the link just as Alek was about to protest. Tamyn looked at Benajim, her eyes narrow and smokey.

"What about primary designation?" Ratha demanded.

"Regents control," Traville said. "That's against the Charter— I *thought* it was anyway—"

"How can they control it without Merrick's imprimatur?" Shreve wondered.

"My, what a lot of dendritic convoluting," Stoan said. "I think we have, conservatively speaking, a crisis in the smoke."

Tamyn raised a hand and conversation stopped. She stared evenly at Benajim. "Well?"

"If I set foot on board the *Jarom*," Benajim said, "I will disappear and you will be attacked and destroyed."

"That's a hell of an allegation," Tamyn said.

"The Regents are trying to maintain control of Sean's corporations. That's why his corporate dataspheres are still intact. It's essential to them—some of them—that they not be dismantled. That's why I can't be allowed to keep *Solo* or be allowed to go free." He leaned closer to Tamyn. "I'm not lying to you, Shipmaster."

"I didn't say you were." She frowned. "He wants a face to face."

"Don't go to him. Have him come here."

"Agreed," Stoan said. "It sounds like he's assumed, or the Board of Regents has granted him, complete discretionary powers. Holding you hostage would not be unexpected."

"If true," Tamyn said, "then it's been done outside the Flow, without public knowledge and consent. Then we invite him here. But first I want to know what's going on, Co Cyanus."

"Please...call me Ben."

"I'll call you bounty and claim the reward for returning you if you don't start answering me!"

Benajim felt chilled. He looked around the bridge at the others, most of whom were watching him—especially Stoan and Kryder. He saw a clean, well-run ship, efficient crew, orderly routine. He was disrupting them; Tamyn Glass would not tolerate that without excellent reason.

"I really am tired," he said. She cocked an eyebrow meaningfully and he cleared his throat. She frowned at that, but said nothing. "You asked how Sean died. Well, I'll tell you. He died in his sleep, just after I shut down his life support."

He braced himself for her reaction. Instead of outrage, though, Tamyn's face seemed to close down. Benajim's fingers ached from the grip he had on the edge of the console at his back. As seconds passed in silence, he willed them to relax.

Finally, she nodded slowly. She stood and looked at him narrowly.

"Come with me, Co Cyanus," she said and led the way to her cabin.

Benajim followed, Kryder close behind him. When her door closed and he was alone with Tamyn and Kryder, he felt slightly better, less on trial, though Kryder made him feel that he was under guard.

"Sean was old," she said.

"Very," Benajim agreed. "Almost two hundred."

"And sick."

"He has been on full life support for the past three years." He watched her pace the length of the compartment, her eyes on the deck. "He was miserable," Benajim added. "If you knew him, you know how active he was, how he hated being kept stationary."

"I would probably have terminated him myself."

"He told me you could be trusted. He told me to deliver that disk to you and get you to help him."

"Do you know what it is he wants?"

"Yes," Benajim said. "He wants to be buried on Earth, where he was born."

Tamyn sat down on the couch and looked contemplatively at the display of the Great Nebula. She shook her head and chuckled mirthlessly.

"That son-of-a-bitch," she whispered. She closed her eyes for a time. "What is Alek trying to do?"

Benajim licked his lips. Trust her, Sean had said. "Not Alek, he's not at the core of this. There's a movement to reopen the Charter and amend it to allow corporations to retain identity after the death of the founders."

"Again?" Tamyn scowled as if disappointed. "Sutter Hall was agitating for that twenty years ago when he thought he was dying. It's old politics." She shook her head. "There's more, of course. Sean wants to be buried on Earth. That's at the heart of the Pan Humana."

"True..."

"So it's a violation of the Treaty of Hominus Valorem for a C.R. ship to cross the border into the Pan. To fulfill Sean's will would require an illegal action. I suppose implementation of the balance of the will is contingent on that?"

"That, and the *Solo* has to be put back into service as an explorer. That is, after he's been transported to Earth."

Tamyn looked startled. "You don't have his corpse"?"

"No, no!" Benajim laughed. "I'm a fair thief, but not that good."

"That means his body has to be..." She laughed sourly. "What made him think *I* was a good thief?"

"Sean always spoke highly of your talents."

"He must not have mentioned my ethics."

"Well, he did say you could be counted on to do the right thing when possible."

Tamyn stared at him as if he were insane. He met her gaze and held it, convinced that the worst thing now would be to show doubt.

She snapped to her feet. "Damnit, do you have any idea what this entails? A sojourn to Earth? Hell, we don't even know if Earth still exists!"

"Oh, it does. I'm sure of that. Sean was, at least. We'd have heard if something had happened to Earth. I don't think the Panners would have kept that to themselves."

"Why not? They don't have any reason to talk to us. We're deviants as far as they're concerned, race traitors. Or didn't you read history? How old are you anyway?"

"I don't know."

Tamyn frowned. "Not born on Miron then?"

"No."

She raised her eyebrows, waiting. "Where?"

"The Frontier," Benajim said uncomfortably.

Tamyn nodded. "Some little agroworld that barely has indoor plumbing, much less decent recordkeeping? No?"

Benajim looked away.

"You're hiding something from me, Co Cyanus. That's not the way to establish a trusting relationship."

"I'd rather not discuss my life."

"All right. You only knew Sean a few years you say? Five? But you got close enough to him to be able to switch off his life support."

"I did."

"What would Sean want with some blankbrained seeder when he could choose from a whole worldfull of people just like himself?"

"He saw potential in me."

"Is that what he said? Did he say potential for what?"

"Business."

"If that were the only thing, he'd never have trusted you."

"Is there some point to this?"

"That's my next question. Is there some point to stealing a ship, leading a police cruiser out here to find me, and complicating my life with nonsense about taking a corpse back to Earth? A planet I've never been to, incidentally."

"If you don't want to do it, Shipmaster Glass, I'll take my leave of you and do it myself. Sean asked. That's all I need. He was a friend. I thought you were his friend, too."

Tamyn crossed the room to him and jabbed her fingertips into his sternum, backing him up.

"Listen, Ben, and try not to be so pompous and self-important. If it was just me there's no question that I'd do it. I wouldn't even ask why. But it isn't. Where do you think you are? *Wicca* is a clipper, a merchant ship. I have crew and passengers on board to whom I have contractual obligations. You're not just asking me. And if I'm going ask them then I have to know who I'm talking to. So far you're just a problem. It's not me that has to present credentials, especially not to prove my loyalties."

Benajim stepped away from her. His hands curled into fists and he consciously opened them. He glanced at Kryder, who remained immobile at the door, watching him.

"If it weren't important," he said slowly, "then why would a Regent come after me personally?"

Tamyn nodded. "That's a very good question. I hope you have an answer." She went to the bar and poured herself a drink. "You want something?"

"Brandy?"

She poured another glass, brought it to him, then went to the couch at the polycom. She sipped her drink, regarding him expressionlessly.

Benajim breathed the aroma of the brandy, then took a mouthful.

"Let me explain one more problem," she said. "Just so we're clear. You brought Alek here, to me. That means the Board of Regents will know I'm involved. How am I supposed to remove Sean's body from wherever it is and leave the C.R. with it now? You've made my job harder, Ben. Didn't you think about that before you came after me?" She frowned at him. "And how the hell did you even know where to look?"

"The, uh...Coro who sold you the data? He did that at Sean's direction. He brought it to Sean first."

Tamyn silently drank her brandy, staring at him, her face expressionless. Finally, she nodded, poured another drink, and sat down.

"Now," Tamyn said softly, "you may start explaining to me why I ought to risk everything on this venture."

"I remember nothing of my homeworld. I arrived on Miron with only recent memories. I'd been running. I felt lost, bewildered. It was such a huge city, there was so much, it was exciting. My senses dragged me on a tour, pulling me from place to place, demanding exposure to the wealth of sensation Miron City offered. Miron, center of the C.R. The city is like an organism, slowly devouring the desert around it, replacing the uninhabitable with its living fabric. Huge atmosphere generators pumping nitrogen-oxygen throughout the tunnels, warrens, and above-ground streets and avenues, gradually changing Mirak itself. In another thousand, perhaps two thousand years humans might walk on the open soil without needing breathers.

"But I didn't know enough to survive and it almost killed me. I nearly starved to death before Merrick's people found me.

"I woke up in a strange room, hooked to a biomed. Shortly afterward an old man in a mobile life support unit rolled in and talked to me. I don't remember what we discussed. Everything. I do remember the sympathy, the interest. The old man gave me a job, a place to live. Later I learned that Sean Merrick was like that, always taking in waifs and doing what he could to make them whole.

Everyone expected it, so no one questioned the presence of another charity case within Merrick Enterprises. What no one expected was how close I became to Sean Merrick. Within a year I was Merrick's personal aide.

"What I didn't expect was how people hated me for that. Dee Clars was Sean's personnel director and he hated it that Sean overrode his choice in a personal aide. Clars, I found out, is the surface of a tremendous problem within Sean's companies. I learned quickly how to live in the corporate matrix, survive the attacks, both professional and personal, and later how to come out the winner in most encounters. It was like a game and I was very adept. Merrick joked that all the neurons that were empty of a lifetime gave me plenty of operating and learning capacity. I only seemed like a prodigy because new data did not have to compete with old.

"On Sean's advice, I founded my own company. Doppler Marketing. I even surprised myself with my alacrity; it seemed natural to me, although Sean walked me through the procedures, helped me set up the charter, the structure, showed me how to operate successfully on a tight budget, did everything but actually run it for me. He even helped me pick a staff and they turned out to be good enough that I don't have to be there to run it. Doppler deals in pharmaceuticals. Lucrative and very dangerous. I kept it small—also on Sean's advice—and began acquiring other stocks and market shares from a variety of companies. Later, I discovered that all those companies were subsidiaries of Merrick Enterprises or divisions of the Mirak Corporation. For all intents and purposes, so is Doppler—but it's in my name.

"Sean grew weaker. I worked for him for almost five years, taking care of correspondence, then later representing him at board meetings, proxying for Merrick at public functions, becoming, in effect, a new persona for Sean Merrick. I had no illusions about what would happen when Sean died. There were many people within and outside the company who wanted me gone. People Clars had hired and placed. When Sean died and the entire structure of his corporations dissolved as a result, I would be in no position to profit by it. Clars' people were being placed to take advantage of the dissolution of Sean's holdings. Doppler Marketing was to be my escape, my shield. Without Merrick, I was too vulnerable.

"I watched the meds work on Merrick. It became clear that they could keep him alive almost indefinitely. Sean's speech was beginning to slur, his ideas jumbled, often incomprehensible, but his heart kept going at the insistence of the machines and the meds. Tissue samples became a daily ritual. It didn't make sense if what I had assumed Clars was doing was correct. Why prolong his life? Why not let him die and feed on the remains?

"I came to see him nightly, sitting with him for hours, talking, sometimes just waiting, holding his hand. Sean was disgusted with his existence. He was the living center of a body of machinery that mimicked life for him and he had no way to turn it off. He tried from time to time. Once he nearly succeeded in issuing precisely the right commands to cause all the support to disconnect, but a human technician was on duty that night and overrode it. Better safeguards were installed after that and Sean had less control. Finally, he wept. He stared at me through most of one night, silent, tears streaking his parchment skin. I ignored the request I knew Sean was making. Ignored it all night, until I left.

"The next night I reprogrammed the biomeds. Sean never woke up."

Benajim's eyes were closed. He did not know when he had closed them, had not noticed until then. When he opened them he saw Tamyn staring at him.

"He was my friend," he said. "Still is. He hurt. Then he didn't hurt anymore."

"And the *Solo?*"

"He verbally granted title to me two months before he died. The problem is that the Board of Regents has declared many objects associated with the Distal War and the founding of the C.R., including the *Solo*, state treasures, to become part of a commonwealth museum after the demise of their original owners. With the cooperation of the owners, of course."

"So you stole her."

"Just so. I used a temporary persona mask to mimic Sean's neural pattern so the ship would recognize me. It had to be done quickly, they only last a short while."

"Were there any witnesses to this bestowal?"

"Yes. A Ranonan named Tej-Ojann. He's an ambassador-at-large."

"And what about Sean's will?"

"Also held by Tej-Ojann. He'll release it into the Flow when he has evidence that Sean Merrick is dead."

"Which the corpse ought to provide."

"Exactly."

"Alek admitted Sean died. If everyone knows Sean has died, then—"

"It's only known to the Board and a few of the directors of Merrick's company. Rumors were starting to spread when I left, but there's an awful lot of Q at stake. A lot of people don't want Merrick Enterprises to dissolve."

"The word of a Ranonan ambassador is as good as it gets."

"Tej-Ojann wants to see the actual body, to verify it, to know that Sean's will is being honored."

"Legally or otherwise."

Benajim shrugged. "If the Board presents it, then the will is being legally honored and Tej won't have to act. If we show up with the body, then Tej knows that extralegal actions are necessary."

"And releasing the will into the Flow at that time will create quite a stir."

"I'd imagine so."

"What's to prevent Alek and whoever he's working with from doing whatever they want with Sean's holdings in the meantime?"

"That's the other problem. None of the corporate dataspheres have begun to dissolve, which they should have when Sean's imprimatur in the Flow failed to validate them after several days. That's why no one outside the Board is really sure if he's dead. I don't know how the dataspheres are still intact. Evidently the Board has come up with a way to prevent their dissolution. In the meantime Ambassador Tej-Ojann is trying to intervene there."

"How?"

"He's filed an amicus with both the Board of Regents and Standing Committee of the Independent Judiciary. An injunction has been placed on all actions pending an investigation. Tej-Ojann is organizing an oversight committee for the purpose."

"That could take years."

"So Alek is trying to arrest me now for violating the injunction. My taking *Solo* before a hearing of the committee."

"If he can make the arrest stick," Tamyn mused, "then he establishes the theft as a foundation to make a claim of legal ownership. And there's no reason why he couldn't make it stick unless you got some independent judicial help." She narrowed her eyes. "Me." Tamyn tapped her fingers against her glass. "Sean was a clever bastard." She grunted. "You said Dee Clars is the surface of a larger problem?"

"None of the people Clars placed worked for Sean. They work for Clars and, I suspect, through him for Carson Reiner."

"Why? She has her own company."

"And Clars is a shadow partner in it."

"That must have been difficult to discover."

Benajim did not respond.

"Do you have any idea," Tamyn asked, "what they're trying to do?"

"I have some suspicions, but I wasn't able to get past the security in certain sections of the corporate datasphere. Whatever is being done, she's using Merrick Enterprises Flow to run it."

"And if Sean's companies are dissolved—"

"That datasphere is gone as well. Or at least not hidden."

Tamyn nodded thoughtfully.

"What happened to your memory?" she asked.

"I don't know."

"You said you arrived on Miron on the run. From where?"

Benajim looked away.

"You expect me to trust you—"

"Because Sean trusted me, not because I open my soul to you, Shipmaster. If what I've told you so far isn't sufficient, fine. I'll take care of all this myself."

"Your memory was wiped, wasn't it?"

Benajim hesitated. "Yes."

"Why?"

Benajim frowned and then saw where her distaste lay.

"I don't know," he said. "That's part of what was wiped."

She shook her head and her expression softened. "I'm Akaren. The idea of tampering with your memory…"

"I'm not too troubled by it," Benajim said. "But sometimes I feel…incomplete."

"I have a Stralith on board. Crej'Nevan has certain talents in these areas. It's possible that if you wish to remember…most mindwipes don't erase memory, they merely block it."

Benajim stared at her.

The door chimed.

"Come."

Stoan entered. "Regent Alek is insisting on discussions now. He's had the *Jarom* moved in closer."

"I'll be out in a minute." When Stoan left, she looked at Benajim. He felt exposed by that gaze. She said, "For the time being I'm going to assume everything you've told me is the truth. I don't have much reason to side with Trace Alek—he's a political cannibal. But I hold final judgement. If you've lied to me in any way, you'll wish you'd never found me."

"Sean said you were the one to find."

She stood. "I've known Sean to be wrong on occasion." She headed for the door.

"I want to be there when you talk to Alek," Benajim said.

"I wouldn't have it any other way."

Benajim began to follow her. She stopped at the door and looked back.

"You tell things well," she said.

"I'm not Akaren."

"Have you considered becoming?"

"Is this an invitation?"

Tamyn frowned.

Benajim shrugged. "No, I haven't," he said quickly. "I have no history of my own. I'm not sure I'd belong there."

"Well. I have a feeling we'll see you compensated for that before we're through."

Chapter Four

Joclen watched the wall of clouds coming toward them over the sea. On the ridge an occasional brush of salted breeze brought a wispy sample of things to come. The sky directly overhead was a rich violet, darkening toward night. Joclen wanted very much to be upwell, on board *Wicca*, but she understood why Tamyn wanted her here, on the planet. Joclen could run a separate command-and-control operation even if *Wicca's* bridge became impaired.

A light flashed on the comm panel. Joclen linked.

Tam?

Things may get very thick very fast up here. Are you set up?

I am. But—

Stay down, stay quiet. I want you in the Flow, running projections. Keep an eye on us.

The link to Tamyn broke and Joclen tapped sensor readings on the approaching storm. The orbital images from the string of satellites they had deposited upon arrival showed a roiling mass about four hundred kilometers across, with winds nearing one hundred thirty kph. She ran a projection and found that it would hit them full on; they would be in the eye in four hours.

Joclen withdrew and looked across the cockpit at Clif.

"Prep us for that storm," she said. "And run another check on our uplinks to the satellites."

He nodded and went to work.

Tamyn tried again to punch through the closed sphere around the *Jarom*. The only gate apparently open was to Trace Alek, and she had spoken enough with him. She wanted to talk to Shipmaster Vollander. It made no sense that he continued to refuse her hails.

Wicca's datasphere had been probed a half dozen times in the last hour. Tamyn could not believe Vollander would attack her without a hearing of some kind, but watching the maneuvers of the police cruiser gave her a sour feeling. She ordered Shreve to start counterprobes to try to find some way to fight back if need be and had Traville release several unused supplementals. The bulky modules floated free of *Wicca's* spine and tractors moved them into a loose and slowly shifting array between the two ships.

Suddenly the dull pewter surface of the *Jarom's* datasphere roiled, shifted to mother-of-pearl, and a slender thread emerged to touch *Wicca's* own envelope.

Shipmaster Glass, this is Trace Alek.

Tamyn resisted the urge to cut the link now—she still mistrusted Alek's intentions and had intended to communicate with him only by commlink or in person. She had been caught probing, though, and could not withdraw without appearing dishonest.

Yes, Co Alek?

I've decided to accept your suggestion to meet with you on board your vessel. This stalemate is doing neither of us any good.

Agreed.

My shuttle will launch in ten minutes.

I look forward to this.

The thread broke, the *Jarom's* datasphere hardened again.

Shreve—

Got a partial reading. I can work with it.

Good. Joclen?

Linked and in the Flow. I've got navcom. You know about the storm?

Traville's been keeping me posted. Can you manage or do you think you should relocate down to the valley?

We're anchored well. I'm just not sure if it's ionized enough to interfere with the link.

Stoan says not.

We'll see.

Tamyn withdrew and rubbed her eyes. The Flow could be more difficult to leave than work through. She often felt diminished after the expanse the interface offered.

"A shuttle has left the *Jarom*," Ratha said at last.

"Have Crej'Nevan prepare a berth, full security. In one of the supplemental bays, not the main one. Kryder, I want you there with her."

Kryder nodded and left the bridge.

In the projection the small boat drifted toward them.

"Mightn't receiving him in a supplemental be construed as an insult?" Ratha asked.

Tamyn drummed her fingers absently, watching the shuttle. Then she stood. "Maybe. But he's inconveniencing me. I'll be down in the dock."

She left the bridge and went straight down the corridor, past the shunt, and into the cabin section. Here the corridor forked and described an oval around a large collection of private compartments. Many were empty, their recent occupants left behind at prior stops in the sojourn. Crew quartered in the cabins that ran along the outer perimeter.

Tamyn stopped at the one Benajim had been assigned and pressed the chime. She waited a few seconds, pressed it again, then knocked.

The door snapped open and Haranson stood there. Behind her, slouched on the lone couch in the small cabin, was Benajim.

"Sorry, Shipmaster," Haranson said, standing aside.

"She was using the cube," Benajim said, smiling and jerking a thumb at the hygienic cubicle. "Being under restraint, I couldn't answer the door."

Tamyn stared at Benajim until he looked away.

"Trace Alek is coming over," she said. "I thought you might like to meet your accuser face to face."

Benajim sat up, eyes intent. "Of course." He looked thoughtful, then smiled. "You want to see our reactions to each other."

"I'm being courteous, Co Cyanus. If you'd rather stay here—"

"No, no," Benajim got quickly to his feet. "I accept your invitation, Shipmaster. I wouldn't miss it."

Tamyn led the way and Haranson brought up the rear. They took a lift tube down a deck, then through a hatch into a broad area in which the shipboard motiles waited in wall units. A wide hatch opened onto an enclosed walkway.

"Orientation changes here," Tamyn said over her shoulder. She grabbed a railing just outside the hatch and stepped through, falling—

—swinging down into an upright position ninety degrees to the other side of the hatch. She turned and looked "down" at the opening to see Benajim hesitating at the edge, Haranson just behind him. Tamyn knelt down and extended a hand.

Benajim scowled and ignored her, taking hold of the same rail. He stepped "upward" and twisted around deftly to land on his feet beside her.

Haranson joined them a moment later. The walkway ran around the inner circumference of the central supplemental shaft. Looking out, the tunnel extended nearly four hundred meters to the far end. Walkways ringed it at each attachment point, where the supplementals linked to the shaft.

"I keep g at constant outward orientation," Tamyn explained as they walked around the ring to a lift platform.

"Do you provide individual g envelopes?" Benajim asked. "Or do you require your customers to provide their own?"

"They can rent them from me or use their own. But everyone is required to do one or the other."

"No such thing as free g," Benajim said.

Tamyn glanced at him and saw an amused smile.

They stepped onto the platform and Tamyn touched a fingertip to the control. They rode up the shaft to the fourth ring, then walked around it to a hatch.

They repeated the maneuver, entering a space with a different orientation again.

"I suppose you get used to that after a time," Benajim said.

At the end of a short access tube, they stepped into an observation blister a few meters above the deck of a cramped docking supplemental. Crej'Nevan nearly filled half the space, her crown extended, multiple limbs poised above a compact control panel. Kryder stood by the lift tube.

Below, an apron ran the length of the supplemental's interior. Five channels ran toward five enormous bay doors, the center one of which stood open to space. From that channel, a long boom stretched out through vacuum. Overhead, almost filling the "ceiling" of the supplemental, clustered maintenance nodes, manipulator arms, ducts, crossbeams, cranes, and other service devices. Flood lights illuminated the center channel.

"Status?" Tamyn asked Crej'Nevan.

"Shuttle is in the cradle," the Stralith said. "Bringing it in now."

The boat from the Jarom perched on the cradle at the end of the boom. As the shuttle came fully into the dock, the bay door closed and atmosphere flooded the chamber.

"How does it scan?" Tamyn asked.

"The boat is unarmed," Crej'Nevan said. "There are three life signs on board."

"Armed?" Tamyn asked.

"Not that I can discern."

"Are you being blocked?"

"No," the Stralith said. "I have a curious reading on one of the life signs. Temperature does not conform to human standard."

"Seti?"

Crej worked at the console. "Not that I can discern." The Stralith raised several appendages in an approximation of a shrug. "I am sorry. My best judgement suggests all is nominal."

"Nominal," Tamyn repeated. She sighed. "Well, Co Cyanus. Ready?"

Benajim nodded and eased past Kryder, Haranson, and Crej'Nevan.

"Kryder, come with us."

Kryder stepped to one side while Tamyn and Benajim stepped onto the platform, then squeezed himself on. Tamyn watched Benajim try to keep space between himself and Kryder on the way down. His eyes seemed feverish, excited. When they exited the lift, his gaze darted around, taking in the bay.

"He's going to be pissed," he said.

"Why's that?" Tamyn asked.

"A supplemental and not the *Wicca's* own main bay? You'd think you didn't trust him." He smiled wryly at Tamyn.

The squat shuttle rested at the edge of the apron, nose forward. Tamyn stopped about five meters away. Kryder kept slightly behind her. After a few minutes, a ramp opened beneath the nose and lowered.

Trace Alek descended the ramp to the deck. Almost two meters tall, slim, and conservatively dressed in dark green, his hair was a striking mass of pale blue, highlights catching silver under the bay floods. As Tamyn neared, his face revealed the webbed evidence of all the uses to which he had put it in a long political career.

"Shipmaster Glass," he said, stopping a meter away from her and bowing politely. His gaze shifted briefly to Benajim, then past him to take in the bay. "Not exactly the kind of welcome I expected."

"We're doing maintenance on *Wicca's* main bay, Regent," Tamyn said. "Welcome aboard."

"Thank you. I hope we can come to an accommodation fitting everyone's needs."

"We'll see, Regent."

Another man stepped from the shuttle. Tamyn stiffened. He was slight compared to Kryder but his function was obvious.

At the edge of her vision she saw Kryder begin to move forward. "Your prophylactic can stay here," she said.

Trace Alek frowned and looked behind him. "This is one of my aides, Ras Gellem. I don't require a—"

Gellem moved too fast for Tamyn to follow. Trace Alek staggered aside, arms flailing. Tamyn felt a solid impact against her left shoulder, spinning her. She lost her footing and fell.

She rolled automatically to a crouch. Kryder lay far at the opposite end of the bay, slammed against the bulkhead, head lolling on his massive chest. Tamyn looked up at the observation blister, but Gellem had somehow smeared the surface with a milky stain and all she could make out within were shadows.

Tamyn got to her feet; her shoulder throbbed. Trace Alek lay sprawled on the deck, legs wide, arms out as if to hold onto gravity. He raised his head and began looking frantically around.

Benajim was gone.

Tamyn hissed and strode toward Kryder, who still sat unmoving against the wall. She tried to think through what she had just seen—Trace Alek descending from the shuttle, his aide appearing, Kryder moving, then—

Kryder breathed ponderously. A thin line of blood ran down from his lower lip, staining his shirt.

Suddenly Kryder jerked once and his eyes snapped open. In the next instant he lurched to his feet and began surveying the bay. He looked around wildly. Tamyn recognized the intense, almost desperate expression: he was forcing himself. Chemical and electronic augments supplemented his native capabilities, and he had triggered all of them. He was hyperaware and very dangerous.

He stared at Tamyn.

"Kryder," Tamyn said clearly, firmly. "Gellem is seti. He's loose on *Wicca*. Locate."

He hesitated. His eyes closed for a moment, then he winced.

"Haranson is dead," he said. "Gellem is in the Flow."

"Tamyn," Stoan's voice echoed through the bay. "*Jarom* is attacking our datasphere. Systems are being corrupted. We're losing defensive cohesion."

"Is Shreve linked?" she asked.

"Yes."

"Kryder, find Gellem. Neutralize him."

Kryder stepped inside the lift tube, pressed arms and legs against the sides, and made a quick crablike climb up the shaft.

Where was Benajim? She called his name and searched the surrounding bay quickly. Only Trace Alek remained, shakily climbing to his feet. He stared at her with mute surprise.

The shuttle hatch was sealed. Tamyn went to a large console at the terminus of the docking cradle. Within seconds, she locked the shuttle to the pad. She set the bay to void its atmosphere as soon as she and Alek left.

"Come along, Regent!" She shoved him ahead of her, starting toward the lift. "Let's hope your weapon hasn't damaged my ship!"

Benajim pried open the control panel on the lock. He touched his fingers to the secondary control contacts, let the data suffuse him for the instant it took to comprehend the override, and ordered the lock open.

The heavy doors slid aside and he stepped into the chamber. The panel on the deck already stood open. He reached down and touched the plate on *Solo's* access. His ID opened it at once. He climbed down the shaft and dropped into the lock and cycled through and hurried onto the bridge.

The speed with which Gellem moved—not human, certainly, and maybe that was the reason the Stralith had been unable to determine with certainty the nature of the three people on board the shuttle from the *Jarom*. Who, he wondered, was the third person? For an instant in the supplemental bay it seemed Gellem was coming for him. At the last moment, the saboteur veered off and scurried up the lift tube, into the observation blister with the Stralith and Haranson. All at once the transparent surface of the blister went opaque.

Tamyn Glass was down. So was Trace Alek. And Kryder had been knocked across the bay. Benajim had taken that opportunity to leave. Only one way out: he clambered up the emergency rungs inside the lift tube, pushed the platform up out of the way, and climbed into the observation blister.

The Stralith had retracted into itself defensively and become little more than a large pinecone-shaped mass, shielded within its mantle.

No alarms had sounded. Gellem was loose on the *Wicca*.

Stupid, he thought impatiently, too stupid to live...

None of them had expected the attack. Not like this.

He brought all the systems up to full and began a check.

Problem? the ship asked through the link.

Yes. Tamyn's ship has been compromised. We have to leave, now. Are we clear?

No one's even noticed us yet.

Good. Start debarkation. On my mark—now.

The connections to the *Wicca* closed off. In a moment the two ships no longer shared peripheral layers of datasphere. Benajim broke the seal with the lock and *Solo* dropped away.

The *Jarom* was very close. Through the sensory shell Benajim could "see" the rippling waves of grapples trying to move the blocking supplementals aside and find purchase on the *Wicca*. *Wicca's* own tractors countered adroitly. He reached out to the dataspheres. Thousands of fibrous lines reached from the *Jarom*, like filamental roots trying to find a way into fertile ground. The dataspheres crackled and sparked with the energy of the exchange.

Best we get out of here, Ben. Can't do much yet.

Benajim powered up and shot away from the pair of dueling giants.

Joclen monitored the *Jarom's* movements while running a subroutine to simulate possible attacks and countermeasures. So far, no missiles or beams had been fired; all the battle raged between dataspheres and grapples. She could not believe another shipmaster, even one working for the Board of Regents, would attack *Wicca*, especially not over something as trivial as a stolen ship. More likely these maneuvers were bluff, bluster. Nevertheless, she ran the simulations just in case.

Shreve's presence in the Flow showed as a brilliant starpoint, hundreds of luminous trails leading to him, continually accessed datanodes supplying him with as much power as he needed to work his own simulations and create a different sort of countermeasure. *Wicca* possessed a few particle beam projectors, a brace of missile launchers and an adequate stock of hull punchers, but Shreve was the first line of defense. If virals got into their datasphere and damaged the control systems, it would not matter what other weaponry they had. Joclen was fascinated by Shreve; she wondered what it was like to be half cybernetic—more than half, she thought, the way Shreve exhibited such a limited range of emotional responses. Stoan was more human, even with his often incomprehensible expressions.

The datasphere seemed organismic. Nodes spun candyfloss trails into and out of collections of static structures that grew from the function centers of the ship. Crew flitted in and out of the whole like insects, making temporary connections between the nodes, forming new constructs to meet new needs. Everything danced together in an elegant chaconne that made perfect sense while one was a part of it.

Suddenly a black shatter-pattern emerged from the midst of a collection of datanodes. Its tendrils plunged into other nodes, causing immediate corruption.

Shreve!

On it.

Shreve sent several thick tendrils toward the disintegrating datanodes. The cables of code entwined each other, snaking in and out. Shreve's countermeasures bound the black lines, absorbed them, and slowly removed them from their victims. Shreve alerted others and brought a few more crew to bear on reconstructing the disintegrating datanodes. None possessed Shreve's skill, but he could not do all this alone.

Another shatter-pattern appeared.

The surface of the datasphere rippled, shockwaves coursing throughout the medium. The *Jarom* sent lances of code to strike at guarded entry points, looking for a way into the corrupted areas.

Joclen powered up the weapons, funneled missiles into launchers, programmed targeting, then activated a back-up datasphere as prophylactic in case Shreve failed. It would not work for long in that case, but maybe long enough for her to get a shot off.

Another black outcrop appeared. Corruption in several major datanodes now caused severe problems in data transfer. Lines of interaction faltered, broke, contacts faded.

Shreve planted countermeasures at each point of outgrowth. But the corruption already in place seemed to be fighting the attempts to replace the spoiled datanodes. Each time a new node was brought in to replace a damaged one the infection spread.

Then one of the primary defense algorithms faltered. An entry point opened and a snake of the *Jarom's* probing code stabbed inside.

Shreve was right there. He encased the tendril, held it in place, then his code traveled back down the tendril to the Jarom.

The entire Flow flickered.

Where's Tamyn? Stoan!

Tamyn is not within the Flow. We are trying to locate the saboteur.

It flickered again. The access paths for the crew were being destroyed. Alternate routes were forged, but it was a slow process and much of the support machinery within the Flow itself was engaged in combating the corruption.

How'd it get in?

Joclen shifted through the volume from point to point trying to find the residual code of the saboteur. At each entry point she found only a familiar presence: Haranson's.

The Flow flickered again. For an instant she was back in the grounded shuttle, the dull thunder of heavy rain in the background.

She pushed her way into *Wicca's* datasphere and started collecting the navcom control nodes. One by one she placed them in the smaller, cramped datasphere of the shuttle. All she needed then was a link to the navcom machinery and she could run the ship. But the link itself was being threatened.

The Flow flickered.

Tamyn dragged Trace Alek out of the supplemental and back toward the connecting hatch. He was not used to the orientation change and fell to the deck retching the first time. She grabbed his jacket collar and hauled him to his feet. He staggered forward under her direction. The man was in shock, for which Tamyn was grateful.

"I didn't know," Trace Alek said suddenly. He looked grim, pale now with a hint of fear in his eyes. "He's my secretary...one of them."

"Do all your secretaries go armed to diplomatic negotiations?"

She took him to the passenger section and searched for a vacant room. A heavy vibration rumbled through the deck. She went to the nearest comm and pressed her fingers to the gate.

Stoan.

System compromised—fighting—virals from Jarom. Someone is trying to shut down the TEG.

A flash of violet washed through the impression. Tamyn jerked herself out of the link. Black starpoints flickered over her vision. Her shoulder throbbed.

The lights went out.

"Wonderful," she muttered. Across the corridor the function lights still shone on the link.

"What's happening?" Trace Alek asked.

"Your secretary is trying to dismantle my datasphere, Regent. He's remarkably adept at it for a secretary." She opened a panel below the gate and reached a finger in to find the contact she wanted. There— a command-emergency lights winked on, glowing sulphurous amber.

A door opened nearby and someone leaned out.

"Shipmaster...?"

"Stay in your cabins!"

"But—"

"In!"

The door resealed.

Tamyn's breath thickened and she glared at Trace Alek. He frowned.

"Come with me," she said.

"Where?"

"Now!" She grabbed his shirt and pulled him along. Four doors further she stopped, opened the cabin, and checked inside. Empty. She pushed Alek through the hatch. "You stay here, Regent, until we have this solved."

"I object!"

"Your privilege." She closed and locked the door and locked it with her personal code.

She headed for the bridge.

Kryder, grim-faced, was coming out as she reached the door. He rushed back the way she had just come.

"The mole is sealed in one of the labs, working the polycom," Ratha said behind her.

"How's he doing that without a system ID?"

Ratha looked ill for a moment. "I don't know how, but he's using Haranson's code."

"Why hasn't Shreve shut the access down?" she demanded.

"Somehow the defense shields have been tied in to the datasphere access," Ratha said. "If we cut Haranson off, *Jarom* can blow us apart."

Tamyn cursed and sprinted after Kryder.

Benajim orbited Pron quickly and changed vector before coming out of its shadow. Solo fell into a long elliptical path that would bring Benajim around the other side of the *Jarom.*

So far the battle was still one of virals and Flow countermeasures. The grapples were little more than distractions, an attempt to overload an already burdened system. The Wicca held her own for the time being, but with a mole on the inside undoing things faster than they could be reassembled Benajim did not think it would be much longer. Once the *Wicca's* datasphere was thoroughly crippled, fire control would not work, nor would the shields, and the Jarom could punch holes in her at leisure.

Benajim found it hard to believe Shipmaster Vollander would attack this way. Benajim had met the man a few times and had come away with the impression of a fair-minded, independent sojourner. Not the sort to engage another sojourner without excellent cause.

As he came out of Pron's shadow, Benajim entered the Flow and reached toward the *Wicca.*

The datasphere coruscated with energies. Flashes rippled across temporary structures, sweeping them aside. The probing virals from the *Jarom* were spreading deep in the *Wicca's* Flow. Benajim probed for something that resembled an operating system.

Benajim found a construct that looked undamaged, nestled between layers of the datasphere. He touched it.

Identify!

Cyanus—

Where are you? You can't use our links.

In my ship.

How—? Transfer coordinates, vector. What are you doing?

Trying to put myself in a position where I'll be useful.

He supplied the data, then waited for a response. All through the *Wicca's* Flow battle raged. As he watched, several auxiliary operating systems assembled out of the rubble of corrupted ones. Black, fungal-like structures almost immediately penetrated them and began sapping their cohesion. The entire datasphere was being maintained by a constant shifting of all the major operating systems, a few moments here, an instant there, choreographed to dump function in a desperate dance to avoid complete collapse. But there was no time to rally for an effective counterattack. This was purely survival. Impressive, but hopeless.

Cyanus, I'm feeding you new coordinates. What weaponry are you carrying?

A quad of particle beams.

Good. Encode and follow through.

Do you have a plan or is this improvisation?

A little of both. Move.

Benajim withdrew from the chaos. He checked the numbers and smiled. They put him right where he had intended to be.

Joclen rode out the onslaught. She knew Shreve was using her projection into the Flow as a template on which to continually reconstruct the crumbling architecture of the datasphere, but she could not comprehend how. Shreve did not communicate with her directly, since driving his own projection back across the intruding viral into the *Jarom's* datasphere took all his attention.

Then she saw the strategy. Shreve was betting on two assumptions: one, that the usual crew was not operating the *Jarom*, and two, that they did not know their mole, their saboteur, was failing to fatally cripple *Wicca*. There would be a narrow window for attack if Shreve was correct. Joclen repeatedly checked navcom and weapons control. She was navcom, holding it within herself, defending it. Weapons control had so far not been touched. Perhaps they thought they did not need to—or that it could not be quickly and thoroughly done. Better to wreck the larger operating systems, render it impossible to use the link system in general.

The weapons all came online, ready. Joclen kept a tendril of attention on them, ready to fire the moment the opportunity came. She hoped she would not need to.

The shunt was inoperative. Kryder stopped at a lift tube that went straight down. The door was sealed. Tamyn kept back. Kryder studied it for a moment, then punched the control panel. On the third blow it cracked and he peeled away the fragments of the coverplate. He reached in, found a connection, and the door shot open.

Kryder looked down the shaft, then jumped.

Tamyn leaned in after him. The lift was three decks down. Kryder landed heavily, and rushed out the open door.

Three decks, fifteen meters. Tamyn shook her head, then swung far out to press her foot against the far wall. She scooted her way around so only her right shoulder pressed one surface, both feet the opposite, and began working her way down the shaft. She dropped the last three meters and rolled out into the corridor.

Here were long stretches of bulkhead without hatches. Machine shops, laboratories, and the library were all located on this deck, along with stores of raw material, stocks of replacement components, and a couple of chambers that had not been entered in many years. It was quiet. Tamyn realized then that the circulation fans had been shut off.

Vollander has a lot to explain, she thought.

Not far down the corridor one of the hatches curled back from its tracks, folded and useless, dangling in the hall. Tamyn started for it.

Her feet came off the deck. She waved her arms for balance, but she turned slowly around until she faced the ceiling. She drifted a few meters toward the ruined hatch, turned full circle again, then abruptly dropped to the deck. The wind exploded from her lungs and her teeth jarred painfully.

She pushed herself up and ran to the hatch, swung around it, and dived through the opening.

Most of the lights had been physically broken. Shadows reared up from function lights and the few remaining emergency panels. Tamyn recognized the physics lab. The polycom would be to the left, over there...

She crouched and skirted the hulking machinery. She heard nothing. She slowed, leery. While she worked her way around the lab she thought about what Ratha had told her. Gellem was using Haranson's code. But Kryder—who should know—said Haranson was dead. They both had broadcast links to the Flow, tenuous carrier waves that acted as a sixth sense for them. Haranson's absent signal was very apparent to Kryder and the only way it would cut out would be by death.

Something shifted across the deck. Tamyn froze, listening intently. She heard another sound, like plastic cable tapping itself. She stood. Gellem was beside the chair before one of the pair of polycoms on the other side of the chamber. He worked on something, stooped over it. Tamyn moved closer. Thin lines trailed from a jack in the back of his neck to the chair.

Gellem turned, saw her.

He started to raise his arm—

Kryder appeared and grabbed Gellem's wrist. He drove his other fist down onto Gellem's shoulder. Tamyn heard the ugly crunch of bone and cartilage.

But Gellem twisted in Kryder's grip, his free arm seeming to grow as he swung it around. The forearm wrapped around Kryder's neck, the hand splaying across Kryder's mouth and chin. Gellem's left leg shot up, the knee driving into Kryder's ribs.

Kryder stepped forward, into Gellem's grasp, and rammed a fist repeatedly up into Gellem's neck.

Gellem's left leg began to twist around Kryder's waist and the hand clasping Kryder's face pulled. Tamyn saw the strain in Kryder's eyes as he struggled to keep his posture and continued to punch, apparently to no effect. Kryder still held Gellem's wrist and now he began to turn it back on Gellem.

Gellem, balanced on one foot, raised Kryder from the deck.

Kryder got the wrist completely bent back. For a few seconds neither moved. Then a brilliant white flash erupted between them.

Gellem's left leg loosened. Kryder dropped to the deck and pried Gellem's hand from his face, then clasped Gellem's head by one hand and pulled the saboteur toward him, fumbling at the cables extruding from the back of Gellem's neck. Kryder ripped them out—Gellem's mouth opened wide, soundless. Kryder took hold of Gellem's chin in one hand, the back of his head in the other hand, and jerked. A sharp, clean crack echoed through the lab. Gellem's eyes rolled up into his head and he fell away from Kryder.

Tamyn hurried to the chair.

Haranson's body was seated before the polycom, her right hand encased in a box with an interface gate on its surface. Her other hand rested on the polycom gate, taped in place. A jack, cables dangling, had been jammed through her temple. Her face was largely discolored and her eyes stared lifelessly at the polycom.

Tamyn pulled Haranson's hands away and pressed her own to the gate.

Mole is dead. Recover and attack.

Benajim moved closer to the big warship. Any moment now he would register on their sensors and some of their weapons would turn on him. So far so good.

Luck's a good captain, lad, and Tamyn's one of the best.

She was getting ripped to shreds five minutes ago.

The way *Solo* responded to him in the Flow bothered him. He knew where it came from, she was Sean's ship, and a great deal of Sean was a part of her, but sometimes—

All at once the *Jarom's* shield winked out. It was clear through the sensors, a beacon by absence. Benajim was startled. A mistake? He was tempted to do a systems diagnostic to be sure the sensors were telling the truth.

Instead he fired. The particle beams lanced into the hull of the ship, tearing open a hole that spewed atmosphere in sparkling crystals into the vacuum.

Chapter Five

The *Jarom* turned away. *Wicca's* guns opened fire. The faltering shields staved off the initial bursts, dissipating the energy. Tamyn kept up a steady assault as the *Jarom* tried to gain speed. A sickly green and violet eruption coruscated briefly over its hull and winked out. The next barrage from *Wicca* tore into the skin of the retreating ship, leaving blackened scars. Another volley, and the skin buckled and split. Atmosphere gushed out, oxygen igniting even as the other gases froze. Tamyn advanced the particle beams forward, section by section. *Wicca* opened another hole in the hull, but the very next section repelled the beam.

Suddenly, a ring encircling the mid-section of the *Jarom* glowed white and energy pulses shot toward *Wicca*. Tamyn jumped, startled by the number of beams. The cruiser should have been more crippled than that. *Wicca* rocked violently.

"Hull breach," Thijs called. "I've got servos moving in to seal it, the section is already closed off." Pause. Then: "Six on-board supplementals compromised...five of them cargo...the sixth one was assigned to Colum Dover's mission, no one there."

"Any casualties yet?" Tamyn asked.

"None reported."

The *Jarom* fired again.

"Another breach," Thijs reported. "Passenger sections."

"Damn!"

Wicca did not have enough firepower for this; the power cells would be depleting soon.

The *Jarom* came about, moving into position to fire all its remaining batteries. Tamyn braced herself.

A brilliant flash silhouetted the cruiser. Two more followed in quick succession.

Abruptly the *Jarom* stopped dead.

"Its shields are down," Stoan said. "Hah! There are minimal energy readings. I think its datasphere has collapsed. Zero function evident." He gave her a wide-eyed look. "Come with your blind step, strangers."

"We have casualties among our passengers," Thijs added.

"See to them," Tamyn said. "Stoan, what about the Flow?"

Stoan moved methodically, checking readouts. He nodded. "We're recovering. Shreve is on it. First indications are we lost nothing vital. Backups uncompromised."

"Ratha, any comm from the *Jarom?*"

"None. Their carrier wave is gone. But I've got incoming from the *Solo.*"

Tamyn turned to the holo. The *Solo* drifted from behind the *Jarom* and rested a few hundred meters off the cruiser.

"On comm."

"*Wicca*, this is *Solo*. Talk to me. Tell me I didn't just attack a police cruiser for no reason."

"This is *Wicca*," Tamyn said. "Good timing, Co Cyanus." She bit back a thank you. "Do you have damage?"

"None. What about you? Can you maneuver or do you need tractor service?"

"Stoan?"

The Alcyone scowled and nodded. "We can maneuver. Joclen kept navcom coherent and our in-system engines are fine."

"Did you hear that, Cyanus?"

"Yes. I want to board the *Jarom* and check for survivors."

"You wait, maintain your station. I want to be there with you for this one."

"You don't trust me?"

"Truthfully, not at all."

"I'm hurt. But I'll maintain position and await your pleasure, Shipmaster Glass."

Hearing that phrase, Tamyn felt an odd sense of displacement. She worried at it for a few seconds, then turned back to her console and the necessities demanding her attention.

A containment field stood between Tamyn and the gaping tear in *Wicca's* hull. Motiles already scurried over the jagged chaos, measuring, sorting, beginning repairs. Three members of a student research team had blown out into space through that breach. Another passenger was in med with a broken arm and four others were in stasis cocoons awaiting treatment. Traville had suffered some nerve damage while in the Flow. One of her shuttle pilots, Steg, had a broken leg.

Stoan deftly kept the other passengers away from Tamyn. Time later for complaints.

Tamyn found Innes in an observation blister above the envelope generator shaft. Beyond the transparency the coils converged away. Halfway down its length the chamber was ripped open to space, broken coil dangling, cable, metal sheeting, and various other components jumbled chaotically.

Innes and Shreve huddled before a monitor to one side, talking in low voices. Innes looked up as Tamyn approached.

"Well?" Tamyn asked.

Innes sucked air through her teeth and shook her head doubtfully. Shreve maintained a neutral expression.

"Bad shape," Shreve said quietly. "Need to replace about thirty meters of coil, then see if the envelope can be stabilized." He pointed at a readout. "Five subsystems, gone. Might be able to patch them together. Don't know what to do about the coil."

"Could you adapt parts from the *Jarom?*"

Shreve nodded quickly. "Need to inventory personally."

"Fine. I'll let you know when we're going."

Shreve turned back to the monitor.

"Even if we can fix her," Innes said, "what do we do about the fact that we just destroyed a Regency police cruiser?"

"Innes, you are one unremittant pessimist."

"A realist."

"What about our guns?"

"We've got maybe twenty percent power. I've got the cells recharging now, but only at a trickle. We need the energy elsewhere more."

"So if another cruiser comes along…"

Innes nodded. "Fucked."

"Pessimist," Tamyn repeated.

"Realist."

Tamyn went to the intercom.

"Kryder, I locked Regent Alek in a cabin in the main passenger section, number eight. Bring him up to engineering observation node one please."

Tamyn watched Innes and Shreve work on the TEG system. Reports appeared on the several small screens they had temporarily attached to the walls and consoles. The burst from *Jarom's* main batteries had torn through here. Shreve had taken the TEG drive offline the instant the datasphere attack had begun, otherwise the unleashed energies would have ripped *Wicca* apart from within, bursting her hull and spilling her contents into space. They were alive, at least, but from what Tamyn could see the TEG system was completely disrupted. The polycom constructs that automatically monitored and controlled the translight envelope no longer existed in any recognizable form. Shreve would have to rebuild it practically from scratch.

Footsteps came up the corridor. Tamyn looked around to see Kryder ushering Trace Alek into the blister.

Kryder's face showed three darkening bruises along the jaw and neck, but he looked otherwise unruffled. Alek, however... hair disheveled, he looked around with narrowed and suspicious eyes. When he saw the gaping hole and damaged coils beyond the transparency, his eyes widened in shock.

"Impressive sight, isn't it, Co Alek?" Tamyn asked. "It occurs to me that an assault like this is in complete violation of the Charter and at least a score more due process accords the C.R. has signed with various members of the Reaches. It will be interesting to hear your explanation before a full court of your staff's actions." He gave her a puzzled look. "I very sincerely doubt Shipmaster Vollander would willingly have engaged in an ambush of this sort. He's an honorable co. I suspect when we talk to the survivors from the *Jarom* we'll find that your staff is responsible."

Alek blinked at her, then scowled. "My staff? That's absurd."

"Did you know Gellem was a prophylactic and a saboteur?"

"N-no..."

"Did Vollander have orders to do this?"

"No! Absolutely not!" He shook his head impatiently. "Why would I give orders to attack if I was aboard?" He narrowed his eyes at her. "Unless you attacked first..."

"That would be convenient for you, wouldn't it?" Tamyn asked. "I'll be more than happy to replay the recordings for you. In fact, I'm boarding the *Jarom* soon. You can review its records as well."

Alek seemed dubious for a moment, then shrugged. "I didn't order this, Shipmaster."

"How many were in your personal staff? Where did they come from? Who were they?"

"I'm not obligated to answer to you."

"Now or before a court. This was your mission, your responsibility."

"Are you invoking judicial status?"

"If I am?"

"Then we can resume this discussion back in the C.R. in the proper venue."

Tamyn stepped between Alek and the transparency.

"We might not leave under our own power, Regent Alek. You can imagine how that makes me feel." She stared at him evenly then.

Alek glanced at Innes and Shreve then looked back at Tamyn. "Is this a threat?" he asked.

"A suggestion."

He breathed deeply and looked away. "Most of them were new staff. My chief advisor is a woman named Frelin Cass. She came to me six months ago, highly recommended. Over the last few months she has augmented my staff with new personnel. They seem an efficient, competent group. Since my older staff members are responsible for the daily handling of Board affairs, I elected to take the new members on this sojourn."

"You didn't personally check their backgrounds?"

"That is what my chief advisor is supposed to do."

Tamyn grunted and turned away.

"I suggest you don't check things very well yourself, Shipmaster," Alek said. "If you did, this wouldn't have come about. You took a thief's word over mine and set yourself in opposition to the Board of Regents."

"So I deserved being blown apart? The flaw, Co Alek, is that you're on board my ship and would have died, too. Unless you were expendable."

Alek frowned. "I don't understand."

"Your 'secretary' nearly collapsed my datasphere. The two barrages you heard were fully charged bursts from the *Jarom's* guns. Every action taken against us was designed to kill us, including you. I'm willing to consider that you really didn't know anything about this. That you were going to be sacrificed along with the rest of us."

"Why, though?"

"That's what the Court will have to discover."

Alek looked past her at the damaged coils. His hands closed once into fists, then opened.

"Your cooperation would be helpful," Tamyn said.

"What can I do to help?" he asked finally.

"You're coming with me to board the *Jarom*. For now, you're a guest on my ship. Kryder will take you to a cabin. You can get cleaned up. I'll come get you when we're ready."

Alek backed away, turned when he reached the door, and left. Kryder followed.

Innes let out a long, loud breath. "Taking him with you? Isn't that...?"

"Isn't that what?" Tamyn shot back. "Stupid? He could always claim altered recordings later. I want him to see with his own eyes."

Tamyn watched the surface of the *Jarom* as Carl brought the shuttle closer. The big ship drifted slowly, lightless and unresponsive to comms. As they approached, the holes punched by *Wicca* became clear, neatly-edged piercings, polished by the high-energy beams, with small trails of ice crystal and debris streaming from each, the detritus slowly collecting into a nimbus of material enveloping the entire ship.

"Nothing this side," Carl muttered, scowling at his instruments, searching for a viable lock with which to dock.

"I'd rather not have to float across," Tamyn said.

Carl nodded. They were all suited up, but Tamyn hoped not to have to rely on them entirely.

The shuttle sailed over the warship. In the distance, the *Solo* waited, like a predator, keeping watch.

"Shit!" Carl hissed.

Tamyn looked at the *Jarom*. The hull here billowed outward along a line from the tail section almost to the nose. *Solo's* guns had ripped it open, the interior exposed explosively. Metal puckered and bubbled along the rim of the wound; the insides appeared dark and cavelike through the floating debris lit by the shuttle's floods.

Solo began to move in closer. Tamyn caught Alek's bitter expression when he saw the ship.

"Found one," Carl announced. He guided the shuttle around the scarred hulk. Near the blunt prow a ring of light glowed dully. Carl brought them up against it. A gentle shock ran through the boat at contact. Precise machine noises followed, ending with a final *shhkink*. A light flashed on the console. "Coupled," Carl announced. "No atmosphere."

"Signal Cyanus," Tamyn said. "Guide him in to dock with us."

"You're letting him on board, too?" Alek asked sharply.

Tamyn ignored him. "What about life signs? Anything?"

"No," Carl replied. "You'll need helmets."

Shreve, Kryder, and Thijs were already fitting their helmets on. Kryder handed one to Tamyn. She fitted it onto the collar ring and checked the heads-up display.

"Let Cyanus know he needs a suit," she said into the helmet comm. She glanced around at the team, all thoroughly indistinguishable in their dark grey suits with green stripes running from shoulder to boot. "Regent?"

Alek had moved in behind her. Unconsciously she touched the butt of her pistol, then reached up to the storage rack and pulled a helmet down for him. He looked unhappy, but wordlessly fitted it in place.

Shreve moved to the lock and cycled the hatch open. He entered and sealed it. A minute or so went by and the hatch opened again. Tamyn peered up at Shreve looking back at her from just inside the Jarom's lock.

She pulled herself up in a fluid motion and braked lightly against the ceiling of the chamber. Her shoulder ached dully through the painblock Thijs had given her. With a gentle push she turned and drifted off to the side while the others emerged from the shuttle.

Weak amber emergency lights illuminated the unoccupied chamber. Shreve drifted to the console that dominated a raised platform to one side of the lock.

"Minimal power, purely maintenance," he said. "I doubt there's enough to reinstate the datasphere."

The access to the rest of the ship opened silently.

"All right," Tamyn said, "move cautiously. Stay together for now, we make for the bridge."

Kryder went through first, then Tamyn. The others swam after. Tamyn missed her estimate on the next turn and sailed clumsily into the bulkhead. She chided herself for not spending more time in zero G.

The passageway was blocked a dozen meters further on. Twisted metal curled inward; loose objects caught in the giant fingers formed a dam. A boot clung to the lip of shorn hull that came nearest the inner wall.

They backtracked to a cross corridor that took them into the main passage. Here power had failed completely. Tamyn's people switched on their lamps. Tamyn stared, a slow, burning revulsion kindling inside, at the bodies floating along the length of the corridor. Their limbs were bent at odd angles and clouds of ice crystals hovered about them.

Someone bumped her suit and she started. She whirled and her momentum carried her up against the wall, hard. The recoil sent her straight out. Two people caught her arms, absorbing most of her energy, though they turned in a silent dance in the middle of the corridor.

"Sorry, Co Glass," Benajim said.

His suit was a much lighter color—yellow, she thought, though in the bright white of the handlamps it was hard to tell. She glimpsed his face through his helmet and thought he was grinning at her.

"I guess I need more practice," she said.

"Tam."

Thijs and Kryder were by one of the bodies. When she drew close she saw that the eyes bulged from their sockets and the cheeks were puffy, engorged. In her lamp the ice crystals had a pinkish hue. Thijs lifted a hand and shone his beam on it. The fingernails were black.

"Cyanosis," Thijs said.

"You're sure?"

"Not positive, I'd have to do a tissue analysis, but there aren't too many things that'd cause this."

"So these people were dead before?"

"Again, I'd have to do a lab workup."

Tamyn shined her light on the row of cabin doors—all stood open to the corridor.

Benajim was making his way forward. Tamyn pushed off from the corpse and swam after him.

Wicca's and *Solo's* beams had failed to penetrate this deep into the ship. Benajim stopped at the heavy door that sealed this section from the forward bridge section. He worked the contacts on the access. Nothing happened.

Shreve moved him gently aside and laid his gloved hand against the panel. His fingers danced for a moment and the hatch began to move apart. A meter open, it jammed.

"Not enough power," Shreve said.

He squeezed through. Then Benajim. Tamyn followed, Kryder right behind her, Trace Alek squeezing in after.

The bridge was twice the size of *Wicca's*. Most of the couches were unoccupied, though. An entire section of equipment had been blown apart. Cooled globules of what had been molten metal and plastic floated freely.

One body hung above the lifeless holo projector. Four others were strapped in couches, and one of the couches drifted, torn away from the deck by the blast that had taken out the equipment. The body in it was pulped, unrecognizable.

A woman and two men occupied three other couches, one by weapons control, the other in the Shipmaster's couch, and the third before biomed. The man at weapons control's hands were burned off, his interface slagged. The woman was in the Shipmaster's couch. Her eyes were bulged out of the sockets and her tongue protruded thickly from her mouth. Her short hair stood out from her scalp in an eerie halo.

"That's my chief advisor," Alek said. "Frelin Cass."

He floated alongside Tamyn and stared down at the dead woman. She went over to the second man, by biomed.

It was Vollander. His left hand was encased in a box similar to the one Gellem had used on Haranson, his right taped to the interface panel. Thin cables ran from a jack in his temple to the back of Frelin Cass's neck.

"Regent Alek," Tamyn called.

The Regent swam over to her. He gazed down at Vollander in silence.

"I want the database salvaged," Tamyn said finally. "Shreve, you see to that first. Then start salvaging parts."

"This," Alek said, "is your fault, Cyanus. All yours."

"I don't see how you can blame your bad judgement on me, Co. I never asked you to intrude in my business."

"Your fault," Alek repeated. "Regardless. Your fault."

Tamyn looked at Benajim. He stared at Alek from the opposite side of the bridge. When Alek did not look at him, Benajim turned away. Tamyn could sense him shaking his head in dismay, even though she could not see it. Somehow it seemed right, familiar, even though she saw it only in her imagination. There was no answer Benajim could give Alek.

The storm still pounded at the shuttle. Joclen was dismayed when she withdrew from the Flow, expecting both violences to be over.

Clif set a cup of coffee in front of her and smiled when she looked up. She nodded, rubbed her eyes, and lifted the cup to her lips. "Thanks."

Clif gazed around at the monitors. "We're okay? The ship?"

"Yes, we're fine. So far."

"I've never been in a battle before."

Joclen looked up at Clif. He seemed worn. While she had been in the Flow, he had monitored the shuttle's moorings and power systems.

"Me neither," she said.

A red light winked on the interface panel, a request to link.

"You take it," Joclen said. "I'm worn."

Clif nodded and touched his fingers to the gate.

"Tamyn wants us upwell, soon as possible," he said.

Joclen groaned. "We ought to wait for the storm to pass."

"I got the distinct impression Tamyn meant now."

"Mm."

After a pause, Joclen drank more coffee, then eased out of her couch. Her back was stiff. She stretched and twisted. Surprisingly, she felt calm. She held her hands up, fingers spread: not a tremor.

"All right," she said, setting her fingers onto the gate. "Retract the anchors and strap in. The ride up might be worse than the combat."

Tamyn looked up when Joclen entered the small makeshift conference room. She nodded to the younger woman, who smiled and took a seat across from her.

"Any problems?" Tamyn asked.

"Not in the least," Joclen said wryly. "You?"

"Nothing that can't be fixed later."

Tamyn had cleared the chamber out of some of the odds and ends normally stored here. A bank of windows looked down on the cargo section that had been wrecked by the Jarom's guns. Ragged metal, conduit, cable, sheets of melted plastic, and charring, broken by views of open space. An impressive, ugly sight, and Trace Alek seemed unable to look away from it.

Benajim Cyanus sat staring into his glass, face set and unreadable. Kryder stood at the entrance. Shreve, Innes, and Thijs worked on linked slates while they waited. A few minutes after Joclen entered, Stoan joined them.

"All right," Tamyn said. "Thijs?"

The med looked thoughtful. "I removed as much of what was inserted into Haranson's brain as I could. There was a lot of it—polyceramo fibers, basically exploded throughout the brain when the jacks were inserted. The fibers attached to the neuronal mesh at thousands of points."

"And the box?"

"Shreve helped me with that. A translator, of sorts. Gellem had set up a scanner loop that read and duplicated Haranson's interface ID. Gellem, linked directly to her brain, was able to use that ID to access our datasphere and actually enter our Flow."

Tamyn frowned. "And Haranson was dead at the time?"

"Yes. But that didn't matter. A small current fed through the brain would produce sufficient activity in the neural net that the link would respond to."

"The same thing was done to Shipmaster Vollander?"

Thijs nodded.

Everyone stared at Trace Alek. Tamyn walked over to the windows and looked out at the wreckage.

"What about Regent Alek's aides?" Tamyn asked.

"The shuttle pilot is dead. Neck broken, I assume by Gellem." Thijs paused. "Gellem was a Vohec projection."

Quick whispers and sharp intakes of breath ended in solemn quiet. Tamyn's fingertips dug into her palms until she made them relax.

"That explains a few things," she said. "Shreve?"

"Ten days. Inventory says there's enough of the *Jarom* left to cannibalize to get us mobile again. Our datasphere is nearly one hundred percent. I still have scours in the system searching for any vestige of the virals. It was a crude attack, really, from a cybernetic viewpoint. They probably thought they didn't need anything too sophisticated what with Gellem's sabotage."

"I want the TEGlink up first," Tamyn said.

"Already on it," Shreve said.

"We're very lucky," Tamyn said. "A Vohec projection...I'm surprised there's anything left of the system." She sighed and turned toward the table. "You said you'd cooperate, Regent."

Trace Alek looked profoundly troubled now. He looked at her narrowly, shaking his head. "I can't help with something I know nothing about."

"Start with the initiation of this mission."

"Well...after Cyanus stole the *Solo*—"

"I did not steal her," Benajim said tightly.

"Removed the ship without proper authority," Alek amended sarcastically. "We met to decide a course of action."

"Who is 'we'?" Tamyn asked.

"Carson Reiner, Sutter Hall, and Hiram Ross."

"Hiram Ross?"

"Sean's general manager," Benajim said, frowning. "What did he have to do with this?"

"The museum is sponsored by Merrick Enterprises and maintained by a staff in their employ. As general manager, the *Solo* was his responsibility. Also, he knew you, his advice was important. Since you were tracked heading for the Reaches, it was his opinion that you were seeking the executor, Tej-Ojann."

"He didn't know me that well, then."

"On the contrary, I think he was very astute. You didn't intend to just run with the ship but to involve yourself in the matter of Merrick's death."

"I was involved."

"Not in the matter of his primary designation."

"Coes," Tamyn said, warning. "So the decision was made to pursue. Why send you?"

"It was decided that an authorized representative of the Board be present should he indeed reach Tej-Ojann."

"Who's suggestion was that?" Benajim asked. "Ross?"

Alek frowned and nodded.

"Why Vollander?" Tamyn asked, glaring at Benajim.

"Uh...that was my choice," Alek said. "I insisted on picking a shipmaster I had confidence in." He looked at Tamyn sharply. "I knew him. You must believe that I knew nothing of any planned assault."

"Which means," Tamyn said, "that no matter who Co Cyanus ran to, your 'staff' had orders to destroy them. If he led them to Tej-Ojann, so much the better, that took care of the executor and the principle obstacle to your intentions. Tell me, Regent, did your chief of staff recommend that you come aboard my ship?"

"Yes."

"So in any event you were to be sacrificed."

"But I don't understand why. Everything we're doing is legal."

"Really? Why don't you have warrants with you? With Sutter Hall involved, they shouldn't have been that hard to obtain."

"There wasn't a lot of time—"

"That's shit, Regent. What's an hour out of a thirty-day pursuit? You aren't paying attention."

Alek shook his head. "But it doesn't make sense, what you're suggesting. A conspiracy by the Board? To do what?"

"Well, let's see. If I understand everything correctly, the Board of Regents has assumed control of the holdings of a dead man. That's obstruction of primary designation, a challenge to the principle of corporate mortality. That's why you have no warrants. How many judges will sign off on that? How long do you think such actions would stand once they became known? Warrants make it public. You were sent to destroy evidence." She frowned at his silence. "Why is Sean Merrick's will being violated? He did grant ownership of the *Solo* to Benajim Cyanus, didn't he?"

Trace Alek looked at her uncertainly. "I...would rather discuss that with you privately, Shipmaster."

Benajim looked up sharply.

"I think you've used up my consideration," Tamyn said. "I've got deaths on my conscience."

"This is not a situation wherein I'm comfortable discussing Board policy."

"Do you intend to honor Sean Merrick's right of primary designation?"

Trace Alek was thoughtful for some time. "It's not altogether certain that he had such a right, considering one of his requests involved a violation of the treaty between the C.R. and the Pan Humana. I mean, can one legitimately request something illegal? I think not. The question follows, then, if that part of the will cannot be honored, is the whole thing invalid?"

Benajim hissed. "This is just an excuse to steal what isn't yours."

"Something you should know quite a bit about, Co Cyanus."

Benajim's hands flexed.

"That means," Tamyn said quickly, her voice rising, "you know the contents of Merrick's will. How? If his death has not been publicly acknowledged—"

"He told us," Alek said. "The gloating old bastard told us what was in the will. He handed us a draft of it four weeks before he died, just after he'd sent a copy to Tej-Ojann."

Sounds just like him, Tamyn thought. But Merrick never did anything simply to be annoying, there was always a point...

"So," Tamyn continued, "because of one apparently impossible clause you're prepared to undo the entire Charter?"

Trace Alek scowled. "Have you ever wondered what the blind adherence to such a right would do in the case of economic giants like Merrick Enterprises and Mirak Corporation? We've been dreading this day since the Charter was ratified. The dissolution of most companies would be little ripples in the ocean. Merrick *was* the ocean! You can't convince me that all the disparate elements of those two companies would be quietly and efficiently absorbed by the rest of the C.R. without enormous upheaval and damage."

"Quietly and efficiently, no," Tamyn said. "That's beside the point anyway. Corporate mortality—"

Trace Alek made an impatient gesture. "Has never been tested on this scale. It's not as if *you* were to die and there was only the reshuffling of your crew and contracts among other shippers. We're talking about Merrick Enterprises and Mirak Corporation. In their own way they're just as 'alive' as Merrick ever was. In fact, at the end they were Merrick. But beyond that, we're talking about one of the largest economic institutions in the C.R. We're talking about economic chaos in the event that these—monoliths—are permitted to go the way of any other small merchanter."

Tamyn shook her head. "I don't even know what we're discussing here. This is so basic to the C.R. that..."

"And it's never been tested," Alek pressed. "It can't be allowed. The effects could be devastating."

"To who?" Benajim asked.

Alek blinked. "Excuse me?"

"To who—or whom—would it be devastating? You? Your sponsors?"

"To the C.R. itself!"

Benajim smiled. "How do you know? It's never been tested on this scale." He chuckled. "There's your answer, Shipmaster Glass. Why all this bother over one ship and a so-called thief? Because someone has decided, in violation of the Charter, that that much power should not be scattered. I have to wonder why. What's it being used for?"

Tamyn sat down across from Alek. "Regent, do you realize that you're talking about violating your oath of office?"

"My oath is to serve the C.R."

"By contravening one of the basic tenets of it?" She shook her head. "I don't think you understand everything that's going on."

"Don't I?"

"No, you don't. You were sacrificed. If they had succeeded, we would all be dead, and none of this could be debated. You're being used, Regent. Whoever sent you isn't interested in the potential harm of corporate mortality, they could care less about the debate. They want to preserve the status quo, even if it means committing murder."

"That's a strong charge, Shipmaster."

"Can you think of a better explanation? Unless you went along with all this voluntarily, even your self-sacrifice."

Alek opened his mouth to answer, but hesitated. Finally, he shook his head.

"Then I suggest you reconsider your mission, Regent," Tamyn said. "It has now become very personal for you."

Tamyn waited in the dark, a drink, untouched, on the table beside her. The light from her polycom gave enough illumination to see her cabin, but not enough to wash away the images of corpses, floating on the dead ship. Her hands trembled slightly.

The chime sounded.

"Come."

Trace Alek entered, Kryder behind him. The door closed. Alek frowned, looking around the room as if expecting someone else to be present.

"Just us, Regent," Tamyn said. "This is your private meeting with me. Your chance to make me understand."

"I don't see any reason to say anything else," Alek said.

"My people have finished going through the *Jarom's* datasphere. Most of it has been corrupted, unrecoverable, even Vollander's personal logs."

After a long silence, Alek said, "I see."

"No, I don't think you do. We found nothing coherent except the trace patterns of some of the crew. We found no warrants, Regent. We found no orders. We found nothing to suggest that your mission was in any way legal, sanctioned, or even real." She cleared her throat. "The datasphere was destroyed when it became obvious that the *Jarom* had lost. Whatever went on aboard that ship will now remain a matter of conjecture. All that's left is your word."

"I did not lie to you about the nature of my mission."

"I believe you. But that makes it worse."

"In what way, Shipmaster?"

"Shipmaster Vollander's log is gone. Destroyed. Do you have any idea what that means?"

"His personal record—"

"His life is gone. Everything. Vollander was not Akaren, there is no record in any lodge for him. When he retired or died, his log would ordinarily be released in the Flow. A permanent record of all his travels, everything he saw and did as a shipmaster. We rely on those records, Regent. They comprise a library of useful, important data, history. Vollander's is now gone."

Alek's gaze was fixed on her. He said nothing, frowning slightly.

"The same thing was about to happen to us," Tamyn continued.

"Shipmaster, I protest—"

"Your privilege, Regent," she cut him off. "Later. This is private. Between you and I. It's important for you to understand what you've done. You came out here, hunting someone for political reasons. That's fine as far as it goes, but you've put my people under threat. For politics. One crew is dead and their legacy is lost, for politics. My ship was nearly destroyed with my crew. For politics!"

She stood and stepped close to him.

"Understand me, Regent, I think politics is important. It's the tool we use to figure out what to do next. You challenge the Charter if you want, that's fine, we'll fight it out in Flow until there's consensus. If you win, fine, I'll abide by the new law. But you put my crew in danger. I don't care if you meant to or were just too stupid to understand you were being used, the end result is the same. You damn near got my people killed."

"But I didn't."

Tamyn drew a deep breath and returned to her seat. She sat down. "That's all I wanted to say to you, Regent," she said. "We're starting repairs. You'll be treated as a guest aboard *Wicca*. If you remember anything else useful that might help me figure out what's going on, I would appreciate knowing it. When we return to Miron, we'll discuss the next step. What I recommend, though, is that you figure out who you can trust and act accordingly."

"Trust?"

"Carson Reiner? Hiram Ross? Sutter Hall? Whoever sent you on this mission was willing to murder. In fact, that was the whole point. I don't think they'll be reluctant to murder a few more."

"Shipmaster—"

"That's all for now, Regent. We can talk later. I just wanted to let you know where we stand."

Alek gave a short bow and Kryder escorted him out. Tamyn lifted the glass. Her hand trembled less now.

Chapter Six

Benajim stepped off the lift platform and found Joclen Bramus by *Solo's* lock. She leaned against the bulkhead, one leg up, foot pressed to the wall behind her.

"I assumed," he said, "that I had unrestricted access to my ship now."

"You do," she said, pushing away from the bulkhead. "If you didn't, Kryder or Stoan would be here. I want to talk to you."

"What about?"

"I'd like to see the *Solo.*"

"You're Shipmaster Glass's pilot."

Joclen nodded.

"So I suppose your interest is professional."

"Not entirely. Tamyn's my friend."

Benajim studied her. He saw a tall woman, young, but with a brittleness in her eyes that belonged to someone much older.

"Come on aboard," he said, touching the gate on the lock.

He preceded her through the hatch.

"Company coming on board," he said as he stepped into *Solo's* lock. A light above the inner hatch went off. A few seconds later Joclen came through.

"Welcome," Benajim said. "You're the first stranger to come aboard. At least, since I've owned her."

She studied the walls, the deck, the polycom console with a pensive interest—reluctant worship, Benajim thought, watching her. Admiration reticent, but undeniable: *Solo* was a famous ship.

A hatch opened to a short corridor that led to a ladder down. Benajim grabbed hold of the smooth metal rods and slid to the deck below.

"This," he said when Joclen had followed him down, "is the common." The large chamber was furnished with couches, tables that rose out of the deck, a food server, polycom, an oversized wall monitor, and crumpled clothes scattered about. "I've been sleeping in here since I left Miron."

Joclen cocked her eyebrows, critically amused, and walked slowly around the room. After she made a full circuit, Benajim gestured to a wide archway.

The connecting passage angled up. He led her onto the bridge— a smaller chamber than the common, but almost as large as the bridge of the *Wicca*. There was no holographic projector in the center of the deck. A pair of couches faced an amphitheater of monitors and readouts that dominated the forward section. A hodge-podge of smaller stations jammed against the bulkheads. The equipment did not all appear to be from the same era; a collection, as eclectic as *Solo's* former owner. Benajim watched Joclen, and noted her puzzled expression.

"Sean kept upgrading her," Benajim said.

"I've heard so many stories about this ship," she said. "You grow up with them. I never thought I'd be aboard..."

"I've heard Sean was quite a legend."

"'Heard'?"

Benajim tapped his skull. "No memory. My oldest recollection is—well, showing up in Miron City." He turned away. "Would you like something to drink? Sean always kept an amazing cellar on board."

"Whiskey?"

Benajim went back to the common and tapped the instructions into the server. A door slid open and he removed two snifters with five centimeters of shimmering copper liquid in each. He brought them back to the bridge and handed one to Joclen.

She frowned at the glass, then shrugged and sipped. "Hm." She drank deeper. Her eyes squeezed shut and she grinned. "Well, a fire, at least." She laughed. "So, you showed up on Miron without a memory. In a way, I think you're lucky. I'd like to forget some things."

"Oh?"

"Mmm." She sat down in the command couch. "What does it feel like to manage a whole ship alone?"

"Oh, I'm hardly alone."

She looked at him questioningly.

"Sean had a full array of semi-sentient programs to augment the link control. They're not people, but they respond like crew."

Joclen's hand poised furtively over the panel in the arm of the couch. Without touching it, her fingers curled and she rubbed their tips across her thumb, down the heel, and opened them again. After a moment she stood and finished her drink. She set the empty glass on the arm of the command couch.

"So, what was it like living with someone like Merrick?"

"What's it like living with someone like Tamyn Glass?"

Joclen frowned at him. "That's not—"

"Exactly. It's none of your business, either."

Joclen's expression hardened.

"Now," Benajim went on casually, "I doubt Tamyn sent you here, so it must have been your own idea. Tamyn strikes me as the sort who if she wants to know something she comes out and asks. If she felt the need to go through the back door she'd have sent someone who's good at it." He sat down by one of the auxiliary stations. "If there's something in particular you'd like to know, Co Bramus, why not follow Tamyn's example?"

"You're an arrogant co, Cyanus."

"Only when I don't know what I'm doing."

Joclen laughed sharply. "I wondered what kind of a co could cause this much trouble this fast."

Benajim gestured around the bridge. "*Solo* was built in the Kronos Shipyards almost a century and a half ago. Originally, she was a diplomatic courier, crew of four, I think. She was decommissioned after twenty years of service and Sean came into possession of her. He modified the envelope generator, added a deck," he gestured downward with a thumb, "and ran her as an independent merchanter. At one time there was a full set of supplemental grapples on the underside of the hull. When the Distal Wars broke out, Sean had her modified again as a fighting ship, and she saw action on the side of the C.R. She's been in dock for the last twenty-odd years. I think Sean was trying to outfit her to accommodate his disability, but he never finished the modifications once he realized he'd never get outside his own corporate matrix."

"So he gave her to you."

"Yes."

"Why? To compensate for your lack of a past?"

"Possibly. What might Tamyn be compensating you for?"

Joclen's eyes narrowed. "I was born on Clannar."

Benajim started. "I would never have envisioned you as a renunciate."

"Neither would I."

Benajim laughed. "Your family is still there?"

"As far as I know. They weren't particularly interested in my aspirations, so I reciprocate. They were well-off, I can tell you that. I left when I was just over six thousand days old."

"Did they pay your way off-world?"

She gave another laugh. "Q spent on anything not relating to the family business or sect? In fact, I had to leave anonymously. I freerode all the way to Miron."

"No way to Miron is free, they all cost something."

Joclen shrugged. "I've done nothing but profit by it. The best was shipping on *Wicca.*"

"How long have you been with Shipmaster Glass?"

"Just over three hundred days. I signed for this sojourn."

"And now you're primary pilot? I'm impressed."

Joclen smiled. "Yes, well, now I've told you mine."

"So it's my turn?" Benajim looked around the bridge. "I was a slave. That's all I know. I don't remember where or for how long. I've been through a mindwipe. All that remains of it are vague impressions. But that's what I was on the run from when I hit Miron."

He felt Joclen's stare but refused to look at her. He filled his mouth with more whiskey, let it warm his tongue, flow down his throat, and distract him from the cold pain that came with confession. Slave. He did not remember the last time he had spoken the word.

"I imagine," he said, "that you'll tell Tamyn now."

"Is anyone looking to claim their property?"

He snapped his head around. "As far as I know, just me. I'd like to have my past back."

"Do you even know where to get it?"

He shook his head.

A few minutes later Joclen stood. "I won't tell Tamyn your private business if you don't want me to. That's between you and her. I might suggest, though, that you trust her. It would only be fair, considering." She gave the bridge a last appreciative look. "Thanks for the tour, co. I'll come back and see the rest some other time, when you feel more like company."

Benajim listened to her leave the bridge. Presently a light winked on a panel and he glanced up: she had left the lock. Benajim went back into the common and refilled his glass.

Benajim stared at flickering data and listened to the gentle clinking of ice cubes in the glass he held. The ubiquitous screens, readouts, and status lights of *Solo's* bridge comprised a single unarticulated environment for him at present. He reclined in the command couch and let sensations pass through him. Bitterness, frustration, an unexpected sadness. In his mind, he replayed the battle, the tour of the *Jarom*, saw all the bodies. After each review he came to the same conclusion: it's my fault. Try as he might, he could not shift it all back onto Trace Alek.

He thought about the conversation with Joclen Bramus and wondered how wise it had been to admit his origins, particularly when he was not sure of them. Sean had told him he had been a slave. He tended not to question Sean, but he always wondered how Sean had known.

That Joclen had come from Clannar was a surprise. Benajim maintained offices of his company, Doppler Marketing, on Clannar, established at Sean's suggestion. Benajim had never been to Clannar and he did not believe Sean had ever been. A whim, maybe, an eccentricity, one of scores from a man who had seemed wholly composed of them. Somehow it amused him to locate the offices for a biotech research company on a world settled mostly by religious orders of a hundred variations. The coincidence of Bramus coming from there troubled him. There was no way it could not be a coincidence, the odds were simply too great, but Benajim took no relief from that obvious truth. Over the years, and especially since Sean's death, Benajim had developed a keen sense of conspiracy.

Thank you, Sean, for the gift of cynicism...

Sean had been the most enigmatic and eccentric man he had ever met—that he recalled having met—and some of his interests had bordered on repulsive. Sean had possessed an extensive collection of erotica from a dozen civilizations; Benajim sympathized with a certain voyeuristic interest in human sexual activities, but Sean had seemed equally taken with seti examples. He had also been deeply interested in memory, how it occurred, how it was stored, how it was accessed. He had complained bitterly once, with a bitterness Benajim had found hard to comprehend, that although cybernetics had gotten to the point of augmenting the human mind, encoding personalities within machine containers, even constructing AI systems that were indeed conscious, no one had yet found a way of simply and completely transferring consciousness and persona from one organic brain to another. "Death," he went on forcefully, "is a necessary border. We can reconstruct a personality in another system, but the original cannot survive the transfer. All we've managed to do is create more precise descriptions of the problem!" Benajim had laughed and asked him what he wanted, immortality? Sean had looked at him with a compact seriousness that had drained the levity from Benajim. "Of course," Sean had said. "What else is all this so-called progress for?"

And I am a partial person, Benajim thought. Am I being lived through vicariously by a dead man? Is that why Sean left this ship to me?

Would I have taken it—accepted it—if I believed that?

He had lied to Joclen and Tamyn. His memory, such as it was, began months before reaching Miron—on Tabit, deep inside the Pan Humana. He remembered the gnomish man who had gotten him passage on a smuggler, taken almost all his Q. He remembered the long voyage, the closeness of the hidden compartment, the smells of ship and sweat and organics. He remembered the shuttle ride down from orbit in a drone, autopiloted to the ground on Miron. But it was a vague, undetailed set of memories, as if his brain had had to learn how to encode memory all over again before it recovered its proficiency. He had escaped the Pan but at the cost of his identity. He did not know where he had been born, how he had been made a slave, or even how he had escaped. That had all been blocked. The occasional image that surfaced only teased him with ephemeral familiarity. If he got the chance he intended to go back to Tabit. With *Solo* he had the chance. No matter what Sean had wanted him to use the ship for, Benajim knew that this came first. He had never told Sean. He felt guilty about that, too, that he had not confided everything to his friend, his benefactor.

More whiskey. It was a taste he had acquired only recently. Benajim raised his glass to the bridge and silently toasted a great, dead man.

He looked toward a small section of the circle of consoles, off to his right. It was a simple place, a fairly recent addition. Merrick had continued to order additions, improvements, alterations to the

Solo up until a month before his death. Trace Alek knew that, so his claim that the ship was a Commonwealth treasure lacked substance. Perhaps if Merrick had left it alone all these years, the idea might have been valid—though still illegal and unethical, since Alek's intentions and actions violated the sanctity of last wills. The patchwork layers of equipment and ideas made her a fundamentally different vessel than the one Merrick had commanded at the founding of the C.R. Benajim waved his glass at that one particular addition. A couch, a small projection plate, and a switch.

"I could ask you what you intended," Benajim said. "But I doubt you'd tell me."

He looked away. Finding nothing else to hold his attention, he looked back at the booth. He sighed, swallowed a mouthful of whiskey and stood, and went, slightly unsteady, to the booth.

With mock ceremony he placed the glass on the right, bowed at the waist, and lowered himself into the couch. He stabbed the switch and leaned back.

The air above the projector blurred, brightened, solidified.

"It's me, Sean," Benajim said. "Yours truly."

Features formed. The old, lined face peered at him for a moment, then creased further around a wide grin.

"Ben! God, it's been an eternity!"

"It's been three days."

"Easy for you to discount three days. For me, stuck inside this box, that's a few hundred trillion nanoseconds or something like that."

"Hello, Sean."

The grin diminished. "What's wrong?"

"I found Tamyn Glass."

"Oh. And?"

"There was a fight..."

"Between you and Tam? Not good. She's to be trusted, Ben, not argued with. I daresay you lost."

"No, not with her. With the *Jarom.*"

"Oh."

Benajim looked at the glass but resisted picking it up. "I—killed some people, Sean."

Merrick's features shifted, eyebrows raised questioningly. "Never an easy thing to do right off. What happened?"

Hesitantly at first, then more fluidly, Benajim described the events leading up to the battle, the battle, and afterward on board the holed and decimated cruiser.

"Trace Alek's still alive, then? I'm surprised at Tam. When she was younger she'd've shoved him out a lock, let him float home."

"She didn't seem any more eager to kill anyone than I was."

Sean looked skeptical. "More likely she wasn't taken with the idea of engaging a better armed ship. You did the right thing, Ben. Tam might've lost without you. Had Vollander been in command, both of you would've lost. But then he wouldn't've attacked."

"You're not very surprised by all this."

"Should I be? I am, actually. I'm surprised anyone could have taken Vollander's ship away from him. He was an experienced, seasoned shipmaster. I'm sorry he's gone. The people who did this were capable. Bastards, but very capable."

"People are dead, Sean."

"People die all the time. Ask me how I know."

Benajim picked up the glass and took a drink. Sean frowned at him.

"If I were you I'd be worrying over who those people were that took a warship from its commander instead of crying in my cups."

"Why is it so easy for you to dismiss what I did?"

"What? Kill someone who was trying to kill you? Would you feel better if you'd let them succeed?"

"No, but—"

"But nothing!" Sean sighed audibly. "I can see that you're confused. That confusion can get you killed. Right now you're flaying yourself because you're not sure what you did was right. Fine. That's a form of learning. But consider this: you're not sure it was right because you wouldn't want it done to you. Your dilemma stems from the fact that someone was going to do it to you and you responded in kind. Do two wrongs, you ask yourself, make a right? It's a ridiculous question under these circumstances and, I assure you, a false dilemma. In the scheme of cosmic intangibles, is the net result moral or immoral? Since they're dead it no longer matters to them. Since you're alive, all that you have to consider are the ramifications of your success. Flaying yourself is just a form of survivor's guilt. If it enables you to act in the future, fine, indulge it, but it's nothing more than a justification to yourself."

"A justification?"

"Sure. As long as you can feel bad about something you can go ahead and do it. That makes it only a little wrong, because you had to do it and you feel appropriately sorry afterward. Next you'll want me to tell you that killing never gets any easier. Bullshit. That's a fairy tale designed to convince us that we aren't all sociopaths. The truth is killing always gets easier with repetition. Discriminate killing is always hard and never gets easier. But that's a matter of responsibility, which may yet turn out to be the only moral criteria."

"Then why do I feel so damn bad about it?"

Sean's features softened a little. "Because when you kill someone you come face to face with the fact of mortality. No one lives forever and sometimes life is really damn short. The true pathological killer is the one who never sees his own death in every victim."

"I'm not sure I want to live in your universe."

"I'm not thrilled with it myself, but there it is." His head shook briefly. "Bah! Philosophy. I always feel like I've eaten something utterly flavorless, dry, and essentially vile when I talk like that."

"Hm. You mean you don't agree with yourself?"

"Don't get personal."

Despite himself, Benajim smiled. "Why'd you give this ship to me, Sean?"

"I'll be damned if I'd let her sit in a museum or a dock somewhere, unused. Of course, I'm probably damned anyway."

Benajim wondered if an encoding could feel ashamed of itself for lying. It was pointless, though, to pursue it; he would get no useful answers here.

"Alek keeps talking about posterity and the heritage of the Commonwealth."

Sean wrinkled his mouth in disgust. "If you can't carry your heritage around in your heart it's not real. The posterity and heritage Alek is talking about is the kind you can use, as in power. He and Carson Reiner and their bunch want to establish the Board of Regents as a governing body instead of what it is, basically a body of advisors and arbiters. A bad idea. The Pan is infected with that disease. Hell, it was handed down from Earth before the Sprawl occurred. Nothing was ever done if it threatened someone's hold on power. Everybody thought the Sprawl would take care of it.

Space is too big for power to operate over interstellar distances. Wasn't the first idea humanity had wrong."

"You remember all this?"

"No, I was born after the Sprawl began. God, I'm not that old!"

"I don't know. It has to take centuries to get a face like that."

"You son-of-a-bitch! Damn, if I had an arm with a fist on the end of it"—!"

Benajim was laughing. Sean watched for a few seconds then joined him, cackling in his raw, old man's rasp.

The laughter died slowly and the two regarded each other in silence for a time. At times like this Benajim felt that Sean really still lived. Part of him, he knew, had not yet accepted the fact that Sean Merrick was dead.

"Feel better?" Sean asked.

"Some. I'm still not sure about all this, but..."

"You'll sort it out. I did."

Benajim finished his glass without comment.

"Speaking of sorts," Sean went on then, "what do you think of Tam?"

"She's not what I expected."

"She never is."

"She's not happy about me. I've damaged contractual arrangements for her and thoroughly upset her life."

"Hmm. When this is all over you'll have to make it up to her."

"Why me? It was your idea to find her."

"How am I going to make it up to her?"

"She's included in your will. Since all this was planned, I expect that's partly compensation."

Sean chuckled. "That will is going to be a shock to everybody when it gets read into the Flow. I'd love to be there when it is."

"If it gets read. The way things seem to be going it may not."

"Oh, I don't doubt there are people who don't want it read. This is, after all, the first real test of primary designation for the C.R. So far nobody important enough has died to cause much of a stir, but Merrick Enterprises and Mirak Corporation are two of the biggest financial entities out here. The disposition of all that property is a matter of considerable concern to a great many people. Some—like Trace Alek—would just as soon the will never be read so the Board of Regents can simply act as executors and smooth everything over. If you just disappear and everyone else gets quietly bought off, the test never arises. The status, so to speak, remains quo."

Benajim listened with half his attention. Sean had gone on about this almost incessantly—obsessively—before his death. Benajim was unsure, though, that Merrick's fanaticism about the right of final designation was really all that important. It made sense that in some cases some other agency—a government, in this case, or as close to a government as the C.R. had—might be more responsible in the disposition of large blocks of property, power, and influence than the individual who was no longer alive to control it.

But where was the line? Below what threshold was it sane and rational to mandate primary designation, and above which did it cease to be workable? The C.R. did possess a government, and it was growing, evolving to answer needs and demands which simply could not be managed by individuals. It seemed only reasonable that limits be set, and set broadly, by disinterested authority. But how could interest be flensed from authority when—

"Are you listening to me?"

Benajim started and blinked at the scowling face floating before him.

"Sorry," he said. "I was thinking."

"Good. I'm proud of you. But if you're going to ignore me then let me get some sleep."

"Do you sleep?"

"As far as you're concerned, yes."

"All right. I'll talk to you later."

"Sooner than three days next time."

"I'll try. Thanks, Sean."

The image smiled and nodded. Benajim touched the contact and the projection dissolved.

He poured another whiskey and went back to the command couch. It was difficult to think of the ship as his when he had to share it with a ghost.

Benajim awoke the following day to find a schedule from Shipmaster Glass on *Solo's* comm. A repair roster, with task assignments. *Solo* possessed more powerful tractors than *Wicca's* shuttles, but the first job Glass set for him was a survey outside the perimeter of the system to see if any other ships lay in wait. Benajim felt fairly certain the *Jarom* had come alone—and he believed Tamyn felt that way, too—but it was a reasonable precaution.

He deposited a dozen small satellites at intervals around the system, each with its own short-burst TEGlink, leftovers from *Solo's* days as a corsair. If everything went well, he would collect them before leaving the system. Then Benajim returned to help with rebuilding the *Wicca.*

Except for the one serious tear that had killed the three students, the main body of the *Wicca* had come through the fight relatively unscathed. Scoring, weakened plates, a few holes here and there, nothing that could not be fixed easily. Most of the severe damage had been done to the supplementals—and the TEG system.

Innes and Shreve supervised the scavenging of the *Jarom.* Benajim spent hours linked into the Flow with them, ripping up hull plating, lifting out components, and moving the new parts to *Wicca.* Shreve was an experienced datasphere mechanic and worked at a high level of efficiency, almost too fast sometimes for Benajim. Innes conducted the inventory and supplied the schedule for transfers.

Unsurprisingly, Tamyn took some of the *Jarom's* guns and the power cells to juice them.

On the fourth day, one of Benajim's satellites sent a signal that a ship was coming in. He took *Solo* out to meet it and came face to face with a Rahalen ship. They had come in response to Tamyn Glass's request for aid. Benajim escorted the vessel in.

He was not privy to whatever communications went between Tamyn and the setis, but by the end of the day the remaining research teams had transferred to the larger ship for transport to their respective destinations, along with the balance of Tamyn's cargo.

Twice the size of the *Wicca,* the Rahalen vessel was a fragile-seeming hemisphere set atop a platform like spun glass. The surface caught and refracted light like oil on water. Each time Benajim saw a seti ship he felt awe and a gnawing compulsion to go to them and touch them, talk with them, learn what they were like. He wanted to travel the Reaches and count the seti races and civilizations. How many of you are there? Enough...

Without ever seeing its crew, Benajim watched the ship leave the next day.

On the seventh day, ahead of schedule, they were ready to leave Pron.

The beep brought Benajim out of a light sleep. He looked around *Solo's* bridge then pushed out of the couch. He leaned over the communications console.

"Yes?"

"This is Glass. Permission to come aboard?"

"Of course."

Tamyn stepped onto the bridge, examining everything, her eyes a little wide, her gaze tentative. She seemed immersed in nostalgia.

"I guess you're familiar with her?" Benajim asked.

"It's been a long time," she said. "Sean hired me when I was fifty-five hundred days old. I worked on a couple of his freighters for a few years, then suddenly he wanted a traveling companion and I was here." She smiled. "He did that then. Just got an impulse and took off for parts unknown. We sojourned for better than fifteen hundred days. When we came back I was handed a ship from his fleet and he told me to make it profitable."

"The *Wicca?*"

"No, a different one, but a merchanter. It was old, in desperate need of repair, and I daresay it was a miracle that it made any Q at all. But it did."

Benajim turned away. "Would you like a cognac? I've got some fine old stuff on board."

"Thank you."

Benajim ducked out of the bridge, into the common, and opened the special cabinet. He took out an ancient cut-glass decanter and poured two glasses. He imagined for an instant journeying with Merrick and wondered what it had been like. An image of Merrick and Tamyn making love intruded for a moment, but he could not take it seriously—his only memory of Sean was as a bedridden invalid.

He returned and handed her the drink. She breathed its aroma appreciatively.

"What happened next?" he asked.

"I wanted my independence. I felt I'd worked off any obligation I had to him. Merrick Enterprises was huge, and there were aspects of life within it that I found...intolerable." She sipped thoughtfully.

"So I went looking to buy my own ship. Sean said he'd back me. It took a while to find *Wicca*, but it was love at first sight. The moment I boarded her I knew she was the ship I wanted. I remember Sean giving me a stern look and saying 'Mind you, Tam, this is an expensive cow you're thinking of buying. The debt burden might not justify your affection.' I insisted and he was as good as his word."

"How long after that did he get sick?"

Tamyn shrugged. "Sean was always sick. He ignored it, thought he hid it from everyone around. Granted, he was good at fooling people. But not those who knew him well. It's been twenty-five hundred, three thousand days since I saw him and he was still walking around then. Two thousand days ago I couldn't get past his security." She gave him an accusing look.

"I didn't control that."

"Sean wants me to make a run to Earth. He never ventured anything for only one reason. Burying him in some family crypt doesn't seem like him. There are other reasons. Do you have any ideas?"

"What do you know?" he asked.

"Not very much. He suggested that it's time to open the border again, thought I'm the one to do it. I can't imagine why when he has such an amazing thief as yourself." Tamyn shrugged. "But then, I have a bigger ship. I can see the business potential in this. And since I'm an independent, there's less chance of a monopoly establishing itself. That's still possible, but..."

Benajim licked his lips and drew a deep breath. "Sean was born on Earth. Did you know that?"

"He mentioned it from time to time. For a while I thought he made it up just to sound important. He wasn't above embellishing."

Benajim laughed. "He was always talking about heritage. Not the way Trace Alek is, but what Sean called a co's own true heritage, what's a part of us, inside. He said you could ignore it most of your life, but at some point you want to know where you came from and why. He said, and I quote: 'The Commonwealth is an orphan. We're cut off from our roots, isolated, as if we'd sprung whole from the head of Zeus. The Pan Humana is a memory and a myth, but we don't really know a damn thing about it. Fact is, we came from there, and we ought to remember that, and we ought to know who they are.'"

Tamyn raised an eyebrow. "Pretty good memory."

Benajim tapped his forehead. "Lots of room." He shifted uncomfortably. "Point is, Sean believed we'd fail if we didn't have our heritage to rely on."

"I can understand part of that. I'm an orphan myself."

"Really?"

"Well...after a fashion. My...parents...sold me to a colonial redistribution agency."

"I'm afraid I don't—"

"They didn't last long for the most part. Right after the wars ended, a lot of colonies were badly wounded. Some failed altogether, other settlements just limped along. A few shippers—Sean among them—established routes between them that kept supplies distributed. Some people used to wonder where Sean got all his goods. He was the best, then. Anyway, the Distals subsidized each other until we were better. It still took a long time for everything to recover and hardship practices that sprang up took just as long to die. One of the things that needed redistribution was people. A few colonies didn't have enough population to be viable, so there was a lot of shifting. Since there were plenty of orphans, that was one source for new colonists."

"But that was what, eighty years ago?"

"I said some things didn't die right away. I was born on Grissom. My birth parents had a plantation. The most valuable resource they had was labor. I had five older brothers. Then I came along, and my father decided to trade me for another son. I was barely a thousand days old, I don't remember much, only that I didn't get where I was supposed to go. A man named Gordon Glass adopted me."

She smiled quietly. "He was a veteran, had a headful of bad neuronal mesh from an accident, so he couldn't link very well. At the time we still didn't have the resources to replace that kind of damage. He did maintenance on the shuttles. I grew up on a space port."

"How did you find Sean? Or was it the other way around?"

"He found me. I was working with Gordon by then and Sean came downwell. He was doing an inspection of his franchises. I was assigned the job of servicing his shuttle. In the middle of the job, he just showed up and started talking with me. I don't remember what about. But we talked the rest of the day. The next morning he offered me a job. Gordon told me to take it, it was my chance to do what I really wanted to do. So I went."

"What happened to Gordon?"

"He killed himself a few years later."

"Sorry."

Tamyn shrugged again and took a drink. She looked around the bridge, her gaze pausing for a moment here, a second there. It occurred to Benajim that she might resent him for possessing *Solo*, that she might feel that she deserved her.

"Anyway," she continued, "I understand about being orphaned. What does that have to do with the Pan?"

"Sean felt we had lost our heritage."

"A pretty ugly heritage."

"True."

"Trace Alek says the problem with the C.R. is we have no direction."

"So Sean believed, too. But—an important distinction, this—he believed we had no direction because we have no history, not the long kind that knowing your roots can give, and without that it will be easy some day for someone like Alek or Sutter Hall to impose direction on us. Sean believed that identity is a need for a people and they'll accept it from any source if they've been without it long enough."

"Very interesting philosophy. But again, what the hell does this have to do with opening up the Pan?"

"You're Akaren."

"Yes."

"Then you should know. Aren't the Akaren dedicated to heritage?"

"After a fashion."

Benajim made a gesture that said well, there you have it, and sipped more brandy.

"That's facile," Tamyn said. She shook her head. "There's more to it. There's a pretty healthy black market trade across the Secant—you can buy all the heritage you can carry. No, there's something else. Sean was sentimental, but not that sentimental. Business always came first." She stood, finished the brandy. "Thank you."

"Shipmaster Glass?"

Tamyn paused.

"Are you going to do it?"

"If I'm not in jail after we get back to Miron? Probably."

Chapter Seven

Piper Van pushed through the crowd on the public observation platform. She worked her way to the edge of the terrace, against the balustrade. To her right as she hurried along, hand sliding on the railing, a panoramic display rose to the ceiling, busy with the traffic around Miron Transit Station. Off to the extreme left of the screen, Miron glowed, reddish-brown and inhospitable.

She reached the gate and touched a fingertip to the small panel set in the rail. Reservation confirmed, the gate opened and she descended the stair into the loges. Her box was near the base of the tiers. The view filled her vision as she sat down.

Huge merchanters moved with relative slowness amid swarms of small tenders. To the far right a boom stretched out to the dark, incoherent mass of a Vohec ship. Sunlight glinted off the hull of a shuttle rising up out of Miron's gravity well.

Piper touched the interface gate beside her and requested the location of the *Wicca* and the *Solo*. She picked out the pair at once. They were still an hour out, waiting for an open lane to dock. The Wicca dwarfed the smaller ship.

Refreshment? the system asked. Piper canceled all service requests and the troll vanished from her perception.

She deepened the interface and the two ships grew closer. The *Wicca* did not match its previous configuration. Piper called up a comparison. Yes, there were differences, particularly the scarring on large areas of the hull, livid blue, violet, and greenish streaks like bruises. Fewer supplementals filled out the space between foresection and the aft cap. She withdrew and gazed at the two ships. The *Jarom* still had not returned and no data was available on that ship's mission.

Piper touched the gate again and accessed the stream of inquiries of incoming ships. More than a dozen centered on the *Wicca* and a quick survey showed most were business inquiries.

One pulled away the moment Piper brushed by. The manifestation seemed familiar, but in so brief a contact she could not identify it. None of the other snaking cords of datafeed had withdrawn from the node.

Piper cast about for possible pathways the Flow-form could
have taken. Beneath a cascade of towering communication nexi she
found the familiar trace. She touched the surface of the node. Direction was imprecise but she did not need more than a hint. She
pursued the fleeing manifestation.

It led to a rippling configuration Piper recognized immediately
as the Reiner Combine sector.

She returned to the communication node. There was no chance
she could infiltrate there on such short notice and it mattered little
anyway. Conjecture, hypothesis, theory—the pieces were falling into
place. That the sentinel code had returned to Reiner Combine rather
than Carson Reiner's regent datanode was important.

She checked docking schedules. The *Wicca* was assigned berth
18, the *Solo* a smaller one, berth 27. Piper quickly surveyed a diagnostic of the two docks. No apparent evidence of tampering, but
that could be done in a moment.

She requested a secure comm and gave a code.

Naril here, her mother answered.

Piper. I'm monitoring Wicca's *progress into dock. Your conjecture
seems correct.*

What about security? Any notifications for detention?

None I can find.

*Stick to Shipmaster Glass's instructions, then. Find assigned citizen
and defend. I'll be in touch later unless something else comes up.*

Piper withdrew and stretched. The ships had grown on the
realtime display. They would dock in less than an hour. She ached
to know what had become of the *Jarom.* No official requests had
gone out to the *Wicca* when the merchanter had dropped out of
translight at the edge of the system. Naril had checked a few days
earlier and found no official dispatch orders for the ship. Piper had
checked the docks and confirmed that the ship had, indeed, left
nearly sixty-five days ago. No destination had been logged and
departure had been fast and secured.

Less than two days after the *Solo* had been reported missing,
Piper thought.

"Co Van, what a pleasant coincidence."

Piper looked up. A wide-faced man with large, moist eyes smiled
at her from the left edge of her booth. Piper casually placed one
foot flat on the carpet, shifted her weight slightly.

"Co Calenda," she said. Now she recognized the Flow-form: Bris Calenda, agent of Reiner Combine.

"May I join you?"

She shook her head. "I wish privacy, Co Calenda. That's why I leased a loge."

"Yes, but we have a proposition to discuss with you," he said and entered her booth.

Another man followed and Piper immediately tensed. He moved with the unmistakable sureness and ease of a prophylactic. Piper released a dose of adrenal-prox, felt her muscles respond to the stimulus, and amped her reflex coordination and percept processing. His eyes appeared normal, the pulse she counted by the gentle palpitation in his neck unenhanced. He was being too sure. Perhaps Bris Calenda had failed to tell him Piper was a prophylactic.

Calenda sat down. "Don't mind my companion, he's only here as a witness. You've shown some interest in the *Solo.* I'd like to extend an offer to discontinue that interest."

"My interest is in the *Wicca,*" she said smoothly. "Shipmaster Glass is a Van client."

Calenda shook his head. "Don't disappoint me, Co Van. We both understand more than appearances suggest. Are you interested in hearing my offer or not?"

"You mean a bribe."

"I mean what I say. An offer."

Piper shrugged, sat up straighter, glancing at the other, who stood at the entrance to the booth.

"One hundred thousand Q," Calenda said slowly, "and we will drop the Eridson infringement matter with your mother."

Piper blinked, startled in spite of herself. "That's a considerable offer. The litigation itself is worth nearly a hundred thousand."

Calenda smiled.

"Why?"

"We have interests in the affair which, frankly, we do not wish to share. The interference of your mother and her estimable family is not welcome. We're willing to pay for your disinterest."

"But you have to realize that you've just piqued that interest. Doubled it, in fact."

Calenda's smile faded. "Three hundred thousand Q, then. The matter doesn't concern you anyway."

"Then why the offer?"

"Because you're trying to concern yourself. If the Q isn't enough to dissuade you, a more direct form of persuasion will be as readily employed."

"Threats, now. This is getting more rather than less interesting."

"And you're getting dramatic, Co Van. This is really out of your area." He glanced up.

Piper moved and a fist slammed into the upholstery beside her head. She thrust up into the prophylactic's diaphragm, but she knew the blow lacked enough force. He grabbed her forearm and pulled her off-balance, then pressed his thumb up into the gland beneath her jawline. The pain was shocking and she closed her eyes.

Bris Calenda's voice was close. "You have a large family, Co Van. They're all vulnerable. If you pursue this matter we may capitalize on that vulnerability."

Piper opened her eyes and looked up into the face of the man holding her. He was intent, paying attention to what he was doing, yet she saw a glint of amusement in his eyes that, combined with the pain he was causing, stoked her anger.

"Now," Bris Calenda said.

Suddenly she was released. She slumped in her seat, her entire neck and most of her head aching. She pushed herself up and back from them, rushed stims through her system, and waited.

Bris Calenda smiled and left the booth. The prophylactic was already gone.

Piper sat back and massaged her neck. On the screen the two ships drew closer.

Wicca dropped from translight at the edge of the system and immediately the Flow grew richer. Immersed in the interface, monitoring transition, Tamyn experienced a moment of vertigo as the datasphere began to interact with the much greater ocean of information permeating the entire Mirak system. Shreve oversaw the integration. Everyone else joined in the Flow could watch, safely awed by the opening out of their apparent senses.

Tamyn sent her ship ID and filed a request for docking space at Miron Transit. She waited anxiously for the response, half expecting an injunction, official request for surrender, an arrest. Instead, a queue number and a bay assignment returned, encased within a standard welcome home.

Tamyn drifted through the thousand details of docking and unloading and ordering service for her battered ship while Joclen concentrated on navigating through the increasingly dense traffic closer to the station. Shreve and Innes had prepared a thorough inventory of parts and services needed and Tamyn signed off and sent them to the proper nodes. As *Wicca* fell sunward, toward Miron, she kept waiting for a sign that some action awaited her. Everything continued routine, though.

As *Wicca* took up a waiting position several hundred kilometers from the station, communiqués began coming through from her clients requesting updates. She was back far too soon and many of them, suddenly alerted to her presence, crowded her with requests for explanations. Tamyn responded to each one as it came in.

She found an acknowledgement from her advocate that the TEGlink communication sent a few days earlier had been received. Tamyn looked for another update at her personal datanode, but found nothing more than a request for contact upon arrival. Nothing to explain the absence of any official censure, retribution, or even acknowledgement of actionable offense. She refrained from checking with the Regent police.

Roster complete, she sent a brief message to her lodge, and withdrew from the Flow.

"I'll be in my cabin," she announced, rising from her couch on the bridge. "Let me know if anything changes."

It felt wrong. She considered pouring a drink, but instead brought up a schedule on her polycom to keep an eye on comm traffic. She watched the alphanumerics and acronyms scroll past for a time, her thoughts drifting through possibilities.

Her door chimed.

"Come," she said automatically.

Joclen and Stoan entered.

Tamyn waved them into chairs. "When we dock, *Wicca* will have a new owner," she said. Joclen frowned and Stoan looked more attentive. "Something's not right. I don't know what's about to happen, but the only one on this ship to whom any guilt might attach—legally, at any rate—is me. I'm not about to have my ship impounded and my crew cut loose over political games. So I'm transferring title to you, Joclen. Stoan is my witness. It will be registered the instant we connect physically to Miron Transit."

"But"—Joclen began.

"It's temporary," Tamyn cut her off. "I have no intention of relinquishing ownership. I'm relying on you to honor this."

Stoan grinned. "And my testimony would validate her future claim. Cleverness incarnate!"

Joclen still looked uneasy. "What if we all get brought before a Court?"

"It doesn't work that way. A shipmaster is solely responsible for what happens under her command. Tamyn Glass will be the one charged, both personally and corporately. *Wicca* will be in your name and therefore cannot be confiscated for any purpose."

"Is that legal?"

"Barely," Tamyn admitted. "Mostly, though, it's a delay tactic. I want to be able to leave quickly. Even if I'm not arrested and charged, I can be bottled up with inquiries from the Regents. We can't risk immobility. So, for a while, *Wicca* is yours."

Joclen blinked. "Damn."

"Indeed," Stoan agreed.

Tamyn went to her polycom and drew out a pair of disks. She handed one to each of them. "Those contain the full agreement, transfer, and my imprimatur authenticating the transfer. Registration in the Flow will be automatic and you'll be able to make command and contractual decisions on *Wicca's* behalf."

Joclen slipped the disk into her pocket. "All right. I guess you expect complications, then?"

"Oh, yes. Especially when I start trying to fulfill Merrick's commission."

As *Wicca* attached to dock, Tamyn monitored the station services linking to the ship, and kept an eye on incoming comm traffic, still expecting police or court action.

She withdrew from the link and looked around her bridge. Joclen was still deeply linked, as was Shreve. Thijs was leaving and Innes was already gone.

Regent Alek entered, Kryder just behind him.

"With your permission, Shipmaster," he said, "I'd like to take my leave of you."

"May I recommend that you accept the hospitality of the Akaren, in my lodge. It might be a good idea to probe the situation from somewhere safe."

He gave her a half-smile. "Safe from what? I appreciate your caution, Shipmaster Glass, but we're back in the C.R. and I am a regent."

"Still..."

"I'll be perfectly safe. I have inquiries to make and I need privacy and freedom of movement to make them. Thank you all the same."

Tamyn nodded, uneasy. "Let me know how your inquiries progress, then. I'll give you any help I can."

He bowed his head politely and turned. Kryder stepped out of his way and Trace Alek left the bridge. Tamyn wished Haranson was still alive; she could send a prophylactic after him. She could send one of Kryder's aides—nonaugmenteds—but she doubted Alek would accept the protection. A prophylactic could not be dismissed.

She touch her gate.

Tamyn Glass, requesting immediate communication with Naril Van.

A few seconds later a communication node flowered.

Tamyn.

Naril, I need a favor.

You need more than that. What have you done?

I'll transfer the data after. I need to have someone protected. I'm having trouble protecting my own right now.

?

Tell you in person. Who? I've already seen to Benajim Cyanus.

Regent Trace Alek.

Why?

I suspect he's in jeopardy. Nothing substantial, but...

I'll see what I can arrange. Anything else?

Where are you?

Downwell.

Need you upwell. At the lodge.

I suggest that you stay on your ship till I get there—

I'll be safe enough in the lodge.

But will you be safe enough on the way?

Naril, I have a promise to keep, and if I wait I may run out of time to keep it. I'll be at the lodge.

Damnit, Tam, you know how I feel about shuttling!
Naril—
I'll be there. I thought I could avoid this.
Situation may become very fluid. Have to keep all options open.
Verification of the transfer of title came to her then.
What have you done, Tamyn?
Covering our asses.
Do you trust her?
Stoan witnessed, but, yes, I do.
I can't wait to meet her...
Tamyn withdrew from the link.

Joclen was absent.

"I'm going to the lodge," she said, standing.

Ratha looked up from his station. "Do you want me to tell anyone you're there?"

"Use your best judgement, but in general, no. I'm taking Joclen and Kryder. Tell Traville he's in charge of ship security. Where's Joclen?"

Ratha touched his gate. "Engineering."

"Where else?"

Ratha chuckled, nodding.

Kryder joined her on the way, falling in quietly behind her.

"You saw Regent Alek off the ship?" she asked.

"I did."

"Anybody waiting for him?"

"Not that I detected. It does not appear that any surveillance has been placed on us, either."

Tamyn stopped by her cabin and packed a small bag of personal items and a change of clothes. She paused before the Pronan statue. Keep an eye on things for me, will you? she requested silently. She laid a finger on its head briefly, then went to engineering.

Joclen was helping Shreve and Innes set up the repair schedules for the station maintenance motiles. She looked up when Tamyn entered the chamber.

"I'm going to my lodge," Tamyn said. "Can they manage without you?"

Joclen blinked, then grinned. "Give me a couple of minutes."

Tamyn nodded. Below, the envelope coil stretched away. Motiles scrambled over its length. A section of the housing above had been cut away and cables hung down into the ship. Tamyn glanced over the readouts of a nearby monitor. The envelope generator had operated poorly. It had taken too long to generate the field through which the ship slipped at translight velocity, and the integrity of the envelope had come dangerously close a couple of times to failing. Tamyn had been afraid of exactly that, which was one reason she had not towed the *Jarom* back.

"I'm ready."

Joclen, her own bag on her shoulder, followed Tamyn through the lock and out of the ship. Kryder walked silently behind them.

Through a wide transparency in the debarkation chamber the entire length of *Wicca* was visible. Motiles swarmed over the hull amid a forest of cables, conduit, and cranes. The cannibalized plating and retro-engineered apparatus gave the ship a patchwork appearance. Burn marks discolored the skin.

They crossed the chamber and exited into the warehouse circuit that ran parallel to the docks. Offices and storage facilities shared space with cheap flophouses and eateries. The tang of oil and ozone filled the air and motiles whined alongside humans and setis, moving pallets, running errands, carrying messages. It was a busy, noisy corridor, fifty meters wide, starkly-illuminated from high overhead. Tamyn and Joclen crossed to the opposite side and entered a narrow passage that let them into the warmer, cheerier light of a main station circuit.

The artery was wide and spacious and in spite of the large number of coes it did not seem crowded. Overhead the ceiling glowed a pleasant blue that mimicked open sky. Islands of thick green foliage and flowering plants followed a staggered path down the middle. Shops alternated with offices, restaurants, private residences.

Four hundred meters along the circuit Tamyn stopped before a plain metal-grey door, three meters tall and two wide. Above it was a pewter hemisphere set in a midnight blue disc. Tamyn stepped close and placed her hand flat against a scanner set in the frame.

The door slid open. Tamyn turned to Kryder.

"I want you to stay near the ship until I call for you," she said. "On the docks, surveillance. Traville has shipboard security. If anything crosses your attention, report to him. We'll be safe here."

Kryder nodded and headed back.

Joclen stared through the open door, her eyes wide and excited.

"Ready?" Tamyn asked.

Joclen nodded quickly.

They entered a quiet anteroom, carpeted in maroon and paneled in woodgrain. The door closed behind them. A small man approached from an archway in the opposite wall. He smiled warmly and bowed.

"Welcome," he said. "You are fellow travelers?"

"I am," Tamyn said. She returned the bow. "I have stories from the nether stars."

"And I have the ears of the homeworld."

"Then we may form truth between us."

"Truth for truth. I am Golles Caplan, marshal. Welcome to Miron."

"I am Shipmaster Tamyn Glass. Thank you. I've brought one who wishes to travel our paths. This is Joclen Bramus."

"A pleasure," Golles said. "It's been some time since we received a petitioner. I'll inform the Lodgemaster. Enter and be at home."

Golles led them through the arch, then gestured toward another. He bowed again and went the other way.

"Is it always so formal?" Joclen asked.

"No, only admittance and the initiations. The lodge attendants tend to become a bit stiff after a while, though, and it does get silly—Golles and I have known each other nearly two thousand days." She shrugged. "You get used to it."

The archway led to a gallery of holographs from other worlds. Some were landscapes, others of cities, some of oceans, others of space. Tamyn watched Joclen pause before each one and study it intently, as if to memorize every detail.

Tamyn felt slightly amazed at the speed with which she had decided to sponsor Joclen. From the first, Tamyn had felt a rightness about the woman, a connection of trust and kinship she had experienced only a few times in her life. Up until the arrival of the *Solo* and Benajim Cyanus, Tamyn still hesitated—but now there was no question. She wanted another Akaren as witness. She was the only one on board *Wicca* who had accepted membership. She had offered sponsorship to several of them and they had all politely declined. Joclen was eager. And Tamyn trusted her.

Golles returned. "The Lodgemaster will see you now, Shipmaster. I'll take Co Bramus to her room and begin her preparations."

The Miron Lodge of the Akaren occupied a four level block. One of the first lodges, it was crammed with history. Along the walls leading to the Lodgemaster's private chambers were paintings, holographs, representations from all over the Reaches, and the occasional portrait of a fellow traveler—*Aka'Ren* in the language of the Rahalen. Tamyn found her way through the maze to the Lodgemaster's private audience room.

She found an old man with bright blue, youthful eyes. A stranger.

"Shipmaster Glass?"

"Lodgemaster."

He motioned to a chair and she sat down.

"I am Sarkis," he said. "I became Lodgemaster in your absence. I'm told you brought a petitioner?"

"My pilot," Tamyn nodded.

"Is there some urgency in her admission?"

"Not that I'm aware...why?"

"Your name is appearing in the Flow in unlikely places. Or, perhaps, not so unlikely if what we've heard about the *Jarom* is true. Did you destroy it?"

Tamyn hesitated. "Yes, but we didn't destroy its master. Vollander had already been brought down beforehand."

"Ah. You're on your way to conflict with the Board of Regents." He smiled contemplatively. "Interesting. In that case, my question stands. You may soon find yourself with little time for lodge matters. How important is Co Bramus's admission to you?"

"It's important. I'm not sure for whom it's more important. But..." Tamyn straightened and adopted a more formal tone. "I am about to embark on a sojourn and the companionship of a reliable witness would make the journey richer."

Sarkis frowned. "A sojourn for one may be a sojourn for all," he responded. "May I ask your destination?"

"Let us talk for a time before I say." Tamyn made herself relax. "I'm not sure myself about the wisdom of this journey."

"I see. I've instructed Golles to administer the preliminary examination as soon as Co Bramus is ready." He narrowed his eyes. "This is all concerned with Sean Merrick, isn't it?"

"Yes."

"Hmm. You were a friend of his. He was never really a friend to the Akaren. Not an enemy, either. His death complicates things. We've noticed some irregular transactions in the Flow concerning his two companies, not least of which is that those two companies still retain their corporate integrity. They should have broken up and dissolved."

"His right to primary designation is being denied."

"An ongoing debate. It was questioned when the Charter was ratified, it will be questioned forever. It is the nature of such principles."

"This isn't a debate now. Carson Reiner and her supporters have invalidated the principle."

"Possibly. That's up to the Flow to determine."

"The Flow isn't being consulted."

Sarkis smiled wryly. "No one invites the Flow to act, it just does."

Tamyn regarded the lodgemaster for a long moment. Her pulse moved quickly, anxiety-driven.

"I may be making a sojourn to Earth," she said.

Sarkis controlled his surprise well, little more than a straightening in his chair showed. "Earth..."

"I need to know if the Lodge will back me."

Sarkis stared at her. "The Akaren believe themselves the keepers of history, heritage, the caretakers of memory...I always found it sad and ironic that we do so on insufficient foundation. The greater part of humanity is cut off from us, we have no knowledge of what goes on in the Pan Humana, and not everything from before the Secession was saved. It's one of our goals to reestablish the connection."

"I doubt this sojourn will accomplish that. I'll be slipping in doing my best to not be caught. A thief's mission."

"But still, you'll be there. You may have an opportunity to retrieve something...anything...of value."

"If the opportunity arises, I'll do that."

"What will you need?"

Tamyn thought for a moment. "Provisions, in case I have any trouble getting them through normal channels. Possibly something in the way of extralegal help."

Sarkis nodded. "To participate just that much in a sojourn to Earth...certainly. You have whatever we can provide."

"Thank you."

"It's settled then. Now." He leaned forward, smiling broadly, his fingers lacing together expectantly. "Tell me some stories. What have you seen?"

The *Solo* occupied berth 27. Piper expected to see station security, regent police, official activity layered around berth 27, but the circuit seemed no different than on any other day. She strolled casually along, studying the coes around her. A temporary sleepover faced the entrance to berth 27 across the concourse. A maintenance motile worked on conduit coming from the next dock. Three carryall motiles unloaded a stack of pallets on a conveyor feeding into a warehouse nearby.

She walked past the access to berth 27. An engineer squatted before an open panel near the next dock, cables trailing from within the wall to an analyzer on the floor. A bored co napped in an information booth outside a locker-lease. Nothing seemed unusual. Piper absently rubbed her neck again; the pain was only a dim, persistent pressure now, absorbed into memory.

She drifted over to a public polycom and touched her fingers to the gate. In a moment she learned that the *Solo* was stationlinked, cleared, with no maintenance scheduled. Piper made a further inquiry and discovered that no engineer had been scheduled for this section of the docks. She looked at the man. He made adjustments on his analyzer and glanced casually at berth 27. Piper studied his face and turned back to the polycom. She dumped the image into the Flow for a match. He was not on station maintenance staff. Berth 28 was leased to an in-system tug independently owned and he did not work for them nor had they contracted with any private company for any kind of dock maintenance. Doubtless she could find a match eventually, but anybody with legitimate business would not be so hard to find.

Piper accessed the comm trunk to the *Solo*.

Co Cyanus, I'm from Naril Van's service. Could we meet?

There was a pause. I suppose. I can't sit here forever. Where?

There's an omnirec not far from you. Sebastien's. Five minutes?

I know the place. How will I know you?

She flashed her image through the Flow and he responded in kind. *He's so young,* she thought, startled. She had imagined anyone capable of being so close to Sean Merrick and stealing his ship to be considerably older, an experienced spacer.

Five minutes, he sent, and broke the link.

As she pulled out of the trunk she surveyed for eavesdroppers. Nothing. When she withdrew she pretended to remain linked. Reflected in the surface of the screens above the gate she could see the opposite side of the concourse. A few minutes later Benajim Cyanus stepped from the access and headed in the direction of *Sebastien's.*

The engineer unhooked his equipment and folded up his analyzer. He replaced the open panel and crossed to the locker-lease.

Piper turned and followed him into the long passage. He had stopped a short way in and was shoving his gear into a locker. When he turned to leave Piper was right there. His eyes flashed for a moment, until she jammed the heel of her hand against his forehead. He staggered backward. She spun him around and pushed him back to where the passage turned.

He started to recover and tried to punch her. She let the blow slip by and thrust her thumb deep into his armpit. He caught his breath sharply; Piper kicked his right leg out from under him and pulled. He dropped to his knees and she took his neck from behind in both hands and pushed her fingertips up under his ears.

"Let's talk, co. Why don't you tell me who you snoop for? Don't bother denying it. You'll just be wasting my time and causing yourself inconvenience."

"I—"

"No lies, now, co. I've got a strand of Ranonan code woven into my DNA. I'm telepathic. I'll know if you lie." She pressed harder.

"I work for Merrick Enterprises—"

Piper squeezed and he gasped. "I don't think that's entirely accurate, co. Try being a bit more specific."

"Hiram Cross." He tried to move away and she tightened her grip. "Hiram Cross! Please—"

"You wouldn't happen to know who Hiram Cross works for, would you, co?"

"Merrick Enterprises!"

Piper changed her grip, found the nerve cluster, and dug in. A few seconds later he passed out.

She laid him down easily. She went to the locker he had been using and with a few seconds had the door open. She went through the contents quickly. Standard polycom maintenance gear. One device—an electron flow monitor—felt heavier than it should. The bottom finally opened and within she found a supply of small surveillance devices that could be attached to the interface lines of any symbiotic ship-to-station system. She spilled them into her hand and slipped them into a pocket, then returned the device and closed the locker. She was already late for her appointment with Co Cyanus.

The Distal War had split humanity into two separate realms. The border between the Commonwealth Republic and the Pan Humana lay between Denebola and Deneb Kaitos, about fifty light years from Sol. The war had devastated not only resources but the image both sides had of themselves and each other; no official contact and little of any other kind remained.

Tamyn had grown up in the C.R. She had come of age in a growing community that shared space with dozens of nonhuman—seti—cultures. The C.R. effectively knew no limits to where they might go, what they might become. No limits on travel and experience save one: the Pan Humana was closed to them, a cloistered empire that wanted nothing to do with setis or the humans who chose to cohabit space with them. For whatever reason—economics, xenophobia, the politics of control—humanity was divided into two separate families, one outward seeking, the other ingrown.

At least, that's how the propaganda portrayed it.

Still, Tamyn could think of no corollary in history where the children had been so totally cut off from the parents. She thought of these things as she watched Joclen go through the initiation rites of the Akaren.

Joclen stood in the center of the round chamber. Above her the ceiling blazed with stars. Panels on the wall all around bore images of worlds, places discovered, explored, or visited by Akaren, interspersed by the various sigils representing seti homeworlds, races, or affiliations. Before these panels stood a ring of chairs, each occupied by an Akaren. Several Rahalen attended, tall and slender and bright in their long robes. Two Vohec projections, distinct from humans only in the solid green of their eyes. Featureless, saffron-skinned Distanti; heavy-limbed, powerful Cursians, a trio of Ranonans, a Menkan, an Alcyoni transmorph (this one sharing traits of human and Distanti), half a dozen others, some in environment apparatus. In the soft opalescent light this gathering represented to Tamyn everything she loved about living here and now.

Sarkis approached Joclen from his seat.

"Memory," he recited, "is the binding substance of civilization. Without memory we have no continuity. Without continuity we have no identity. Without identity we have no purpose. Whatever else you have heard about the Akaren, this now is the truth: we are pledged to memory. We do not forget. We gather, protect, and keep alive memories. All other aspects stem from that central purpose.

"We are not a secretive order. We do not hide or conceal what we do. Everything we are, everything we do is open to all. To become Akaren is a choice, an act of will. We offer sanctuary, companionship, and a community. What we ask in return is a commitment to continuity and truth. We ask that you never turn away a fellow traveler who asks aid in the name of the Akaren. We ask that you accept us as we accept you.

"Do you feel that you can freely make such a commitment?"

"Yes," Joclen said quietly.

"Do you wish to?"

"Yes."

"Who speaks for the petitioner?"

Tamyn stepped forward. "I do."

"Your name?"

"Tamyn Fitzgerald Glass."

Sarkis looked at her. "Do you pledge to instruct the petitioner in the truths of the Akaren?"

"Yes."

"Do you pledge to stand by the petitioner, shouldering equally both the responsibility and the pleasure of her acceptance?"

"Yes."

"All present have witnessed the petition and pledge. Do any challenge?" Sarkis turned slowly round, looking from one to the next. "Good. The petition is accepted. The petitioner is on the first step of a journey." He smiled at Joclen. "Welcome, Joclen Bramus, to the Order of Travelers known as the Akaren."

Tamyn squeezed her fists, savoring the surge of pride.

"Thank you," Joclen said.

Everyone closed in on her then, congratulating her, hands touching her. Joclen turned around within the group embrace until she caught Tamyn's eye. She reached for her and Tamyn took her hand and squeezed. For a moment Tamyn remembered her own initiation almost thirty years ago and the pleasure and happiness she felt at being welcomed among the Akaren. For her it had become a home after years of homelessness. She did not know Joclen's reasons for seeking admission—she had not asked—but from her expression Tamyn could see how important this was.

Someone patted her back and she turned toward the offered hug. She found herself embraced by the smothering warmth of a big Cursian, smelled the musky tang of the seti. Here there were only the boundaries of inner privacy; none others mattered.

Joclen lay awake on the suspensor bed and stared at the paintings on the ceiling. It seemed to her that all of history was depicted in the lodge. Images hung everywhere. Above her was the story of the colonization of Eurasia, one of the first colonies settled by humans in the initial surge of the Migration, or Sprawl as some liked to call it. Ships, harsh Tau Ceti, the unforgiving landscape, the enormous canyon in which the colony first survived, then thrived.

She tried to sort out her feelings. I'm Akaren now, she thought, and chased after the associated sensations. Something else to attach herself to that was apart from Clannar and the stifling expectations of her family and neighbors. Home? Maybe. Tamyn had already offered that, but Joclen had wanted more. There was nothing worse, she believed, than not belonging. If you belonged to no one it meant no one wanted you. What could there be about someone that no one wanted?

Perhaps, she thought, Benajim Cyanus knows.

Joclen gnawed her lip and hoped she never knew—never had to know—such a truth about herself.

Chapter Eight

Benajim listened. The woman spoke with quiet authority. Around their booth both human and seti crowded the omnirec; the din of voices and the thundering music from the next section masked their conversation, giving them a degree of privacy.

"My mother is Tamyn Glass's advocate," Piper explained. "I've been retained to be your prophylactic."

"Your mother assumes I need one?"

Piper—she was almost delicate-looking, with a rounded face, large, black eyes, and short reddish-brown hair—nodded. "It's the safest assumption, Co Cyanus."

Benajim glanced into the crowd. "I haven't exactly had good experiences with prophylactics, Co Van."

"Because you've never had one working on your behalf."

"That's a point," he said. "Are you good?"

"I've worked two other assignments, both successfully. I think I am." She smiled modestly.

"And what do you do between assignments?"

"I've been in university. Two years now."

"Here?"

She nodded. "History is my interest. I've taken a secondary in anthropology."

"Have you completed your degrees? I wouldn't want your studies to inconvenience me."

Piper stared at him blankly, then frowned. "It's not a problem, Co Cyanus. All I have to do is protect you until I'm told otherwise. It would be to our mutual benefit to work willingly together, but I don't require your appreciation."

"Good." Benajim sprawled in the booth and studied her. She did not appear strong enough, but he knew that was deceptive—prophylactics came with a compliment of augments that more than compensated for any natural limitations. "Would you like another?" He gestured at her empty glass.

"No, thank you, co. But go ahead, don't let me impede you. Maybe with a few more drinks we might both find out why you're being such an ass."

Benajim winced. "Maybe. What would you like to know?"

"You might start by telling me about the theft of the Solo. Then go on from there. I was only asked to do this less than a day ago. I'd like to have some idea what I'm involved in."

"Fair enough," Benajim said. He leaned forward and began talking. Piper listened intently, even though her eyes drifted away constantly, watching the omnirec and its everchanging assortment of patrons. Benajim had the impression he was the focus of a very wide sphere of attention.

Tamyn entered the Flow and followed a familiar path to an old node.

I need consultation, old friend...

She waited while the black, purple, and azure crenelations shifted on the surface of the node, suggesting that the life within it stirred now, disturbed, and awoke slowly. A crack widened and bronze light glimmered from within.

Enter...

Tamyn pushed her way through the crack, into the pool of golden light. Silver and blue-tinged pockets swam about like protozoa. No one shape emerged out of the stew and Tamyn waited for further recognition.

Tam...long time, sojourner...

Too long. Forgive me?

What's to forgive? You're here now. You have stories, no doubt?

Many.

But you aren't here to tell me tales.

No...

A spike of red lanced from the midst of the golden soup and out the fissure through which Tamyn intruded.

You're back early...with a familiar ship in train...you want to know about Sean...

I need to know...

You've made promises?

Conditionally, but yes.

Unfortunate habit, that. You should know better by now. Get paid for your trouble first, then—

Please.

A lump of blue darkened, grew briefly, and faded out to silver.

Sorry.

Sean's will hasn't been read. He's dead, but his corporate dataspheres are still intact. True or false?

All true. No explanations forthcoming. There's confusion about the dead part. He still manifests every cycle to sustain his dataspheres. A few jurists and more than a few advocates have been trying to bring the issue to court, but some new rules have complicated that process. If you try it that way, you'll get bogged down, too.

I'm being asked to break the law.

Will you do it?

Not without knowing why and whether it will do any good.

Safe answer. Partially true, but I wager there's more?

Well...

Something personal, of course.

Of course. But—

You like most of the C.R. believe that a bad law ought to be broken. That attitude got you into a lot of trouble at one time. Now that you're just about recovered from that, you're thinking, is it worth the risk a second time?

I'm wrong?

Not in theory. We all want to be law-abiding citizens. Sometimes the only way to do that is to let illegalities stand.

That's a contradiction.

Is it? We went over this years ago. You were a stubborn student then and maybe you still are. Where's the contradiction?

The contradiction lies in complicity. To allow a known crime to stand is to approve the crime, becoming complicit in it.

But if the only way to expose the crime is by a criminal act?

In an open system, no such act is necessary. Revelation renders exposure absolute, leading to—

And if the law is wrong at the outset?

Challenge in open court produces a new consensus, again mitigating the need for extralegal actions.

Argued like a true advocate.

And the problem with that is...?

Advocates argue law, not principle. An advocate does not question the underlying assumptions of a law. When contradiction occurs, the answer is always either compromise or new law. Both fall short of principled ideals. The contradiction is in assuming that obedience to bad laws makes for good citizenship. That is a prima facie ridiculous notion, but civic inertia makes it a legal bulwark. So if the prescription for citizenship is to agree to a status quo which allows unprincipled actions because they adhere to legality, then it follows that permitting certain crimes to go unchallenged is in fact the action of a good citizen.

All right, but in this case I don't see how it applies. The principle of corporate mortality is being violated in this instance. How does that adhere to the law?

We base all our principles of citizenship on identity. Possession of identity is the standard and key. If an identity can be made manifest in the Flow, who is to say legally that the person in question does not exist and retain the rights of citizenship? We don't have consensus on discorporate identities. I believe Sean Merrick is dead. But he manifests in the Flow. Which aspect of his condition is the valid one?

There's law on persona copies—

And it has always been possible to tell the copy from the original. An imprimatur cannot be used by a copy.

This manifestation is not a copy?

Apparently not.

There's more...

There always is.

I've been asked to fulfill a last request.

And the problem?

It violates the law.

Again.

Sean wants to be buried on Earth.

Ah. Tricky bastard. So you have another apparent contradiction. The law says one thing, the Charter says another. Which do you choose? Tell me, is this the promise you made?

...yes...

Then what does the law have to do with it?

Am I a good citizen if I fulfill my promise?

Seems we already went over that. There's a different question you need to ask here.

What?

Are you a good person if you don't.

It shouldn't contradict like this!

Should, would, could—Sean was one of the ones who set up this system.

So?

You think maybe he might have seen something like this coming?

Can you help me?

Depends. What do you need?

Is Sean dead? If so, where is his body? Why is his primary designation being...restrained?

Sean's dead. The proof will be in the corpse. For that, I can't help you. The security around his dataspheres is massive. As for the last, you figure it out. If I just tell you, it won't help you decide what to do. Assuming you haven't already decided.

How do I find him then?

Stay out of the Flow. Trolls are everywhere. Use Teaker. If he can't find a body, no one can.

Tamyn felt the substance around her stiffen. She was pushed out of the sphere. The crack closed up, sealing her away. As she pulled back, she thought, *I'll never retire...I'll take my own life before I turn into an isolate like that...*

...before I give up the stars...

Tamyn opened her eyes to a knock on the cubicle door. She stretched and swung her legs over the edge of the narrow bed.

"Yes?"

The door opened. One of the acolytes peered in.

"Pardon, Shipmaster, but there are two police officers wishing to speak with you in the reception lounge."

Tamyn squinted at the acolyte. "Police? Did they say what it's about?"

"No, Shipmaster."

Tamyn sighed. "Tell them I'll be there in a few minutes."

The door closed. Tamyn reached to the gate on the comm panel at the head of the bed. Her advocate was out of the Flow. Tamyn tapped into Naril's message node and told her about the police. Then she stepped into the shower stall and let the sonics scour her body for a minute.

Tingling and awake, she pulled on pants, a pull-over, half-boots, and a jacket, then headed for the lodge reception hall.

The pair of station police wore dark grey and heavy belts. The grey ill-suited the soft-furred Ranonan, its large amber eyes much too gentle for the stern image the uniforms projected.

"Shipmaster Glass?" the human, an older woman, stepped forward. Her face was grim.

"Yes?"

"I'm Leece Granna, station police. This is Laj-Travas. Do you mind coming with us?"

"May I ask why?"

"We need to ask you some questions."

"Pertaining to?"

"Please, co—"

"You're required to tell me the charges."

"There are no charges," Granna said.

"Then...?"

"Cooperation would be appreciated," the Ranonan said. "There is a matter concerning a death. We wish to ask about your involvement."

"Whose death?"

"Please, shipmaster," Granna said, stepping forward. "We have the authority to detain you for questioning—"

"Not without an explanation."

"It is to do with Regent Trace Alek," Laj-Travas said, drawing a glare from Granna.

"Trace Alek..."

"He was a passenger aboard you ship," Granna said. "True?"

"Yes."

"Then we have the authority to detain you for questioning."

"All right," Tamyn conceded. "But I won't answer any questions without the presence of my advocate."

Granna closed her eyes wearily and nodded. "Of course."

Tamyn left word with the lodge acolyte for Joclen to inform Naril of her whereabouts, then went with the police. Her scalp tingled and she wished she could bring someone, perhaps Kryder, but in police custody—in fact if not form—she could not do that.

They took her to a nearby shunt station where a small car waited. The human sat opposite Tamyn and the Ranonan beside her. After a short ride, the car came to a halt and the police ushered her into an austere chamber with a large workstation surrounded on all sides by hatches. Two humans occupied the station.

"Glass, Tamyn F.," Granna informed one of them. "Shipmaster, *Wicca*."

The attendant nodded, eyes slitted, her mind half in the Flow. "Cell twelve-C."

One of the hatches in the circle opened.

"I thought I was here to be interviewed," Tamyn said.

"Move forward, co," Granna said.

"Am I now under arrest?"

Granna touched Tamyn's shoulder. "Move."

Tamyn balked. She looked at the Ranonan, hoping for an explanation at least, but Granna prodded her once more.

"Hold on," a new voice snapped.

"Move," Leece Granna repeated, nudging Tamyn between her shoulders.

"Officer, you will wait," the voice said.

Tamyn turned. She saw a slender woman, with a headfull of thick black hair, shot through with silver, and a large, jagged nose, heavy lips, and small, piercing dark eyes at the edge of the workstation. She raised a hand in greeting to Tamyn.

"I am Advocate Naril Van," she said, handing a chit across the desk to one of the attendants. "I represent Shipmaster Glass. This is my bond and a court-verified release for my client." She looked directly at Granna. "Assuming she is in custody. Is she?"

Leece Granna glared at Naril while the attendant went through the documents. Finally, she returned the chit, nodding.

"All in order. Let her go."

Tamyn looked at Granna, then at the Ranonan. "I was brought here to be questioned concerning a death. What was that, a pretext?"

"That was my understanding as well, Shipmaster Glass," Laj-Travas said. "Our apologies for the inconvenience."

"Will you"—Granna began, then clamped her mouth shut and walked away.

"Tamyn," Naril said, gesturing for her to follow.

Tamyn sighed nervously and joined Naril in another shunt. The hatch sealed and the car began to move. Tamyn's hands trembled.

"Thank you," Tamyn said.

"Sorry it took me so long. I wish you'd stay in one place for more than ten minutes when you get to port." Naril glowered.

"I know, I'm an inconvenience." Tamyn refrained from reminding Naril that she had been at her lodge for hours. "Maybe if you didn't have such a phobia about shuttles—"

"Never mind. I'm in this for the excitement anyway." She touched the gate and her eyes unfocussed briefly while she issued instructions to the shunt. She cleared her throat loudly. "Be that as it may, we have a serious problem."

"That's an understatement. I was damn near in a cell," Tamyn said, hearing the impatience in her voice. "What is going on?"

"No more questions," Naril said, holding up a hand. "Wait."

Tamyn bit back her impatience. She knew Naril well enough to trust her, but she hated being uninformed. She made herself relax during the shunt ride.

They stopped in an office circuit. Naril led the way down the sparsely-trafficked corridor to a broad door labeled Van and Associates, Civil Advocacy. She touched the gate below the plaque and the door opened. Lights came up as they entered. A desk stretched along the wall opposite the entrance. Behind it hung an enormous neomimetic pictorial of an imagined First Landing on Miron, a bulbous ship slamming dust into the yellow-tinged air above a dismally barren landscape.

When the door closed, Naril waved Tamyn to a chair. "My trolls informed me on the way up. Regent Trace Alek was found dead two hours ago."

She leaned over the desk and touched the polycom gate. An area of the floor in front of the desk glowed and then a holo appeared.

The room displayed was a short-stay hostelry, a one-nighter with the bare minimum of accommodations, now crowded with people.

In a corner, Trace Alek sat in a highbacked chair. His eyes stared glassily out at the room, his blue hair disheveled. A hole marred his temple, a thin line of dried blood ran down the side of his face.

Equipment filled the round table to the right of the body. Technicians were conducting scans of the walls. Tamyn studied everything for several seconds before looking at Trace Alek's body again. Frozen in death, his face, rather than surprise or fear or anger, wore an expression of regret. Tamyn stood and stepped into the holo, crouched before Alek's body. and wondered what his last minutes had shown him.

"Who are all these?" Tamyn asked, gesturing at the technicians.

"Police," Naril said. "I smuggled this out of the direct feed to headquarters."

Tamyn looked appreciatively at her advocate. "Is there audio?"

Naril fiddled on her desk. Suddenly the sounds of too many people in too small a space filled the air.

"Can they dig a memory retrieval out of him?" someone asked.

"No, he's been dead at least seven hours."

Tamyn stood, shaking her head. The sound ceased.

"This is getting complicated," she said.

"What did you say before about understatement?" Naril asked. "When did Alek leave *Wicca?*"

"A litle over eight hours ago. I took Joclen to the lodge. We've been there since."

"How long? Alek left eight-plus hours ago, you left when?"

"Shortly after that."

"You went straight to your lodge?"

"Yes."

"That can be verified then. You stayed there the whole time? What about comm? Did you use the Flow?"

"Once. Most of the time was spent initiating Joclen."

Naril blinked. "That was quick. You've only known her how long?"

"Long enough."

Naril shrugged. "Anyway, you were in the presence of witnesses all that time?"

"Pretty much so. Kryder escorted us to the lodge. I talked for at least an hour with the Lodgemaster. I took a nap after the ceremony."

"Then they can't charge you with this."

"They were about to put me in a cell, Naril. Not an interrogation room. A cell."

"I recognized the architecture, Tam." Naril sat down behind the desk. "Correction, they could charge you with this, they just couldn't make it stick."

"What would that accomplish?"

"Keep you inactive for a time. Give them cause to search Wicca."

"No. *Wicca's* not mine. Joclen owns her."

"Excuse me?"

"Didn't you check all your messages? I transferred title before we docked. Stoan witnessed. It's temporary."

"You hope. Who is this person? I hope you don't expect me to trust her absolutely."

"I only expect you to trust me. Joclen's my pilot. I trust her to fly *Wicca*, what more is there?"

Naril's eyes narrowed. "Probably more than I want to know." She pursed her lips thoughtfully. "Good move just the same. They can't search her unless they charge Joclen. At least, not right away. By the time they get a second warrant, maybe we can cover you for this. They're putting all their efforts into fouling you up right now."

"Okay, who's they?"

"Whoever murdered Regent Alek, I assume." She leaned forward, folding her hands on the desk. "So why don't you start at the beginning. How did he end up on *Wicca*?"

"And how did Regent Alek come to be on board your ship?" the police advocate asked.

Tamyn glanced at Naril, who only tapped her lips once with a fingertip. They had rehearsed all this. Naril insisted that an act of cooperation would be helpful as she made the connections to the police authority.

"He came aboard from the *Jarom*," Tamyn said.

The advocate frowned. He occupied a chair that seemed too small for his size, but the rest of the chamber from which he conducted the interview remained undisplayed in Naril's holo projection.

"The *Jarom*? You mean, the regent cruiser?"

"Yes," Tamyn said, keeping her expression neutral.

"Why?"

"I'm afraid that must remain confidential. The visit was official. Board of Regents business. You'll have to ask them. I'm bound not to discuss it."

The police advocate shifted in his chair, looking distinctly unhappy. "Did Regent Alek give you to understand that his life might be at risk?"

"No. I offered, of course, to escort him to my lodge if he wished privacy in the conclusion of his business, but he demurred. He left *Wicca* without reluctance."

The advocate sighed. "I'll have to make inquiries with the Board, then...I'll have to suspend your access to the Flow until I can clear this matter."

Tamyn had expected this, but she still disliked it. "I have business to do. Will this take long?"

"Depends on how forthcoming the Board is. I'm sorry, Shipmaster Glass. You must understand—"

"Absolutely. You have your duty. You may inform the Board that I have no reservations about their discussing any aspect of this."

"Thank you for your cooperation. I'll get back to you through the office of your advocate as soon as I hear anything."

"Of course."

The projection faded out. Tamyn closed her eyes and leaned her head back, feeling the tension across her shoulders.

"So he doesn't know anything, either," Naril said. "The police are out of the loop."

"Well, this one is, anyway."

"I found nothing in the Flow about the *Jarom*. Nothing. Not even a departure time. But the docking logs indicate that the ship is out. No data about the *Solo* being stolen, either, which is how Co Cyanus was able to dock unchallenged." Naril stood and crossed to her desk. "Might be another matter entirely getting out of dock."

"What now?"

Naril shrugged, studying a flatscreen on her desk. "As far as the Flow is concerned, no crime has been committed. Not by Cyanus, not by you, not by the Board."

"So why was Trace Alek murdered?"

"From what you told me, he was about to dump it all into the Flow." She looked up, thoughtful. "He was new, not even eight months on the Board. Some of the older members put him up to this mission and probably had no reservations about appealing to his untested sense of public cause."

"In other words, they used him."

"That's what the young ones are for, isn't it?" She gave Tamyn a sardonic grin. "That same naïvete helped get him killed. You're probably right, none of them were supposed to come back. So the entire crew of a police cruiser plus a member of the Board of Regents were sacrificed to hide...what? The fact that they don't want Sean Merrick's empire to disintegrate?"

"The fact that they have a way to prevent it."

"Still, I'm not altogether convinced Charter purists could win that fight right now. Trace Alek was right about it never being tested on this scale. My take is, consensus would agree to let it stand. I'm sure they have the same data I do. Why not just go public?"

"Merrick's last request?"

"It's illegal."

"It's a Charter right."

"Would you be willing to spend the rest of your natural life fighting for it in court?"

"Of course not. I'd pay you to spend yours fighting it."

Naril smiled thinly at the joke. Both of them knew Tamyn could not afford that retainer.

"Which I wouldn't," Naril said. "Sometimes a more basic principle comes into play—common sense. The C.R. isn't going to start a war over a last request like that."

Tamyn felt annoyed at Naril, but knew her advocate was essentially correct. "All right, so if it isn't over corporate mortality or primary designation, what's left?"

Naril sat down. "Maybe the same things, but for different reasons. Assuming everyone on the Board is long past the kind of idealism Trace Alek might have possessed, then what reason would they have to violate the Charter and keep their involvement secret?"

"I have no idea."

"Nor do I. But that's what we need to find out. And maybe that's what Merrick wanted by asking you to do this."

"I don't quite follow."

"Let's assume," Naril said, smiling, "they're using something like that device you told me about, that was used on your prophylactic. Evidently they need the actual brain."

"We're not absolutely sure about that."

Naril waved a hand impatiently. "Trying to maintain a viable imprimatur with a copy has been tried endlessly. It doesn't work. If they've found a way to do it, it probably requires the actual organ. Why? Ask a neuropathologist. I have no idea. But if it does, then they're using Merrick the same way."

"So by stealing his corpse—"

"—the dataspheres collapse. Voilá—all is revealed."

Tamyn nodded. "Find Cyanus."

"It's a good thing we got rid of all our cargo," Shreve said, gazing at the array of screens behind his station. "There've been eight attempts at penetrating our datasphere since we docked, all of them concealed in standard manifest requests from our clients."

"How effective?" Tamyn asked.

"If they'd gotten in, very," Shreve said. "Sophisticated stuff. *Wicca* would have been rendered so much scrap within twenty minutes."

Tamyn sighed and looked around the bridge. Joclen sat in her couch while Benajim Cyanus stood, arms folded, with his back to a bracing. Near him, Naril's daughter, Piper Van, stood watching everyone, arms behind her back, legs slightly wide, opposite Kryder, who maintained a nearly identical posture.

Besides Shreve, Stoan sat at his station, and Innes stood by the entrance to the bridge. Naril leaned on the back of an unoccupied couch—Thijs's.

"Evidence?" Tamyn asked.

"I've got the specs on disk," Shreve said. "I can demonstrate that an attack was intended, if that's what you mean."

"That's what I mean. Can you trace the original source?"

Shreve shook his head. "They were all routed through legitimate clients. Can't get past their security without a big mess."

"Hah!" Stoan barked. "Determinably antiappreciable. Holes bigger than patches can hide worlds."

"Can you keep *Wicca* safe, Shreve?"

Shreve shrugged, then nodded. "All the invasive shells are basically the same type. Masking them this way limits their configuration. I don't even have to be here. I've been setting up an algorithmic defense for Stoan to run, just in case."

"Naril," Tamyn said. "What are we looking at timewise if I pursue this through a court?"

"Weeks, maybe months. At worst, years."

"That won't do," Tamyn said. "What about finding Ambassador Tej-Ojann?" She looked at Cyanus. "You could have gone looking for him instead of coming to find me."

He shrugged. "Sean suggested otherwise. Besides, they followed me to you, they would have followed me to Ojann. With him dead, there are no viable witnesses to Sean's primary designation."

"Perhaps," Naril said, "we should try to do that ourselves now."

"No," Tamyn said. "If we succeed, that provides one target instead of several."

"You don't think they'd try to kill a Ranonan ambassador," Naril objected. "Do you?"

"They murdered a regent. What's the difference? And if they keep us bottled up here, they can get us one by one while we're tied up with legalities."

"That's a bit paranoid," Naril said.

"Practical," Cyanus said. "They've demonstrated intent."

Tamyn saw Naril watching her, eyes narrowed.

"You've already made up your mind," Naril said. "Haven't you?"

Tamyn paced the bridge. "What we need to do is find Sean's body. I need to get downwell to do that."

"Tam—"

"Then we need to find a way to open this to the Flow. Under injunction like this, I can't. That will be your job, Naril."

"Tam—"

Cyanus grinned at her. "You're going to do it, aren't you?"

"What I am not going to do is sit still while Sutter Hall and Carson Reiner take careful aim."

Tamyn stepped from the shuttle lock, blinking in the furious brightness, hesitant in the wash of sudden heat. The low domes of the terminal shimmered through mirages; distant thunder from shuttles drowned all other sounds. The sky above was yellow-white, cloudless, ending at a jagged horizon line to the east comprised of towers and pyramids and myriad other architectures; to the west, the line of the planet was straight, a vast plain undisturbed by visible geography.

A light touch on her shoulder reminded Tamyn to move. Behind her, Naril and Joclen waited impatiently. Kryder emerged last, apparently unbothered by the sharp change in ambient comfort. Tamyn tried to hurry down the ramp and up the path to the terminal entrance.

As soon as they pushed through the air wall into the cooler spaces of the terminal the babble of hundreds of voices broke on them like a wave. A single row of service islands ran left and right down the center of the terminal. Travelers huddled around each of them, those who could not find an available polycom or simply preferred dealing with a living being, harrying the quartets of coes who worked them with questions and demands. Polycom terminals were everywhere, all continually occupied.

They worked a path through the crowds to the opposite side and entered a broad tunnel. Voices from behind echoed off the curved walls, mingled with a different collection of living sounds at the midway point, then became inaudible amid the chorus from ahead. The tunnel rose slightly and let them out on a wide slab of 'crete that ran the length of the terminal. Cabs waited for passengers on the slab. Beyond was the port plaza.

People writhed, jammed, among each other, in and out, sandwiched between tents, prefab kiosks, and tall public service stalls that dotted the plaza. Stelae rose above the meleé with messages, proclamations, poetry, commemorations, and temporary graffiti covering their hexagonal surfaces. Banners snapped in breezes created by the interactions of pumped air from the ducts on the other side of the plaza and the backwash from the constant arrivals and departures of shuttles. The smells of foods, perfumes, humans, and setis mingled. Beyond, a hazy mass of structures coagulated into a single smear of indistinct detail, a blue-grey curtain, backdrop to this unroofed polis.

Miron City was a collection of impressions—odors, textures, noises combined to form a distinct though unnamable mélange. Port town, its lifeblood was mercantilism. Everything orbited around the port and commercial districts that surrounded it. To the north and west of the field were residential sections; south and east were more warehouses, offices, manufactories, and bazaars. Enormous oxygen pumping plants marked the stages of urban growth like the rings radiating through the core of a tree; atmosphere was pumped throughout the four hundred fifty square kilometers of the city via huge ducts, contained by a system of energy fields that allowed a certain amount to spill over, outside the immediate perimeter of the city. Such a high percentage of oxygen was toxic to the few native plant forms that clung tenaciously to the hard, miserly soil, so as the city grew a band of barrenness preceded it.

"Now I'm hungry," Joclen said.

Tamyn glanced at her. "I guess we have time."

Naril frowned. "We should get to my office. I can order something delivered."

"No," Joclen said, stepping forward. "It wouldn't be the same."

"She's right," Tamyn said, and followed. "Come on. This one's on me."

"But—"

Helplessly, Naril trailed along.

Tamyn squeezed through the press, quietly reveling in the gestalt. In this one place, it seemed, all of civilized space was represented.

Joclen found a long booth from which drifted a dozen exotic scents. A trio of Vosh scurried back and forth from a stack of meter-wide spheres and the counter. The Vosh were squat and covered with fine cilia that they could extend and retract at will, similar to the Stralith, giving them the appearance of big, deep-green sponges. Joclen stepped to the counter and one of them scooted up to her. A mass of cilia extruded and covered Joclen's face for a few seconds, then retracted. The Vosh moved to the stack of spheres. Each sphere had a small hole. The Vosh picked up a plate from the table below the stack, then reached into four of the spheres and removed something, arranged it all on the plate, and returned to the counter.

Tamyn joined her. Plate in hand, Joclen took a small brownish chunk of something doughlike, swished it in the honey-colored gravy, and popped it into her mouth. There was a violet sauce and a white sauce as well.

"Good?" Tamyn asked.

"Mm," Joclen nodded, eyes closed.

Tamyn looked at the Vosh. The cilia came forward. It felt like a pleasant massage. Briefly, before she was even sure it had happened, some of the strands entered her mouth and nostrils, making her want to sneeze. Then the Vosh hurried away. It returned with a plate of greyish dough bits and red, orange, and pale blue sauces.

"I had no idea that's how they did it," Naril said.

Tamyn looked at her. "You've lived here all your life and you didn't know this?" Naril frowned at her and Tamyn shrugged. "How do you get it?"

"I just order it delivered," Naril said, "tell them what colors I want."

"And how does it taste?"

Naril shrugged. "Sometimes all right. Sometimes...flat."

Joclen chuckled. "You better try some the right way. They have to take a sample of your enzymes, then contour the sauces to you personally. When it's done right it's some of the best stuff you'll ever eat."

Naril shook her head and took an unconscious step back. "I'll get something from the Rahalen *krish* booth."

Tamyn dipped a nugget into the blue sauce and bit it. She closed her eyes for a moment and let the flavors wash her mouth: tang of citrus, an underflavor of rich red wine, and sweet-sour aftertaste for which she had no name. Slowly, she finished the plate, then fished a couple of coins from her pocket and set them on the payment tray.

Naril stood by the high, lavish tent of the Rahalen *krish* vendors. The dignified-looking Rahalen who owned the booth stood to one side while a gangly apprentice waited on Naril. The apprentice was an unaltered Rahalen, tall, almost gaunt, with greenish eyes set wide apart in a large head. From the cheekbones up, he looked nearly human. From where a human nose would end down, a complex arrangement of flaps and cords tapered to the upper chest; no ear cups, no jawline, no hair. He diced the bright red flesh, scraped the bits into a pan, added a sauce, some yellow powder, and set the pan on an open flame. The Rahalen claimed to have learned to cook this way from humans, but Tamyn had her doubts.

Joclen stood beside Naril, watching the preparations with open skepticism. "You actually eat that stuff?"

Naril frowned and nodded. "It's very good. I understand it's a delicacy."

"Mm. If you're a connoisseur of entrails of a deep sea mollusk, I suppose it is."

Naril looked at her uncertainly, then glanced at Tamyn. "Look," she said suddenly, "I'm not letting you spoil my appreciation for something I've been eating for years. Play your games with someone else."

Joclen looked offended. "I thought you knew."

Tamyn stepped away from the debate and moved over to the proprietor. He watched her approach from unblinking, solid blue eyes in an almost human face; he had altered his appearance from Rahalen norm, adding a very human mouth and a sharp chin. No hair, though, which Tamyn approved—Rahalen with hair simply did not look natural.

"Greetings, co," she said.

"Greetings, sojourner," he said. "It's been a while, Tamyn."

"But you're still dealing in effluent."

He smiled. "And your people are still buying it. What can I do? We choose to serve."

"You've got another new face, Follish."

A long-fingered hand came up to stroke the chin. "Merely modi-fied. My last jaw was too small and my smile disturbed some people. This one is better. Yours never seems to change."

"It does."

"You're in trouble, Tamyn. So I hear."

"I've been caught unprepared by unexpected complications."

"How can I help? If at all."

"Do you know where Teaker stays these days?"

"Teaker never stayed anywhere that I felt comfortable sending anyone. He's in the Vacants."

"Can you get word to him that I need to talk?"

"Easily. Is there anything else?"

"I may have trouble getting back off-world."

"And you will need to?"

"Perhaps sooner than I expect."

"I'll see what avenues I can open."

"Thank you, Follish."

"Travel well, travel far."

She drifted back to Joclen and Naril, who were still arguing over the merits of different seti cuisines. Naril's face was com-pressed in a look of revulsion.

"—Scanvi blanblaffs," Joclen said, pointing for emphasis at the Rahalen chef. He nodded politely. "Best fungal derivatives that ever graced a ship's mess."

"Especially," the Rahalen said, "when sautéed in guamesh."

Naril shook her head. "You two eat stuff unfit for anything but homicide."

"I never eat it," the Rahalen said. "I only prepare it."

Naril saw Tamyn. "Can we go, now? You really shouldn't be walking around like this."

"They haven't arrested me yet," Tamyn said, popping a last Vosh bit in her mouth. "Besides," she motioned toward Kryder.

"Kryder can't cover you all the time and even a prophylactic has certain legal limitations."

"All right," Tamyn conceded, "let's go."

The press of vendors and consumers seemed to thicken as they neared the opposite side of the plaza. But then the crowds abruptly ended at a set of ten steps that ran the length of the plaza. Tamyn walked up to the next level. A broad boulevard separated the bazaar from the city proper.

Tamyn saw herself briefly, reflected in the silvery windows of a shop across the way, standing alone at the head of the stairs. Behind her the terminal stood in slightly warped grandeur. A shuttle lifted off then, its thrusters brilliant white, turning her into a silhouette for a few seconds. Then the light was gone and she was not alone. She could not identify the feeling with which the image left her, except that she was even more concerned for what was happening in the C.R. Perhaps pathos, perhaps a certain *déjà vu,* or even *presque vu;* as she tried to pin it down it eluded her.

A police cruiser sailed by. She let Naril urge her on.

Chapter Nine

The cab flew west over the city, to the opposite side, and let them out on the roof of a sixty-story hexagonal tower. Tamyn walked to the eastern edge and looked down into the center of Miron City. Buildings rose up like spikes; around them sprawled domes, pyramids, squat blocks, a dozen other architectures, human and seti. Directly between her and the port was the trio of wedge-shaped towers that housed Merrick Enterprises, Sean's import, export, shipping, and distribution company; off to the right was the shorter, bullet-shaped building of Mirak Corporation, his manufacturing firm.

Formerly Sean's, she reminded herself.

The cab lifted off. Tamyn watched it curve gracefully away from the building and head back into the city proper, returning to the port.

A thin breeze stroked her face briefly. She did a slow survey of the cityscape, stopping when she caught Kryder at the corner of her vision, solidly immobile, alert, waiting.

Naril and Joclen crossed the broad deck to a row of private elevators. Naril touched the contact on one and the door whisked open.

"Are you coming?" Naril called to Tamyn.

Tamyn and Kryder joined them.

When the door opened again, soft ivory light flooded the car.

"Mammo! Mammo!"

Naril stepped out and scooped up a small child, drawing him into a hug. The child pressed against Naril's face, laughing gleefully. As Tamyn and Joclen left the elevator more children ran up—Tamyn counted six of different ages. The younger ones gathered around Naril while the older ones hung back and studied Tamyn, Joclen, and Kryder.

The hallway widened quickly and let out into a broad, terraced chamber. Panels in the ceiling gave off the restful light. A narrow stream ran from high on one wall, down a sculpted path, into a pool on the far side of the room. A young man swam back and forth, apparently oblivious to the excitement.

Naril put the child down, only to pick up another. Her face, when she turned to Tamyn, was beatific. She laughed and blushed slightly. The child she had set down jumped at her playfully. Two of the older children ran off singing "Naril's home! Naril's home!" Naril kissed the little girl in her arms. "Can someone else have a turn now?" she asked.

"Are you staying for a while?" the child asked.

Naril nodded. "Oh, yes. But I wasn't gone that long this time, though, was I?"

The child shrugged. "Long enough. Sure." And she squirmed out of Naril's embrace. When she stood on the floor, she pointed at one of her siblings, whom Naril hoisted and nestled on her right hip, then reached out to one of the older girls to run a hand through long, thin golden hair.

"Seji's front teeth fell out," the girl reported. "And Coralyn passed her entry exams for Anselm's School."

"Great! Where is she?" Naril glanced at Tamyn. "Before you arrived in-system and dragged me upwell I was practically living in the offices of Camphart and Ajira, the auditors. I've been gone five days."

Tamyn felt like an intruder. She gazed uneasily at the children, who kept looking at her with questions in their eyes. She could think of nothing to say. When she glanced at Joclen, though, she saw the younger woman smiling. One of the smaller children motioned for Joclen to bend down, and when she did the child whispered in her ear. Joclen nodded in reply and the child laughed and danced away.

An elderly couple, their long silver hair coiled into buns at the crowns of their heads, approached, accompanied by the two children who had run off to announce Naril. The old man reclined in a floater, his legs dangling and useless, while the woman walked alongside, holding his right hand. Two adolescents followed in their wake.

The boy in the pool continued to swim.

"Is Leeg around?" Naril asked the girl with the long blond hair.

"No, he's at Jame's," she said. "Want me to get him?"

"No, not yet."

Tamyn cleared her throat uncomfortably.

"I'm sorry, Tam," Naril said, laughing. "This is the homecoming ritual. Every time, you'd think I'd been gone a century."

"Are you going to show me a proper dismount on the bars?" a boy asked.

"Sometime," Naril said, sighing. "Let me make introductions." She set the boy down and started pointing, first at the blond girl. "That's Crijy—she's forty-one hundred days old and keeps track of everyone for me. Next to her is Hane. He's..."

"Four thousand one hundred and ninety days," the boy supplied.

"Right. He'll be a good mechanic if he ever learns to remember how things come apart and where he put all the pieces."

The boy laughed.

"This is Dana"—

"I'll never remember their ages," Tamyn said.

Naril nodded. "Dana has pretensions to art."

The petite young girl gave Naril a mock scowl, then smiled at Tamyn. "Naril can't draw a straight line with a pattern transcriber."

Naril squatted down then and hugged the little boy she had just released. "This is Timru." She hugged a little girl in her other arm. "Marg." She pointed at the one she had picked up first. "Reese."

The old man in the floater came to a halt just outside the circle of children. "It's about time you got home," he said.

Naril arched an eyebrow. "This is my father, Coral," she said. "And Archer, Coral's companion."

The woman smiled and nodded at Tamyn and Joclen. Coral scowled impatiently. "You've got business to tend to."

"I'm tending to it. This is Tamyn Glass, Shipmaster of the *Wicca*, her pilot, Joclen Bramus, and her prophylactic, Kryder." She looked pointedly at Coral. "Business."

He nodded. "I know. There've been three communications from Regent Reiner, pertaining directly to the *Wicca*." He grinned lopsidedly at Tamyn. "Glad to meet you. Anyone who can irritate Reiner is welcome. You must be someone special."

"I'm sure I'm just a side issue," Tamyn said. "Reiner is easily irritated."

Coral laughed hoarsely. "Absolutely! I—"

"The one in the pool," Naril said, interrupting, "is Kevon. You'll meet him later. There are a couple of others missing." She moved around Coral and leaned over to whisper. He frowned, then nodded. Naril kissed his cheek.

Another child—Timru—tugged on Joclen's jacket hem. She squatted down to his level.

"Are you a sojourner?" Timru asked.

Joclen grinned. "Yes, I am."

Timru looked at Joclen with wide, serious eyes, then at Tamyn. "Are you one, too?"

"Yes," Tamyn said. "Shipmaster Tamyn Glass, of the Wicca."

Joclen nodded. "She tells me where to go and I figure out how to get us there."

"And the big one's a bodyguard?" Timru asked.

"Tam," Naril called. "You want to come listen to this?"

Tamyn nodded gratefully.

"One of you get rooms ready," Naril said, walking away. "Tamyn and Joclen may be staying awhile."

"Aren't you going to be staying on your ship?" Crijy asked.

"Not for a couple of days." Tamyn worked her way through the gathering. The two teenagers who had escorted Coral and Archer walked alongside Tamyn.

"Nary forgot us," the boy said. "She usually forgets someone."

Naril glanced over her shoulder. "Sometimes it's on purpose."

"I'm Josh," the boy continued, "and that's Breve. We're twins."

"Leeg's not here," Breve said. "And Seji and Coralyn are out celebrating Coralyn's exams."

"The fish," Josh pointed at the pool, "is Kevon. If he ever comes up for air you'll meet him."

"Naril mentioned Kevon already," Tamyn said. "But she never told me about all of you."

"She only tells close friends," Breve said. "It's nobody's business, she says."

"Matter of principle," Josh said. "You must be a close friend."

"Or maybe just a friend in need."

They reached the opposite end of the long room and Naril stopped at an arched doorway. "Or maybe just a client with certain privileges," she said. "Privacy."

Josh pursed his lips, then nodded. He gave Tamyn a short bow and strode off.

"We can find out later what's going on," Breve announced, laughed, and danced after her brother.

"My staff," Naril grinned.

"They're all...?"

"None of them are biological offspring. I adopted them."

Tamyn glanced back and saw four of the children gathered around Coral, who worked on a broad projection slate on his lap now. A geometric form shimmered in the air above the slate and the children gazed up, rapt.

"Tam," Naril called.

Tamyn turned away and followed Naril, Kryder close behind.

Naril's office overlooked the corporate section of the city. She went to her polycom and touched a fingertip to the interface. Light flickered over her face briefly from the screen as she sat down.

"You can stay here while we sort through all this," Naril said. "I've got the whole floor, plenty of room."

"You never told me about your family," Tamyn said.

"Hmm?" Naril shrugged. "It didn't seem important to you." She looked up from the screen. "You never struck me as the family type."

"I'm not comfortable around children," Tamyn admitted. "But..."

Naril waited for more. When Tamyn remained silent—what was there to say? she wondered—Naril returned her attention to the screen. She raised her eyebrows. "This is going to be interesting." She punched a few buttons on her console, glanced at Tamyn. "Okay, we've got some work to do. Ready?"

Tamyn went to the window and gazed out at the city, trying to sort her feelings. She felt uncomfortably annoyed at Naril. The casual exclusion disturbed her as much if not more than the enforced exclusion from the Flow. She had known Naril almost two thousand days, as long as most of her crew. In some ways, Naril was crew. How, she wondered, would I feel if I learned that Thijs or Innes or Clif had an extended family I knew nothing about?

It should make no difference...

But it did. I'm being unreasonable, she thought, over-sensitive and out of line. The feeling persisted.

"Tam?" Naril prompted.

Tamyn could not quite keep a sulking tone from her voice. "Sure. I'm expecting word from a Rahalen named Follish. Till then, you have my full attention."

Piper sat back in the chair and scowled at the seti across from her. The private meeting room felt cramped—the Thaxan filled almost half of it.

"Come on, Quoris," she said, "there's got to be more than that." The Thaxan shuddered. It was a mass of filaments, not quite spines, not quite hair, over an eight-section articulated body capped with a membranous disk that seemed filled with pale yellow gelatin. When it moved, the bluish-grey segments of its body rolled in a way that gave the illusion that they swapped positions. For all that it seemed like it should, it did not resemble an insect.

Quoris's portable translator produced a pleasantly sexless voice. "Apologies, Co Van. I am certain there is more, but it cannot be found." It shuddered again—an emotive gesture, Piper suspected. "This Benajim Cyanus appeared on Miron quite suddenly, began working for Sean Merrick, became quickly important to Co Merrick, and now has caused considerable excitement in the Flow."

"But where did he come from? He didn't just appear out of thin air!"

"No. Not likely. And the air in Miron City is not thin. He reputedly originated in the Frontier, but I can find no birth records or transport documents. No doubt he possessed a different name. He has only been Benajim Cyanus for eighteen hundred and fifty-eight days."

Piper shook her head. This was becoming frustrating. Who was she protecting? She had to suspend her studies until this was over and Naril had been less informative than usual.

"What about rumors?" she asked.

"Rumors come in degrees," the Thaxan said. "What I have already found are the most reliable."

"Give me your second tier, then."

Quoris shuddered. "Based on source, it is rumored that he came from the Pan Humana."

Based on what source, Piper wondered. If Quoris were willing to say, she would know already. "How would that be possible? First you said the Frontier, now—"

"Rumor. Be discriminate. Does it matter more than the fact that Merrick took him in and made him valuable?"

"Good point. But it would be interesting to know how he crossed the Secant."

"More interesting still, if true, how Merrick found him. A fact—
if Benajim Cyanus could be proven a Pan citizen, others would have
acted on that already. It remains rumor."

How do you know someone hasn't, Piper thought. The *Jarom*
incident could very well qualify...

"A favor?" Quoris asked.

"Of course."

"Information for information."

"You haven't been especially informative."

Quoris shuddered. "Even the lack of data is informative after
a fashion. My resources are extensive."

"True. I was being facetious."

"Granted. Still, I will provide information of a more solid sort
in exchange for similar quality."

"All right."

"Sean Merrick is dead yet his holdings are still functioning, still
extant, and no will has been released. When inquiries are made, it
commences a long sequence of circular algorithmic nonsense. It has
become as difficult to learn anything about this as it has been to find
the substance behind your Benajim Cyanus."

"It's true, there are problems."

"Merrick still manifests in the Flow."

Piper nodded.

"Only long enough each day to validate business transactions,"
Quoris continued. "Many coes are becoming increasingly uneasy
dealing with what they believe is a corpse. Moral issues emerge, not
to mention the questions of legality."

"He's being...mimicked. Merrick himself is dead."

"Can you substantiate that?"

"I don't know. Maybe."

"So far it is little more than rumor that he is dead. Rumor many
accept as true. For myself, I believe you. But the uncertainty is
detrimental to the market, to the Flow itself. Proof one way or the
other would be a valuable thing."

"There may be a way," Piper said. "We're working on it."

"Does this involve Benajim Cyanus?"

"It does."

"I see. Then I will give you my information. Those who are
sensitive to such aspects of the Flow have noted that this Benajim

Cyanus shares certain qualities with Sean Merrick. His manifestation in the Flow bears similarities to Merrick's imprimatur."

"That's...interesting. But wouldn't the Flow recognize that?"

"I said 'similar', not identical. But the similarities are strong enough to intrigue and unsettle my informants."

"So...what do you want in return?"

"Proof. Merrick's corpse, Benajim Cyanus's origin. Not where he came from but how he came to be. Revelation. Begin with how the dead can still act within the Flow."

"We don't—I don't know what's behind it. Something is wrong. That's part of why I needed information on Cyanus. Tell me, what sort of business is being transacted through Merrick's constructs? There can't be a lot."

"Very limited, very specific. Quantities are large as always. Pharmaceuticals, small technologies, other goods Merrick concerned himself with very little." Quoris paused for several seconds. Then, another shudder. "Perhaps this is important. Merrick transport sails empty, returns laden, yet no colony or seti system reports a shipment scheduled. Also, none of it has come through Miron."

"Merrick's entire fleet?"

"No. Numbers are inconsistent. A third of the fleet or less."

"Then where's it coming from and going?"

"That is a question in need of an answer."

Merrick Shipping being used for illicit transport? Or just by someone else...

Piper nursed her own suspicions, as did her mother, but without proof no action could be taken. Merrick had known, she realized. In which case, Cyanus might be the key to the entire puzzle.

"I'll do what I can to find it for you," Piper said.

"Thank you. Information for information."

"I—"

Quoris went on. "The dead require consideration. Every species provides this according to its own concept. We thought we understood humans in this. Not much different from, say, the Rahalen or the Menkans. It is important that basic consistencies be observed. There is deviation now. Many are confused. There cannot be truth between the confused. Without truth, we cannot interact reliably. This matter of Merrick's death-not death is disturbing.

It is likely many among the Reaches will cease dealing with humans until the confusion is resolved."

Piper listened to the statement, hearing it more as a formal pronouncement than a revelation of secrets. Quoris was relaying the essence of some resolution that had already been made.

She swallowed drily. "Tell whoever you need to that we're trying to correct it. Some few among us want to change things. We're trying to stop the deviation from progressing."

Quoris shuddered a last time and moved around to head back to the lock that separated the Thaxan section from this meeting room and the human section.

"Thank you, Quoris," Piper said.

The Thaxan hesitated, then said, "Please succeed." The lock cycled and Quoris tumbled through.

The warehouses rimming the southern edge of the port formed layers. First, corporate buildings—domes, quonsets, blockhouses, and towers bearing innumerable logos. Then the smaller companies—limited partnerships, sole proprietorships, communal and aggregate affiliations—with more modest structures. The layers overlapped, eddied, backwashed, and further from the port proper became more spartan, less affluent, finally dingier, bleaker, meaner. Worse places existed, Tamyn knew, worse to look at and worse to be alone in, but the quality of desperation here gave an edge to Miron's back alleys found nowhere else. People came here to succeed, all optimism and ambition. Those who failed clung to slimmer hopes, reduced expectations, and struggled for the smaller opportunities that remained. It resulted in a stunted, aberrant sham of commerce, as little by little possibilities died.

At the bottom were the Vacants. The old buildings formed canyons, high walls where rust and graffiti grafted onto each other so that they became one message. Some structures did not rust; others would hold no graffiti, pigments sliding off, evaporating, or melting into the peculiar molecular structure of the walls. These just turned ichorous with molds, algae, wet growths, and the damage of time. And always sounds: drippings, distant scrapings, unidentified percussives, mostly faint, just below the threshold of awareness, but some close and unnatural.

Even here, a few coes found success...

Tamyn led the way up a flight of broad metal steps to the catwalk bolted to the wall of a boxy building. Gaps in the wall showed a skeletal interior lit indifferently by the late afternoon sun, sky above faded to a cottony white. The sudden scurrying of feet stopped her; she stared into the shadows that flowed across the dark alley pavement and the striated discolorations of the walls.

"Fobes," Joclen said after a few seconds.

"Hey, coes."

Tamyn looked up. A dark-complected man leaned out of a mansized gap in the wall above the next landing. He smiled at them broadly.

"Teaker," Tamyn breathed, relieved.

"Follish said you were looking for me. You've been away a while." He ducked back inside.

Tamyn and Joclen, Kryder close behind, followed Teaker into the body of the abandoned building. Teaker led them deep into the framework of old, empty racks, walkways, crane supports, and offices. The shredded roof let light filter in like dripping water. Teaker had laid new flooring in one of the larger office areas and draped off the walls. A few desks interrupted islands of workbenches, all filled with gadgets and pieces and parts that had grown together like an evolved beast, asleep now, waiting. Teaker unfolded a pair of chairs and gestured for Tamyn and Joclen to sit. From an enormous cooler he pulled a couple of bottles of amber liquid.

"When did you drop down?" he asked, offering the bottles.

"This morning," Tamyn said, accepting. "We got into port the day before yesterday."

"And the port authority has you bottled up. What's that all about?"

"You mean you don't know?" Tamyn twisted off the cap.

Teaker sat on the edge of a workbench. He rested his chin on his thumb, elbow on knee. "What I know is that certain members of the Board of Regents have been talking a great deal with some board members of a couple of corporations, and that between them they have altered the decent procedure for putting the dead to rest. Merrick's imprimatur manifests in the Flow. Identity extending beyond life is contrary to the way we live. I know that Merrick's boat was stolen about seventy, seventy-five days ago and that a police cruiser was sent after it. I know that you have returned early from sojourn in company with Merrick's boat and now you're bottled up by the people who have been talking to each other. I know that Merrick's will is in the hands of a Ranonan legate, waiting for proof of Merrick's death and the disintegration of his corporate dataspheres. I'm sure there are alternate instructions if the current situation goes on long enough. I know that a couple of members of the Board of Regents are not happy with what the others are doing, but so far haven't had much cause to act." He grinned. "How am I doing so far?"

Tamyn laughed. "Not bad. Maybe between us we can fill in a few of the gaps."

"What can I do for you?"

"Besides general data—who's talking to who and about what— I want to know where Sean Merrick's body is."

Teaker whistled and rolled his eyes dramatically. "What am I offered?"

Tamyn took a pull from the bottle; it was bittersweet and rich. "Standard fee plus a bonus."

"You're always understanding, co. I also want a couple of dock motiles. I'm going to have to vacate the Vacants pretty soon. Also, understand, things are a bit edgy these days. Data pertaining to this subject causes discomfort in certain areas."

"You're in trouble?"

"Goes and comes. All depends on how much edge a co can buy for himself. Presently I'm expensive."

"Then double your standard fee. The bonus depends on what you tell me."

"Always reasonable," Teaker nodded. Between one second and the next his expression changed. The grin vanished, a tightness crept around his large brown eyes. His voice came out less inflected. "The data I can't confirm is evidently what the trouble is all about. Merrick is dead but not dead, as I hear it, and I can't make a lot more sense out of that, except that Merrick Enterprises is still doing business. No moratorium, no stasis, no halt in transactions except in-system. A lot of traffic has been running through Merrick's infra-structures—don't know what it is or where it's going. Tej-Ojann's injunction hasn't been effective elsewhere in the Reaches and hasn't done a lot of good here. So while nobody locally is doing deals with them, the outer Reaches are still trading, as well as a few of the other C.R. worlds. It's business as usual. Locally, stock transactions have acquired the flavor of paranoia. Keller Industries has been openly buying all stock that comes available for any of the subsidiaries of either Merrick or Mirak. Keller happens to be held in majority by Reiner Combine. In the last ninety days several attempts have been made by factions of both Merrick Enterprises and Mirak Corporation to dissolve and reform as something else, but a lot of Q and a lot of data have changed hands to persuade those factions to remain. Unconfirmed."

"When did Reiner Combine acquire so much of Keller Industries?" Tamyn asked.

"Most of the stocks were acquired within the last fifteen hundred days, through blinds."

"Keller leased shipping exclusively from Merrick."

"And still does apparently. The trouble is, I can't find out where those ships are going now. Their itineraries are all within the Merrick dataspheres and so far no Jurist has been brought in to demand public declaration. Till that happens, schedules will be confidential."

"And if a jurist does become involved," Tamyn mused, "the dataspheres can be dissolved according to tradition and the information lost legally."

"That would be extreme but certainly possible."

"What do you know about Benajim Cyanus?" Tamyn asked.

"Nothing. He came out of nowhere and was suddenly Sean Merrick's eyes, ears, arms, and legs."

Joclen said, "How is the Flow dealing with this?"

"Flow doesn't seem to know what to do yet. There's no consensus. But there are grumblings. If Reiner's not careful the Flow will shut them out."

"If they are careful?"

"Might never make any difference again."

Kryder hissed. He held up a hand and turned his head from side to side, eyes intense, listening with an almost delicate grace.

"Stay here," he said and slipped out of the workshop area.

"We heard Fobes outside," Tamyn said.

Teaker nodded. "Like I said, some data is unwelcome. I have to move soon." He jumped off the bench. "I'll find out what I can about Cyanus—if there's anything to find out. Finding Merrick's body won't be that hard, but I don't know what you can do about it when I do. Where are you?"

"With my advocate, Naril Van."

"As good a place as any," Teaker said.

Kryder appeared a few meters away, ghostlike in the dark.

"Go to the exit," he said, then backed away, vanishing.

Teaker took something from a pile on another bench and brought it to her. "When you go out, throw these down the alley." He handed her three flat grey disks. "Then get the hell out quickly. I'll contact you at Co Van's place when I find anything."

"I'll see about your fee then. What are these?"

"Nerve scours."

"Ow! Nasty." She laughed and hugged Teaker briefly.

She stepped through the doorway and stopped. Swinging gently in the shafts of light coming through the gaps in the wall a body hung from a noose of metal cable. Tamyn tried to make out detail in the chaotic shadows of the warehouse. Imaginary motions frustrated her.

A sharp cry, cut off as abruptly as it began, echoed through the building.

Outside on the catwalk, Tamyn stood very still, looking up and down the alley. Night was coming on quickly, the sky already dingy grey and streaked with sickly yellow clouds.

Joclen touched her shoulder and pointed to the right. She took one of the disks and descended the stairs before Tamyn could say anything. Tamyn watched her, moving fast and silent toward an intersection. Tamyn swallowed over the lump forming in her throat and looked across at the opposite building. Dead face, ancient and scarred, a structure that was gradually becoming a natural part of the landscape.

Someone stepped out the door behind her. She turned. He wore a chameleon mask, undulating shapes and colors obscuring his features. He raised a pistol—

Kryder gripped the forearm from behind and twisted it quickly. Cartilage crackled, the hand opened, letting the pistol fall. Kryder grasped the chin and jerked savagely. The neck gave with a faint snap. Kryder tossed the body over the railing.

"Any more?" Tamyn asked, her heart hammering.

"There were five. All accounted for now."

Then Joclen was running back. Tamyn saw the tight smile and wild look on her face. She slowed only a moment to take in the bonelessly sprawled body on the alley floor, then gestured wildly for

Tamyn and Kryder to follow. From the intersection she heard running feet. Tamyn thrust one of the disks into Kryder's hand.

A movement caught her eye. She looked across at the building again. A tall, narrow window, all black within, contained one small face staring across at her, chin resting on the sill. Tamyn froze for an instant. The face vanished.

Tamyn palmed a disk and launched it. She watched the smooth arc as it sailed toward the opposite building, then through the open window. She heard it clatter somewhere inside.

Then she was hurrying down the steps, heedless of the noise. Joclen was already fifty meters ahead of her. She reached the bottom, turned as Kryder launched the last disk toward the intersection. She did not wait to see it land.

Joclen had slowed for her and she caught up. Then they were both pumping their legs to the point of failure while Kryder seemed to jog along effortlessly. As they made the final intersection before the edge of the Vacants, Tamyn felt her entire body suddenly tingle as a high keening whistle began to modulate up and down a quartertone scale. Flat, her ears shouted, flat—then sharp, but not quite. It covered her in ice. Half a block further on she could no longer feel it.

Music thundered up and down the street. Neon, holos, lasers, phoscandescence all set the night aglow with an eerie familiarity. If she squinted, Tamyn imagined she was linked, running with the Flow. Instead it was only one of several entertainment districts just off the port plaza.

Coes conducted life here with as much intensity and in much the same way as they conducted business. Tamyn tried to imagine anything different and all she could find were images of other races, seti cultures. But really only the forms were different. In the drive to live all coes were the same, human, Rahalen, Alcyoni, Menkar, Ranonan—life in search of living.

Was it really any different across the border?

Probably not, Tamyn decided, but we don't know. We can't see it or touch it, so we make things up about it. Except the privateers, the border runners. They knew.

An old man sat at a table on the apron of an outdoor cafe, drink in hand and half a dozen young spacers gathered around listening to his yarns. He looked ancient, his thin face creased with the evidence of a life well lived. No ship anymore, retired, but welcome on board any vessel anytime. Tamyn reflected that in another fifty years she would be much the same, one of the honored old, taken care of, cherished for her wisdom and experience. The C.R. was young and needed such people. The Commonwealth was only a little older than she was.

Merrick had seen both sides. He ought to have been among the cherished old. Perhaps he was, but his final wishes were being violated. How much different could it be from abandonment"?

"Thirsty?" Joclen prompted.

"Hm? Yes, I suppose."

"Where are your thoughts?"

Tamyn shook her head. "Fragility."

Joclen steered them toward a nightclutch. The music pounded Tamyn's ears until they reached a booth and keyed the baffle. The sound diminished to a vague rumble.

"I've been thinking," Joclen said. "All the theorizing I've heard between you and Naril, you and Stoan, you and Cyanus—it's pointless. You're trying to figure out the motives of someone you don't know."

Amused, Tamyn asked, "What would you recommend?"

"It's clear what Reiner and Hall are doing. They're violating primary designation. They're trying to make it so that a co's word means nothing and death is not final. Something obscene about that."

"Y-yes..."

"So instead of trying to understand them, just do what is necessary."

"And what's necessary?"

"What were Merrick's requests?"

"That he be buried on Earth and that the *Solo* be returned to active service in the hands of someone of his choice, namely Benajim Cyanus. Whatever else is in his will."

"So fulfill the conditions he asked you to. Reiner's faction will have to do something openly then because the dataspheres will start disintegrating and the Ranonan ambassador will act on Merrick's will. They'll have to declare the will null and try to make it stick."

"What, I should just steal Merrick's body and run the border with it?"

Joclen cocked her head as if to say "Isn't that obvious?" then turned to the menu screen and ordered a drink. "It's not like you don't want to anyway," she said, looking at Tamyn evenly. "You want to cross the Secant so bad..."

Tamyn leaned back and stared at Joclen. She's talking piracy, she thought. I'd be risking every damn thing I've got. My ship, my reputation, my life...

And if Reiner and Hall succeed? she asked herself. If they succeed, I have nothing anyway, and everything I know may well change.

Tamyn did not fear change, but she did not care to have it forced on her, either.

"The initiation," Joclen said then. "All that beautiful talk about memory and what it means to have continuity and new knowledge. The gap is the Pan. We don't know much about it anymore. I spoke to Lodgemaster Sarkis about it. One of the great hopes of the human Akaren is to fill in gaps. Bringing that history back is important, something that any Akaren would understand."

"So why hasn't it happened yet?"

Joclen shrugged. "Who says it hasn't? We know some things about the Pan, but—Merrick wants you to go to Earth. I don't think that's been done since the end of the war. And if it has, it's not public knowledge. We have a chance here to do something important for the Akaren, for the C.R., for—"

"For what?"

"Everything." Joclen leaned across the table, smiling a conspirator's smile. "If we go, that will be the reason. All the rest..."

"What?"

"Spice, seasoning, gravy."

Tamyn felt a grin begin to take over her face.

"The right thing," she said carefully, "would be to challenge this in court, invoke my authority as an independent jurist—"

"Which only solves part of the problem," Joclen said. "And risks having consensus turn against you. Safer to just act."

"Kind of reckless."

"What have you got to lose?" Joclen asked.

"Everything. And nothing." Tamyn laughed. "Not a thing," she said. "Not a damn thing."

Chapter Ten

Benajim stepped from the shunt into a dry, cottony heat, and shrugged out of his jacket. The circuit looked little different from any other dock access on the station, except that it was unpopulated. Piper Van, Stoan, and Traville followed him. Piper's head swiveled in a quick scan of the area. Then she pointed.

"That way."

Benajim and Traville stayed a pace behind Piper and Stoan, and moved down the circuit. Benajim saw Piper's hyperalertness in the set of her shoulders, the way her arms swung a few centimeters further out from her sides than when she was relaxed, the almost silent tread of her boots.

She brought them to one of the large hatches lining the left side of the circuit and touched a fingertip to its gate. A few minutes passed in silence. Traville took off his jacket and draped it over his shoulder, hooked by a thumb. Stoan stared fixedly at the hatch, hands clasped behind his back, fingers lacing and unlacing rhythmically.

Finally the access opened.

"Come on," Piper said.

They descended a short umbilical to another open hatch.

"God," Traville wrinkled his nose.

Benajim grinned against his own reaction. "What's wrong, co? A little Cursian stench bother you?"

Piper gave him a critical look but said nothing. Stoan stared at Traville. They went through the second hatch into a high-ceilinged, broad chamber.

The light was terribly bright. Three Cursians stepped ponderously toward them, a smaller Orioni in the lead. The Cursians looked like massive collections of cloth piled over a rocky form. Gold and platinum in different sizes dangled from various places on the multihued fabric. Except for deepset eyes that glimmered like oil, no part of their bodies was bare.

Like Rahalen, the Orioni appeared disconcertingly human at first glance. Nearer, the fine reticulation of his skin was evident and the thick head of ebony hair proved to be a cowl of dense, bonelike substance.

The Cursians stopped several meters from the humans and the Orioni crossed the rest of the distance. He was easily two heads taller than Traville, who stood nearly two meters.

"Welcome, coes," he said in a nasal voice. "I interpret for Longhauler Kee Ru-Esk. I am No One. Ignore me."

Stoan looked at the trio of massive forms beyond No One and laughed. Benajim cleared his throat. The light hurt his eyes, but Stoan looked unblinkingly at the Cursians.

"I am Benajim Cyanus," Benajim said. "This is my assistant, Piper Van...Stoan, cargomaster of the *Wicca,* and his assistant, Traville."

"Welcome, welcome," No One said to each in turn. Then he spoke to Stoan. "We remember the *Wicca* with pleasure. The race was rigged, but Glass won anyway. Because of that we owe a debt of face to you. How may we pay?"

Stoan nodded toward the Cursians, not looking at No One. "Straight lines need bending sometimes. Hah! We require two services, one of which will be to your profit, as well as ours, the other which will test your mettle as competent coes."

The three Cursians shifted pensively.

"State the first."

"We have cargo obligations on the ground, from various places, from various persons. Our last sojourn was shortened. Now we're under quarantine. Deliveries must be met, regardless, and our next obligation may take us nowhere. We do not wish our clients unserviced due to our inability to fulfill contract obligations. It would serve us both for you to claim the contracts at a reasonable fee and sell it as your own."

"You have a manifest?"

Stoan pulled a disk from his breast pocket and handed it to No One, who inserted it in a reader at his side. The device fed directly into his neural link.

"Exemplary clients, Co Stoan," he said finally. "What is your reasonable fee?"

"Amended!" He shook his head impatiently. "Access the second file."

A few seconds later, No One said, "All provisions for a long sojourn. All for Co Cyanus, none for the *Wicca?* This is not reasonable, this is robbery. We will be accused of stealing from you!"

"A trick of phrasing, winked through slit minds," Stoan shrugged. "Note the capacity of Cyanus's ship and add the sums."

No One stood silently a few seconds longer. "There is trickery here. You are correct, the *Solo* cannot contain so much." No One looked at them. "Even so, the record will still appear overbalanced in our favor, and face may be damaged further."

"The second request will more than compensate us," Benajim said.

"Yes?"

"First, though," Traville interrupted, "could you dim the lights?"

Stoan gave Traville an odd look and laughed.

As they left, Traville shook his head dubiously, rubbing his eyes. "I've never felt comfortable dealing with Cursians. They always do something to send everything tangent."

"That's why we offered the contracts," Benajim said. "Greed will keep them close to their bargain."

"Honor bribed, competence baited," Stoan mused. "Small seeing in deep troughs."

Benajim glanced at Stoan, then leaned close to Traville. "I admit next to no experience with Alcyoni Transmorphs, but—"

Traville shook his head slightly. "Look at it from his perspective. Seti shoved into human form, living with humans, but still seti."

Benajim nodded. "I guess I'd be a little..."

"Exactly."

"Anyway," Benajim continued, "don't worry about the Cursians. They'll be there."

Traville gave him an uncertain look, then shrugged. Benajim smiled, but admitted to himself that it was a weak bargain at best. Cursians tended to operate on a slightly skewed time sense. The idea of linear sequentialism slipped around them; events happened, as they would anyway, they argued, so why be upset if one happened sooner than later? Benajim hoped that by keeping the cargo as an anchor Longhauler Kee Ru-Esk might find it easier to act in concert with them.

"I'm just not clear," he said then, "why I had to be present during the negotiations."

Stoan gave him a round-eyed look. "Holes in expectations abound. You know so much about Cursian ethics, it surprises me you don't know Cursian tradition."

"They won't make a deal," Piper explained, "unless all the principles are present to speak for themselves. You're being used to hand off supplies to us. That makes you indispensable."

"Punctuation complete," Stoan said. "Be honored. They accepted the proposition."

The shunt took them through the body of the station, directly to the opposite side in less than two minutes, letting them out near *Solo's* berth. Benajim found himself grateful to be among people after the stark vacancy of the Cursian section. The docks on the far side of the bulkhead serviced small ships like *Solo:* scouts, explorers, couriers, stage one merchanters hoping to one day expand to full-service transports like the *Wicca*. Mostly humans, Benajim saw a small seti presence—Menkan, Coro, a lone Distanti.

As he came in sight of *Solo's* berth, he slowed, then stopped. Two men in station maintenance utilities worked the access on his lock. While he watched, the hatch rolled aside and they entered.

Benajim started forward. A hand closed over his right bicep, halting him. He looked around to find Piper Van holding him. He tried to pull free, but her grip held.

"Stop," she said.

Her eyes did not blink as she scanned the circuit. Within a few moments, she pulled Benajim closer, turned him so that he walked alongside her, his arm firmly in her grip. She smiled up at him, then looked at Traville. She made a gesture Benajim did not see, then brought her free hand around to place over the one on his arm.

"Walk," she said, smiling.

Traville was moving off, toward a man standing at a public polycom terminal. Benajim glanced back, looking for Stoan. The Alcyone was gone.

Piper walked him calmly by his lock. Several meters on, she stopped them before a public lavatory and let go of his arm. Benajim rubbed it.

"I want you to just go to the lock as if nothing is wrong," she said, still smiling. She gestured toward the lavatory entrance. "Casually, like you always do. Don't look back at me." She stepped toward the door.

He started back toward the lock. He glanced at the polycom. Traville was nowhere in sight and the polycom was unoccupied. Where was Stoan?

He reached the lock, paused, and raised a hand to the access panel. His heart quickened. There were at least two people on the other side. What about behind him? He touched the gate and issued the command. The hatch opened.

"Let's move on through," Piper said in his ear.

Benajim's nerves screamed with the effort not to jump. His scalp went briefly numb and he turned slowly toward her.

Piper's nostrils flared slightly and her eyes glinted, pupils dilated.

He walked down the umbilical to the outer dock. No one waited on the platform. A moment after Benajim and Piper stepped through, Traville and Stoan joined them. Traville held a palm-sized handgun now.

The room was a five-by-five meter space. Motiles hung immobile on the walls, awaiting instructions.

"They must've entered the ship," Piper said. She advanced to one of the motiles. "Damn, they're persistent."

"Wait," Benajim said. "That won't be necessary."

Benajim hurried to the umbilical. Piper caught him, but he blocked her way.

"My ship," he said. "She knows me."

Reluctantly, Piper nodded.

He found the two in *Solo's* lock, on the deck, unconscious. Benajim sighed, then went to the link on the bulkhead.

We have company, he told the ship.

I noticed.

More, friendly.

Ah. I'll hold my punch.

Do that.

Piper was going through their pockets when Benajim turned around.

"They're getting bolder," Traville said. "We'd better move soon."

"We will," Stoan said. "Very soon."

"Nothing," Piper said. "I suggest we stow them until we can do a proper disposal. Can you?" She looked at Benajim.

"Sure." He opened a small locker just off the foyer and helped her move the limp coes into it. "Do we keep them alive?"

"Until I can do a trace-and-identify," Piper said.

"Quickly, then," Stoan said. "We leave tomorrow."

"What?" Benajim said. "I thought three days—"

"Longhauler Kee Ru-Esk also thinks three days. He'll bring his tug around and claim the cargo tomorrow, hoping to reclaim face at Tamyn's expense." Stoan looked at Traville, who seemed puzzled. "I have dealt with Cursians before as well."

Piper laughed.

Tamyn manifested in the privy chamber as a silent presence, constrained from interaction. Naril's face, larger than her own within the Flow, spoke on her behalf. Judge Culstan listened, but it became clear to Tamyn from the length of time he listened without comment that nothing would happen.

"Your Honor," Naril concluded, "we suggest that the restraint put on my client is a violation of basic Charter principle. Both her ability to answer charges and her ability to conduct her business are materially harmed by these motions. It seems incredible to me that—"

Culstan manifested a hand, palm out, and Naril fell silent at once. "I know what you're going to say, Advocate, and I agree with a lot of it. Seems incredible to me, too. But it may also be in Shipmaster Glass's best interest to wait for the pleasure of the court on this matter. A prolonged discovery period might be in all our best interests. Motion denied."

Tamyn stared at Culstan's magisterial image, her thoughts carefully distant. She had told herself to expect exactly this—had gone about making plans for exactly this contingency—but it still came as a shock. Till now, she could have stopped everything, terminated the arrangements being made. Till now...

Culstan looked at her. "Shipmaster Glass. You've got to understand that what we have here is extraordinary. You claim to have destroyed a Regent police cruiser. You claim that the...*Jarom*...was sent illegally with the sole purpose of destroying both the *Solo* and your ship. Now you're filing charges against a member of the Board, demanding an exculpatory hearing and disclosure of Board minutes. I admire your carbon, Shipmaster, since you've been implicated in the murder of a regent. This has never happened before. I think extraordinary measures are in order."

Tamyn tried to speak, but the restraining code prevented it.

"I'm granting the request for disclosure," Culstan said. "Regent Hall is being informed. Since there's no record of the *Jarom's* destination—indeed, no record of when it left—I must take your word that the events presented to me are factual. Based on that, I have no choice but to proceed as requested. Until, however, further evidence emerges, I will permit your exclusion to stand. Your advocate can interact on your behalf."

Culstan manifested a gavel, banged it once, and faded from the Flow.

Tamyn blinked at the polycom station, suddenly kicked out of the interface.

"Son of a..." Naril muttered. "He's really going to do it. I would never have expected Culstan, of all people...how did you know?"

"Hm? Oh, Culstan may be conservative as a rock, but he's a strict interpretation thinker. Members of the Board of Regents sending out assassins may sound extraordinary, but since the *Jarom* is missing and there's a dead regent, he suspects too much to deny the motion. I figured he'd be the one. He'll tie Hall up for months once disclosure begins." Tamyn cleared her throat and stood. "So then we go ahead."

"Maybe you should change your mind about this," Naril suggested, a hopeful note in her voice. "I mean, since you've got the ear of the Court now—"

Joclen stood at the office door, leaning in. "Teaker's here."

"Good," Tamyn said. "We'll be out in a few minutes."

Naril looked at Tamyn crossly. "I still think you should fight this thing through court."

"Yes, well," Tamyn said, shrugging, "that's inappropriate."

"Would you mind explaining that?"

"Very simple. There isn't time. We don't know what Reiner is using Merrick shipping for and we don't know how Hall's Charter amendment will go."

"I think it's a safe bet that it will fail. Stall, at least, once this gets out."

"I disagree."

Naril scowled. "You've already made up your mind. You want to do this, you're just going through these motions to buy time."

"Why shouldn't I go through with it?"

"Oh, no reason! Except that you'll be breaking laws that are legal according to the Charter. You may never be able to come back."

Tamyn looked away. "Yes, well," she repeated, then walked toward the door.

"Is this some Akaren thing?"

"No. Not...entirely."

Naril just sighed, shook her head, and waved Tamyn through the door.

Teaker lounged on one of the enormous sofas, watching the water in the pool lap delicately against the rim. Joclen stood behind him, arms folded over her chest.

"Teaker," Tamyn said. "What do you have for me?"

"Lot of grief, co," he said lazily, "if you really intend to do something about anything." He stretched and yawned. "I been up twenty-two hours now, pushing stimulant through my brain like a bad dream. Two times somebody got in my way." He raised a hand, two fingers extended. "Two times. Good thing you're paying premium on this, otherwise..."

Tamyn sat down beside him. "Are you just working me, Teaker, or were there serious problems?"

Teaker looked at her evenly. "The Fobes you took care of on your way out were just watching. When I left, the real trouble showed up. Two teams, three each. I'm not certain, but I'd swear they had a Vohec with them." He stared out at the pool. "Second one was waiting at one of my stash holes. One co, maybe a prophylactic. Wired funny anyway." He looked at Tamyn again, a faint smile on his lips. "Not anymore."

Tamyn caught Joclen's frown. "Did they keep you from finding what I asked?"

Teaker made a disgusted noise and sat forward. "I am a professional, Shipmaster Tamyn. That's why you use me, is it not? No one keeps me from getting what I'm hired to get."

Tamyn waited, watching him.

He yawned, stretched, and stood. "He's under the pavilion in Merrick Courtyard." He pulled a disk from his pocket and dropped it into Tamyn's lap. "There's some security. Nothing that can't be dealt with. I already have people working on it."

Benajim slept in the common, fully clothed, as he had done since taking *Solo* from the museum. He opened his eyes to the sound of voices and found Piper and Stoan by the samovar. They fell silent as he sat up.

"Is that coffee?" Benajim asked, stumping groggily toward them.

"You snore," Piper said.

"A hobby," Benajim said, filling a cup. "What do you do?"

"I was about to roust you. We're getting set to move."

Benajim blinked at the time on the autochef. "You let me sleep that long?"

"You evidently needed it."

Benajim sipped the hot drink and looked around. "Where is everybody?"

"Shreve and Innes are in the station lock," Stoan said. "I will soon be elsewhere than here." He pointed toward the bridge. "There."

The Alcyoni walked off.

"Station lock?" Benajim asked.

Piper shrugged. "I'll be on the bridge, too. I want to make sure we can defend ourselves if anything goes wrong."

"You're kidding."

Piper raised an eyebrow, then followed Stoan.

Benajim ran a hand through his disheveled hair. He finished his coffee and went to one of the cabins. After a quick shower, he pulled on fresh utilities and went out through the lock, into the connecting umbilical.

Innes stood below an open hatch, staring up. Benajim stopped beside her.

"Morning."

"Is it?" Innes asked.

Benajim gestured at the opening.

"Shreve," Innes said. "He's circumventing the bay controls, funneling control through the *Solo*. Also making sure no other sabotage has been done."

"Ah. I understand we're about to leave?"

"According to Stoan." She looked at him curiously. "How did you get out of the station the first time?"

"As long as *Solo* is manned the automated dock systems respond to her," Benajim said. "Since technically only Sean could be operating her, the station had no reason to deny the request to open the doors. I'm sure that oversight has been corrected."

Innes gave him a curious look. "Wouldn't that mean the *Solo* would have to recognize you as Sean Merrick?"

"Well, yes, I suppose. But Sean had already transferred ownership. I imagine he changed the recognition code on *Solo.*"

"That's a fairly complex procedure," Innes muttered, puzzled. "Even more difficult from a medunit bed."

Benajim stared up at the open hatch, his scalp warming, very aware of Innes beside him, watching.

"Innes," Piper's voice broke in.

Innes lifted a comm to her mouth. "Here."

"We need you on the comm board, monitoring station traffic."

"Be right there." She called up to the open hatch. "Shreve, we're going on board. You need me?"

"Check the remotes from the bridge," Shreve's voice came out of the darkness. "See if power is coming through. They might have put some blocks in between here and there."

"Right." She pocketed the link and nodded at Benajim. "Time to go."

Benajim led the way to the bridge. He dropped into his couch and keyed the master controls. Piper waited in the copilot's couch beside him.

"By the way," she said conversationally, "in case you're interested, our intruders worked for Keller Shipping."

"Reiner's company?"

"The same."

Benajim thought about that. Then: "You said 'worked'?"

Piper only smiled, grimly, and continued studying the monitors.

"What's the status?" Benajim asked finally.

Piper looked up. "Longhauler Kee Ru-Esk has already left his dock and is coming around. Innes?"

She worked the comm console briefly. "We have five minutes, people." She winked at Benajim.

"So where are we going once we get out?" Benajim asked.

"First," Piper said, "we get the *Solo* out of here. Stoan will take care of freeing the *Wicca.* Once we're offstation and free, he'll tell us the rest."

Innes went to the engineering station. "Got it," Innes said. She touched a contact. "Okay, Shreve, get your imprinted ass in here." She looked around. "We have bay door control."

Benajim swallowed drily. He was excited and he liked the edge all the adrenalin gave him, but the sour undercurrent of fear kept interjecting the wish to be done with it and away from everything. He activated the agravs and checked his systems again for sabotage. Sean had built some very efficient datasphere scours into the *Solo's* Flow.

"It doesn't seem anyone's noticed we're here yet," Piper said.

A minute later Shreve entered the bridge. He went directly to a polycom console.

"Anytime you're ready, Shipmaster," Shreve said and set his hands onto the gate.

Benajim licked his lips and started *Solo* down the tunnel.

"Ah," Piper said. "They noticed now." She laughed.

The domed pavilion in the center of the courtyard formed by the trio of towers glowed dimly from within, casting a dull amber light on the surrounding pavement. Tamyn flexed her hands, curling her fingers into fists and opening them, like flowers blooming and dying. Every sound made her start.

"Hey, co."

Tamyn whirled. A dark figure towered behind her in the gangway. A light winked on and she saw, briefly, Teaker's features. He grinned, glancing at Kryder who held the light.

"You better listen better than that, co," Teaker said.

Tamyn's heart thundered. She looked back to the dome. "Is everything in place?"

"Perfectly," Teaker said. "Power should go off in a few minutes. As long as Joclen doesn't—"

"She won't be late." She studied Teaker as he moved closer to the edge of the wall. She felt calmer now. "If things are still difficult I can give you a ride out."

"Thanks, co. Always thoughtful. I actually thought about that, and decided to stay. Things in the Flow are already changing. Subtly, mind you, but change is change. So I'm staying to see what happens next." He passed a packet to her. "This is everything I could find on Cyanus. There's not a lot and most of it's allegorical and third hand. One interesting bit of data— and I'm not too sure what to make of it—has to do with security inside Merrick's corporate matrix. Seems on several occasions Hiram Ross tried to encode blocks to keep Cyanus out, deny him access. Every time the encoding failed. Drove Ross to vexation, from what I hear. I was told that the system continually identified Cyanus as Sean Merrick and rejected any attempt to exclude him."

Tamyn stared at him. "What do you make of that?"

"Not sure. I've heard of consanguinity problems before with ID systems, but nothing so thorough that a simple sight-only program wouldn't work. Does anybody know what Merrick looked like when he was young?"

"Not that young. Thanks, Teaker." She slipped the packet into her pocket. "You don't have to stay here if you have other things to take care of."

Teaker sighed. "I'm going in with you. I have to see Merrick's corpse myself."

She nodded and looked skyward. The rich atmosphere clinging close to Miron City set the stars a-sparkle. She sent a silent hope that everything was going well with *Wicca* and *Solo*.

Teaker touched her shoulder and pointed. The light in the dome flickered and went out.

She sprinted across the courtyard. They had an estimated five minutes before security descended on them. Everything within the Merrick Enterprises compound on several major circuits was out—security would have to come from the police garrison at the port or M.E.'s security station in the warehouse district. Right now internal security could not even open a door.

As she reached the perimeter of the pavilion an explosion cracked the air. Above, one of the huge panes in the dome wall shattered and collapsed. Hovers descended. Several black-clad shapes ran toward her from every corner of the compound, converged on her as she reached the entrance to the pavilion.

She aimed a lamp into the dark of the pavilion. A botanical display filled much of it. Twisted shapes and multihued leaves from various worlds rose up, each world's presentation in its own containment field—now shut down. Insects buzzed and chattered throughout the dome. A hover slid through the hole, drowning them out with its agrav whine.

Teaker led them through the displays to the center of the dome, where a raised platform held a circular bench. He gestured for the closest hover to set down nearby.

Joclen leaned out of the vehicle. "One minute," she hissed.

Three people dropped from the hover and moved around the platform. Teaker's people, Tamyn noted. She heard tools clink. Suddenly, the entire platform rose up on stout pylons. A stairway led down.

At the foot of the stairs was a security door. One of Teaker's assistants opened the link panel beside it and peered into the circuitry within. He connected cables to four places, then Teaker splayed his long fingers across the panel. The door slid open soundlessly.

It was cold on the other side. Tamyn shone her light in. The beam played over a bier covered by a transparency. Within the coffin lay Sean Merrick, naked, ancient, unmoving, cables snaking from his skull to receptacles in the smooth walls around him.

"Figured," Teaker said.

"God," one of his friends whispered.

"They've got him plugged in. Latent patterns are scanned, reinforced, and fed back through this thing. His brain is acting as a template for an AI presence in the Flow. This is why his imprimatur still manifests out in the Reaches. Probably why his own datasphere hasn't shut down."

Tamyn swallowed. "Cut it."

A team of three guided a heavy sarcophagus down the stairs. The agravs hummed gently. Teaker's people went to work separating Merrick from the machinery. Tamyn glanced at the trio with the sarcophagus and recognized Naril's oldest, Leeg, Kevon, and Coralyn. Coralyn nodded reassuringly to her.

"Thirty seconds left," Joclen called.

They placed Merrick's body into the sarcophagus. Coralyn closed the lid and activated the freezer. Then they hustled it back up into the dome and aboard the hover.

Everyone scattered. Tamyn squeezed Teaker's shoulder and he brushed her face with his fingertips, then was gone. She climbed aboard the hover. It was overladen, but Joclen managed to gain altitude and fly back through the opening. Several more hovers waited outside and shot away in as many directions, decoys.

They left the area just as the first security hovers arrived.

Benajim laughed as the bay doors opened on his command. He edged *Solo* forward slowly. So far only automatic systems had detected their movement. Queries came in from observation AIs, but no sentient being had yet asked any questions. Benajim's hand moved toward the TEGlink board.

"Won't need that," Piper said.

Benajim glanced at her, then looked up at the screens. Space outside the dock was blotted out by an enormous, angular mass. Benajim almost stopped *Solo's* egress.

"Longhauler Kee Ru-Esk," Piper said. "Right on time, two days early." She smiled. "Good estimate, Co Stoan. My compliments."

Solo drifted out of the dock, toward the waiting Cursian vessel.

"More notice," Innes called. "Stationmaster is requesting an explanation from the Cursian. I don't think anyone's connected us to them yet. Shreve?"

"Countermeasures will break down in another three minutes," Shreve said. "Then we'll be a big bright blip with an ID on their monitors."

"Find the bay," Piper said.

Benajim touched the gate and entered the Flow. The Cursian trader filled his awareness with its mass and geometries, the fields coiling around it like watery ripples. Benajim piloted *Solo* around it, to the other side. There, one bay stood open to vacuum.

That's it, Piper said

I know...

He maneuvered through the close opening, into the pitch darkness of the Cursian cargo bay.

Stationmaster's pissed now, Shreve informed them. *Wants to know what authority Ru-Esk has to be by a restricted bay.*

Restricted how? I docked in a public—

—more than AIs are in our dock, we've got security trolls—they just reported that Solo has left the station.

As the bay door sealed behind them, Benajim switched on Solo's exterior light and found a docking cradle secured to the deck below. He settled *Solo* into its new berth. Clampons locked down automatically. Benajim turned off the lights and withdrew.

"Now let's hope Longhauler Kee Ru-Esk doesn't overly enjoy arguing," Piper said.

Joclen flew the hover north according to Leeg's direction, skirting the port.

"By now they'll have security up to max in the port," Leeg said. "I found an alternate route."

Tamyn sat beside the sarcophagus. It was warm in the hover and a drop of sweat rolled down from her hairline, followed her jaw. She stared at the sleek, black surface. In the flashing of passing lights it was a mirror reflecting a twisted night world. Joclen descended almost to street level and the reflections were fewer, farther in coming, and it was only a dark slab.

I hope I'm long gone before I'm too weak to resist unwelcome decisions, she thought.

"There," Leeg whispered.

The hover slowed, settled to the pavement. Tamyn looked out the window.

They were in a narrow alley. Tamyn stepped from the hover and looked up. A wide band of night was visible between the edges of the roofs. The only artificial lights were handlamps and old yellowed function lights on a nearby warehouse door.

Kryder and Kevon eased the sarcophagus out of the hover.

"Now where?" Tamyn asked.

Leeg went to a set of hulking doors that angled out from the building. He worked intently at the locking mechanism until it released with a loud crack.

Grating metal teeth slid inside corroded slots. The doors lifted up and out. Tamyn drew a breath of musty air.

"Where does this lead?" she asked.

"Underground tunnels," Leeg said. "They haven't been used in years, not since these warehouses have been closed down. There's a network of them under the port to the various shuttle pits."

"Whose warehouse is this?"

"Mirak Corporation."

Kevon, Coralyn, and Kryder brought the sarcophagus up. "Come on," Kevon said, "we're behind schedule."

Kryder shined a light down the entrance. A ramp angled down about four meters, then levelled off. Tamyn walked down. It was cool and clammy and, except for a couple of pale green liquid light panels glowing at irregular intervals, abysmally dark. Debris crunched delicately beneath her feet, echoing distantly.

They reached a cross corridor. Tamyn glanced at Leeg, who pointed left.

Kryder went first, now, his handlamp tracing out the walls, the detritus, the dust. Briefly his light fell across old graffiti.

SCANS LOK SETI DIE FUCKFILTH SETI SUCKSILT!

It was a pallid brown stain against the grey-green wall. Other phrases were too faded or obscured by newer writing to read.

The echoes of their steps sounded like dripping water. The darkness became denser, like a shroud, clinging, and their handlamps did little to cut it. Tamyn was oppressively conscious of the sarcophagus behind her, guided now by Kevon and Coralyn, and how unnatural that they should be trying to bury a corpse instead of simply recycling it or disposing of it.

She coughed. The sound rippled around them.

"The ventilators probably don't work," Kevon said.

The air was acrid, thicker. "How much further?" Tamyn asked.

"Just up ahead," Leeg replied.

The corridor opened onto a platform. The air cleared slightly and Tamyn felt a faint breeze. With a sharp click a series of blue-white lights flickered on overhead. The light filtered inconsistently through encrusted grime, shedding a dusky illumination. At the edge of the platform Tamyn looked down on a series of thick metal rails that ran down the tunnel.

Flatcars stacked along the rear wall, against which the rails ended. Leeg, Kevon, and Kryder unbolted one and eased it down onto a rail.

"You're sure that's the right one?" Coralyn asked Leeg.

"Absolutely."

"All right," Tamyn said. "Get the sarcophagus loaded. Let's get moving."

"Where is this taking us?" Joclen asked as she helped ease the bulky coffin onto the flatcar.

"Pit 31," Leeg said. "It's about four kilometers out." He crawled underneath the car and after a minute there was a loud click. He emerged grinning.

Everyone stepped on and Leeg, at the front, reached down and activated the car. It began rolling ponderously down the track.

"I hope it moves faster than this," Joclen said.

"It's progressive," Leeg said, frowning.

After several meters it picked up speed.

The lights overhead flickered by, inconsistent. Lichenous growths marbled the walls and occasionally a small animal scurried out of their path. The wheels rumbled steadily and sent a vibration through the floor of the car.

Tamyn grew anxious. Several of the rails on either side veered off into other tunnels, many of them dark. She was persistently aware of the closeness of the walls. These tunnels had been built in the early days of Miron City, some of the first structures on the planet, before atmosphere generation had produced a breathable mix above ground. It was all port, then, and very little else. Warehouses, shuttles coming and going, a constant stream of trade goods. They were riding beneath the inevitability of commerce, the result of humans being humans. A city built where none had been before, lives lived in ways unthought of till the place was settled. Forgotten corridors, stale air, the stench of neglect, a tomb of memories no one cared to remember. She thought of the stories left down here, undiscoverable now because the builders were gone and the rest had other things to do.

Suddenly they were in blackness. Tamyn looked back and saw a dwindling circle of light, receding swiftly, and her throat caught. Ahead she saw nothing.

For an instant she was thoughtless, empty. Air moved past her, hair tickled her face and neck. Nothing surrounded her, nothing defined her. A cry pressed against her teeth. Behind, the light was only a pinpoint now, a star, still shrinking. Then the car turned, to the left, and there was complete darkness.

She reached out and felt the cool, smooth surface of the coffin and it seemed that the chill passed up her arms, into her mind. She pulled her hand away.

The car turned another bend and ahead lay murky light. The walls were closer still, the tunnel narrowed to contain only one car now.

"Tam?"

Joclen knelt beside her. Tamyn groped for her hand and squeezed it.

"I'm here," she whispered.

Joclen nodded uncertainly.

Chapter Eleven

Tamyn, Joclen, and Kryder rode with the sarcophagus in a cramped cabin aboard a Cursian tug. Kryder stayed alert while the others tried to sleep, but the best they could manage were short naps. It always sounded like massive pistons were slamming home somewhere aboard the boat, or huge wheels on corroded shafts turning, or unsecured cargo shifting across metal decks.

Finally, the hatches opened and motiles brought the sarcophagus out. An Orioni translator gestured for them to follow.

An umbilical stretched to another ship.

Gravity resumed the instant they reached the lock. Tamyn's insides felt wrenched out of place and her head throbbed. But the lock was clean, spacious, and the ship was quiet, an immediate relief.

The hatch sealed and the umbilical withdrew. On a large screen Tamyn saw the boat that had hauled them out here: a short-range cargo hauler, oblate, the surface scarred and streaked with age and wear and looking incapable of hauling anything— like most Cursian ships.

"Welcome."

She turned. A tall, elegant Ranonan stood near the hatch, long golden robes falling from narrow shoulders. Large, liquid amber eyes regarded them unblinking, set in a head covered with soft, pale fur.

"I am Shipmaster Tamyn Glass of the *Wicca.*"

The Ranonan bowed slightly. "I am Ambassador Tej-Ojann." He gestured to the sarcophagus.

"Merrick's body," Tamyn said.

Tej-Ojann turned to the bulkhead and touched a contact. Almost immediately two Vohec projections entered. These wore the shapes of Orioni. Their all-green eyes took in everything in the lock.

"Remove this," Tej-Ojann said, gesturing at the sarcophagus, "to Qrath Herin's lab for analysis."

The projections took positions at both ends of the sarcophagus, and guided it from the lock.

"Please," the Ranonan said, "enjoy the hospitality of my ship. I trust we can do better than a Cursian tug, although it is remarkable that Longhauler Kee Ru-Esk kept to a schedule. I hope I've made the appropriate preparations for you. Follish's message gave little time to put everything in place, although I've been waiting for some time for this."

"If I may," Tamyn said, "I'd rather be present at any analysis of Merrick's remains."

Tej-Ojann stared at her, motionless, large eyes unreadable. The Ranonan were telelogs, universally employed as ambassadors, translators, and arbiters throughout the Reaches and by many private companies. Tamyn wondered if it were possible to feel them exploring the mind, the way Crej'Nevan's touch was definite and visceral. The symbiote nanopoles through which they operated infected most citizens of the C.R. and, she believed, of the Seven Reaches as well.

"Time and truth for a fellow sojourner?" Tej-Ojann said.

"Truth for truth, then time is endless. You're Akaren?"

The Ranonan nodded. "Come along. We'll watch Master Herin's proceedings."

The sarcophagus was open beneath a soft light. A Menkan, ropelike tendrils emerging from a thick trunk adorned with strips of metal and fine cloth, bent over the body. Monitors stood just behind Qrath Herin. Tamyn could barely see Merrick's pale, alabaster face within. He had been so robust in life that the shrunken remains seemed a lie, an insult.

"Herin will attempt to establish that these are Merrick's remains," Tej-Ojann explained quietly. "We use a combination of technologies in such instances. We leave as little to chance as possible."

"What happens once you've established that this is Merrick?" Joclen asked.

"Then we challenge the actions of the Board of Regents concerning both Merrick Enterprises and Mirak Corporation, and release Merrick's testament of primary designation to the public, through the Greater Flow. Hopefully his removal has also begun the disintegration of his corporate dataspheres."

"Then all hell breaks loose."

"One may hope."

Tamyn grinned at Tej-Ojann and thought: one may hope in certainty. Suddenly the Ranonan raised a hand.

Tamyn looked at Herin. The Menkan's probing tendrils encased Merrick's face and skull, moving small probes in slow increments. The monitors registered frantically in their seti fashion and the Menkan jerked slightly twice, three times.

"Verified," it said softly. "This was Sean Benjamin Merrick."

Tej-Ojann nodded. "Now we may break hell loose."

Benajim stared at the Stralith. It functioned effortlessly within the confines of the control blister despite its apparent bulk. Crej'Nevan filled the blister, yet moved as if all of space were available to it, the translucent mantle undulating slowly. While working, Crej'Nevan occasionally sang, weaving intricate polytonal constructs that drifted in and out of pleasing to human ears, and occasionally chatted to anyone who was within earshot about anything that occurred to it at the moment. Often, it was quiet. The Stralith possessed profound grace. Benajim was entranced.

Crei also frightened him.

He knew about Straliths, what they purportedly could do within the mind. Benajim had heard it suggested here and there that Crej'Nevan performed such services for various members of the *Wicca's* crew. Disentangling, they called it. Straightening out the knots that twisted the insides into tight, hellish jams. The prospect scared Benajim. He was afraid of remembering, even though he wanted to, desperately.

In theory—and, depending on how good the neuron mechanic was, in practice—all his memories were still there, just blocked, inaccessible. The blocks could be removed.

He would remember in a flood.

Benajim was more twisted about that than anything else. He hated not remembering where he came from, how he had left there, and who he really was. If the blocks were lifted he might emerge with a deep self-loathing. Perhaps some things were better left alone.

Like a child drawn to fire, though, he hung around the docks and listened to the aimless prattle and alien music of the seti, trying to sort through his desires and needs. He wished Tamyn had never made the offer to let Crej'Nevan work on him.

Do I want to remember?

Yes.

Do I want to go through the process of remembering?

No...

Perhaps, he decided, it's time to leave.

Piper felt a peculiar relief when the door to Benajim's cabin opened and he stepped into the corridor. He pressed against the bulkhead and remained motionless. In the dim lights of nightcycle he was a thick shadow. She had expected him to run—hoped he would, in fact—and confirmation felt satisfying.

When he moved he was silent and quick. Piper tracked him easily with her enhanced senses. She admired his unmodified grace and stealth.

He reached a shunt and went on past. Deftly, he removed an access panel to a service duct and slid in, pulling the panel back into place. Piper knelt beside it and listened till she was certain he could not hear her, then pulled the panel off. He had attached a gummy substance to two corners that would hold for a few days. She cleaned it off and bolted the panel.

She took the shunt. She laughed to herself: Benajim was being too stealthy, avoiding the shunt in the belief that he was covering his trail. In the station that might be a worthwhile endeavor, where shunt usage was logged in the station Flow, but here...

Besides, Tamyn did not have a full crew compliment now. Many of the people normally aboard were temporary, signed on for one sojourn only. There were only her fifteen permanent crew on board now, too few to effectively police the big merchanter.

She left the shunt and sprinted to the engineering section, just behind the lock to which the *Solo* was attached. No one was on duty. She slipped through the service access into the bulkhead and through to the lock.

She had beat him by seconds. He crawled out of an air cycler vent and stayed motionless against the bulkhead below the observation blister. No one was there, but he could not see that from his position.

Piper walked across the deck toward him.

Benajim's eyes widened and he bolted for the lock. Piper caught him at the entrance.

"Where are we going, co?" she asked.

Benajim wrenched out of her grip. "I'm leaving."

"I can see that."

He frowned. "I'm leaving."

"We're leaving, or this conversation ends now and you can sleep off a headache in your cabin. I'm your prophylactic, remember? I can't very well do that if I'm left behind."

"I'm relieving you of that duty. You don't have to watch over me."

"You're not paying my fee. I stay with you till the terms of my contract are fulfilled."

"When will that be?"

"Hard to say. I expect I'll know when the time comes."

Benajim pulled away. "No! I don't want anyone with me!"

"Any moment now we'll trigger some alarm somewhere and you'll be explaining this to Stoan. Make a choice. I go or you stay."

He tried to punch her. Piper ducked the blow and grabbed his elbow. She stepped on his foot and pulled him off-balance, held him like that.

"You surprise me, Co Cyanus," she said. She stretched her free hand to the lock control. "It's sealed against unauthorized access. Seems all this was for nothing."

"Kindly let go and I can open it."

Changing her grip to his wrist, she also took hold of his neck, turned him. He touched the control. The door opened. Piper walked him into the lock.

The door sealed and they descended.

"Damn!" he shouted. She let him go and he spun around. "All right!" He jabbed a finger at her. "My ship, my rules!"

Piper held up her hands. "I'm just the prophylactic."

They rode down in silence. Benajim walked quickly up the umbilical to the *Solo*.

"Company on board," he said as they entered the ship.

He led the way to the bridge in stony silence. He dropped into the command couch and linked. For several seconds he was immobile, his head back, eyes slitted, immersed in the Flow.

Abruptly he took his hand from the gate and leaned forward. He was pale and his eyes looked startled.

"Co Cyanus...?"

"We're leaving," he said and glanced at her.

She nodded. "Where?"

"Tabit."

"That's in the Pan."

"Uh huh."

"On the wrong side of the Secant."

"That's right."

Piper sighed heavily. "What did you find out? What were you accessing?"

He busied himself checking monitors. "Sean's dataspheres are breaking down. Shipmaster Glass succeeded and she's on her way here with Sean's body."

"You accessed the Greater Flow from here?"

He nodded.

"That's as good as a beacon. Regent police will be here right on Tamyn's tail."

"No. My access is shielded."

"You can't do that."

He looked at her. "*Solo* can. If anybody tries to trace the access they'll find it originating from a score of places, all over the system."

"How—?"

"Grab a couch and let's get out of here."

Stunned, Piper sat down. In theory she knew the capability to mask access to the Flow was possible, even probable—an extension of secure-coding datanodes—but she had never heard of anyone actually creating the machinery.

"Why Tabit?" she asked.

"That's where the answers are," he said, then linked.

Wicca had rarely looked so good to Tamyn. The ship was dwarfed by the mountain of ice off which she hung, but the dim starlight of Miron's primary splintered through the frozen gas and water and shed spectral shadows across her hull. For a moment all the colors of nature spread like gentle hands around her. Just for a moment—Tamyn caught her breath—and the mountain moved and the fissure through which the light funneled passed, leaving *Wicca* visible only by her running lights.

Tej-Ojann's ship approached slowly. Tamyn sat beside Joclen on the bridge of the Ranonan vessel and watched *Wicca* grow on the wide flatscreen.

"Where's the *Solo?*" Joclen asked.

Tamyn shrugged. They were coming toward *Wicca* from "above" and could not see if Merrick's ship was linked to the belly. "Can we get comm?" Tamyn asked the Vohec projection beside her.

"They aren't transmitting," he said. "We're signaling now."

The shallow arc of a suspensor field upon which Tamyn, Joclen, two Vohec, and Tej-Ojann sat was all that occupied the "bridge". The ship was controlled elsewhere, presumably by Vohec in their natural forms, and information funneled through the two projections.

"Some damage was done at the station," Tej-Ojann said. "The escape was successful, but unsubtle. Reputations have been impugned, a few security vessels were jostled while trying to board the Cursian. Longhauler Kee Ru-Esk was less than graceful. I will tend to it after we have parted, but your ship is sought."

"You've been most kind, Co Ojann."

The Ranonan turned to her and seemed quizzical. "Please understand our motives in this. A war was fought to establish a place where we could interact with humans. There are aspects in these abrogations on the part of certain members of the Board of Regents which lead us to believe a return to the form of government against which human and seti struggled is inevitable. We do not wish this. If we can prevent it without violence—at least without war—then we will do whatever is necessary." Tej-Ojann's large eyes glistened with humor. "We Ranonan are a very utilitarian species."

"It's still twelve light years to the border," Joclen said.

"You will have a Vohec escort that far."

Tamyn frowned.

"We have comm," the Vohec announced.

"—*Wicca*, Supercargo Stoan here. Please clarify your intentions."

"Put me on," Tamyn said.

"Done."

"Stoan, this is Tamyn. We made it."

Tamyn stepped onto the bridge. Her crew watched her, waiting, smiles competing with worry, waiting for direction, orders, guidance. Crej'Nevan was oddly still, limbs wrapped about its trunk, mantle partly retracted.

"First things first," she said and turned to Joclen. She held out her hand.

Joclen, grinning, placed a disk in Tamyn's palm. "I return legal title and ownership of *Wicca* to you. The crew is witness."

Tamyn closed her hand on the disk. "Thank you." She swept her gaze around the bridge.

"We're going across the border," she said. "I have a commitment to fulfill to an old friend. Let me explain it to you and then you can decide. I won't ask anyone to come along who doesn't want to. If you want to leave *Wicca* the Ranonan ship will take you off and see to it you have berths on other ships. If I return and can still operate, you have a place on my ship."

No one said anything. She began to explain, as best she could, everything that had transpired in the last several days, from the confrontation with Trace Alek and the *Jarom* to their hastily arranged and illegal exit from Miron Transit. She spoke evenly, quietly, and no one interrupted. When she was finished everyone continued to sit and watch her.

Tamyn felt their anxiety, but none of it was directed at her.

"Once we move out there's no chance of getting off," she said.

No one moved. An odd pressure built behind her eyes, in her sinuses, that seemed joined to a similar sensation in her throat and lungs. She swallowed thickly.

"Very good," she said quietly. "Thank you. Pilot Bramus, let's get moving. Everyone to stations."

All at once everyone moved. Several left the bridge, a few squeezing her shoulder as they went by, all of them grinning at her. Tamyn felt a childish glee. She held herself firmly; tears, she thought, would be inappropriate.

When everyone was at station, she crossed the bridge to her couch.

"Where's Benajim?" she asked Stoan.

"He left, hah! Insolent humility notwithstanding. We rendezvoused as scheduled, he stayed a day, and then took off."

"Where?"

"He left a heading and a location for you." He looked up at her as if to say "but how can we trust him?"

Tamyn sat down. "Let's worry about getting outsystem first. Then we'll find him."

She flowed into the datasphere eagerly. It had only been a couple of days, but the intense relief made it seem longer. A vast part of her had been inaccessible. There seemed to her no crueler punishment than to isolate someone from the Flow. Thinking about it now brought her to a dull seethe. Might as well cut off a co's air, food, friends.

She touched the Ranonan ship and bade it safe travel. Then she let Joclen take *Wicca* outsystem.

They moved out of the ice field.

Sean's face formed before her.

"God, Tam, it's been an eternity!" Sean's encoding said. He grinned at her. "Good to see you!"

"Sorry. It's been a little more chaotic than I thought." She began telling him—it—about the last few days. The image listened wordlessly, its expression intent and unchanging.

"But it's done?" he asked after she had finished. "We're on our way?"

"Yes. Your...body...is on board. We're leaving Miron System."

The eyes closed, an expression of gratitude suffusing the aged features. "And my corporate dataspheres?"

"Are in a state of collapse. There's no telling yet what the effect will be in the Flow, but—"

Sean closed his eyes. "It's done. Finally." He sighed loudly. "You should access the emerging data. There's plenty of interest. Some of it may be useful."

"What sort of data?"

"Oh, the sort of data one finds it expedient to hide." The eyes opened. "Data about expedient actions. The reason Carson Reiner wanted to keep everything intact." He chuckled. "Now I can go to my grave content that she won't have a monopoly on it."

"You haven't told me everything, have you?"

"You can be a stickler for legalities at times, Tam. I didn't know how you'd react to helping a criminal—"

"I've always known you were a criminal, Sean."

"When we get to Earth and you find the place where I want to be buried, bring this disk along."

"Why?"

"Don't you wonder why I sent a full persona encoding along instead of just a message?"

"To convince me, I thought."

"That, too. And to make explanations. Has Benajim left?"

"Yes. You knew he would?"

"He had to. He has a different job to do than you, but when you're done I want you to find him and help him."

"When I get done burying you I'm turning around and heading home. I've got enough trouble now without lingering in areas where I don't belong."

"Please, Tam. He'll need help."

"Then he should have stayed and explained."

"He couldn't. He won't know till he gets there."

Tamyn stiffened. "Sean..."

"There's a lot of nested data in his skull."

"You know how I feel about that."

"Sure, but this was the safest way to do it. Now you really ought to access some of the emerging data from my dataspheres. You'll find it very instructive."

"Can't. I don't want to risk a trace."

"But—"

"No. We're taking your body to Earth and coming back. That's it. There's nothing in your conditions about helping Benajim or cannibalizing your dataspheres or involving myself in any other way."

Sean scowled petulantly, then nodded. "True. But that pertains to my will, Tam, not the other reasons to go through all this. And you're curious as hell or I've misread you for decades. There are aspects to this you don't know yet."

"You mean like Carson Reiner using Merrick Enterprises as a front for her own illicit activities? And the fact that she and her other associates have been using your death as an excuse to reopen the Charter to make changes?"

The face grinned. "I knew you were the one for this job. Yes, I mean all that. And you'll need the data I have to fish out of the ruin of my empire."

"It can't be that important or you wouldn't have risked my being stubborn and refusing to access the Flow at this point. You already have it."

He started chuckling. "Clever. You always were clever. That's why I trusted you with this."

"Flattery won't change a thing."

"Would you believe it coming just from this encoding?"

Tamyn pursed her lips and studied him narrowly. She had known Sean probably as well as anyone. He was arrogant and smart and suspicious. He could never stand being out of control.

"You'll have to let me do this my own way, Sean. I'm committed to this run now and I won't let anything get in my way. You've dangled information in front of me through this whole thing. I've stopped taking chances I don't need to." She jabbed a finger at the projection. "You're dead! I'm damned if I let a ghost run things for me."

Sean glared at her.

Tamyn reached for the switch.

"What are you doing?" the image demanded.

"Closing down. You obviously have nothing else to say, so you can sit the run out until we reach Sol."

"Tam—"

The image disintegrated and disappeared. Tamyn stared at the empty space above the projector. I hope like hell I'm making the right decision, she thought. Then she touched the comm.

"Shreve, I want to talk to you."

"We're going to owe the transit station quite a lot in fines," Stoan said matter-of-factly. "Transferring title to Joclen got us out, but they'll know it was ruse by now." He grinned maniacally. "But the ride is worth the price of the ticket, I think."

"Mmm," Tamyn ran the tip of her finger over her lower lip. They were gathered in her quarters—Stoan, Joclen, Kryder, and Shreve.

"But the proceeds from the last—shortened—run are being held by the Lodge. The Rahalen have already made delivery and collected fees and transferred the Q, per agreement, to our designated arbiter, the Cursian. They even said nothing about the Pron stalk. I've already confirmed that Longhauler Kee Ru-Esk was prompt in payment. No one can touch them till we return."

"That couldn't put the Lodge in danger, could it?" Joclen asked.

"Who knows?" Tamyn said. "The Lodge can take care of itself, though, and I doubt Reiner would be foolish enough to challenge them over something as trivial as *Wicca's* Q. We can try to clean this mess up when we return. What's our projected run time to Sol?"

"Well," Joclen said, "assuming the Pan hasn't moved the system, we're looking at a thirty-two day transit."

"Border crossing?"

"I need a few hours monitoring time," Shreve said. "Stay near the Secant and scan for Pan comm traffic. Once I tap into it I can analyze their patterns and duplicate them. Unless there's visual contact I can mask us as a Pan vessel."

"Time to the Secant?"

"Three days," Joclen said.

Tamyn nodded. "Now, one more matter. Where's Benajim Cyanus?" She looked at Stoan.

"We made rendezvous. All of them came on board *Wicca*. Sometime the next day he and Piper Van slipped on board the *Solo* and left. He claimed his destination to be the Tabit System."

"And no one saw them?"

"Frankly, no one expected anyone to leave the ship. During the incident with the *Jarom* he must have set a code override into the lock system so he could get out when he wanted to."

"Don't worry about it. He's...damn, he's slipperier than I expected." Slipperier than he has any business being, she added to herself. "All right, we'll assume he's gone where he says he has. I don't think he's a threat, but I'm not going to assume he's an asset, either. We'll keep our options open regarding him. We proceed with what we have. We're going to Earth to bury Sean Merrick's corpse. Afterward, we return for the reading of his will and see what happens then. Simple enough."

Joclen chuckled dryly.

Tamyn continued: "I want a constant monitor on surrounding space. I want to know the instant it looks like someone is following us."

"You don't expect Reiner to send C.R. police after us, do you?" Joclen asked. "Especially not with Vohec escorts."

The two small ships trailed at extreme range, guarding *Wicca's* flanks. Tamyn was both glad and nervous about them.

"I'm not sure what I expect anymore. Eyes and ears open. What about stores? Did we have time to get provisioned for this run?"

"We have sufficient provisions for a seventy-three day run with full crew," Stoan said. "We're running with only primary crew, so stores are doubly adequate. The Lodge was thorough and efficient. Longhauler Kee Ru-Esk provisioned the *Solo*. Co Cyanus didn't complain, so I suppose he is equally well-provisioned."

"That gives us a little leeway, then." She nodded. "Fine. If it turns out that this will take longer than we expect, we can forage. You all have things to do."

She watched Stoan and Kryder leave. Shreve and Joclen remained. The door closed.

"Shreve, have you thought about my request? Cracking persona encodings?"

Shreve nodded. "I can do it if you don't mind losing code integrity. I can open it up, sort out all the contents, scoop it all back together, but it's never the same afterward. Something gets lost in disassembly."

"Hmm. Fine. That's it. I need sleep."

Shreve left.

Tamyn closed her eyes and leaned back in her chair. She let all the tension that she had been storing, wielding, and juggling for the last few days flow into her limbs, spread out around her. It was both uncomfortable and relaxing, like the rictus of stretching maintained too long, till the point of spasm and cramp.

Unasked, strong fingers dug into her shoulders, worked at the taut, hard muscles.

"I thought you had duties," Tamyn said.

"Uh huh."

"How does this qualify?"

"You don't have a bit of excess on you," Joclen said, ignoring the question.

"Oh, yes I do. You'd be amazed." She groaned. "That's nice."

Joclen worked her shoulders and upper arms, then her spine, moving efficiently, expertly, and silently for several minutes until Tamyn began to feel the effects.

"Have you thought about getting back out of the Pan after we've finished?" Joclen asked then.

"And you were doing so well," Tamyn said.

"You don't want to be so relaxed your brain shuts down, do you?"

"It's tempting." Tamyn stood and stretched. "You're assuming we finish. I give us low odds."

"There are pirates crossing the border all the time."

"That's the thing, they only work the border. I've never heard of anyone who went all the way to Sol and came back."

"I don't believe it. You mean you're actually doing something reckless?"

Tamyn laughed quietly. "You were the one who started this by being so logical. What are my options? Stay and watch Reiner and Hall dismantle the Charter? Have my property stripped in restitution for my crimes, possibly end up mindwiped?"

"They don't call it that anymore. It's known as Personality Reconstitution. And it only applies to pathological criminals."

"Mmm. Would I qualify for that?"

"Certainly. You're pathological as they come. A stickler for rules."

"I think you're joking."

Joclen shrugged. "Besides, I didn't start anything. You were decided long before I brought any of that up. I think you might even want to be the one to add to the Exile Texts."

Tamyn said nothing. She went to her bed and laid down. A moment later, Joclen resumed massaging her, fingers digging at Tamyn's lower back.

"What do you think of Cyanus?" Tamyn asked.

"I don't know. He's inconsistent with himself. His actions and how he feels about them don't match."

"Do you like him?"

"Yes. Against my better judgement, but I do."

"So do I."

Tamyn gave in to the relaxation Joclen fed her through her fingers. There was more to say, more to analyze, but the edge was dwindling, worked out of her system, subdued. There was time later.

In a direct line between Miron and Sol, marking the border between the Commonwealth Republic and the Pan Humana, lay a huge station called Hominus Valorem. It had been constructed before the Distal Wars as a sort of meeting place between humankind and the seti races. Vast, it was a world in itself. The purpose for which it had been built vanished with the Distal Wars; no great conferences ever took place there and only the signing of the treaty formally severing the two human civilizations testified to its original intent.

Hominus Valorem converted easily into a tremendous military base from which the Pan patrolled the border.

Tamyn intended to avoid it by a wide margin.

A beacon broadcast from Hominus Valorem defined the border. It was easy to pick up on most electromagnetic bands and comm channels, as well as a tachyon marker that stood out like a vast pearl wall to a ship slipping through space at translight. Joclen brought *Wicca* to within a few hundred kilometers of it and turned the ship on a parallel course, away from the station.

In the Flow, the border wall rose up like a rippling, infinite sheet. Interference patterns expanded through it with each sensor-touch.

At least there's no C.R. version of the same thing, Joclen observed.

Waste of Q, Tamyn returned, *since the Pan was kind enough to provide one. Shreve, it's all yours.*

A sharp blue line lanced out through the sensors, stabbed the wall, and penetrated.

Ratha, keep alert for approaching ships from the C.R. side.

On it.

Traville—

Everything's standing ready.

Tamyn was pleased. She did not need to remind any of them, but she had found that the practice eased anxieties and drew the crew closer into a unit. They knew she was paying attention to them, not just the system status.

Contact points flowered from Shreve's node. The others touched one each. Data opened for them.

No ships. No comm traffic. Empty space.

Where are they all?

At the station, maybe?

Turn us around, Joclen, head back to the station.

Maybe we ought to just slip over now, while no one's looking—

If we were just border smugglers, fine, but I want better odds for where we're going. Shreve, maintain your probe.

The ship turned to the opposite heading and made for Hominus Valorem. Shreve's probe still showed no artificial presence beyond the wall. As they neared the station, Tamyn expected to find a shell of comm traffic, some sort of overflow, distorting the electromagnetic field around it. But nothing changed.

Probe the station, Tamyn directed. She felt the sharp questioning reaction of the others.

Shreve touched Hominus Valorem.

A ripple of high speed chatter coursed through the link briefly, then silence. The station was still, impenetrable. Shreve ran through the gamut of sensors and found them all deflected.

Somebody's home, Joclen commented, *but they're pretending not to be.*

Can you make something out of the burst, Shreve?

Maybe. I've never encountered a completely inert carrier before. This is odd.

Turn us around again, head back the other way. Analyze that burst, let's see what we can come up with.

Joclen brought *Wicca* around again.

Contact, Ratha announced.

Three forms approached from the C.R. They were still distant, but moving quickly. The two Vohec escorts had already turned toward them. Tamyn hoped they would just divert the C.R. ships.

How soon before they get here? Tamyn asked.

Less than a day, Joclen said.

Translight. Shreve, break it off for now.

Smoothly, like a single organism, everyone responded. Wicca accelerated up to transition speed, hugging the wall, and then sheathed itself in its envelope and slipped over into translight velocity. The wall rose up to starboard, shimmery white, while space around them streaked by.

The three shapes, as far away as they were, tracked her and changed vector, despite the presence of the Vohecs.

Over the border, Tamyn ordered.

Wicca veered. For an instant they were immersed in the nonform of the wall, bathed in white and silver and pearl multihues, static blocked sensors, they were blinded by too much vision—

Then they popped through and new space greeted them.

Now we're committed, Tamyn commented. *We're going home,* she added, though it gave her no comfort, and filled her with ill ease.

Chapter Twelve

Benajim watched the structure grow on the monitors, his pulse picking up.

"Why are we still in-system?" Piper asked. "I thought we were heading for the Secant."

He glanced at her. "That's next. I have to see what's happening here."

Piper frowned. "What is that? It looks old."

"TEGlink amplifier station. It is old, one of the first in the system. It's no longer used as a main conduit, but it hasn't been taken fully offline yet."

"You're risking detection."

"I already explained that. Besides, I don't think anyone can catch us now, we're too far out."

"Overconfident, are we? I know this ship is fast—"

"My call."

Piper lapsed into silence and Benajim guided Solo close to the ancient satellite.

He brought the ship within a few tens of meters, keeping the station physically between Solo and Miron, nearly a billion kilometers away.

"You watch our immediate area," he said. "I have business to take care of."

"Right," Piper replied dully.

Benajim pressed his fingertips to the gates and fell into the Flow.

The station appeared as a series of overlapping grids, connected by bright conduits of yellow-white energy. Beyond, though, stood the unused segments of what had once been a huge complex of communication paths, now dim and barely evident. He reached out to one link and read the pathway, pulled back, and tried another and another until he found one that would take him directly into the Greater Flow around Miron.

The pathway seemed to snatch at him, pulling him vertiginously into the system, and within an instant, piggybacked on the translight shortcut the relay provided, Benajim entered a small, inconspicuous portal at the fringe of the Flow.

Immediately the possibilities multiplied as he touched junction
after junction in the nonEuclidean tangle. He paused, letting the
confusion settle around him, until he made sense of the routing
choices. He had entered through a machine link, an automated
datafeed that linked the AI network surrounding Miron. Normally no other human or seti traffic came through here. In moments he found a channel into the oversight network and from
there into the interface—an alarm system tied to the diagnostics.
His presence registered as a routine inspection and so he moved
on, ignored.

He found his way into a security database. Rifling through files,
he discovered that the co using this cache conducted his investment
portfolio through it, and so had a direct link into the mercantile
dataspheres. Benajim slipped out by way of a monitoring routine
that kept track of changes in certain stocks—and from there, to a
troll program that wandered randomly, gathering data.

The corporate dataspheres loomed around him now like worlds
brought into the bright confines of a single brilliant star. He could
read the patterns coruscating over their surfaces, recognized each
one, and guided the troll toward the Merrick constructs.

In the three days since he had escaped in the belly of the Cursian
freighter, the Flow had changed. Configurations showed new aspects, segments detaching and rearranging, colors streaking the surfaces of several dataspheres in patterns that broke down the reliable
geometries that usually prevailed, and the spaces between the
dataspheres were filling with flecks and shards of loose component
elements. Benajim made his way through the labyrinth of connections until Merrick Enterprises came into view.

What had been a vast, slightly oblate sphere, bronze and silver-
streaked, now looked burned and disease-ridden. The flotsam
careening through the surrounding freespace came from enormous
pitted patches of the datasphere, pieces flaking off as Benajim
drew closer.

Swarms of sentinel constructs swam around the disintegrating
datasphere. As large fragments split off, they tried to envelope them
and herd them off, but a short distance away another set of larger
constructs waited, challenging the sentinels, and wresting the enveloped fragments from them. Benajim realized then that this was the
pillage of Sean's corporations, the breakup of his empires.

He moved in, slipping through a gap in the ranks of the sentinels, and skimmed close to the surface. Fissures opened in the once impregnable shell. Benajim peered down the deep crevices into the flesh of the datasphere, ragged walls rippling with code that no longer responded to a coherent matrix. Sean's imprimatur, the personality imprint that imposed order by constantly validating the structure, no longer held it together. Without it, the internal architecture degraded rapidly, releasing the contents in more and more disordered chunks.

The process took time. The vultures had yet to arrive in real force, but already significant pieces of Merrick's former holdings belonged to other corporations, mostly younger entities who accomplished more pilferage by sheer number than the largest competitors could manage. Architectural and access code fell off first. The sentinels belonged to those bigger companies, who hoped to retrieve a key fragment that would allow them to access parts of the datasphere before dissolution broke them loose.

Benajim searched now for a configuration on the shell, a specific design, to which he held the key. Sentinel constructs began swooping around him—he doubted they could identify him, given the way he had entered the Flow, but they sensed his presence.

There. A polyhedral pattern that, when he touched it, deepened into a complex hyperhedron. Code exchanged through the interface and he suddenly knew where to go within the huge expanse that still remained. He pushed through, rattled down a tortuous pathway, and dropped into the central volume.

A cluster of small, multihued orbs hung just off of the malformed core structure. Coddled in their midst he found a pearlescent ball. The other orbs drifted aside at his probe and released the pearl. He enveloped it, and immediately the cluster closed in on him.

Recognition flooded him, an awful feeling of Knowing. Nothing specific, no details, just a sudden, infinite certainty, and the conviction that, for these few moments, he knew exactly who he was and what he wanted. A part of him understood that data was being fed into him via the interface, filling parts of his brain, and although he could decode none of it at this instant he knew it would become accessible over time, like distant memories.

Frightened, he reeled among the orbs, tugging at his flow-presence, trying to free himself. Something seemed to work, for the orbs shrank away, then fell apart. As quickly as it had begun, the frenzy ended. He rushed back up the pathway, the pearl firmly encased in his grasp, and the only thing he recognized now was the need to get away.

Emerging from the datasphere, he dodged a school of sentinels and moved out to a safer distance. Looking back, he saw that things had changed even more. He did not know what the pearl contained, but he could not help believing that it was more important than all the rest of Sean's dataspheres. As if its removal had been a final command, the entire edifice of Merrick Enterprises, including the smaller construct of Mirak Corporation, began to split into irregular masses and drift apart. The dissolution came faster. The sentinels, overwhelmed, gathered around these larger pieces, tried to guide them away, and failed. The fragments moved according to their own momentum. Larger engines appeared now, summoned by the quickening frenzy, and the dismemberment proceeded with scavenger grace.

Benajim moved with cautious speed out of the corporate districts. He slowed near a public news node, weighing time and discretion against ignorance. He reached out to touch the node and copied the current feed, then continued on to his exit.

Off to his right, from behind a column of machine-code anchors, a scavenger construct emerged, moving to intercept him. Only one, but fast and festooned with traps, all it would have to do would be get close to him and it could snatch him out of the Flow.

Find Naril...

Benajim left the pathway and shot across the Flow, the scavenger changing course to pursue.

Naril Van's datasphere appeared as a deep green anemone, tendrils waving in slow, exploratory circles, plucking trolls from the Flow, releasing them, emptied, changed, or untouched. Benajim dived for a space nestled deep amid a cluster of the long threads, sending an ID signal ahead.

The shadow irised open and he entered a crowded dataspace.

Over there, noninteractive.

Benajim was shoved aside, into an alcove. Before him, in the arena formed within a kernel of the Van datasphere, codeshapes danced around and between each other, a fast ballet of dizzying complexity.

Gradually, Benajim began to recognize a few of the representations. Three or four were members of the Board of Regents, one of which was Sutter Hall. He identified Carson Reiner, too, and at least three of her advocates, and Jedora Haversill, Commonwealth Justice. Naril's own construct was a brilliant crimson rod that flowered into spikes from time to time. A few other corporate owners mingled at the fringes of the main interaction, as well as half a dozen independent jurists.

Benajim considered tapping into the stream to hear what was happening, but a touch distracted him. Another construct beckoned him down a newly-opened pathway.

The guide construct attached itself to him and pulled him along. The shape of the path eluded him, but he emerged from another section of Naril's datasphere, into the Flow, and across a gap into another construct.

Trojan shell...

Who?

I work for Naril.

It felt honest, but there was little he could do now. Waiting for the next transfer, he puzzled over why he had sought out Naril Van— and how he had recognized all those flowforms. He still held the pearl, and thought briefly the recognition, even the instruction, had come from it, but he received no confirmation...

The shell opened up and Benajim shot into the Flow. It took a moment to get his bearings—not far from his original entrance. The scavenger construct was nowhere near. He hurried into the pathway and back up the series of connections, out of the Flow, across the TEGlink connection to the relay station, and—

—opened his eyes on the bridge of *Solo.*

"That was quick," Piper said.

He stared at her, his mind roiling with information. "Um..." He licked his lips. "Your mother says hello and good luck. It's working. Sean's dataspheres are collapsing." He looked around at the monitors. They were still alone, still unnoticed. "We're leaving."

He touched the gate and issued instructions—

Did you find it?

Yes.

Do you have it?

See for yourself.

Ah...
Benajim pulled out.
"Something wrong?" Piper asked.
"No. Nothing."
Solo drifted away from the station, oriented itself to a new course, and accelerated.

Benajim sat on the edge of the bed in the small cabin, glancing up at the mirror above the sink from time to time. He had looked once at his reflection since entering the room and locking the door. The mirror both attracted and repelled him just now. He rocked occasionally, hands clasped, dangling between his knees.

"Gotta manifest in the Flow to maintain your dataspheres," he said. "Can't do that if you're dead. But you can't be absent when you're alive, unless you have a very small datasphere nobody cares about that doesn't require special care. But you can travel by investing temporary ID in a special construct that has to be renewed every thirty or forty days...I forget which...but you have to renew it in person, you can't comm it in...that way you have to be there to take care of business...unless you're a merchanter, like Tamyn, then you carry your primary datasphere with you."

His head felt under strain, as if a cord encircled his skull and grew tighter, slowly crushing him, except for the balancing pressure from inside, pushing back.

"Same technology," he murmured, "ghosting the brain patterns, pumping code through old neuronal pathways, just like imprinting a temporary persona, only no conscious participation...must be what they did...seti tech...maybe, maybe not." He shuddered. "Imprint it on a blank disk, no reason you can't imprint it on a blank brain...do it with a dead brain, hell, a live one should be easier...but it's so beside the whole damn point!"

He rubbed his face, his eyes, and sighed. He wanted to lay down, sleep, but he feared his dreams.

"Immortality is a bad idea, big is innately evil, corporate cynosure is antithetical to political viability...all bold sayings, every kid in the C.R. grows up hearing them, but what do they mean? They mean a corporation can never be given more power than an individual and the only way to make sure about that is to make sure corporations die like individuals. Sounds like so much crap, Sean, I mean, they're different things, and you had the two biggest examples of everything you claimed was bad for people." He touched his forehead in a mock salute. "Kudos for trying to see to it even your companies lived up to your rhetoric—or died accordingly, however you want to put it—but I don't think that's why you did it, not for a fucking second do I think that! You just couldn't stand them continuing on without you. Merrick Enterprises and Mirak Corporation mustn't outlive their creator, must they? If you couldn't be there to have all the fun with them, you wanted your toys taken away from everybody else. I suppose it's a good thing your ego coincides with principle so neatly. But I have one question, Sean—one big one, a thousand little ones, but we'll start with the biggest first. If that's how you felt, then why build them in the first place? I mean, if corporations are intrinsically bad, then why even make one?"

Benajim stood and started to step to the mirror, then stopped. "Can't answer that one, can you? Because the only answer there is one you don't like." He sat back down. "But all these people are getting hurt. Tamyn's supposed to be your friend, what are you doing to her? You're playing with all of us, Sean...why?"

A knock came at the door.

"What?"

"It's Piper, Ben. Are you all right?"

"Of course! Where are we?"

"Still en route. Can I come in?"

"No. Let me know when we get close to the Secant."

"Ben—"

"When we get close, Piper. Understand?"

After the silence continued for a time, he shook his head. "And me, Sean, what did you do to me? What am I? You're playing with me. My mind...I can feel it...bigger, better...maybe...too much. What did you do, Sean?"

He lurched to the mirror and stared at himself. He appeared frantic, but, relieved, he saw himself.

"You're a self-centered, hypocritical old shit, Sean, and you can't stop using people, can you? You're using us...don't lie to me...you're using us. And you're dead, you son-of-a-bitch, so you can't even feel guilty about being caught at it. I want to know why, though. I want to know why." He spread his hand against the cool surface of the mirror. "And I will...won't I? Because it's all in me now, isn't it?

You put it there...and I can't get to it till you're ready to let me. How inconsiderate can a co be?" He nodded to himself. "About that inconsiderate...just about that much...which is pretty bad."

He leaned closer, till his eyes filled his vision.

"What's at Tabit, Sean? Why do I want to go there so bad?" He let his forehead fall against the mirror. "I know... I'll know when I get there. You fuck."

Piper heard his heavy tread come up the ramp onto the bridge. When he appeared, she worried. Dark circles rimmed his blood-shot eyes, and his hair lay flat and oily against his skull. Barefoot, he wore the same shirt and pants he had been wearing the day they left Miron system.

He stopped at the top of the ramp and slowly studied the bridge. When he saw her, seated at the sensor array console, he frowned as if he did not remember her. Then he blinked and went to the command couch.

"How far from the border?" he asked, and before she could answer, he pressed his fingertips to the gates. "Soon," he murmured.

Piper touched the interface gate on the console briefly, caching the work she had been doing in the pocket she had created within the *Solo's* datasphere. Then she crossed the bridge to the copilot's couch and studied Benajim until he looked up.

"You look like hell," she said.

"I am hell," he said, smirking. "Another half day, we'll be there."

"Do you know what we'll find?"

He shook his head. "We're crossing, though."

"Into the Pan?"

"Are you surprised?"

"I thought we might try to link up with the *Wicca*. After all, Shipmaster Glass has Merrick's body. I thought you wanted to attend the funeral."

"I attended his funeral long ago, Co Van. Now I have to save his life." He looked at her suddenly, eyes intent. "You've been trying to reengineer the datasphere so you can operate it without my permission. You might've just asked."

Piper returned his gaze evenly. "I haven't been spying on you."

Benajim nodded slowly. "I know." He turned away suddenly. "You couldn't, anyway. *Solo* won't let you. But I appreciate that you haven't tried." He touched his gate. "I'm granting you access to several systems, just in case."

"You brought something back from Miron. Something from the Merrick dataspheres."

"I did."

"May I ask what it is?"

"Sure. But I don't know what it is. Something...necessary." He sighed. "When we get to Tabit, maybe I'll be able to answer you, but right now..." He waved a hand ambiguously.

"If it appears to me that you're putting yourself at risk," Piper said, "I'll intervene. Do you understand?"

"I've been putting myself at risk."

"Not fatally. My job is to keep you alive."

Benajim looked up at her. "I'd appreciate it if you'd leave my bridge now."

"Ben—"

"Now."

Reluctantly, Piper pushed away from the couch and walked down the ramp, into the common. Behind her, a hatch slid solidly in place.

The *Solo's* larder was impressively stocked; Longhauler Kee Ru-Esk had provided amply. Piper punched up an extravagant meal and sent it to the cabin she had taken.

The meal was in the hopper, waiting. Piper let it wait and stripped out of her utilities. In the center of the cabin she spun through a complex series of turns and kicks, stretching her muscles, bones, sighting imaginary targets in difficult combinations, and working herself in five minutes into a heavy sweat. She stopped and checked her pulse. Only slightly increased despite the speed and exertion, all without using her augments.

Satisfied, Piper took her meal and stretched out on the couch to eat.

Sweat coolly evaporating, Piper toyed with questions, enjoying the puzzle. She glanced at the polycom. There were areas of the *Solo's* datasphere closed to her. Benajim had brought something back from the collapsing dataspheres of Merrick Enterprises, but had offered no explanation and she could not access it.

It was difficult to protect someone who gave no trust, but not impossible. It was harder with someone who gave it and withdrew it unpredictably.

She had been given too little time to prepare. She was more annoyed than perhaps she should be, but it was largely because she had been intentionally kept in the dark about it. Naril had known for a long time and only told her about the commission when the *Wicca* and the *Solo* had returned early from Shipmaster Glass's sojourn. Even so, she believed she knew more about what was happening than Benajim. Much more had been kept from him.

Piper wondered, for instance, what he would think if he knew that her commission had originated with Sean Merrick, well over four hundred days past, when Merrick had also retained her mother's services.

Benajim touched the pearl hovering in the web of protective code. Its surface scintillated, but yielded nothing. He had been flooded with information while in its presence in the Merrick datasphere, but here it gave him only a mystery, a koan.

What is it you're going to give me when the time is right?

The pearl did not respond.

He felt calmer immersed in the Flow, as if the extra pieces in his brain had uses here and left him alone. He knew his actions looked irrational and that Piper Van was practicing considerable restraint by letting him work through it this way. He felt curiously safe knowing that she would intervene if he became too erratic. There was comfort in knowing he could only fall so far...

Pay attention, we're coming up on the Secant.

Benajim shifted his attention to the sensor net. Ahead, space appeared bisected. An impossibly long steel-white line cut it in half.

He signalled Piper and opened the bridge, then withdrew from the Flow. He rubbed his face and ran his hands over his hair. He needed to clean himself and sleep.

"What is it?" Piper asked, hurrying into the bridge.

Benajim pointed at the monitors. "The Secant."

Piper dropped into the second couch. "Where?"

"Can't see it in the visible spectrum," he said. He indicated a screen off to her right. "It's up in the TEG range. Translight."

Piper stared at the screen. "That's...a lot of energy consumption. What's generating it?"

"We'll find out soon enough."

"Don't you think we ought to slow down, then?"

Benajim glanced over the array of readouts. "Maybe...no other ships in the area."

"As far as you can tell."

"If they were out there, *Solo* would find them."

Piper frowned. "Do you think you should put so much trust in an old, obsolete ship?"

Benajim touched the gate and dropped *Solo* out of translight. The Secant flickered, gradually fading to invisibility at sublight speed. Now it appeared as a vast fan of electromagnetic radiation on instruments only. He kept his gaze fixed on the screens, ignoring Piper. A light flared on one panel and he touched the gate again.

"Found the source," he said.

"One?"

"One, yes. There's one source."

"This thing stretches light years. There should be relays."

"Check it."

Piper pressed her fingertips to her own gates. "One. It's just a giant beacon."

"Three hundred and sixty degrees of beacon. Interesting, how it always looks like a wall stretched horizontally to your orientation." He watched. "There."

On the center screen, a shape began to emerge against the background of stars. As *Solo* fell closer, it took on irregular features, quickly becoming a station.

"Big," Piper said.

"Mm."

The station looked like a broad plane perched on a collection of shafts and spheres. Benajim magnified the view. The surface showed a lot of scarring and more than a few holes and impact indentations. Small structures huddled here and there across the four thousand kilometer expanse.

"Any comm?" he asked.

"Quite a bit," Piper said, "but nothing directed at us." She let her eyes close as she went deeper into the Flow. "Odd...all machine language...alphanumerics...digital multilinear code..." She pulled out. "No sentient transmissions at all."

"No one home?"

"If it's just a relay station—"

"Big relay station."

"All it seems to be doing is transmitting that one signal." She glanced over. "You're getting pretty close."

"I want to see if anyone will notice."

"I don't think anyone is *there* to notice."

Benajim altered course and let *Solo* drift past the station.

"We're crossing the Secant," Piper said. Then: "We are officially in violation of the Hominus Valorem Territorial Accords. Congratulations, Ben, you're now a criminal in two polities."

"If you're going to do something..."

"...do it well?"

Benajim felt himself smile. "Something like that. See if you can detect any other comm traffic."

Piper slipped into the Flow for a few seconds. "Yes. About two light years away..."

Course coordinates scrolled up on Benajim's screen. "Let's go see what it is."

"Seems similar to what we have here. More machine language, no organic analogs."

"Doesn't make a lot of sense."

Piper grunted. "Add it to the list."

Benajim took *Solo* back up to lightspeed, and made transition smoothly, following Piper's coordinates.

"I've heard," Piper said when he came out of the link, "that Sean Merrick was the first human to explore the region of the C.R."

"Mm."

"I heard he did it in this ship."

"This was his ship."

"So why would he give it to you?"

"I don't know. We got pretty close, especially toward the end. But I still don't understand why he did everything he did."

"Did he ever say where he found you?"

"On the streets, in Miron City—"

"Uh uh. You were brought to Miron on board a Merrick ship. You were found elsewhere and brought directly to him."

Benajim's ears warmed. "How do you know that?"

"I'm good at what I do, Co Cyanus. I don't do prophylactics for someone I don't know anything about."

Benajim forced himself not to look at her. "That's not how I remember it."

"Really. That's interesting, too." She sighed. "He had to know how much shit it would cause, giving you this ship."

"I think that's precisely why he gave it to me."

"Even though he could have accomplished his last requests in simpler, more legal ways?"

"That's questionable."

"Maybe." She pushed herself from the couch. "I'm hungry. Let me know when we get close to those machine sources."

Benajim located the source of the machine data: a group of ships moving at an angle through the Alpha Fornicus system, in the direction of 82 Eridani, deep into the Pan.

The ships were bloated, clumsy-looking masses traveling in a tight cluster. Benajim counted twelve of them. Sensors had reached out to touch *Solo* as she neared, then diminished to the most tentative contact, as if the convoymaster had dismissed *Solo* as insignificant. Benajim sent nothing; if they wished to ignore him, fine, all he wanted to do was look them over.

"No markings," Piper said, "no flashes, no ID numbers, nothing."

The hulls were old and scored, but Benajim found nothing to indicate that they were in disrepair.

"What now?" he wondered.

"We could introduce ourselves."

"Sure, we just tell them we're representatives from their long lost brothers out in the Reaches."

"They already know we're here," Piper pointed out. "They have to surmise that we're not the usual Pan traffic."

"Why? We're just a private ship on a parallel course."

"Then we just follow them and see what happens."

Benajim glanced at her. Piper's expression was carefully neutral.

"They scanned us once," he said, "and then nothing. They're keeping a track on us, but it's not enough signal to derive any information from. Is it enough to follow down through the Flow, though?"

Piper frowned. "I don't like that idea."

"Why not?"

"They could have system prophylactics we know nothing about. We could trip alarms, get locked into their dataspheres, open *Solo's* systems to their intrusives."

"So we just follow along until maybe we run into something bigger and little more curious?"

"I said I don't like that idea. Doesn't mean I have better one."

"Mm."

"Maybe if I understood what we're looking for I could give you better advice."

Benajim ignored the remark and considered his options. He touched his gate.

The Flow opened around him. He found the contact point of the Pan sensor, a pale flower against the membrane of *Solo's* own shields. The wire-thin trace extended back to the cluster of big ships, to one nested in the middle of the convoy. Benajim decided that they must be cargo haulers, probably unarmed and incapable really of dealing with any kind of threat.

He studied the sensor touch. There seemed nothing in it designed to prevent feedback. An open invitation, really, to use it for access into their datasphere.

Go cautiously, lad...

Benajim felt Sean's presence, a guiding intelligence all around him. The pearl he had retrieved came closer.

What's this? he asked.

Information. Accept it. You need it.

He touched the pearl and it changed, the surface roiling with data. It hung before him, a brilliant violet jewel, and he knew all he had to do was dip into it. Just...enter...

He probed deeper.

The node dissolved instantly. For a moment Benajim was awash in information. No single item registered on his consciousness long enough for recognition, but it was all there for him when he needed it.

The flood ended.

He turned his attention again to the Pan sensor trace. It looked more familiar to him now, like something he had seen long ago. It was a simple enough probe, just a carrier wave to create an echo, not much more. The frequency was easy to read.

He spiralled down the beam effortlessly. No sentinels caught him and he reached the projector undetected.

The datascape he found was depressingly uncomplicated. Gross geometric patterns represented the information nodes and the interconnections were straight, uniform lines. Across the dull greyish expanse he saw no splashes of color, no unusual shapes, nothing at all to indicate the presence of a creative mind.

The data core would be to his right and down. Benajim moved easily amid the rigid structures.

He passed close to a square node. Several lines ran from this in various directions. Benajim tapped into it and skimmed through the data within.

Drone merchant ships, automated fleet, mixed cargo, twenty-one stops along a loop covering half the worlds in the Pan.

Not a human on board, probably not in the entire fleet.

He found the manifest and copied it into his own code to review later. Then he studied the channels running from the node. He wanted that one, to the systems overseer section.

He moved from node to node, copying interesting data, until he felt he had enough. He made his way back up the sensor beam, into *Solo's* Flow, then sent an instruction to the drone to cease tracking. The beam winked off. Satisfied, Benajim withdrew.

"You've got data here on ports, orbital facilities, procedures." Piper whistled at the menu on the screen. "Damn, how did you find all this stuff?"

"No security systems," Benajim said. He did an inadequate job of not looking smug. "Easy."

"Yes, but it's a completely different datasphere arrangement. How did you know how to get around?"

He shrugged. "Seemed self-evident."

Piper looked at him sharply, then returned to the data. "I wonder if the whole merchant fleet in the Pan is automated."

"Possibly. But I don't see how they could change the whole system over in less than a century. There were a lot of independents in the Pan."

"Uh huh," Piper said. "And most of them ended up in the C.R. after the war."

"Why would they build an automated merchanter fleet? It doesn't make sense."

"This one is carrying a little bit of everything. Fabrics, pharmaceuticals, raw materials, food stuffs, electronics. There's even something here called a 'Hostile Environment Civic Module' and a prefab power station, slated for Eurasia."

"That's 40 Eridani," Benajim noted.

Piper blinked at him. "Did you look that up?"

Benajim frowned at her.

"The convoy is headed for 82 Eridani first," Piper continued, "so it's logical to conclude that 40 Eridani is next after that. So: do we follow it?"

Benajim glanced up at the screen containing the image of the convoy. "I'm going to drop in among them and go along, yes. I want to see a system besides Tabit first, before we go on."

"You're the pilot." She stood. "Excuse me, then. I'll be in my cabin."

Piper felt him watch her as she left. She slowed, heard him chuckle, then hurried on to her cabin. She had no idea how good the internal prophylactics were on *Solo*, so this would be the test.

She plugged her small monitor into the polycom and activated the snoop she had left on the bridge. Then she settled back to watch.

Benajim eased *Solo* in the midst of the big merchanters. They hulked around the smaller ship like a school of whales, but he had switched off their interest in him, so no scans questioned his presence. *Solo* kept her own distance from them.

Benajim withdrew and studied the telemetry, then went over to the projection plate.

"Sean," he called quietly.

Merrick's face coalesced before him. The old man smiled pleasantly.

"You look like hell," he said. "A little sleep would go a long way toward making a lump of plasma fully human."

"A little free information goes a long way toward keeping me up."

"Such as?"

"The datanode."

"Ah. You found that, did you?"

"No, it was handed to me." He frowned. "What are you doing with me, Sean? What was in that datanode?"

"Useful information. Things I knew you'd need."

"I don't like being fed things without knowing what they are."

"Didn't have time to be polite about it."

"I don't like having things implanted that I don't know about, either."

Sean raised his eyebrows, but said nothing.

Benajim leaned forward. "And I don't think I like how much interaction you've got in this ship!"

"It *is* my ship, lad."

"Was! You gave it to me, or doesn't that count?"

"It counts. But you can't expect me to vacate it completely. You don't know her yet, don't know what she's capable of, all her little idiosyncracies—"

"I can find all that out for myself."

"If you were running her under normal circumstances I'd let you. These are not exactly normal, are they?"

"No, but—"

"But nothing. The last thing you need if you get into trouble is to be trying to figure out something you didn't know about 'your' ship. Now, settle down and accept my help graciously, or by my word I'll take this ship away from you."

"You're more than just an encoding."

"Did you ever know me to do anything half way? The fact is, I *am* this ship. Don't mistake me for Sean Merrick the human. I'm *Solo*, it just happens that this is how I manifest in your sensory matrix."

"My sensory matrix...?"

"You know it as reality. You manifest as code in the Flow, I manifest this way out here."

Benajim fell back in the chair. He felt defeated, but he had not known the nature of the contest. Sean was cheating him of something, a fact which made that something all the more desirable.

"So what happens next?" he asked.

"Don't be so glum. Things are moving along nicely. Tam's on her way to Earth with my—Sean's—corpse and we're on our way to undo the rest of Carson Reiner's machinery. After I'm satisfied that everything is the way I want it to be—"

"I hope the order of nature is up to your specifications."

"—then I'll quietly, more or less, leave you to your destiny. Whatever that might be."

"I don't believe you."

"Too bad. You'll have to live with it. You can't kill a ghost."

Sean frowned. "Why are we heading for 82 Eridani?"

"I wanted to get a look at another system than Tabit before going there."

"Waste of time. Head for Tabit."

"I don't really want to."

"What has that got to do with it?"

Benajim grunted. "Why would I really want to go there?"

"Answers."

"I can get those answers elsewhere."

"No, you can't. Not the answers I need."

"You?"

"There are two threads to this puzzle. One of them, Tamyn Glass is taking care of. The other requires you to take me to Tabit. Now change course."

"You're giving orders now?"

Sean's eyes narrowed. "Why the sudden reluctance to go to Tabit? I thought this was settled."

"I don't know. Maybe I don't want to risk being a slave again."

"Whoever said you were a slave?"

"You did."

"No, I didn't. I said slavery was practiced on Tabit—"

"And I'm from there."

"I didn't say that, either. I said as it happens, you *were* found on a ship with a Tabit registry. You might have come from there. The only way to find out is to go back."

"And risk you being right?"

"No one there will identify you as anyone they ever knew as a slave. Not now."

"How do you know?"

"You'll have to trust me."

"Problem is, I don't!"

"And just what choice do you think you have?"

"I can have the datasphere purged."

Sean shook his head. "Then I wouldn't be the same ship."

"What are you doing to me? I don't even feel the same way."

"You've got a head full of new data. It feels different, having a full mind. You'll access it as you need it. Should be interesting."

"That's not what I mean. I feel different. Not myself."

"Of course you do. You just don't know you as well as I do."

"I'm scared, Sean."

The old man's eyes softened. "I know, son. Trust me. Everything will be fine."

The alarm brought him out of a deep sleep. Benajim had to fight his way to full wakefulness. He staggered to the bridge, trying to drive sleep from his brain.

Piper arrived a second after he did.

"What is it?" she demanded.

"I just got here." He scanned the telemetry. "Ships. A lot of them, coming in from several directions. Looks like an assault pattern."

"Military?"

Benajim shook his head. "Attacking their own territory? Doesn't make sense."

"Unless they're coming for us."

Benajim linked.

The drones issued a barrage of warnings to the swarm of smaller ships, little more than declarations of ownership, destination, and possible consequences for unauthorized interference. Benajim counted fifteen attacking ships. The huge cargo drones began moving closer together, an automatic response to the presence of the smaller, hostile ships. He estimated the space available between them and hoped they would not group too closely together.

A pair of attackers, dwarfed by their targets, dove through the gap between two drones, arced around one of them sharply, and Benajim saw beams slice across the comm lines between that drone and the rest. Very rapidly the links were cut and the commlines were sealed off. More attack ships moved in; code shot into the vacancy left by the severed links.

It was all over quickly. The drone was cut from the group and herded off like some great animal. The convoy rearranged itself to fill the gap.

Another squadron came in and cut loose another ship.

Benajim slipped *Solo* out of the group and shot quickly away. Sensors tracked him for a short distance, a pair of attackers even started after him, but then fell away and returned to working over the convoy. Benajim circled around in a huge arc, all the way to the opposite side of the operation, and came within range of the stolen merchanters.

Each ship was tended by six of the smaller craft. As Benajim watched, two of them settled on opposite sides of the hull while the other four took positions around it. Beams cut into the hull and umbilicals were attached. Then the whole group moved off, at an angle to the original convoy course.

The remaining three ships flew intricate patterns around the pair of captive merchanters, buzzing close to *Solo*. Benajim pulled away a few times until he realized they did not intend to engage him, then he just maintained a discreet distance. A few times sensors tried to penetrate his barriers, but the effort did not seem sincere.

You're losing the convoy.

I know.

Why?

I'm curious.

Of pirates? You'll get us killed.

I don't think so.

Piper lapsed into agitated silence then, maintaining a spiky presence nearby in the Flow. He ignored her.

They made transition shortly. Benajim had little difficulty following them in translight; the merchanters made huge tachyon wakes with the need to displace mass.

Benajim checked the trajectory against his charts. They were headed in the direction of P1-3 Orionis, much closer than 82 Eridani. P1-3 Orionis—Tabit.

It's one of the old colonies, Piper noted.

Ah. You've decided to help then?

!

Thank you. We're among all "old colonies"; can you be a little more specific?

One of the original twelve, I think. The principle members of the Directorate Forum.

I didn't realize you were an authority on the Pan Humana.

I told you I'm studying history.

Mmm. So why would pirates head straight back to a primary system, which is sure to have a military or police garrison?

Piper said nothing.

They didn't attack us, Benajim remarked. *In fact, they were most eager to get away from us. Odd.*

Odd, yes. Something you seem to be an authority on.

Piper withdrew from the flow.

How did you manage this? Benajim shot at the datasphere. When no reply came, he withdrew as well.

They dropped below translight and entered the Tabit system. Benajim moved closer to the small fleet, and two ships detached to block and pace him. As they fell through the system, they shed velocity, altering vector toward one of the gas giants orbiting at a distance of a billion kilometers from the sun. The pirates broke off and veered into orbit around the huge, luminously striped sphere. As Benajim rounded it to the dark side, he saw their destination.

The station was tremendous. A collection of mismatched sections, wedded in a marriage of convenience over time. Bulbous sections abutted cubes, and new construction thrust out like the spines of an exotic anemone, the whole massing easily as much as a moderately-sized moon. The corsairs disappeared in the forest of struts and booms, the two pickets following quickly. Benajim changed course to come into a parallel orbit, keeping his distance.

We're being commed.

Benajim accessed the signal.

Identify, state purpose of visit, intent, comply or be challenged.

Sound friendly, don't they?

Benajim sent *Solo's* Pan registry.

Minutes passed. Then:

Rejected. Do not approach.

That's that, then, Piper commented. *So much for visiting scenic Tabit.*

Benajim resent the registry, but received the same warning. Sean had been so sure about this. Too much had changed in the time between his last visit—before the Secession—and now. Perhaps Sean's assumptions no longer counted. The thought gave Benajim an oily satisfaction.

Solo sent a different sequence.

What was that? Piper asked.

Benajim did not answer, uncertain himself.

Minutes more passed.

Welcome, Solo, *to Tabit Freeroamer Orbital. You may approach and dock. Follow the beacon. Our apologies for the delay in recognition. We look forward to greeting you.*

Chapter Thirteen

Tau Ceti shone yellow in the center of the holo field. It was remarkable only in that it was the right size and temperature to support a family of planets, one of which was human habitable.

"Shreve?" Tamyn said softly.

"A moment," he said, concentrating. Then: "I have it."

A spherical grid encompassed a tremendous volume of space around the star. The main framework was white. Then green bars began filling in the sections. Blue bars ran from corner to corner in each square, then red lines stretched from the major white apices to cut across the internal volume. It grew into a lovely, intricate webwork.

"Complex," Stoan commented, nodding.

"Old system," Tamyn said.

Yellow lines interconnected stations within the sphere.

"Inventory coming up," Shreve said.

Tamyn turned to her console. On one of her screens a list appeared. She scanned it, growing more and more amazed.

"...Five hundred and seventy major orbital habitats...three hundred twenty-one manufactory orbitals...ninety-four research stations...forty-five communications stations...sixty military platforms...six thousand eight hundred twenty monitor stations...estimated data transmission systemwide is eight hundred trillion iterations per second..."

"Impressive," Stoan said. "I wonder what they chatter about so voluminously? Hah!"

"I'm getting interrogatives," Ratha said. "Requests for ID, destination, origin..." He frowned. "They're demanding we turn over control to system administration."

Stoan clapped his hands. "Strikes coy to the belly! Waste more, want more?"

"Shreve?" Tamyn called.

"Got what I need."

"Fine, let's get out of here."

"Tracking six ships on intercept," Traville said.

Tamyn looked at the holo. Brilliant violet dots arched out from the perimeter.

"Shreve, how deep inside their shell are we?"

"Hardly touched it."

Tamyn touched her gate. Space opened for her. Faints wisps of signal extended out from the solid wall of code that comprised the Tau Ceti perimeter, cilia to sense the first hints of approaching craft. The six ships resolved visually now, sleek black and menacing—warships, there was no mistaking their appearance; humans had always built threat into the appearance of their battle machines— and moving very fast.

Joclen...

On it.

They began to move, veering away from the system and the approaching ships. A tendril nearby thickened and took on substance, whipped toward them. Wicca picked up velocity. The end of the tendril touched the datasphere perimeter. Tamyn could see bright splashes of code attempting to find a way in.

The ships fired. Brilliant bolts, seemingly in slow motion, fell from the six vessels toward her.

Traville!

Shields up, no problem.

The bolts struck, exploded brightly; *Wicca's* shields warped under the impact, then resumed their shape. The tendril jabbed code at them. Shreve drew close to it, reached out his own sensor. It bulged out of the envelope. The tendril turned to the pseudopod Shreve offered it, stabbed, and the tip was engulfed by Shreve. Tamyn watched while jumbles of code poured into the receptacle Shreve had prepared. The tendril pulled back and Shreve withdrew within the envelope.

Joclen took them to translight then and shot away from Tau Ceti.

Patterns interlocked, pulled apart, revolved around each other on Shreve's screens.

"This is all machine language," he said.

"Of course it is," Joclen said. "That's all code is. Conversions of organic language into something the Flow can use—"

"No, no," he waved his hand impatiently. "I mean that's *all* this is. No trace of human interfacing. What I mean is that there are no organic constructs here. The reason this code couldn't get into our datasphere is because it was speaking in a very different type of language."

"But—" Joclen began.

Shreve turned to her. "This is machine originated. We probably didn't come into contact with a human datasphere analog through the whole time. Even those ships...I doubt they were manned at all."

"Automated?" Tamyn asked. "Completely?"

Shreve shook his head. "No, not...automated. That implies no intelligence, just repetition of instructions. No, this was adapting as it probed us. It might even have found a solution eventually, but..." He turned to them, his eyes bright. "I heard once that all the worlds of the Pan possessed their own AIs, that machine intelligence was at a high state of development here. Maybe we just came into contact with a world mind."

"I heard those stories, too," Joclen said. "I thought they were inventions to frighten gullible audiences."

"There are such world minds among seti," Stoan said. "Many."

"But you interact with them," Tamyn said. "Treat them as coequals."

Stoan nodded. "They are very different, but they are still participants with us." He shrugged. "Most of them."

"So where are the people in this system?"

"Didn't detect any," Shreve said. "Not in any part of that network I tapped. All machine activity."

"With all those habitats, there must be someone living there," Tamyn said. "Can we navigate these systems?"

Shreve nodded. He gestured at the screen and the patterns. "I can mimic this. By the time we reach Sol I can get us in."

"Can you get us back out, though?"

"We'll have to wait and see." He grinned at her. "But it's fascinating, isn't it?"

"I hope you have enough to play with," Tamyn said. "We aren't staying to get more. We go in, bury Merrick, and leave."

Shreve nodded, his attention on the screen.

Tamyn returned to her couch and stared at the monitors, unseeing. A touch on her shoulder made her jump.

"Don't you think you need some sleep?"

Tamyn looked up at Joclen, ready with a sharp remark full of resentment. She knew her limits, she knew her responsibilities, and it was presumptuous of the pilot to remind her. But before she spoke she knew that she would not normally say things like that to Joclen, or anybody else. She was tired.

"Not sure I can," she said.

"Try. You won't do anyone any good like this."

Tamyn nodded and surveyed the rest of the bridge. No one was watching; apparently no one had heard. Tamyn stood.

"Wake me in five hours."

Joclen raised her eyebrows and said nothing.

Tamyn held a finger up. "Five hours."

Nine hours later she awoke, annoyed at the coddling of her pilot and crew. But she showered and dressed and ate a bar of compressed nutrients, and by the time she emerged onto the bridge, coffee in hand, she knew Joclen had been right to let her sleep.

The holo field was alive with ships. Hundreds of them, all moving in groups of six and heading in the same direction. Huge vessels, bigger than *Wicca* even with a full load of supplementals.

"Was anybody going to bother telling me about this?" she asked.

Stoan looked around from Joclen's station. "No bother. We just found them a few minutes ago. Co Bramus is in her quarters."

Tamyn went to her couch and touched one finger the gate. "No sensor scan? One comm signal?"

"Yes," Shreve said, "a comm signal. A carrier wave, continuous transmission, minimum content. A beacon."

"To us?"

"To them. Just something to follow. I think the entire convoy is automated."

Tamyn gazed at the dense collection of ships, then pressed her hand to the gate. She reached out through *Wicca's* sensors and found their data envelopes, close to the skin of each ship. There were links between ships in each group, then lesser ties between groups. She touched a signal and found basic ID code and little else—guidance parameters to keep them in formation, a reinforcement of the carrier wave the entire group was following. Merchanters—merchant ships, anyway. She withdrew, dismayed.

"Automated," she agreed. "Unless some of them are carrying passengers..."

"We found their manifests and itinerary," Stoan said. "Both are part of their ID packet. They're heading for Sol."

Tamyn felt a spike of excitement. "Might be our way in...what do you think, Shreve?"

"I can mimic their pattern easily enough. Might be simpler than trying to lie to a system mind, if that's what that was back at Tau Ceti."

"All right," Tamyn said. "Let's blend in."

Stoan touched his gate. Tamyn watched in the holo field as they moved closer to the nearest collection of ships. Nearer, nearer, finally they entered the formation. Stoan put them in the middle of one of the groups of six. One immense ship was before them, one behind, the other four to the sides.

"Shreve has constructed a false envelope around us that reflects back to each ship the same code they are all sending to each other," Stoan said. "For all practical purposes we do not exist. A mirror for echoes and hollow lappings."

"Good. Let's hope it stays that way." Tamyn stood. "Passive datafeed, let's record as much about these ships as we can without tripping any alarms. Let me know if anything changes."

She left the bridge and headed down into the cargo bay. Crej'Nevan was on duty, but seemed dormant for the moment, tentacles withdrawn into her trunk, mantle closed.

The bay was dark, most lights off. The shipping nacelles and crates made ominous shadows. Tucked against a bulkhead, connected to a cooling line, was the sarcophagus.

Tamyn still did not know if she approved of this ritual. Some cultures buried the dead, but most recycled what body parts were still usable, the rest went into a general resource pool of organic compounds for replication, processing, and distribution. Some burned their dead, a few ate them. Putting the corpse in the ground and honoring it with a tomb was not rational.

But if that was what Merrick wanted, she owed him an obligation of friendship to fulfill it.

"We're almost there, Sean," she said. "What do you want me to do after?"

A couple days later they touched the perimeter of Sol. Tamyn remained linked during the approach.

Within the immediate vicinity, fifteen trains of ships converged on the system. Hundreds of the mammoth vessels, all silently following the simple carrier wave. The security perimeter presented almost a solid wall, the interweaving of signal and code forest-dense, shimmering pearl-white. Little was perceivable behind that wall. There were none of the wispy sensor tendrils that had been at Tau Ceti. The impression was nothing less than of a vast fortress. In realspace the starfields shifted and shimmered as in a heat mirage. Direct observation within the system was pointless.

Shreve, is there a way to compensate for the distortion?

No. It's random.

Each train met the wall and passed beyond seemingly without a pause. Small remote stations kept watch at the apices of the net. Then Tamyn saw a primary station. At least, it had to be, it was immense. The huge sphere hove into view, just outside the net, a few lines connecting it to the whole. Tamyn estimated that it was easily four times the size of Miron Transit Station.

No interrogatives came. Their convoy reached the perimeter wall, the first ship disappeared through, then the flank ships began to pass...*Wicca* touched it. Code crackled through their envelope. Tamyn sensed Shreve gathering as much of it as he could. And they were through.

Wait, she cautioned, *give us some distance from the perimeter before leaving the convoy.*

The other side of the wall shimmered, faintly yellow. Dimmer lines stretched down into the system. The field of view was clearer now. They passed the orbit of Pluto. Tamyn felt a glimmer of optimism.

"There are at least twenty-five billion individual orbital objects within the volume," Shreve explained.

They were gathered in Tamyn's cabin. Only Stoan seemed unchanged. The others exhibited varying degrees of anxiety—Traville chewed at his thumb knuckle; Innes's mouth flexed compulsively; Joclen kept looking from one face to another, scowling—and Tamyn struggled to keep from drumming her fingers constantly. Despite her confidence in this crew, she believed luck played a larger role in their success so far than skill. She hated that. She never relied on luck. Joss was something invoked when all ability failed, and usually that meant success was lost.

But they were here, in Sol System, close to Earth. Close to Earth...

They had broken away from the convoy when the train itself had begun to disintegrate, different groups heading to different places. *Wicca* now rested just beyond Neptune, close to a shard of a moon that did not even have a name in their records. The rock was dense with nickel, iron, and manganese; Tamyn hoped it was sufficient to hide them for the time being.

"They range in size," Shreve continued, "from about fifty centimeters in diameter to three thousand kilometers. The perimeter station was twenty-six hundred kilometers across. There may be many hundreds of thousands not listed in the data I tapped."

"Doesn't sound like there's any empty space here," Joclen said.

"Humans have been in space here for four centuries," Stoan said. "It's bound to be cluttered. I would suspect a good many of them aren't even operative anymore." He met Tamyn's gaze. "Humans are notorious for not throwing useless objects away or recycling them. You just pretend to each other that some day you'll use it again and then bitch when someone else cleans it up for you when you're not watching."

"Hmm." Tamyn looked at Joclen, who laughed. "So, there's no reason we can't just go straight to Earth and land. Is that what I'm being told?"

"Not in *Wicca*," Shreve said. "But a shuttle should be able to slip through easily enough."

Tamyn studied each of them. Stoan, Joclen, Shreve, Ratha, Clif, Kryder, Traville, and Innes. "Has it occurred to anyone here that this has been incredibly easy so far?"

"Maybe," Joclen said, "we're just incredibly good."

"Nonsense. The last thing we can afford to do here is underestimate them or overestimate ourselves." She crossed to her polycom and called up the encoding. "Sean, it's Tam."

The old face solidified in the projection field and grinned.

"About time," he said. "Have you rethought what we discussed?"

"No. I need advice though." Tamyn moved aside so Sean could see the others present. "Sean, meet my crew. Some of them, anyway." She went round the list, all the while watching Merrick's expression. He looked uncomfortable and unhappy.

"Pleased to meet you all," he said dryly and looked at Tamyn. "I expected a little more privacy, Tam."

"They're risking their lives. I think they deserve to know for what."

"I'd imagine they each have their own reasons."

"True, but they also think they share a common reason. You're it. Now, why don't you tell them about it?"

"Where are we?" he asked.

"Just off Neptune."

His eyes widened. "My god, you got through."

"My people are beginning to feel over-confident."

"Mistake. Here's where you'd best be most alert. Getting in may have been simple enough, getting out's going to be another matter. Once you enter the communications perimeter around Earth they'll know you're here. Won't matter how clever you are then."

"I can mask us like any other Pan vessel," Shreve said.

"Doesn't matter. The only Pan vessels that set down on Earth are the dedicated shuttles from the Earth-Mars Transit Station and the military traffic. No others are permitted. None."

"Shreve?" Tamyn prompted.

"No problem. Part of the convoy is heading there now. I can slip us in with them."

"So we have what we need," Tamyn said, looking at the projection. "Except all the reasons we're doing this."

Sean looked uncomfortable. "I told you to scavenge my dataspheres—"

"We did." She made a nasty smile for the encoding. "I lied. Shreve?"

"I pulled a number of interesting datanodes out just before distance made it impractical. It seems Co Merrick has been doing business across the border for a long time."

Everyone straightened, attention heightened.

"Carson Reiner," Shreve continued, "discovered this fact and started using it for herself. A business arrangement?"

"Well," Sean said, "it could have gotten nasty if she'd let it into the Flow. After all, I was one of the Founders. It wouldn't have looked very good that I was trading with the enemy."

"For how long?" Traville asked, frowning.

"Oh, since the beginning. It never really stopped." Sean looked around at them all and raised an eyebrow. "Before you all get on high moral horses and start thinking unflattering things about me you might want to consider that the C.R. was born out of a revolution that damn near destroyed us. We weren't ready to be a nation. Nothing like it. And our key production worlds had been hit very hard by Pan fleets. It was an ugly, wasteful war and we took the worst of it. We needed resources. We needed food, machinery, medicines, all the stuff the Pan still possessed in abundance. A few of us who still had merchanters that could haul sizable loads went back and made deals with a few coes in a few systems and started bringing those resources out of the Pan. That was before the Charter, before the law said no contact, before the Treaty. After all that legal structure came into existence the C.R. still needed what we were delivering. We never stopped. We hid the fact and kept the runs going until they weren't needed anymore."

"When was that?" Joclen asked.

"About thirty years or so ago it stopped being necessary. But it was pretty lucrative. I thought I'd keep it up for a while, till I got tired of it. Then I got sick."

· "Then Reiner found out," Tamyn said.

"Then Reiner found out. She made a deal with me. I let her conduct business through the same pipeline in exchange for support on the Board. I thought, hell, if she gets herself too involved then we have each others' fates. I was sick anyway, so it didn't matter to me. But she damn near beat me. She set up an entire ghost corporation inside my dataspheres and even I couldn't get at it. The sicker I got the deeper she worked her way in. Then new faces started showing up. Pretty soon I wouldn't have control anymore and then she'd have it all."

"Who's she trading with?"

"I don't know."

"Who were you trading with?"

"Tabit. I'd pared it down to one system. As far as I could find out she still used that as a starting point, but merchandise from more systems than that came back."

"Your corpse was jacked into the Flow," Shreve said. "Your imprimatur was artificially manifested daily."

"A nasty piece of technological perversion, wouldn't you say?" He chuckled. "I died too soon. She still thought she could pull this off. She was setting up a new corporation, preparing the ground to acquire those parts of my holdings she already used after corporate mortality manifested. It fell apart for her when I handed *Solo* to Benajim. *Solo* was the last piece she needed and I took it away from her."

"What's so special about the *Solo?*" Joclen asked.

"Oh, nothing much, except it has the key to the Pan in it." He laughed at Tamyn's startled expression. "It's a Pan ship, after all. To do any kind of open, legal business inside the Pan, she needs the access *Solo's* codes can provide. *Solo* also represented the only real threat to what she intended. Reiner had her people trying to figure a way to open her dataspheres up, but I had her docked where she couldn't get to her."

"Until you died," Joclen said.

"Uh huh. So I gave it to Benajim. I imagine I sorely tried Carson Reiner's patience."

"She thought she could gain access to Pan dataspheres with the *Solo,*" Tamyn observed.

"Oh, she could have," Sean said. "See, *Solo* served many functions for me. One of them was as spy. There are security access codes in her dataspheres even the Armada didn't know I had. Doubtless they've been changed—but you know how algorithms work, and how machine intelligences tend to optimize routines. *Solo* could interpret any new codes and reconfigure herself. Easily. Keys to the kingdom, so to speak. When I still could, I periodically dipped inside the Pan just to update her database. With *Solo* either opened up or neutralized, Reiner would have no barriers to working her own deals inside the Pan. On top of that, if Reiner could have opened the Charter for emendation then everything would very neatly have fallen into her lap. She'd have had my company, my trade routes, and all my connections. She would also have established a power base that could not be dissolved by death." He grinned. "But with *Solo* loose..."

"There's only one problem," Joclen said, leaning forward. "She's assuming—and so are you—that the Pan *wants* open trade with the C.R."

"They want trade," Sean said. "Open or otherwise. But I really think they'd prefer to keep it illegal and funnel it all through one pipeline. Because whoever on this side of the border is dealing with her wouldn't want that monopoly endangered any more than Carson Reiner would."

"And if it had all been kept secret," Tamyn said, "then it would have gone on in just that way."

"And on and on and on. Oh, someone would have eventually figured it out and challenged her. But by then such a confrontation could conceivably tear the C.R. apart. I'm not sure it'll survive this."

Everyone was silent for a long time. Finally Tamyn said, "All right, we're here. You said you wanted the encoding brought down as well. Why?"

"Let me give you the coordinates. There's a family tomb. This encoding is to be placed in the tomb with my body. When you get there you'll see a place for it."

"Why?"

"That's personal, Tam." The face scowled. "Personal enough that I don't even know. I just know it has to be this way."

"Sean—"

"Don't blame me, I'm just the copy."

Tamyn looked at the others. "Any questions? Any doubts? Now is the time if anyone wants to pull out. We can still leave."

Joclen scowled with mock gravity. "This close? You've got to be kidding. I want to see Earth."

The others nodded, although Tamyn saw the doubt in their eyes. They wanted to go forward, but it scared them. Getting out, that was the question. But at this point, it seemed silly to leave before the finish.

"So how do we proceed, Sean?"

Mars-Earth Transit was a globe easily twice the volume of Miron Transit. Shreve blended *Wicca* in with a herd of automated ships and, as they neared, began probing the Mars-Earth datasphere. Tamyn remained linked, sitting quietly in the Flow watching Shreve work. His code jabbed gently at various points in the colorless, rather flat station datanodes. Finally a point flowered in faded pink and pale yellow and Shreve changed vector.

I can arrange it with the station apparats to supply us with a shuttle down, he told her.

The section of Earth-Mars Transit they docked in was, as far as anyone could determine, all automated. Tamyn was beginning to think the entire Pan was populated by machines and ghosts. Her fascination was turning to trepidation; she wanted to be done with the run and go home.

Tamyn and Joclen went down to the cargo bay. Crej'Nevan had moved the sarcophagus over to the main bay door. From the control room they decompressed the chamber and opened the hatch. As they watched, a troop of black-bodied robots rolled through, took positions around the sarcophagus, lifted it, and, as if in parody of a funeral procession, removed it. Crej'Nevan closed the bay and repressurized it.

"I'm not happy," Joclen said. "If you insist on going yourself, I'd rather go with you."

Tamyn did not answer. She had made her decision, her choices, and discussion was over. She had to go, as Sean's appointed agent. And she would not pass up a chance to stand on Earth...

"Let's get this over with," Tamyn said. She touched the pouch on her belt unconsciously. Inside was the Merrick encoding. She had not thought yet that this would be the last she would ever see of her old friend. Good-byes were for Earth, the tomb. She could put it off till then.

"It would still be best if you didn't go," Kryder said.

Tamyn shook her head.

An umbilical had attached itself to one of the locks. Tamyn, Innes, Clif, and Kryder donned environment suits and crossed over to a small, dark debarkation chamber. Crates, old furniture, and machinery were stacked in the room.

Several meters along Tamyn found a small port. Below plummeted the geometric jumble of bare machinery, braces, cables, and umbilicals. *Wicca* rested on a cradle, attached to a number of lines, high over a precipitous drop seemingly the depth of the station.

"Shipmaster."

Tamyn turned and saw Clif beckoning to her. He stood by a railing on the opposite side of the platform. Below the procession of motiles moved along a conveyor with the sarcophagus.

They descended a ladder a short distance away and got on the conveyor behind the procession. The conveyor took them through a maze of structures the purposes of which Tamyn could only guess. None of it seemed made for humans. It possessed an ineffable machine quality.

The conveyor ended at a platform that ran above a long row of black disks. The motiles took the sarcophagus to the nearest one. A lock opened and they entered. Tamyn and the others sprinted to the lock and entered before it sealed.

"Still airless," Innes announced.

The interior was cramped. They had to stoop. The sarcophagus and its machine pall-bearers filled a good portion of the cargo bay.

Innes and Clif worked their way forward.

"Not much of a control room," Clif said. "There's an override panel, but the controls aren't familiar."

"Innes, can you figure it out?" Tamyn asked.

"Sure. Just need a few minutes."

"It's likely going to be a rough ride," Clif said. "No need to be gentle if the only things on board are machines."

"Aren't there any people here?" Innes wondered.

Kryder was inspecting the bulkheads and assorted panels. "Ah," he said suddenly and punched a button. A panel flowered open and retracted and a couch slid out. It was thin and seemed flimsy, but it was obviously designed for humans. Kryder found three more.

"We're moving into position to embark," Clif said. "I don't know what kind of g we're looking at."

They strapped in and waited. Suddenly there was an intense pressure. It maintained for a few minutes, then dissipated.

Clif and Innes quickly returned to the control room. Tamyn studied the motiles tending the sarcophagus. They seemed purely utilitarian. She found no voice response mechanism. They must, she decided, be controlled from a central source, completely automated. Tamyn wondered if Earth was inhabited or if only the machines were left.

"Got it," Clif announced. "I can fly this thing."

Tamyn moved forward. The control room, such as it was, had little space. There was barely enough for Clif and Innes to work around the consoles.

"Are we blind?" Tamyn asked.

"No, but there's no interface either," Innes said. "All instruments."

"You're sure you can fly this thing, Clif?"

The shuttle pilot nodded. "Not as well as one of ours, but well enough."

"Don't subvert the system yet," Tamyn said. "Wait till we get close to the ground."

He nodded again. "Do you know where these coordinates are taking us?"

"Somewhere on the Indian subcontinent, a place called Orissa. Northwest of a city called Cuttack."

"The quicker the better," Innes said.

Joclen watched the shuttle depart and begin its fall toward Earth. Tam will be all right, she repeated to herself, Kryder can manage, she can manage, they'll all get back...

Finally she looked away from the dwindling image in the holo and sighed heavily. Her hands shook slightly: anger. Fear? Yes, she admitted, fear, a lot of it. The cure for fear, the channel for rage, is work.

When she looked up she saw Stoan watching her.

"The Stralith," he said softly, "offers considerable benefit at such times."

Joclen was not sure she approved Tamyn's use of Crej'Nevan. Joclen had used other means to achieve similar results—relaxation, peace of mind, composure—but she did not know how she felt about using another being for that purpose.

"Thank you, Stoan," she said. "But I think I can manage."

"I'm sure you can."

The Alcyone turned back to his console. Joclen did not know how to read him—no one did—so she chose not to hear the sarcasm implicit in his words. He meant well. She could not afford to let her anger and fear muddle her judgement.

Perhaps the Stralith would be a good idea.

She turned. "Shreve. I want to be able to break out of here at a word."

"I've been working through the station systems," Shreve said. "Another hour and you've got a guaranteed door."

"Ratha, I want to know the moment anything changes in the shuttle's signal."

Ratha nodded.

Joclen stood. "I'll be in my quarters."

She descended to the next deck. Her cabin was right off the lift. There, she paced, then touched a finger to her multilink and sent a request for Crej'Nevan's presence.

Several minutes later the door chimed and Joclen admitted the Stralith.

"How may I help, Co Bramus?"

"A few answers, co. Did you have an opportunity to, uh, commune with Benajim Cyanus when he was aboard?"

"No. It seemed imminent. He was fascinated by me, almost to the point of rudeness. I thought he might be xenophobic, but that wasn't the source of his interest."

"What was?"

"I don't know. I am sensitive to a small extent—Straliths aren't Ranonans, although a part of us is a part of them—and I can usually acquire the grosser emotions. Specific thoughts, unless I am in congress with another, do not translate. Only feelings. In Co Cyanus's case it was peculiar." Crej'Nevan paused. "This bears on our purposes here and the safety of the ship?"

"It may. I understand your reluctance to discuss personal matters."

"It's a small issue of propriety. But in this case I've been troubled by what I felt from Co Cyanus. It's a relief that you have asked. What I felt was a profound emptiness within him."

"I don't think I follow."

"I'm not sure I can describe it. It is almost as if he has vast gaps in his persona."

"He'd had a memory wipe."

"Memory wipes hide substance, never destroy it. Co Cyanus seems never to have had this substance. He's a personality in the simplest sense, just enough there to give him an identity and little else, plus the past few years spent with Co Merrick. I sensed an empty place where his past ought to be."

Joclen thought of her brief interactions with Cyanus. He had seemed to possess ample character then.

"That doesn't make sense," she said. "You're suggesting he isn't human?"

"No, he's very human. But more like a young child than the adult he appears to be."

"Would you have told us any of this without our asking?"

"A small matter of propriety, Co Bramus. We are discussing the content of another being's mind."

"But—"

"There was no threat in him that I could detect. If he's a danger to anyone, it is to himself."

The shuttle jarred when it hit atmosphere. They could not see Earth but they felt the inexorable pull.

The machine rode a carrier wave down through the thickening air. At the last moment, Shreve deleted the shuttle from the traffic control system. Clif broke the prescribed flight pattern and turned north. Flying by instruments and aided by Shreve who monitored them from Mars-Earth Transit, Clif took them to the coordinates Merrick had given them.

The lock opened and brilliant daylight poured into the cramped hold. The machinery glistened oilily.

Outside, green grass stretched away, up a rise. Twisted trees, thickly leaved, shared the ground with a forest of crosses, statues, and ribbons that fluttered in the breeze. Tamyn stepped out beneath a blue sky broken by faint wisps of cloud. Right and left as far as she could see the small monuments stretched. Far to the south she saw metal glinting and towers with spinning wheels. A flock of birds turned overhead, then flew away. Tamyn's sense of direction was off—she could not remember which way Earth rotated, so this might be mid morning or mid afternoon.

The grass was damp; the soil yielded pleasantly underfoot. Tamyn opened her faceplate and the humid air kissed her like an old friend. There was a fetid odor, though, undercut by a faint tinge of smoke. She stooped down and dug her fingers into the ground, prying loose a clump of dirt.

Earth...

The motiles brought out the sarcophagus. They seemed to know where to go.

"I'd love Shreve to take that encoding apart," Innes said. "I'd love to know what all was in it."

They followed the motiles up the slope. When they crested the
hill, just below, on the other side, was a long white mausoleum. The
inscription over the entrance was in a language Tamyn did not know.

"Kryder, are you recording all this?"

"Yes."

The motiles carried their burden to the mausoleum. One of
them detached briefly and opened the door. A light came on
within.

Inside the main chamber stretched for fifty meters. Blue-white
seals hung along both walls, each with a different inscription. Names,
Tamyn realized with an odd mingling of nostalgia and uneasiness.
Immortality, in a way. The motiles stopped just inside the opening.

"Who present speaks for the deceased?" a voice asked. It was
strangely accented Langish, but understandable.

Tamyn stepped forward. "I do."

"You are?"

"Tamyn Fitzgerald Glass."

"Relation to the deceased?"

"Friend."

"Name of the deceased?"

"Sean Benjamin Merrick."

"Do you carry his legacy?"

Tamyn frowned. "I don't understand?"

"His history, his life, his record—"

"Yes," she said, pulling the disk from her pouch.

"Enter it."

A disk cradle extruded from the wall near the entrance. Tamyn
set the disk in it, understanding now why Sean had used such an
archaic medium. The cradle retracted.

"Sean Benjamin Merrick is welcome here. Have his remains
interred where indicated."

Further down, a square door opened and a slab emerged. The
motiles carried the sarcophagus down and placed it on the slab, then
filed out of the mausoleum, their function complete. The slab took
the coffin inside and the door closed. Tamyn approached it and
stared at the blank panel. What now?

"Please stand aside," the voice said.

Tamyn stepped back. A white hot beam lanced out from a
projector in the ceiling and splashed against the panel. It cut

inexorably for about a minute, then shut off. Unreadable, glowing letters now adorned the blue-white panel.

"Survivors?" the voice asked.

"I don't understand."

"Family?"

"None that I am aware of."

Tamyn waited for more. It had been, she realized, the first communication she had had with any intelligence within the Pan. Now it was over and she was vaguely sorry she had had nothing better to say to it.

"I guess we're finished," she said.

They left the structure and started back to the shuttle.

Done. Tamyn paused at the top of the hill and looked back. As simple as that. Kryder had the recordings, the body was buried, they had no further obligations. She could now concentrate on getting her ship out of the Pan Humana. She felt as if something were missing, that she was overlooking something.

"Shipmaster?" Kryder called.

"Go on," she said. "Get ready to lift off. I want to check something."

Kryder handed his recorder to Clif and came after Tamyn. She smiled at the singlemindedness of the prophylactic. He followed her back to the mausoleum.

"Tomb," she spoke to the walls. "Can you hear me? I have questions."

"I can hear you. Ask."

"Name me the others buried here. Who were they?"

"The family Merrick and associates. The first is Conner Merrick, born A.D. 1989, died A.D. 2082. Beside him rests his wife, EmLing Chi Merrick, born A.D. 2002, died A.D. 2101. The second is their firstborn, Raphaela Merrick, born A.D. 2031, died A.D. 2140. Beside her is her husband, Tannen Benjamin, born A.D. 2034, died A.D.2130. Opposite Raphaela is the secondborn of Conner and EmLing Chi, Ryan Merrick, born A.D. 2035, died A.D. 2050. Beside him is the thirdborn of Conner and EmLing Chi, Daniel Merrick, born A.D. 2038, died A.D. 2155. Beside him is his wife, Shawna Seabright Merrick, born A.D. 2040, died A.D. 2155. Beside them is their firstborn, Stephen Merrick, born A.D. 2075, died A.D. 2202. Beside him is his first wife, Ann Shephard, born A.D. 2072, died

A.D. 2155. Next is his lifemate, Singli Talek, born A.D. 2105, died A.D. 2249. Beside her is—"

The roll went on, mate after mate, children born, deaths, the litany of a family that had somehow managed a cohesion that kept them buried in one tomb. She did not know how many others there were that had never been buried here. The mausoleum said nothing of them, but somehow Tamyn was certain the primary family members, the central figures of the family in each generation, were here.

Sean was the son of Nathan Merrick and Sian Delip. The mausoleum did not know if Sean had ever fathered children. Sean was the last. Tamyn did not say that there would be no more.

She was sad when she left the tomb. Sean had stolen something from the Republic by demanding burial here, but Tamyn did not know exactly what. It seemed an act of finality. Likely as not this tomb, the family of Merrick, would drift into an irredeemable obscurity. No one would remember, no one would know. Perhaps that was the best kind of privacy.

"Tamyn," Clif's voice came over her comm. "We have problems."

Tamyn started to ask what, then looked up. From the south a flock of shapes grew visibly.

"Damn. Clif! We're on our way!"

She broke into a run. Halfway down the slope the first blasts fragmented stone and wood, sent dirt spraying at them. Something heavy slammed against her. She staggered through the litter of effigies, rubbing dirt out of her eyes.

Explosions broke all around her. She crouched low, tried to pinpoint Kryder or the shuttle.

"Tamyn!" her comm blared.

"Off! Get off! I'll fend for myself!"

More blasts. The attack vehicles circled overhead, making crazy shadow patterns dance around her. She ran.

Kryder stood in an open area, a weapon in hand, firing up at the small craft.

"Kryder, move!"

He glanced at her for a moment, looked back, and a bolt sliced through him. He looked confused for a moment, then dropped, limp.

The shuttle was hovering off the ground, but the hatch was open. Innes stood framed in the circle, waving at her.

She started forward.

An explosion threw a cross at her. It glanced off her head, spun her around, and she fell. Dizzy, she crawled. She could not see. She kept moving, moving, forward, she hoped in the right direction.

The ground beneath her erupted and she remembered—vaguely—flying among the black boats and crosses.

Chapter Fourteen

The beacon led *Solo* into the forested tangle growing over the surface of Tabit Freeroamer Orbital. The irregular assemblage looked
like a massive project abandoned before completion. Gaping canyons, deep depressions, latticed sections like deck work open to
vacuum, amid booms and cranes, struts and buttresses, and the un-
cleared debris of older construction long forgotten. In the expanded
imaging of *Solo's* sensors, Benajim saw that scores of smaller orbitals
had been jammed together, joined incongruously to the growing
structure. Herds of motiles scurried over the plating, pouring from
crevices and holes.

"This doesn't strike me as smart," Piper said.

Benajim ignored her. After a short slalom through an outcrop
of twisted struts, they spilled over the edge of a vast lip and entered a widening cavern. A few hundred meters in, the walls became contoured by deep ravines. Within the encircling depressions, Benajim found ships. Hundreds of them, most in apparent
disrepair. A new signal shot from an empty niche, latching onto
Solo's sensory envelope.

"I don't like this," Piper said. "If you're interested in my opinion at all."

Benajim glanced at her, staring stonily at the monitor array. "I'm
assuming you could have forcibly asserted your will at any time, so
your protest is noted but seems disingenuous."

Piper frowned. "In the first instance, no, your ship would not
allow me to assume control. *Solo* has some very good prophylactics
in the datasphere. In the second place, my job isn't to interfere
unless threat is imminent and potentially lethal. In my opinion, you
could still leave."

"After we dock?"

"That changes the level of difficulty, but yes."

Benajim's awareness was partly in the Flow. He detected no
other scans but the beacon signal.

"See if you can use that signal to get into their datasphere,"
he said.

Piper hesitated, then placed her hands on the gates. Her eyes slitted, rolled back into her head.

No...it's just a beacon...isolated from everything else...

Then we dock.

Benajim let Solo follow the beacon into a berth. He watched a lock extrude from the wall of the berth to press around *Solo's* lock, some sort of bond that, to his surprise, managed to be airtight.

Piper sighed. "All right, up to this point everything you've done has left you with the option to get away. If we leave the ship and go into this place, I have no idea what we'll find, but that option reduces dramatically."

"So now you assert your duty to protect me by requiring ...what?"

"You have to explain what we're doing here."

"To you?"

Piper raised her hand toward the bridge around them. "Do you see anyone else?"

"Or what? You won't let me leave the ship?"

"Even after the explanation, I might not."

Benajim laughed uncomfortably. "I knew I should have come alone."

"You didn't have a choice about that."

"I know." He stared at the monitors, thinking, *all this power and I still can't just act...*

He cleared his throat. "It's hard to explain," he said.

"Try."

"I'm not...complete. My memories...there's a lot of empty space in my head."

"So I understand."

Benajim looked at her. "But there's less now. Since I took that node from Sean's datasphere. I don't know how, but it...added things. Maybe it opened things up, I don't know, but I feel like I'm more complete now than I was before."

"In what way?"

"Ways. I don't know, it's not in discrete packets. Things feel more familiar, things seem to make more sense. But it's not all there yet."

"And you think you'll get the rest here? Is that what you meant by all the answers are here?"

"I'm not sure what I meant exactly. It's not working that way, but—yes, I think I'll get more here. It's fairly clear to me—deep knowledge, the kind you just know—that Tabit is key to what's going on in the C.R. And maybe to me."

Piper was silent for a long time. A comm chimed. Benajim ignored it.

"You've got to know," she said finally, "what absolute nonsense this sounds like."

"Of course. But it's not."

Piper nodded. "Then we go in." She blinked at another chime. "They're calling. Better reply."

The umbilical, attached hermetically to the hull of *Solo,* was without gravity. Benajim pulled himself after Piper down its slightly curving length, and tumbled out onto his buttocks when gravity abruptly resumed at the far end.

Piper had rolled gracefully to her feet, attention focussed ahead, until Benajim stood. The wide chamber, open at the opposite end, possessed no detail. It looked as if one wall had been removed and the contents emptied.

Benajim began to walk forward. Piper's left hand shot out, chest height, and stopped him. Several figures approached from the gloom shrouding the distance, suddenly providing perspective and threat. Benajim's pulse picked up and he saw Piper's eyes widen and the vein in her neck pulse thickly, her entire system preparing.

Before the committee reached them, another figure came hurrying after them. They stopped and turned toward the newcomer. For nearly five minutes they spoke, often gesturing, their voices muffled by distance.

Abruptly, the first group left, leaving the lone figure watching them. When the others were no longer visible, this one approached Benajim and Piper.

A woman, Benajim saw.

She wore loose, dull-yellow coveralls cinched by thick belts around the waist, the right bicep, the left thigh, and both ankles; sandals, and a brilliantly colored sash around the neck. Her hair billowed darkly around a lean face made longer by vertical blue and white stripes on the left half. Her right eye was artificial, a dimly glowing green, and the cheek below it bore an ornate sigil.

Piper took two steps forward and the woman stopped about three meters away.

"You are from *Solo?*" she asked, her voice sharp, almost harsh; the accent gave the "r" and "l" slightly drawn-out pronunciations, barely a beat but noticeable.

"We are," Benajim said.

"You are not...?" She frowned and shook her head. "Representatives, no doubt. Apologies for the delay, the misunderstanding. Long time since...I am Leris op Elen, advocate to trade for Merrick Intersolar."

Piper gave Benajim a quick look.

"I am Benajim Cyanus, shipmaster of *Solo*. This is my associate, Piper Van."

Leris op Elen's green eye seemed to churn briefly. She nodded. "It is the *Solo* then? The actual ship? It took time for the registry to filter through and our offices are no longer fully staffed. There was disbelief. Naturally."

"Naturally," Benajim agreed. "It's been some time since *Solo* visited here."

"Forty-two years. I checked. But the company is still authorized, still credentialed, so Orbital Oversite cannot object." She gestured around at the empty chamber. "We removed the accommodations fifteen years ago, when other arrangements superseded our own." She frowned again. "There is confusion over your visit now." She took a step forward. "You are not Merrick."

"No. I'm...we represent his interests."

"Corporate?"

"And personal."

"Ah." She stepped back, nodding. "Then I assume your visit will entail change. Come with me. Better place to talk freely."

Benajim and Piper followed Leris op Elen half a pace behind.

"These bays," Piper asked, "belong to Merrick Intersolar?"

"Still, yes. We reduced fees by leasing some, by auctioning unused equipment, by using others as storage space." She glanced at Benajim. "We are concerned at the change of attention. No word came over unsatisfactory service. We assumed..."

"Sean never actually terminated his contract with you," Benajim said. "Did he?"

"No. But no exclusivity exists, so of course he was free to engage other clades. There was a termination clause, therefore we also assumed that this meant only an alteration of arrangement, not severance. You are not here to sever?"

"No. Merrick never intended to."

Leris op Elen nodded, but her expression—difficult to read under the paint—seemed even more worried.

"There are explanations?" she asked.

"There are. In time."

She seemed satisfied with that and led on in silence.

The space stretched into the body of the station a good hundred meters before they came to any features other than bare walls. Huge forms bulked, interspersed by conduit and railing. Leris op Elen brought them to a blocky hatch assembly. Through the already open door, they entered a narrower corridor that ended at another hatch. The first door rolled shut behind them. A fine mist filled the close space as they approached the second hatch. Benajim sniffed at the pungent aseptic odor.

"Breathe deep," Leris op Elen said.

The inner hatch opened at their approach. They stepped into a large round chamber, about four meters in diameter. The hatch sealed and the lift began to descend.

The door opened to the dense sound of a populated circuit.

They entered the press of people moving along the wide space. Above, the ceiling was shrouded in mist and brightly-colored banners suspended from the walls of three and four story high structures crowded together. Ramps led into the maws of omnirecs and shops and tributary corridors. Rich smells filled the air and Benajim heard music from several sources.

Leris op Elen looked back often as they wound a ragged path through the throngs. Benajim saw elegant tunics, lace, shorts and vests, naked bodies painted thickly with designs. Many possessed an artificial eye like their guide, though the color varied. He heard the accents of half a dozen dialects of langish and a few languages he could not name.

Leris op Elen brought them to a ramp that led into a narrow structure. A complex pattern adorned the lintel over the door, similar to the sigil on her face. He paused to study it more closely: three parallel lines of unequal length canted at forty-five degrees running through a circle; the upper righthand segment of the circle contained a stylized M and a Delta symbol; the lower, lefthand segment contained a seven-point star with a Pi symbol in its center, all in brilliant azure against a dark grey background.

"Please."

Leris op Elen stood in the doorway, beckoning him.

He entered and the door slid shut. The room remained unlit and all Benajim could see were shadows, until Leris op Elen turned toward him and her green eye glimmered.

"This way," she said, and another door opened behind her.

Benajim stepped through into a densely furnished room. Heavy couches, end tables, and tapestries gave it a close, cozy feeling. The sourceless light was warm and pleasant.

Leris op Elen went to a large, ornate hutch, opened the double doors, and beginning pouring glasses of what appeared to be brandy.

"We were followed," Piper said quietly.

Leris op Elen brought a glass to each of them, frowning. "Of course." She returned to the hutch to fetch her own glass. She raised it in salute. "Welcome."

Benajim sipped at the liquor—not brandy, this had a cinnamon underflavor. Piper pretended to drink.

"I am Elen for convenience," she said.

"Thank you," Benajim said, raising the glass. "You aren't surprised we were followed?"

"Your coming stirs interest," Elen said. "Please. Sit." She studied them. Her artificial eye roiled briefly. "You have no optil," she said, tapping her temple next to the green eye. "No link into the datasphere. What do you use?"

Benajim held up his left hand, fingers splayed, and retracted the sheathes over the caps. Elen nodded.

She curled into a large chair. Benajim sat on one of the sofas, but Piper remained standing, near the door.

"Competitors," Elen said, gesturing vaguely toward the outside.

"The same ones who were coming to meet us?"

"A few. Mostly, they were Orbital Oversite, wondering at the new arrival." She studied Benajim. "There was confusion over your initial challenge."

"The challenge?" Piper asked.

"First contact, ID and announcement. It failed to penetrate the orbital comm sentinels. You registered as enemy. Your last challenge, though, penetrated to our comm. I confess I am still confused. Why the first?"

Benajim raised his glass to his lips, trying to untangle Elen's explanation. "Just testing," he said finally.

Elen nodded. "I must test also. May I?"

"Test how?" Piper asked.

"Would you trust business that proceeded blind? I must know who you are."

"But—" Piper began. Benajim raised a hand to stop her.

"We're from Miron," he said. "Other side of the Secant."

"Understood. You work for Sean Merrick?"

"On his behalf. He's dead."

Elen blinked, startled. "How long?"

"Recently."

"Can you verify this?"

"I have *Solo.*"

Elen seemed to consider this for a long time. "Convincing but insufficient. Possible you stole it."

"Unlikely."

"But possible. Why have you come? To tell us there is no corporation? Or explain why Merrick shifted his trade to others without word? I expected to hear of his death, but I expected to hear years ago, when traffic fell off. Then I find others doing business with Merrick Enterprises. Betrayal seems a Merrick trait. If someone stole his ship—"

She stopped abruptly and closed her natural eye. When she opened it again she seemed once more in control.

"Why have you come?" she asked again.

"To see about the traffic you mentioned," Benajim said. "But we have to know who we're dealing with, as well."

"Fair, of course." She frowned. "It was expected that Merrick himself would come. Either to resurrect our agreement or shut us down officially. I'm at a loss in this instance."

Silence stretched. Then Piper said: "Somebody has to prove something to someone. What verification do you require, Elen?"

She looked up. "Do you bear his mark?"

"Mark?" Benajim asked. He pointed at her face. "You mean like that?"

"Merrick would send someone with his mark."

"I don't—"

Elen returned to the hutch. She set down her glass and opened a drawer. She took out a slim device and brought it over to Benajim. Piper suddenly stood between them. Elen backed up, startled, and stared at Piper. After a few moments, she held out the device. "Not a weapon," she said. "A scanner."

Piper took the device, examined it briefly, and pointed it at Elen. She pressed a contact and waited. Nothing happened.

"What does it scan for?" Piper asked, turning it over. "I don't see a screen or projector."

Elen extended her hand. "Please."

When Piper continued to examine it, Benajim cleared his throat. "We're not finding anything out this way."

Piper glared at him, but returned the device.

Hesitantly, Elen stepped closer to Benajim. She aimed the narrow end of the device at his face. He felt himself tense, hoping that he had judged correctly. She pressed a stud.

A tingling crossed his face. Piper stared at him, wide-eyed. Something seemed to occlude his vision, like a cataract. He blinked and tried to focus.

Hovering before him, about twenty-five centimeters away, shimmered a white holograph: a circle, transected by three parallel lines at a forty-five degree angle, similar to the symbol on Leris op Elen's face and above the entrance to her domicile. Benajim raised a hand and brushed his fingers through it.

Elen smiled. "From Merrick," she said and switched the device off.

The symbol vanished.

"Fifteen years ago, Merrick ships abruptly stopped routing through our bays," Elen explained as she keyed data onto large flatscreens. "There was no explanation given. One day, a shipmaster simply said there would be no more. Other contracts had been engaged. There was no avenue for question."

"Because the trade was illicit," Piper said, watching the charts come up.

"All trade is illicit," Elen said. "Tabit Freeroamer is not Pan sanctioned. We assumed first that relations with the C.R. were normalizing. But that was not the case."

Benajim whistled. "These numbers are huge."

Piper glanced at him where he sat on the other side of Elen, gazing at the screens.

"Prior to the breach," Elen said, "our firm employed six hundred and ninety people. Now there are twenty."

"Who took over?" Piper asked.

Elen pointed. "Ryna Clade. You see? Within two years they owned our numbers and now are larger."

Benajim frowned. "Why? I mean, no one in the C.R. knew about this anyway. Why switch it?"

"The contract we had with Merrick terminates on his death."

"He was enforcing corporate mortality on this side of the Secant?" Piper asked. She laughed. "But when the trade shifted..."

"A new contract without that provision wasn't offered?" Benajim asked.

"No," Elen said. "Merrick himself would have needed to come."

"Imprimatur," Piper commented.

"Was your contract with Merrick legal here?" Benajim asked. "I mean, within Tabit Freeroamer. Did Orbital Oversite know about it and approve?"

"Yes."

"Leaving you with no recourse," Piper said. "You couldn't very well cross the border to complain. Could you?"

"It is not permitted," Elen agreed. "But the contract is still open. By our law, we could not shut down entirely. Maintaining an operative status is required." She shrugged and looked embarrassed. "But it's been long. Waiting has bled resources. We shifted our attention to other areas, to compensate. Your signal took time to get to me. There could be a fine."

Benajim sat forward, intent on the screens. "All this material...almost none of it seems to be luxury items. A lot of exotics—alloys, isotopes, complex equipment—but a lot of it consists of the kind of stuff you need for terraforming and settlement. Is this what's still going through the new vendors?"

"I don't know," Elen said. "Don't you?"

Benajim shook his head. "No. Merrick was...ill for several years. He didn't know."

"But he died. You said."

"Yes."

"Then Ryna Clade no longer has a contract with him."

"They have a contract with someone," Piper said. "We just aren't sure who."

Elen looked at her anxiously. "But not with Merrick. He died."

"That's right," Benajim said. "Is that important?"

"If you can show proof, yes. Leris Clade can terminate the contract legitimately and shift interest to something lucrative."

"Proof..." Benajim mused. "What would satisfy?"

"A certificate? A proclamation?"

"From the C.R.? Would that be accepted here?"

"Tabit Freeroamer accepts the existence of the C.R., even if we cannot go there."

Benajim chuckled. "Doesn't matter. We don't have one. Unless *Solo* qualifies."

"Merrick is dead," Elen said, "but there is no proof?"

"His death was kept a secret even within the C.R. Whoever is dealing with your competitors doesn't want anything changed on either side."

Elen looked from one to the other of them. "Then...why are you here?"

Benajim stared at the screen for a long time. "How," he asked finally, "is the contract validated here?"

"There is a verification with each convoy."

Piper smiled. "Imprimatur."

Piper came awake instantly out of the meditative state she used instead of sleep when she worked. The room around her, plain walled and simply furnished, was dark. She sat up in the bed, back to headboard, and listened.

Benajim had the next room—his insistence, he did not want to sleep in anyone's presence—and Piper had found no way to eavesdrop on Elen's systems. Piper opted to forego normal sleep and keep herself amped and on standby.

The building creaked.

Piper accessed the two minutes prior to her waking, searching for the trigger. The only thing in her memory augment was a single sharp snap, marginally louder than the other structural noises.

Not enough information; could be anything.

Why would a structure inside a station move so much?

Everything she had seen on the way from *Solo* had seemed make-shift, added-on, afterthoughts. Tabit Orbital—Tabit Freeroamer Orbital, she corrected—was very old, older than anything human-built in the C.R. If she understood Elen correctly, they were nomi-nally at war with the Pan Humana.

"Freeroamer" was misleading, Piper thought, since they clearly aren't allowed to go where they wish. Why the restriction on travel to the C.R. if their stated ethic demanded freedom of movement?

It would not be the first time, she knew, when ideals and ideol-ogy conflicted in a system...

Another snap.

Piper opened her door and stopped breathing, amping her hear-ing even more.

An almost sound, a tiny pressure wave that changed the texture of the stillness, moved past. Someone was in the building.

Piper moved into the hallway, leaving the door open behind her. She lowered her body temperature and increased her visual range, extending it into the infrared, and walked sideways, close to the wall, to the head of the steps.

A dim glow, almost the color of clay, outlined the archway at the bottom, shifting slowly.

It increased in intensity. Piper backed up to the wall.

A figure, bright orange face, duller umber body, came into view, his presence illuminating the foot of the landing in Piper's enhanced vision.

Not Elen, not Benajim.

He mounted the stairs.

He came within arm's length and started to walk past her. He hesitated and she heard him sniff.

He turned toward her.

Piper's right hand grabbed his neck, her thumb jamming up just above the larynx. He made a rasping, breathy sound just as she rammed her other thumb against the hinge of his jaw. He slumped against her.

Piper deftly lowered him to the floor and descended the stairs.

A light was on in Elen's office.

Piper pressed against the wall beside the door then silently slid down till she was almost in a sitting posture. She carefully looked around the edge of the door.

Two men, one standing before a broad screen, going through text, the other standing in the center of the room, arms akimbo, watching. She pulled back as he started to look in her direction.

She heard the footstep a few moments before he reached the door. She shifted her weight to her right foot, waited, then spun, left leg snapping out, driving her foot—

—directly into a kneecap.

He sucked his breath sharply and caught himself against the edge of the door as he staggered back into the room. Piper followed closely and came up from below, driving the heel of her left hand into his chin. The impact shocked her, the muscles of his neck and shoulders tensed to counter, but cartilage crackled and he staggered back.

Still holding onto the doorway, he tried to throw a punch at her, but missed. Piper dug fingertips deep into his armpit, making him flinch back, then kicked down into his other knee. Bone caved in, he groaned, and collapsed, his hand sliding down the jamb.

Piper punched him twice in the throat. Blood splattered from his mouth.

In the pair of seconds all this took, the other man managed to turn away from the screen to see what was happening. Piper crossed the distance before he could take more than a step back. He was reaching for a shoulder holster. She caught that hand, twisted it under until the wrist snapped, and almost gracelessly kicked him in the groin. He curled around the pain and fell to the floor. Piper rolled him over and removed the pistol from his holster just as he began to vomit.

She hurried back up the stairs to the first man. He was beginning to stir when she reached him, trying to climb onto hands and knees. She clipped him in the jaw again and he dropped.

A door along the short corridor opened and Elen stepped out. Lights came on. Piper damped her visual enhancement.

Elen, naked and cleansed of her face markings, stood over the unconscious man.

"How many?" she asked.

"Two more downstairs," Piper said.

Benajim came out of his room, zipping his utilities.

"They were going through your records," Piper said. "Here," she tossed the pistol to Benajim and ran back to Elen's office.

The third man had managed to sit up, one hand pressed into his groin, the other wiping at the moisture around his mouth. In normal light, the infrared glow no longer muddying facial features, Piper looked at him. The tips of his fingers looked smooth. She grabbed his hand and tugged at one tip till the sheath rolled back, revealing the polyceramo interface.

"You're from the C.R.," Piper said. "Welcome to Tabit."

"Two of them are Ryna Clade," Elen said. The first one Piper had taken down in the upstairs hallway now sat on the floor beside the others. His face bore smeared remnants of green crosshatching across the right cheek, below red and blue triangles across his forehead. The clade sigil on his left cheek was an unrecognizable blur: he had tried to obscure it.

Both his eyes were natural.

The dead one possessed an optil.

Benajim stood over the third man where he sat on the floor, cradling his broken wrist in his lap. Dried vomit speckled his black tunic. Benajim stood there until the intruder looked up.

"A little far from home, aren't you?" Benajim said. "Taking in the sights?"

The man did not reply. He looked at Piper, then across the room at the body.

"Yes," Piper said. "You made an error in judgement."

"Nothing to compare to your own," he said. "Fuck you all. I have nothing to say."

"Do you have a name?" Piper asked. The man looked away.

"What happens," Benajim asked, "if we turn them all over to Orbital Oversite?"

"Nothing," the intruder said. "Without evidence of malfeasance, they won't risk losing the Q."

Elen went to the screen and touched a number of contact points. The screen cleared and a new image appeared. It showed the three intruders breaking into her offices.

The man blinked, frowning.

"Proof," Elen said. "But he is correct about the Q. Too much traffic. More than likely, this one will be barred from return, but our case will be ignored."

"Too much Q," Benajim mused. "The traffic he represents is about to end. When we left the C.R. the Flow was learning all about what Reiner Combine was doing."

The intruder grunted. "Won't change anything there, either. Still too much Q."

"Unless we can demonstrate that the Q will continue to flow." Benajim tapped Elen on the shoulder. "I have a proposal to take before Orbital Oversite along with our challenge. I wasn't sure it would work before, but these coes have handed me a guarantee."

"You're bluffing," the man said.

"You hope." Benajim gestured for Elen to follow him.

When they had left the room, Piper continued to stare at the intruder.

Finally he looked at her. "You better think about your family, Co Van. You aren't there to protect them."

Piper straddled his legs. He tried to push back, but she grabbed his face, fingers squeezing at the jaw until his mouth opened. She reached into his mouth and pulled his tongue out, tugging at it till his head followed. His eyes went large and he looked up at her.

"One more threat of any kind," she said, "and I'll tear this out by the roots." She made a smile. "A bit melodramatic, I know, but don't misunderstand me—I just don't want to listen to your shit anymore."

She released him and wiped her fingers on his sleeve. "Who else is here? From the C.R.?"

He pointedly looked down at his wrist.

"Doesn't matter," Piper said. "We'll find out soon enough."

Twenty minutes later, four men entered Elen's domicile, all bearing the Merrick Company sigil on their variously-decorated faces. The corpse was efficiently bundled into a long sack which became rigid at a touch. Two of the men carried it out.

The other two conferred with Elen for several minutes while Benajim and Piper waited outside her office.

Finally, the door opened and Elen gestured for them to enter.

The two intruders lay together, unconscious, in the middle of the floor between two sofas and Elen's chair.

"Benajim Cyanus and Piper Van," Elen said. "These are clade. Leris op Jary and Leris op Nois."

Benajim nodded politely to each one.

"You bring a new contract?" the one named Jary asked, voice thick and liquid. The left side of his face was adorned by a spiral of pencil-thin blue against an amber background.

"Depends," Benajim said. "Would it do any good on this end?"

Jary frowned at Elen. "Ryna," she said.

Jary nodded. "That problem stays here. We handle it. You," he jabbed a finger at Benajim, "must guarantee our actions count."

"I can't guarantee anything if your Oversite doesn't accept our challenge."

Jary scowled and turned toward Elen. "Trouble. Not worth it."

"Listen," Elen said.

"To what?" Jary stepped close to Benajim. He stopped when Piper moved closer. He frowned, but continued talking to Benajim. "Ryna rises. The ships come to them, not us. Oversite favors them with merchandise, not us. What do we offer to convince them to end current arrangements? Your word that Merrick is dead and those who come now do so illegally? Illegal by C.R. law, not ours!"

"As we understand it," Piper said, "that's not precisely true. The contract requires validation on both sides. If the proper guarantees cannot be given by those now dealing with Ryna Clade..."

Jary now seemed intrigued.

"It's about to end anyway," Benajim said. "Reiner Combine has been exposed in the C.R. Before long, action will be taken to end the caravans. How will Ryna look then? Will Orbital Oversite continue to favor them when they can't maintain the traffic?"

Benajim caught the scent of sweat beneath the slightly sweet smell of Jary's paint.

"We should do nothing," Jary said quietly. "Let them fail. Then..."

"Then? What? Start all over? With what? I can offer you a potential. But I need Tabit to repudiate Reiner Combine and the clades dealing with them."

"Ask for a sun in a glass jar next time," Jary said, moving away. "Easier."

"Then let's just disrupt it and see what happens," Benajim said. "I've offered to stand with you before Oversite and demand that the contract validation be presented. They can't. Not now. When they fail to do that, what will happen?"

Jary regarded him with an expression of shock mingled with fear.

"I can offer you," Benajim continued, "a legitimate contract as a designated successor to Sean Merrick's enterprises. Once Reiner's activities are generally known in the C.R. they'll be censured. Even if the Board of Regents and the Flow arrive at a consensus to continue the trade, it won't be Reiner conducting it. Ryna Clade will lose it."

"And if consensus is to continue the boycott?"

"Then we pick up where Merrick left off. Reiner Combine still loses in the C.R. and I can step in."

Benajim caught Piper's startled look and hoped she would stay silent. She did and Jary paced the room.

"Cletus will hate us," Leris op Nois said, the first time he spoke.

"He already does," Elen said.

"But not with cause. That changes."

"Who's Cletus?" Piper asked.

"Ryna Clade chairman," Elen said. "He also sits on Orbital Oversite."

Jary stopped, his eyes on Benajim. "But he doesn't control it." Then he looked at Elen and Nois. "It would be pleasure, though, to see him choke." He nodded. "Details." He gestured at the pair of intruders. "When Jush and Plona return," he said to Nois, "see these two are removed. Elen."

"Privacy, please," Elen said to Benajim and Piper. "We will let you know."

Benajim ascended the stairs and returned to his room. As the door began to close, Piper slipped in.

"What are you doing?" she asked.

"I thought I'd get a little more sleep—"

"I mean with them," she said, waving a hand. "You're promising them things you can't deliver."

"I didn't promise—"

"A legitimate contract? How does that work? What Sean Merrick was doing happens to be illegal, too! Just because Reiner appropriated it doesn't make his actions or your cause legitimate!"

"It's legitimate here."

"This isn't the C.R."

"I noticed that."

"Then—?"

Benajim held a hand up and went to the bed. "How long do you think it would be before someone challenged the Secant as a monolith? Another year, another generation? It's ridiculous. The only reason it's stood this long is because it was assumed no one worth trading with on the Pan side of the border wanted to do business. Now we know that's wrong. Once the Flow begins to assess the potential profit—"

"The Charter—"

"Get over it! The law is what people say it is today. Tomorrow it will be something else."

Piper blinked at him. "I suppose you'd toss out corporate mortality along with the separation clauses?"

"The separation clauses recognized a reality, they didn't create it. And corporate mortality isn't threatened because it serves the interests of too many people."

"So it's all context for you?"

"No, it's all context for everyone. Carson Reiner was there when the Charter was ratified, she's no less a patriot than Sean was."

"Or no more."

"Granted. But look at them. Two of the Founders, breaking the laws they set up. Sean did it out of pragmatic necessity, Carson is doing it out of greed. Change your viewpoint and they could switch places, Sean the greedy one and Carson simply taking advantage of a necessary situation."

"And what about you? What are you doing this for?"

"More reasons than I'm willing to give you. But the one you need to know, the only one that matters, is that Sean wanted the monopoly ended. He wanted what Carson Reiner is doing exposed and the smuggling brought into the open. He wanted the field disrupted. I'm promising these people nothing. I'm offering them whatever I think I have to, to fulfill Sean's wishes. I don't care if any of this actually happens, I just want the whole thing busted up. What we do after that I'll leave up to the Flow. But I'll guarantee you they won't shut it down. Not when they realize what it's worth, what they'd lose."

Piper nodded. "Maybe you're right. I needed to know, though. I don't like the way you're doing it, but under these circumstances—"

Benajim sighed wearily. "Stop it. You and I both know that how you kill someone is unimportant. What matters is your willingness to do it. After that it's just expediency."

"You're a cold bastard."

Benajim grunted. "Maybe. I'd like to think I wasn't always, but I may never know."

Benajim looked up at the knock on his door. He considered ignoring it and pretending sleep, but after the second knock he got out of bed and answered it.

Elen stood in the dark hall. Her optil glimmered faintly. Across from them, Piper stood in her doorway, watching.

"Yes?" Benajim said.

"May I speak?" Elen asked. "Privately."

Benajim gave Piper a slight nod and stepped aside.

Elen sat down and Benajim returned to the bed, crossing his legs.

"We have arranged a hearing," she said. "Cletus protested, but no one else. We believe others on Oversite are jealous and suspicious of Ryna Clade, so given a chance they will stand against them. There will be a first hearing, admitting only clade members. Then, if successful there, a second, and you will speak."

"Good."

Elen studied him. Her expression seemed different, now, less clinical. "Why are you here?"

Benajim grunted, uneasy. "You keep asking me that. Isn't it apparent?"

"No. You hide yourself. You say what you want but not why you want it. Merrick is dead and you are here to speak for him. Why?"

"I'm..."

Benajim blinked, his mind suddenly filled with a heightening immanence, as if on the verge of understanding something. He caught his breath, hoping the onslaught did not show. But it did, he could see it in her face.

"I'm...Sean's friend," he said, groping. "He trusted me."

"Yes?"

"But I don't know why."

"How can you not know?"

Benajim stared at her. "I have no memory of my life before I knew Sean Merrick. He found me, saved my life, and gave me a purpose. I killed him. He was sick, he hated living more than anything else, he asked to die."

Elen frowned. "A friend would listen and do what friend-ship required."

"I believe that. But I don't know why he—I don't understand where that trust came from, why—I can't know till I remember myself."

Elen was still for a long time. Then: "You came here for answers?"

"Sean told me that I was once a slave. I came from here. I think—I believe—that there are answers here. But..."

"But you think asking may be painful."

"Yes..."

Elen nodded. "We can help. Maybe. We have a genome li-brary. If you ever lived here..."

Benajim swallowed thickly. "What do you need?"

"Tissue. Time."

Benajim closed his eyes. The storm in his mind subsided and a kind of clarity seemed to settle on the surface of this thoughts.

"Let's try," he said.

Chapter Fifteen

Tamyn came awake with complete awareness, as if someone had switched her on. She faced a man sitting behind a plain-looking black desk who vaguely resembled Stoan. The differences flooded in before she said anything: shorter than Stoan, broader across the shoulders, his chin weaker, and his wide-set eyes a startling pale green. His lips turned inward so that all she saw was a compressed, uneven line. Faint greyish fur covered his pate.

Then she noticed that she could not move.

He smiled at that point. "Neural blocks," he said softly, his accent odd. "No need for you to be able to move anyway. I want to talk, not fight. I am Commander Moss Fisher, Armada Intelligence. You are?"

Tamyn glared at him.

"Come," he said. "I can loosen your tongue the same way I've frozen your body. I'd like to be civilized about this."

"Tamyn Glass."

"Ah. No rank? No title?"

"No."

"I suspect you're lying, but we can find out about that later. What were you doing in that cemetery?"

"Saying farewell to an old friend."

"You have old friends on Earth? I'm impressed, even if they are dead. Why that cemetary?"

"That's where my old friends are buried."

"Your accent is odd, I'm not familiar with it. I've been to forty-eight worlds, learned the dialects of a hundred subcultures, but I've never heard yours before. Where are you from?"

"Out."

"Ah. How far? A system name would be nice. We are remaining civilized here, aren't we?"

"I don't know. Where I come from it's impolite to hold guests immobile while interrogating them."

Fisher laughed and slapped the desk. "What do you think of Earth now that you've been here?"

"I haven't seen much of it."

"First time?"

"Yes."

"And you came uninvited, slipped past our security perimeter, hid out, and redirected a shuttle. Manners must be elastic where you come from." He raised a finger. "That man with you. Nasty fellow. Quite a collection of augments he had. I'm sure we missed a few when we cut him up. I've never seen that particular type of physiological modification, that gland joined onto his adrenal. What was it for?"

Tamyn stared at him. I will not cry, she thought, nothing for him.

"Nothing to say?" Fisher prompted.

"I hope he was dead before you started cutting."

"Quite. Couldn't take him alive. If you ask me they looked like seti mods. Were they?"

"You're making this up as you go along."

"No, not really. Most people don't believe in the seti anymore, but I know better. You're from the boundaries, aren't you? Pirate. I had no idea you were getting quite so sophisticated, though. Pirates don't usually come in this close."

"How would you know? I erred in judgement, that's all."

He laughed again. "Now who's making it up?" He leaned forward. "I'll tell you what we've found. We've found that your weapons don't conform to any currently known design, but they're not unfamiliar. We can extrapolate back to older models, figure out where the changes were made. Your companion had a lot of technology built into him we have seen prototype proposals for, but not for some decades. The extra glands are a problem, but not unlikely theoretically. Everything about you so far says pirate, but there are a number of oddities that don't add up. Pirates don't visit graves. Also we can't find your ship. We will, it can't get out of Sol now that we know it's here. We also found wiring in your head that dates back to the War and hasn't been used in awhile. So you're from a spacer clade, that's sure. Which one? I'm guessing, and I'll admit it, that you're a boundary runner. Dealing with seti, human filth, and deviants of all sort, political and otherwise. Got anything to say to contradict me? You better think of something because on just my say-so you can die."

"Why tell me then?"

"Because you won't remember any of this later. I'm curious, I'd like some answers."

"You seem to have your mind made up already. Why should I contradict you?"

"Because I can also be generous. I need a reason, though."

"I have no reason to give you anything. My companion is dead. The reason I came here is fulfilled. I can die content."

"No one's happy to die."

"I said 'content'. There's a difference."

"You won't have either. You'll die not even knowing who you are." He leaned back. "I'll tell you what I'm going to do."

"Why?"

He shrugged. "I'm sadistic. And intensely curious. You might even like me, I have certain interests that are unique, arcane. But never mind that. I'm going to tell you what I intend to do because I want to see what falls out when I shake you up. I'm going to find out everything I want to know eventually anyway and I have the luxury of time. You see, you achieved something for me that I on my own might never have achieved. You got my predecessor out of the way. You embarrassed him. He couldn't explain you. I don't actually have to do that. All I have to do is make sure you don't happen again."

"Doesn't that necessitate explaining me?"

"In time. I'm convinced of two things, though. One is, if you're a pirate, then you're acting on your own. Brave, very brave, something I doubt any of your peers are, in sufficient degree to bring them following you. Your ship will be found soon enough in that case and destroyed, so the interlude ends."

"And the other?"

"The other is more interesting to me. If you're not a pirate, then you are certainly a very long way from home. Your ship will almost hand itself over to me while it tries to locate you. Same end result. No one will likely follow you. My job is secured. As long as I have you I can take my time explaining you. I intend to do that. You have my curiosity."

"I seriously doubt you'd believe the truth. So why should I waste my time trying to convince you?"

"Because I can let you live as well. I can give you a new life. A life of Peace."

Tamyn was glad of the neural blocks. She did not want Moss Fisher to see her shaking. She was terrified. The more she looked at his eyes the more frightened she became and she was glad she did not have to control her own responses.

As if reading her thoughts, he smiled at her.

Shreve emerged from a deep link and blinked as if he had never seen the bridge before. He shook his head and looked up at Joclen.

"Well?" she snapped, immediately critical of the sharpness in her voice. Everyone felt it, though, and she did not envy Shreve. He was the only one capable of decoding the Pan cybernetics. He was their oracle.

"Nothing about any arrests, no actions reported, and I can't detect any overt moves against us," he said. "It's all routine."

"Not good," Stoan said. "Hah! They expect us to be lazy. Or worse, reckless." He looked from person to person, then back at Shreve.

Joclen licked her lips and nodded. Reckless was precisely what she wanted to be. When the shuttle came back without Tamyn and Kryder, an ugly mass inside her began generating rage. So far she had managed to hold back her immediate impulses. *Wicca* was not a warship, no matter how powerful her teeth, no matter that so far they had fooled every Pan system they had encountered, and no matter that their anger was justified.

"Recommendations, anyone?" she said.

"You won't like this, but we have to find Cyanus," Stoan said.

Joclen stared at him startled. "Why?"

Stoan looked at her curiously. "Because he has the *Solo,* which is principally a Pan ship. I imagine Merrick stored a considerable quantity of information about the Pan in her datasphere. And it gives us something to do that we *can* do!"

Joclen worked it through. Part of her rage included a deep dislike for Benajim Cyanus, but, she told herself, that was irrational. Stoan might be correct about the Solo, and in that case they did need Cyanus. For a while, anyway.

"All right," she said. "First thing then is to get ourselves out of the Sol system." She looked at Shreve. "Can you?"

"Y-yes, but..."

Ratha cleared his throat. "Once we get out can we be sure to get back in?"

"Hah!" Stoan barked. "Cyanus will do that! Twisty bit of indulgent manifestation, thoroughly unconscious, but the right co for the sacrifice."

"If Stoan is right," Joclen said warily, "then yes. If he's wrong...we aren't doing any better right now anyway." She looked at Shreve. "Get us out." Joclen stood. "When we find Cyanus we come back to get Tam. Is everyone agreed?"

Nods answered all around. Joclen had hoped for no less, though she believed that what most of them sincerely wanted was to leave the Pan Humana, soon, ship intact, and without further loss. Adrenaline and confusion might have been the only things sealing their commitment. But for the time being, she knew she could rely on them completely.

"At your convenience, Shreve," Joclen said. "I'll be in my quarters. Let me know if anything changes."

She walked off the bridge stiffly, aware of being watched, perhaps judged. No one had actually called her Shipmaster yet, but command had fallen to her. She still technically owned *Wicca;* although the crew had witnessed Joclen returning title to Tamyn, the transfer had yet to be recorded in the Flow, and therefore remained only symbolic.

Joclen relied on Stoan because she had expected him to assume command, but he was content to advise. She was not sure how his orders might come out, though. Even so, others who had been with Tamyn longer bowed to her authority.

She reached her cabin and locked the door behind her. She stood in the darkness. Confusion, fear, bloodlust...that surprised her. She had always been quick to anger, just as quick to let it go. This was different.

Joclen touched her polycom and with a thought summoned Crej'Nevan. The tangles were suffocating her.

The room in which they put Tamyn was pale blue and featureless. The light was constant and pleasant, but there was nothing on which to fix her attention.

At first she was restless. The neural blocks gone, she exercised, flexed her body. The surfaces of the room yielded slightly. She whirled and kicked through her martial disciplines until, sweating and muscles burning, she became flushed with euphoric exhaustion. No one came to speak to her, look at her, or touch her. When she was not looking the same bland porridge appeared once each day. She found no seams to the room. The perfect prison. She relieved herself in a corner and sometime in the next few minutes it was somehow absorbed, not even leaving odors behind. She awoke after short bouts of sleep cleaned. Her exercises became the only thing on which she could focus.

She had no idea what technical capacity her captors possessed. They could possibly read her thoughts, though she doubted it. The Pan was an insulated polity, peopled by insular people who had demonstrated their unwillingness to accept challenges to what they were by learning the nature of anyone else. It did not seem reasonable to Tamyn that such people would be interested in reading minds. Or was she being naive? Moss Fisher of Armada Intelligence did not strike her as particularly squeamish.

They had disassembled Kryder—not the act of squeamish people.

There was no way out. Time could not be accurately marked in her blue cell, so she could only estimate when she reached that conclusion, sometime during the fourth or fifth days. She continued her exercises with the dim hope of using her skills on Moss Fisher. He watched, she knew.

She felt the same as when kept out of the Flow. No contact, no sensation except that which she could create for herself. Isolation. How could they stand it as a people? The synonym for Panners was isolationists. Ever since entering the Pan they had found contact with no one. Machines ran everything, or so it seemed. Perhaps even Moss Fisher was a machine.

After fifteen sleep-wake cycles her time sense was completely destroyed. She had no idea how long she had been in the cell and she began to suspect that she was either being undernourished or drugged. Her thoughts were skewed, incoherent at times, uncontrolled. She thought of her father. Gordon had not been her biological parent, only the one who had raised her and loved her and given her the tools she needed to be who she was. She had not thought of him in years, not deeply, not like now. She pictured his face, his beard, remembered his laugh, his bitterness, his pride. His love. She believed he would be proud of her. She had always tried to earn that, even after it no longer mattered to him.

"You're breaking me down," she said quietly. "Very good. Giving me nothing to fight, nothing to resist. Sap, sap, sap." She smiled enigmatically and slept.

She came awake with a start. Across the room a man squatted on his haunches, his dark eyes fixed on her. His skin was a mottled yellow, his grey hair short. He appeared sinewy; a large greenish bruise covered his right thigh.

Tamyn glanced about. No food or water. She imitated his posture and met his gaze.

"My name is Tamyn Glass."

His eyes flickered, but he remained silent.

"Do you have a name?" she asked. "Do you speak Langish?"

A shadow of pain and resentment crossed his face. For a moment he averted his eyes and Tamyn expected him to cry. But he regained control and resumed staring at her.

They went on this way for some time. Tamyn felt it would be a mistake to turn her back on him or show any sign of tiring. Her legs soon felt on the verge of cramping.

She stood.

He stood, his eyes widening in alarm.

"I'm not going to hurt you," she said. "If you understand me, nod." She stepped toward him, offering her hand, palm up. "If you can't speak—"

He jumped forward. Before Tamyn could react he slammed a fist into her shoulder. She spun around, crouching, and kicked him in the back of his left knee. The leg buckled and he fell, hard, on one knee. Tamyn followed through with a sharp punch just below his right ear. He sprawled face down, unconscious.

She retreated across the room, breath fast and hard. Her shoulder throbbed. When he did not move for several seconds she rolled him on his back.

His mouth hung open. Within she saw the fleshy stump where his tongue had been.

While she watched he sank into the floor and disappeared. Tamyn thrust a hand at the spot, but it was solid, impenetrable.

Her food and water had appeared in a corner.

She kneaded her aching shoulder, then picked up the bowl and ate, watching the room for another surprise appearance. By the time she finished her meal she realized that it had been drugged. She fought sleep till she became sick to her stomach. Consciousness faded quickly, then.

When she awoke he was back.

His left leg had been amputated at the knee.

Tamyn stared at the pink stump.

He wore a shocked expression. The cold reserve that bordered on anger was gone, the vitality leached from his eyes. Tamyn approached him and he only watched her. He seemed to plead, the way his head lay back in resignation against the wall.

"Why?" she asked. "What did you do?"

His hands rested on the floor. Gently, Tamyn touched his right hand, stroked it lightly. When he did not draw back or move to strike her she held it, trying to convey comfort.

Tears traced paths down his cheeks.

Her water cup was still where she had left it.

"Water?" Even if drugged, perhaps sleep would be welcome to him. She went to fetch it. When she turned back he was gone.

He reappeared while she napped. She sensed his presence.

His right hand was gone.

Tamyn clenched her teeth against the scream. She looked around at the walls, avoiding his eyes as long as possible.

He wept freely now.

Tamyn resisted the impulse to go to him. She pressed herself back against the wall.

"I'm sorry," she said. Her voice cracked.

As he receded through the wall his mouth opened and a garbled scream, hoarse and pitiful, filled the room, cut off the moment his head was swallowed.

When he appeared again his eyes were gone.

Tamyn turned away. Sobs shuddered through her, but she squeezed shut her eyes and struggled for control.

He made mewling sounds. Tamyn did not look at him. She concentrated on ignoring the sounds, imagining tantras and exploring their intricacies. The sounds stopped. He was gone again.

She saw him reappear. He emerged from the surface of the wall, like someone floating to the surface of a pool of milk. He made no sounds this time. Instead he moved his head slowly, in vague, circular motions.

Where the bulge of his adam's apple had been now was a deep depression, the skin puckered.

Tamyn shouted in rage. She stood and looked up at the ceiling. "Why? What's the point to this?"

He had stopped moving his head. Her heart hammered as she looked at him. *How far would it go, she wondered, and now that I know what they're doing at what point am I complicit?*

Swiftly she knelt beside him and took his head in her hands.

"I'm sorry," she said. She shifted one hand to his chin. With a quick, hard twist she snapped his neck. The body slumped over on its side.

She backed to the opposite wall and slid to the floor. After a time her crying stopped. She did not notice when she fell asleep.

Joclen felt much calmer now. She sat at her station on the bridge and watched the holo as Shreve took them closer to the convoy streaming toward the perimeter stations.

They had threaded a crooked course from point to point in the system. It was the third day since leaving Mars-Earth Transit. Everyone was impatient. Shreve intended dropping them into the midst of another convoy and masking again, the same way they had entered the system. All the comm they had monitored continued to be machine language. There had been no mention of intruders.

The holo displayed their approach to the monstrous cargohaulers. *Great beasts,* Joclen thought, *mindless and servile, pack animals.*

Wicca dropped between two of them and settled into place in the hole.

The cargohaulers shifted. The big ships began closing in. Joclen linked.

The group in which they rested was slowing, closing in, and shifting away from the pack.

Shreve—

No signal, no change in comm, nothing—

What about their guidance comm?

Working.

Shreve's code lanced through the simple signals passed among the big ships. They were closing up the escape passages for *Wicca,* forming a huge cage to trap the invader. However the order had been given it was a clever, terribly simple and elegant trap.

One of them started moving away from the others. Joclen wanted to laugh. She seized navcom, though, and plotted a path out of the group. *Wicca* surged through the widening gap.

A score of small ships hovered around the convoy. Joclen tracked them as they closed with *Wicca.*

Stand by on weapons, Traville, she commanded. His code vibrated anxiously. Joclen issued instructions through navcom.

Wicca veered sharply and sailed tightly around the group of cargohaulers. The big ships moved apart now, widening the gaps between each other to their former positions. *Wicca* came around a pair still close together. The small ships had scattered, some following, others moving around to cut off any escape route.

Joclen's perception whipped vertiginously sideways as the ship fell through the narrow gap between the cargohaulers. She powered up and pushed straight through the hole before them, out into less crowded space, then straight toward the convoy.

Wicca quickly gained a significant fraction of lightspeed. The small fighters fell after her, but were losing ground, unable or unwilling to match velocities. Joclen hoped nothing would force her to turn now. Without the translight envelope, the torque would sheer off parts of *Wicca.*

A large shape appeared ahead and to the right, a big mass, dark and swift. She calculated their convergence quickly.

They were falling toward the shallow border of the system. She gave up any attempt to hide or mask their presence.

A bolt of brilliant blue-white streaked across their path. The heat washed over their sensors and Joclen winced. The converging ship fired again, closer. Warning shots, she realized. They wanted *Wicca* intact if possible.

Velocity jumped again. Joclen felt, at the same time, vulnerable and completely in control.

She changed vector, a small change, not even a full degree, but Joclen "felt" the stresses throughout the ship. Things gave way, braces collapsed, the hull seemed to tighten from the forces squeezing it. A quick diagnostic told her the motiles could manage repairs easily. Then she noticed that all the shields were up. Not projected outward to fend off incoming debris, but inverted, directed at the hull itself, through it, and within, a close field of projection that acted as an underskin of immense durability. The stresses from the turn suffused the shields, bled off—not completely, no, but enough to keep *Wicca* from crumbling like the fragile eggshell she was.

They shot by the warship and caught it in their wake. It should have had no effect at all, except the shields suddenly reversed again just as they approached it and caught it in a gentle brush stroke that spun the big ship around, like a leaf in a storm.

They left the system, shooting out from the plane of the ecliptic and achieving transition speed. The envelope surrounded them and they fell into interstellar space at translight velocity.

Good flying, Pilot Bramus, Stoan said.

Yes, it was, she returned. *Traville, what was that maneuver with the shields?*

Something I picked up along the way, he returned.

Good move. Next time, though, let me know what you're going to do, she said. Still, she was glad he had done it. The vector change had been a necessary gamble, but she would never have thought of using the shields that way.

Tamyn had an excellent crew.

Tamyn opened her eyes to a different room. She was in a comfortable bed. Sunlight splintered through louvers and dappled the deep green carpet; a table with chairs, a couch, two easy chairs, a couple of abstract pictorials completed the furnishings.

Tamyn's skin felt too tight, the way her skull felt when she concentrated too long and hard on one thing. The pains of her wounds lingered, but faintly. Cautiously she pushed herself up in bed.

A door appeared in the opposite wall and Moss Fisher entered.

"Well, well," he said. "May I sit?"

Tamyn did not know what to say. She stared at him with growing revulsion. He shrugged and sat on the couch.

"You'll be fully recovered in a few days," he said. "Recovered enough to travel, anyway."

"Travel where?"

"Ah. You can still speak. I will probably always wonder if you'd have bitten your tongue out in time, too."

Tamyn tried to get out of bed. Her legs did not respond. She looked down at them with an intense sense of betrayal.

"Neural blocks," Fisher said. "I didn't quite trust you to be civilized. Interesting fighting style you have. Where did you learn it?"

"What was the purpose of that exercise?"

"Oh, manifold. I learned a great deal from that. My predecessor never appreciated the full potential of the isolation cells. He just used them to torment people."

"You use them to learn."

"Yes. For instance, I learned your limits of concentration. I learned a great deal about how you cope with despair. I learned whether or not you'll kill. I learned how far you have to be pushed before you do. You're a very rational person, Glass. You expect rationality from those around you. Your companion was completely irrational, there was never a possibility of reasoning with him. He'd been kept in isolation for about two years."

Completely irrational, she thought. You don't understand as much as you think you do, Commander Moss Fisher.

"Why?" she asked.

"He was political."

Tamyn frowned. "Who isn't?"

Fisher's eyebrows went up. "Ah. I've learned something else now."

"I doubt that."

"You also expect justice."

"Doesn't everybody?"

Fisher shrugged. "It's an arguable point. Perhaps. The naïve actually believe they can get it. Are you naïve, Glass?" He leaned forward, hands folded on his knees. "Where are you from?"

Tamyn looked away from him, to the window and the pleasant sunlight. He pressured her. His presence was insistent. He also possessed the luxury of control.

"Travel to where? Where am I going?"

"Questions answered with questions. You're not a pirate. Not like any I've seen, anyway. Doesn't matter what you learn now, you won't remember it later anyway. I'm sending you to Peace."

She looked at him. He frowned.

"You don't know Peace?"

"What kind of peace?"

He sat back. "My, my. I wanted to know where you were from and now I've learned. Where did you learn your sense of ethics?"

Tamyn was growing irritated now. She thought it through as best she could. It had been easily fifteen to twenty days since her capture. If they had found *Wicca* Fisher probably would not be wasting his time with her. In fact, she would probably be dead. A reaction now might be useful.

She looked at him. "In the Reaches."

"The—where?"

"Now I know where you're from."

He looked baffled for a moment, then angry.

Tamyn smiled. "The Seven Reaches, out beyond the Distal Colonies. Among the seti."

For a few moments he still looked puzzled. Then his eyes widened slightly and he seemed to lose a little color.

"That's impossible," he said.

"Where did you think I was from? You said you knew."

"I thought—" He stood abruptly and headed for the door. "This is better than I expected. You've given me something, Glass, that...anyway, it has been interesting knowing you. I'll be seeing you again, later, on Peace. But for now, good-bye."

He left the room.

Later four people in white uniforms entered. The neural blocks robbed her of her arms and they lifted her from bed and placed her on a gurney.

Outside were pale corridors. People spoke in hushed monotones, consulted each other briefly, and parted quickly. There was a sense of urgency, expectation, work all around. It felt very much like a med facility.

The gurney rounded a corner into a broader area and she saw Moss Fisher speaking to two people, a man and a woman, who were dressed differently. They wore bright colors, cut with obvious luxury, and when they looked at her she saw distant coldness in their eyes. Under their gaze she felt more like an object than she had ever felt before. Aristocracy, she thought, they must be, that must be what it looks like...

Fisher glanced at her, said something to them, and stepped alongside the gurney as it went past the two aristocrats.

"You'll enjoy this trip, Glass," Fisher said. "You're going to lose your mind on it. Most of it, anyway. Don't worry, you won't miss it much." He patted her lifeless hand; she was glad she could not feel his touch. He left then, and walked off with the pair of aristocrats.

They went down another corridor.

Benajim Cyanus walked by. He looked at her curiously, as if he had never seen her before and wondered what was wrong with her. Then he was gone and she wondered if it had been a hallucination. She gnawed her lip and thought about Fisher's claim.

She knew she was on board a ship. She could sense it. They had brought her aboard asleep, lifted off before waking her, but she knew anyway.

But other things were hazy, unclear. People moved in and out of her view, doing things with the equipment surrounding her, attaching things to her. The neural blocks were still in place so she could feel almost none of it, but something was different.

She caught herself staring at a piece of equipment. She should know what that is. It confused her. So familiar, yet...

Losing your mind.

Fisher's voice rang in her head.

She screamed.

She watched her memories being pared away, layer by layer. She figured out what they were doing just in time to forget it. They were placing blocks on synapses, closing off access to various memory nodes in her mind. Piece by piece they closed her off to herself.

This is what happened to Benajim, she thought.

Then: *Who's Benajim?*

I am Tamyn Fitzgerald Glass, Shipmaster of...Shipmaster...I am Tamyn Glass. I know that. I was born...Shipmaster...Tamyn Glass...

I'm frightened.

She was being drowned in forgetfulness. The waters of Lethe, easing away the sorrows and burdens of an overfull soul...

I am Tamyn Glass. Tamyn Glass.

Submerged.

Sean, what have you sent me into? I buried you like you asked, now get me out of here. I'm in your will. I am...Tamyn Glass...

Where have I been? Where have I gone?

I don't remember.

She drooled. She was embarrassed, but she did not know why. Someone wiped her face for her.

I am...someone...

The drool mingled with her tears. Someone wiped both of them.

The cobblestone street was lined with pleasant two story houses with fences and gardens. It looked like something out of ancient history, part of the stories her father used to tell her. When she thought of him she felt a warm glow inside and a smile came to her face.

Her thoughts were muzzy, indistinct. She was sleepy. They had released her from hospice this morning and told her to take her pills every few hours to keep the pain away. She could go home, they said, but she was not sure where home was.

People worked in their yards, a few waved to her. They moved carefully, intently.

Ahead, a carrier turned onto the street. She stopped and watched it approach. One of its turbines whined sorrowfully, out of tune. A redbearded man drove. He set the carrier down a few meters before her. She watched him anxiously. He stepped from the carrier, his hands out from his sides, and a quiet smile on his weatherworn face.

"My name's Ryan Jones," he said. He spoke Langish, but with an odd accent. His voice was a pleasant baritone. "You look a bit lost. Can I help?"

"I, uh...can't seem to recall where my..." She chewed her lip uncertainly. She wanted to trust him. Her head pounded and her thoughts were confused. Information floated randomly through her head, unattached to anything meaningful.

"I'll handle this, Jones."

A shorter man, dark-haired, with a round face that matched his overall heaviness, stepped off the sidewalk behind her. She backed away a few steps.

"My name is Del Robello," he said, holding his hands up and gently patting the air as if to calm her. "I'm the Interface representative in the community-at-large. I want to welcome you to Peace."

She glanced left and right, as if looking for a place to run. That did not seem correct, though. What was there to run from? The other people along the street had stopped to watch.

Robello moved closer. She sidestepped him, moving toward Ryan. Robello frowned.

"Would you like to come to my place?" Ryan asked. "It's out from town a ways. It's quiet, you can sort things out there."

"You're interfering, Jones," Robello said.

"Hey, look, Del, things can be scary first day out, you know that. I'll take her to my place, get her away from the crowds."

"I think it would be best if she stayed in town."

She edged closer to Ryan. A few people left the sidewalks and began gathering behind Robello, who did not see them.

"Why?" Ryan asked. "Something special about this one? Interface ask you to watch her?"

"This isn't any of your business, Jones," Robello said and stepped toward her. He lunged for her, missed, and smiled testily.

"You're throwing your weight around again, Robello," a woman said.

He noticed the gathered crowd then and turned a full circle, glaring at them.

"This is an Interface matter," he said.

"Bullshit!" the woman who had spoken first snapped. She stepped up to him and jabbed a finger at him. "Mind your own business, Robello. She wants to be with Ryan, leave her alone. She's old enough to make her own choices. Hell, we're all old enough!"

Laughter peppered the air.

Robello reddened. "Now, look!" He made another grab for her.

Ryan pulled her behind him and stuck out a foot. Robello caught it and fell headlong to the cobblestones, landing with a grunt. Quickly, Ryan turned and ushered her into the carrier. He jumped behind the controls and played with them, cursing softly at the complaining turbine. The machine lifted off the ground and he backed it away.

Robello sat in the street, nursing his left arm, while the crowd gathered around him, loudly chastising him for being nosey, officious, pompous—then the transport carried them out of hearing range, and turned a corner.

Her head throbbed.

"You look like you could use a nap," Ryan said. "We'll be at my place soon enough. Relax. Welcome to Peace."

"Thanks," she said. This is exciting, she thought. Then: who am I?

Chapter Sixteen

Twenty-two billion people lived within Tabit Freeroamer Orbital. Leris op Elen dropped the number casually, just another fact, equal to any other, as she guided them through local precincts. Wasting time while Leris op Jary went through the complex process of petitioning Orbital Oversite for the hearings.

As they stepped out on a long walkway, Piper asked, "What's the population of the planet?"

"About eight billion."

Benajim leaned on the railing above a farm. Tiered platens tended by people and machines jammed a space that stretched away to a vanishing point.

"Is all your production used here?" he asked.

"There are surpluses," Elen said. Her optil glimmered. "With the Circumvention, there are few outlets for export. I don't have numbers, but several commodities no longer ship at levels before Ryna took the Merrick trade."

"But other items have increased?" Benajim asked.

"I don't have numbers."

"What do you do with the surplus?"

"Store it."

Benajim turned to her. "Why not cut production?"

Elen gave him a dubious look. "What would these workers do? They must eat."

"You just said you have surpluses."

"So we give them the surpluses? Immoral." She turned before he could respond and walked off.

"Touchy subject," Piper commented.

"Doesn't make sense."

They caught up to Elen in an ascending corridor.

"What brought on the Circumvention," Benajim asked.

"Directorate arrogance," Elen snapped. "Homestead encroached our markets. Protest went to the Forum and the Chairman. We were told that Homestead had precedence as one of the Primary Twelve. That was foolish. We are Primary Twelve. We knew it was only because Homestead owned more reps in the Forum. We pressed our protest. Then, when nothing was done, we declared that any Homestead merchanter caught invading Tabit markets without Tabit licensing would be taken. The Forum censured us and the Circumvention came."

"How long ago was that?" Piper asked.

"Sixty years."

"Negotiation hasn't resolved anything?"

Elen shot her an odd look. "No negotiation. They refuse. We no longer exist to them."

"But you keep taking shiploads of goods," Benajim said. "How do they explain that?"

"I don't know. No one cares. When the Directorate recognize us, we'll negotiate. Until then—"

"Until then you live in a devastating population-resource spiral," Piper said. She looked at Benajim. "I studied this sort of thing. With no outlets to production, a negative feedback loop establishes itself as production outstrips demand, surplus stockpiles, and no mechanism is in place to curb the one or absorb the other. You end up starving in the midst of plenty."

Elen frowned at her.

Benajim said, "So what happens when the Directorate gets tired of you stealing ships from the trade lanes?"

"We never steal."

"Appropriate for use, then. I don't care what you call it, you're irritating them. What happens when they've had enough?"

"I don't know." She shrugged. "They have done nothing yet."

"Any idea why?"

"Machines. The Directorate has plenty of machines." She looked at him. "It would cost them more to acknowledge our existence and try to stop us than the ships and cargos cost."

"Hmm."

They exited the corridor on one of the main residential circuits. The walls on both sides were mosaics of windows and doors. Down the center ran an electromagnetic rail system. At irregular intervals the overhead lights had gone out, leaving stretches of twilight along the length of the circuit.

Elen turned right and crossed the track. A few people nodded at her, one called a greeting to which she waved back. After thirty meters she went through a curtained doorway. Benajim had to duck under the low arch.

The corridor was barely two meters wide and jammed with people. Benajim reached behind him to take Piper's hand, but she did not take his. He glanced back and saw her keeping up, face determined.

The passageway split in three directions—straight ahead angled up, and two new corridors went left and right. Elen took the left. The crowd thinned. Benajim smelled sweet, narcotic smoke, a bluish pall clouding the dim light. Presently the corridor opened into a circular plaza about twenty meters across. Lamps hung on the walls with live flames in them, casting oily orange light through time-stained glass. People clustered in small groups. Several watched Benajim and Piper as they crossed the space to one of eight doorways set in the wall.

A black field covered the entrance. For the fraction of a second it took to pass through, Benajim was blind. He emerged in a dark room about five or six meters wide.

On a raised dais a dancer spun through impossible gyrations. Colored laser light whipped about the slender, sexless body, striking the mylar sheathing the dancer wore. In each hand a silver sash lashed in an intricate choreography of counterpoint to the facile contortions of the performer. The dancer stood in one spot, never moving from that center, and undulated to a breakneck rhythm.

Around the stage Benajim saw a few faces, one or two optils catching stray light. A couple of people entered the chamber after them. Elen motioned for him to sit on the pillows beside her. He lowered himself, unwilling to take his eyes from the dancer. Elen's hand rested briefly on his thigh.

Someone handed him a glass from behind. He sipped the sweet liquid absently. The performance went on for several minutes. At first, it seemed changeless, the same series of movements repeated over and over. Gradually, Benajim noticed that modifications slipped in, variations took over, the set movements repeated more as refrains than theme, and by the time the dance ended it was entirely different.

The dancer snapped into a final position. Benajim waited for the collapse or explosion from the backlash of instantly stopping so much energy, but the dancer held position perfectly. The music gave a last bar and crashed to silence.

The audience sighed loudly in applause. The dancer straightened, smiled 'round at everyone, and left the stage. Quieter music came up and a whirl of holographic abstracts took the dancers' place, to which no one paid any attention. A few people left.

Piper leaned across Benajim and touched Elen's leg. "We've been followed since we left your dom."

Elen frowned and Piper indicated by a nod two men across the room. She bowed her head for a few seconds, her optil shifting.

"Cletus's people," Elen said. "Jary is progressing. Your hearing is scheduled."

"Are we in any danger?"

"Always," Elen said. She smiled reassuringly. "But I think nothing will happen till after the challenge is presented. Ignore them." She waved around. "All this I've shown you is Leris Clade dependency. The idleness has worsened gradually since Merrick's trade shifted to Ryna." She looked at Piper. "We do not allow starvation. But each clade must care for its own."

"Am I supposed to feel more responsible?" Benajim asked.

"No. More informed. It's best to know all possible consequences of decisions."

Benajim caught her eye. "I don't intend to damage anything that doesn't require it."

She smiled briefly.

"Information is never worthless," she said. "I thought you should see."

"So if we restore the traffic to Leris Clade," Piper said, "all these people go back to work?"

"Many. Maybe all. With the loss of employment from the interface directly, many ancillary activities ended. I—" She stopped abruptly and gazed off. Her optil glowed while her natural eye almost closed. In a few seconds, she sighed and her eyelid came back up. "Mmm."

"What—?" Benajim began to ask, then a movement caught his attention. The pair of shadows had risen and now left the club.

"We should continue," Elen said, standing. Something in her face had changed, but Benajim could not read it.

Benajim and Piper followed her from the theater. As they left the cul de sac Benajim glanced around, but he saw nothing of the tail.

Elen took them to another connecting circuit, then onto a public platform where she accessed a private shunt.

She sat close to the control panel and touched a contact. A pale reddish beam shot into her false eye for a moment, then the shunt began to move.

"Cletus," she said, "is competing to be chosen successor to the Chairman of Orbital Oversite. The man holding that position now is Colis op Ulor. He and Cletus have been rivals for decades. Your presence creates the possibility of upsetting Cletus's position. Should he lose the traffic from the C.R. he will lose the advantage to become Chairman." She hesitated. "Before the traffic changed hands, Jary was in line to be Chairman. Ulor has been reluctant to decide. He preferred Jary to Cletus on several grounds, but resource is paramount. Your coming has revived Jary's chances."

"If we restore the trade to Leris Clade, Jary stands to be head of Tabit Freeroamer?"

Elen nodded. "That choice could still be overturned by a caucus of other clademasters. Cletus has been building influence with them. It may not be enough. You are a problem for Cletus."

Piper asked, "What qualifies someone to be Chairman? That is, if the succession is left undecided by the current Chairman."

"Reputation. How much they provide on a hunt. Status among their immediate clients."

"When a hunter takes a Directorate ship is there some central receiving area where it's brought to?"

"No. Each hunter maintains warehouses, docks, distribution centers."

"Just out of curiosity," Piper continued, "what is it about Cletus that bothers you? I mean, besides being head of a competing clade. Would he be a bad leader?"

"He favors initiating negotiations with the Directorate. He claims to have a way to do it, but he never discusses it."

"Wouldn't that be convenient," Piper commented. "The clade dealing with Merrick, opening trade with the Pan...Cletus could end up owning Tabit."

"Perhaps," Elen said, nodding. She glanced at the control panel. "Ah. Our stop."

The car slowed, then came to a halt with a heavy jerk. The hatch opened outward.

They stepped from the shunt onto the soft surface of an open field. Above, fibrous clouds streaked pale blue sky. Clusters of trees and bushes punctuated the slightly rolling landscape. Elen was halfway to a brook.

"Impressive," Piper said.

"Expensive," Benajim added.

When they caught up with her, Elen stood at the bank of the pleasantly noisy stream.

"This is one of the compounds of the clademasters," she said. She stared across the stream. Benajim thought he saw a flash of light. Directly opposite, on the far side of the water, a vertical seam appeared, then widened into a doorway. A walkway extruded across the brook.

Elen led them into a small, spartan compartment. The light was soft. An L-shaped couch faced a hulking mass that resembled a polycom. Two doors opened off of the main room.

"The cubicles are for common use," she said, "although few know they exist. This area is maintained by Pelas Clade, friends of Leris. This place is for your use."

Elen faced the polycom. A series of wire-thin pulses passed between her optil and the console. The light brightened a bit, changed hue to a gentle yellow tint. A countertop extruded from one wall; music began to play, a low, sonorous melody.

"You're hiding us," Piper said.

"The next hours are high risk," Elen said. "Actions might be taken against you. Once Ulor decides..."

She left the sentence hang unfinished. Then: "Are you hungry? Thirsty? We're now completely screened from eavesdropping, too."

Elen leaned back and gazed at the ceiling thoughtfully. "We didn't tell you any of this at first because we wanted you to acquire a sense of Tabit. Power is a slippery thing, especially when you don't understand the pathways it travels."

Benajim leaned forward on the couch. "Cletus's claim about opening negotiations with the Directorate—why doesn't anyone investigate that?"

"This is not a popular idea," Elen said, nodding. "But no one questions him because no one believes he can do it. The Directorate has no reason to acknowledge us."

"Unless Cletus is already doing business with the Directorate," Piper said.

Elen nodded. "We thought at first that you might be from the Directorate, hence the initial challenge to your ship."

"If we had been, our purpose in a visit would be to...?" Benajim asked.

"Study weakness, ascertain Ryna Clade's dependability."

"But we came in Merrick's ship."

"That weighed in your favor with Leris Clade and with Orbital Oversite. Otherwise, you would be dead."

Benajim sat back, letting that idea wash through him. He cleared his throat. "Ulor distrusts Cletus. It can't be simply because of the trade with the C.R. since he favored Jary. We're getting a hearing, you said, which surprises me a little. I didn't expect that so soon. Ulor is moving this along quickly. There has to be something else. A reason Cletus is a viable threat and a problem for Ulor."

"You see a great deal very quickly." Elen was silent for a long time, her expression unreadable. "The traffic Ryna Clade sends to the C.R. does not all originate here. Cletus has another source."

"He hunts well, you said."

"But no hunter can guarantee his take every time," Elen said. "Cletus seems to know when he goes out what he will find in the caravans."

"He's being fed information," Piper said. "He's already in contact with the Directorate."

"Or some faction within it," Benajim said.

"Does it matter? It's illegal."

"But no one will challenge it," Benajim said, "because it's also profitable."

"Disruption now is the only way Jary can succeed," Elen said.

"What," Piper asked, "will Jary do about Cletus's contact with the Directorate?"

"End it."

"Really? Why not take it over?"

"Jary is honorable—"

"And he steals," Benajim said. "On the hunt. Just like everyone else on Tabit. Which I suppose makes him a model citizen. The question that you want answered is whether he'll keep the Directorate at arm's length. The trouble with that is, they may already be

here, at Cletus's invitation, which means Jary will have to throw them
out. He may not want to. But any choice is going to have to include
coming to terms with what Cletus is actually doing. I can tell you
about the people he apparently is dealing with. That's a start. That's
part of what Sean wanted me to do anyway." Benajim gave her a
mischievous smile. "How close am I?"
		Elen laughed harshly. "Truth for truth?"
		Benajim started, surprised. "Then time is endless."
		"You seem to know us better than we know ourselves."
		Yes, Benajim thought, but how? The phrase was Akaren. But
he had never been...

		Benajim lay on the couch, his temples throbbing from a nascent
headache. Hours of talk and argument fueled the pressure. He
pretended to sleep, but his thinking roiled excitedly.
		Their hearing before Orbital Oversight had been canceled. Jary
arrived with the news. Benajim got the sense that this was not in
itself a bad thing, that at this point his personal testimony meant
little. Events had taken a different tack.
		The politics were hopelessly complicated. Jary and Elen had
patiently tried to explain the interconnections, but it became obvious that understanding required living in Tabit Freeroamer Orbital. Piper hammered at it longer than he. She insisted that it
make sense. Benajim admired her perseverance, but his own limits
had been reached and passed.
		"Cletus distributes goods throughout the orbital," Jary had ex-
plained. "He buys surpluses and in return provides commodities
we do not produce."
		"No one has bothered to ask where he gets them?" Piper asked.
		"Most assume from the same sources as I and a score of
other hunters."
		"But you don't conduct trade. Cletus obviously does."
		"No one asks."
		"Why not?"
		"We need what he provides."
		"So you don't question the source. He threatens the power
base here, but because he does so with essential goods you look
the other way."
		"We would challenge him regardless," Jary insisted, "with proof."

"Proof that the traffic will not end?"

Jary spread his hands, conceding the point. "We are a practical people. If the trade in fact continues, even shifting to Leris Clade..." Benajim wondered why someone did not simply kill Cletus. The trade route might end completely in that case. No, that would not do.

But it was unclear why Cletus would want to risk Tabit's reabsorption into the Pan by opening negotiations with the Directorate. Unless he expected to come out at the head of any such repatriation. And Carson Reiner? Siding with Cletus and handing Tabit back to the Directorate, she could have the border restrictions modified. She could pursue almost unlimited trade throughout the Pan Humana and herself become a principle force within the C.R. Between Reiner and the Directorate, Tabit could become a captured prize to be carved up for mutual profit.

Carson Reiner would be the first generation of a new oligarchy, what in the Pan was known as Primary Vested...

Did Cletus believe himself clever enough to use Carson Reiner and avoid the trap? Perhaps he thought Tabit would continue on as the exclusive pipeline between the C.R. and the Directorate. Benajim was willing to bet, though, that Reiner would be offered a better arrangement directly with the Pan, cutting Tabit out of the loop, and the price of admission into that club would be the betrayal of Tabit to its political death.

The rest of the answers were in the Directorate, with whomever was in contact with Cletus. Or Reiner. Earth.

Bits of the discussion chased each other around Benajim's brain. Eventually he slept. His dreams were vague forms that refused to coalesce into anything identifiable. He came awake slowly, to a pleasant pressure on his chest and around his neck.

He opened his eyes. Elen leaned over him, gently massaging him.

"Sorry," he said. "I was tired."

"The others are asleep now," she said. She ran a fingertip over his forehead. "Arrangements are made. We have time for a different dialogue...if you wish, if you trust..."

Benajim swallowed. Tingly warmth spread through his torso. The possibilities latent in the next decision made him anxious. Hesitantly, he reached up and touched her cheek. "Yes..."

She took his hand and pulled him up. He followed her to the door on the left. It opened on a short hallway. At the end there were three more doors, one facing them, the others facing each other on left and right. She opened the one directly ahead.

The room was dimly-lit. To the left was a hygiene cubicle, directly opposite the door a wardrobe. Immediately to the right was a curtained area.

Elen drew aside the curtains to reveal a long shelf, belly-height. She climbed in, gesturing for Benajim to follow.

It was a broad, low-ceilinged chamber, high enough to sit up in, too low to stand. Benajim heaved himself over the lip.

Elen wriggled out of her clothes. Benajim watched, fascinated. The horizontal lines on her face continued on down the right side of her body, both front and back. Her ribs showed in deep relief. Her breasts were small and high. The muscles of her belly rippled sinuously as she twisted out of her clothes. The body decor switched sides at her hips and red rings covered her left leg.

Benajim hesitated until she raised her eyebrows. Then he undressed. He wondered if she found his undecorated body less attractive or more. She watched him closely, her mouth twitching in a nervous smile. When he was naked she offered her hand. He took it and she pulled him to her.

It was over very quickly. She seemed to draw him in. It shocked him for an instant; it felt as if he had entered her before he reached her and suddenly he was deep inside her. Then his entire body clenched in orgasm. He exhaled explosively. Her hands ran up and down his back, his buttocks, his arms. He continued thrusting, but lost his rhythm several times as though she moved in intentional asymmetry. He gave up finally and let her dictate the motion. It was strange—her hips and belly moved against him in one cadence, but he slid back and forth within her in another.

She gripped him powerfully. Her mouth opened wide as her head arched back. Soundlessly, she came.

Slowly, she relaxed, and sighed. He kissed her chin, her neck, the point where her jaw met her ear.

Body art smeared along her stomach. A red streak crossed her navel. He touched her labia and felt for her clitoris. As his fingers brushed the opening of her vagina, it seemed to retract.

"It isn't finished," she whispered.

Elen grasped his penis gently and ran her thumb up and down its underside until it became erect. Then she straddled him. He looked down. As he watched, a moist, fleshy tube extruded from between her legs. A mouth opened wide at its end and surrounded the tip of his penis. A moment later it engulfed the whole shaft. Benajim lay back, shaken by the sight and electrified by the sensation.

Her vagina sucked at him.

His body shivered, his eyes closed, his thighs tightened.

He opened his eyes again and saw Elen above him, the colors on her body running together. She leaned down and kissed his neck, collarbone, chest, and smiled at him.

Exhausted, Benajim's breath came heavy, and he was covered in sweat. He ran his fingers over her torso, her breasts, down her belly. He found a raised patch, about five centimeters long, on the underside of each breast. When he touched them she sucked her breath in, shuddering. He found another pair on either side of her navel, and a third set on her inner thighs, close to her pelvis. Each patch produced an exhalation of pleasure when caressed. He sat up, placed an arm around her lower back, and eased her onto her back. He kissed and licked at the patches, gradually increasing pressure, amazed at the reactions. Elen squirmed, panted, laughed. ("How do you go through a day with those? Aren't you stimulated constantly?" "They only emerge when I'm aroused...") Her prehensile vagina pulled at his penis until he moved down to the patches on her thighs; she stroked his face with it then, filling his nostrils with her pungent musk. He took the vagina in his hand and squeezed gently. Elen arched upward against him. Benajim ran his tongue around the rim of the vaginal mouth; the organ vibrated in response. He looked at her and saw a startled expression on her face. Her mouth was open, her chest heaved. Benajim took the vagina in his mouth; Elen's eye closed and her head went back. Her body shook. She wrapped her legs around his head. Benajim drew on the salty-sweet organ while she rubbed her thigh patches against his ears.

Suddenly she seized up. Her hands clutched his forearms. Her body strained, riding the orgasm.

She relaxed. Her vagina withdrew. Benajim examined it closely. It resembled an unmodified genital now.

Elen pulled him up and hugged him. She kissed his face, then lay back and fell asleep.

Benajim stared at her, amazed. The impressions that chased each other through his mind, centering on Elen now like an anchor, seemed at once familiar and alien.

"Benajim."

He opened his eyes. It was nightcycle, the domicile was dark.

"Benajim, it's Piper. We have to go."

He sat up. Piper wore black, neck to foot.

"Put these on," she said, unrolling a bundle on his pallet.

Unquestioning, Benajim slipped into the oversized black togs.

Outside, Elen led them out of the arboretum, down the shunt tracks to an access set into the ground. She descended the stairs into a dark passage, lit intermittently by old panels, to an ancient shunt that smelled of oil and musty disuse.

"Where are we going?" Benajim asked.

"Things have gone wrong," Elen said. "Jary's challenge has been met with rejection. Cletus has threatened to withdraw from Orbital Oversite and sever his clade from Tabit."

Benajim looked at Piper, who shrugged.

"We have recruited supporters among the independent clades," Elen said. "Several of Cletus's agents have been taken and interrogated. Reprisals have already taken place. It may not be safe for you to stay anymore."

"But—" Piper began.

"We have what we need from you. Cletus's reaction has demonstrated his culpability. We succeed or fail now on our own."

"We're not done here," Piper said. "Unless Jary has the all proof he needs."

Elen remained silent and engaged the shunt. The walls vibrated delicately, a low howling just beyond them. Elen continued her silence and kept her eyes on the small screen at the head of the shunt that displayed position.

The shunt carried them for several minutes before it began to slow and finally come to a halt. Elen went to the hatch and motioned them to stay back. She left for a few seconds, then returned and waved them after her.

Benajim noticed a difference immediately in the very feel of the place. Supports, struts, and braces defined the shape of a vast, complex area; the sharp, even sounds of machinery dominated, and the air was full of metallic and electric odors. Bright lights stabbed through the darkness here and there, leaving dark spaces between harsh oases of brilliance.

Elen kept them to the shadows. At one point they crossed over a grate. Benajim looked down through the loose mesh into a cavernous drop between walls of metal and through a maze of cables and conduit. He swallowed and forced his gaze up, straight ahead, into the next patch of darkness.

A small light flicked on. Elen ran the beam of her lamp around them, found a ladder, and motioned them up.

Benajim climbed quickly until he ran out of ladder. He stepped off onto a narrow walkway. Piper came next, then Elen. She switched off her light. A pale yellow glow gave the walkway a vague definition. Benajim could see Elen as a shadowy outline. She pointed direction and nudged them forward.

The walkway ended in a cramped observation blister. Dust and grime coated the transparency and the small room was made smaller by stacked boxes and furniture and equipment.

"You require the proof now," Elen said. "Then you must leave Tabit." Elen wiped soot from their view. "Down there."

Below was a wide loading dock. Conveyors entered the area from the left, out of their field of vision. Crates and nacelles moved along them to where crews—humans in exoskeleton multipliers—took them to be stacked on the dock for others to carry them to a warehouse that defined the far right limit of what they saw. Benajim counted perhaps fifty people working.

"Cletus owns this area," Elen said.

"Ben," Piper whispered, "those nacelles..."

"They look like C.R. manufacture. Can we get a look at the ship they're coming from?"

"Through here," Elen said, and shoved a stack aside to reveal the opposite doorway.

The walkway was jammed with discarded junk. Benajim wondered if they ever threw anything away here, but said nothing as he worked his way around the obstacles.

The walkway ended at a heavy hatch that stood open. They entered a long chamber that was less cluttered. Elen switched on her light and picked out the details of an exterior access room; environment suits hung in racks against one wall, facing a row of consoles and screens. At the far end, to the right, was an airlock.

Elen tried to close the door, but the controls were useless. "Let's see if the monitors work," Benajim said.

Most of the consoles seemed powerless. Two of them activated, though, and Benajim held the light while Elen worked the controls. One of the screens flickered on. It showed a large patch of star-filled black and a smooth horizon line of station surface. A camera number appeared on the console. She tried other camera codes. Three more screens winked to life, but the first one cut out.

"How often do you do maintenance on these systems?" Piper asked facetiously.

"We don't," Elen said. "This section is technically vacuum. It took a hit many years ago from a raider. No regular maintenance is scheduled at all."

"Then Cletus—"

"Is using this facility secretly." She looked up at them, her optil catching light from the screens. "It's an open secret among the clademasters. Ulor knows, and obviously Jary and I know. Several others. But it hasn't been...expedient...to expose Cletus. No one would oppose him in this openly."

On two of the screens were different views of the same thing. A huge merchanter hung snug to the torn open wall of the station by four large umbilicals. Dangling inside the ripped section Benajim made out the misshapen remnants of berthing cradles and service cables. The umbilicals were retrofits, bypassing all the normal, now-useless docking mechanisms.

"That's a Mirak Corporation ship," Piper said.

"How much comes in this way?" Benajim asked.

"A ship like this arrives every eight days," she said. "Sometimes two of them."

"Laden with what?"

Elen shrugged. "Cybernetic components, fabrics, exotic foods. Much goes directly to Tabit Prime, we never see it. We couldn't steal Directorate ships as easily until we began receiving new code and the tools to implement it. Nothing we haven't benefited by."

"All right," Benajim said. "We've identified that as a C.R. ship. What else?"

Elen tapped instructions into another panel. A second screen flickered on, showing a different ship.

"That looks like one of those big Pan merchanters," Benajim said. He pointed. "But what's that?"

A dark shape drifted near the mass of the merchanter. Elen enlarged the image. A sleek, black-skinned ship hung fifty meters off the merchanter's bow.

"Armada," Elen said. "Directorate." She looked at them. "Now you must leave. Come."

Elen stepped back into the first observation blister. As Piper entered she looked down on the scene below and stopped.

"Wait." She pointed. "Those two."

A pair of men were following another across the dock.

"Who are they?" Benajim asked.

Piper smiled thinly. "Proof positive. That's Bris Calenda and his prophylactic." She looked at Elen. "How do I get down there?"

"Who's—?" Benajim started.

"I wouldn't recommend going—" Elen said.

Piper raised a hand. "It's necessary. Show me the way down."

Elen gestured for them to follow. "This way."

Piper looked back up the length of the lift shaft. Light from Benajim's lamp split and splintered through the thick cables, splashed against grimy walls. The air smelled of mold and machine oil. Piper stood on top of the car amid a thicket of chaotically tangled cable, the bulk of which leaned against the sealed doors.

She pulled at the cable and a pile of it fell, twisting out of her grasp to crash against the opposite wall. The impact echoed up the shaft.

Piper switched on her own lamp and traced the outlines of the doors. The bottom ledge was hip level. Piper aimed her light upward and flashed it twice, then turned it off to wait while Elen tried to activate the door controls from above.

The low hum of power through servos filled the darkness. Piper tensed. The sound grew louder for a moment, then died. A second later it came again, followed by a sharp metallic crack and the rattle of bearings on plastic. The doors lurched apart. Piper stepped back. The rattle stopped, the doors parted only half a meter. The electric hum continued for a few more seconds, then ended. She flashed her light upward once more: okay.

Piper peered through the opening. A bare wall was directly across from her. To the right it grew darker; to the left was brighter. Piper amped and filtered her hearing, occluding the loud noise of heavy dockwork and sorting through what remained. The articulated sounds of the exoskeletons mingled with the softer human sounds, voices, clothes shifting, footsteps.

She pulled herself through and scurried to the far wall. There the light was broken by angular shadows. Piper moved silently to the end of the wall, where a short gangway led directly to the dock proper.

Jagged clusters of twisted metal and plastic blocked the exit. Piper cursed and stepped up to the barrier.

Through the cracks and crevices of the debris Piper looked across the scarred deck of the bay. There was a slight warp to the entire floor and the workers in their multipliers cast insect shadows that rippled over the frozen waves. Far on the opposite side huge sheets of plating had been welded in place over the ripped bulkheads. An onion-shaped portal opened into the umbilical to the merchanter. Off to the right was the warehouse. To the left the deck ended at a deep channel.

No one seemed to be near the mass of debris. Piper examined it for a way through. On her hands and knees she squeezed down a tight tunnel that constricted even more. She turned sideways and worked her way through. It widened, then narrowed again. She crawled over a sharp mass and continued on. Light filtered through the canopy of shards. She was about to give up and go back when her hand plunged down into nothing, bringing her down hard against her ribs.

When she recovered her wind, Piper shone her light down. About ten meters below the beam glinted dully off worn metal. Rails ran down the center of the wide canal. She realized then that she had reached the channel she had seen.

The mass of debris had partly spilled over the edge. It was sufficient to give her hand-and-footholds down almost halfway. She dropped the remaining distance, landed in a roll, and came up against the wall.

The channel seemed to have been part of a cargo transport system. A series of ten rails covered the floor. To her left it ran up against a door that was part way open. At the opposite end it had been sealed off with the same patchwork expertise as the rest of the bulkhead.

Ladders ran up the wall every twenty meters.

Piper stayed close to the wall and sprinted to the ladder nearest the repaired bulkhead. She climbed up and eased her head above the edge.

Two multipliers were on their way to the warehouse with their burdens. An empty one was just starting back. Three people emerged on foot from the umbilical and headed toward the warehouse.

From here she could see the row of observation booths high above and to her left where Elen and Benajim now waited. They hung in the dark above a dismaying jumble of debris that had been shoved up against that wall. Broken, shredded, bent, and mangled structures heaped high into the shadows near the ceiling. The warehouse was an enormous quonset standing against more wreckage.

It was cold here. Piper could see her breath.

The empty multiplier reached the umbilical. In the distance the other two reached the warehouse, the three men fast in their wake.

The multiplier worker wore a protective helmet and goggles, but was otherwise clothed in the same black utilities Elen had provided.

He was also not strapped securely in his seat. He rested his hands on the control gates, his legs dangled, crossed at the ankle.

Piper came over the edge, her reflexes and senses amplified, and walked matter-of-factly to the umbilical. She waved at the worker congenially, glanced up the tube and saw no one. For a few seconds they were alone.

She crossed in front of the exoskeleton. The operator did nothing different, just came ahead. He did not recognize her as other than someone who was supposed to be here.

Abruptly she changed direction, jumped straight into him. She landed with her knee in his stomach. The multiplier shuddered until she wiped his hands from the gates. He opened his mouth in pain, then. Before he screamed she crushed his larynx. She pulled his helmet and goggles off—he was very young, short, blondish hair—and put them on herself.

Piper dropped back, to the floor, and pulled him out of the seat, rested his weight over her back, and walked him to the edge of the canal. She turned and let him fall. She heard the thud just as she reached the multiplier.

Control of the machine was simple gate induction. It was not as complete an interface as the Flow, but after a few seconds she controlled it as easily as her own body.

She strode up the umbilical.

As she passed through the lock into the hold of the merchanter a heat spread through her torso, up her neck, and over her scalp: fear, excitement, the thrill generated by the mingling of the two.

"About time!" someone shouted.

Piper glanced to the right. A foreman sat behind a console, glaring at her. Six more exoskeletons waited to pass through the umbilical. There was only room for one at a time.

Inefficient, Piper thought. She moved on by the foreman. She received instructions through the gate and turned down a row of nacelles. She lifted one easily and returned to line.

A screen beside the foreman shifted through a number of scenes, both internal and external. There were two other umbilicals through which cargo passed from different holds. The scene changed to show an external view of the umbilical link to the station. The damage was even more evident. The entire section must have been collapsed. Molten surfaces butted against new sections of plating where the skin had been sheared away. This was the best lock mechanism this section of the station could provide.

Her turn came around again and she walked back into the bay.

The multipliers kept about fifteen meters between them. Piper sauntered along. Two empty exoskeletons went by.

She entered the warehouse.

Overhead, harsh lights ran down the center of the ceiling, casting deep shadows amid the stacks on both sides. Piper trailed along after the other multipliers. She queued up and left her load with the rest, then turned.

Above the doors hung a row of observation booths. The lights were on in one. Stairs ran up the wall below them. Piper walked the machine back until she was near the entrance, then stepped aside, into the aisle between stacks. At the end of the aisle, near the wall, she powered down and left the multiplier.

Piper moved purposefully to the stairs. No one was nearby. A cluster of workers lounged in the deep shadows of the stacks, but none of them seemed interested in her. She climbed the stairs.

The stairs let onto a walkway behind the offices. She looked into the first one—empty—and entered.

The room light was off; everything was illuminated by the warehouse lights. She made out a desk with a console, a pair of chairs, and a small cabinet in one corner. The warehouse stretched out below.

She amped her vision and went to the desk. The console was a comm unit of some kind. Numbered contacts ran across the face. Fifteen of them. She checked her memory and counted ten offices comprising the observation blisters. She touched the first one.

"—OVER BY BAY NINE—"

She took her finger away and the voice died. There were three verniers below the contacts. She turned them all to zero and touched the contact again. No sound. She turned up each knob until the voice returned, much quieter now.

Satisfied, she tried each of the rest. Most had nothing.

Then she hit number twelve.

"—be unwise to let anything complicate the situation."

Piper smiled. Bris Calenda possessed such a distinctive voice.

"My people are moving to contain the problem."

"Good. I hope you do. It was sloppy to let these people have such free run of the place."

"That was not my place to decide otherwise. Soon enough it will be."

"Sloppy. I don't care for sloppiness and neither will my sponsors. Our agreement with you is for exclusive trade rights."

"I was under the impression that you had the sanction of the Founder."

"So?"

"So these two have thrown some doubt on that."

"Does it matter? As long as the route remains open and business is good, do you really care with whom you're dealing?"

"As long as I'm treated honestly, no."

Calenda laughed. "Honestly? You people lie to each other so casually I'm surprised you even have a word for truth. Now. These two mustn't leave Tabit. They're trouble for us, and that means trouble for you."

"I'm not anxious for them to leave, either. It's being seen to."

"Good. I've been instructed to remain here until this problem is satisfactorily resolved."

"You don't trust me?"

"Such a question!"

Piper switched off. She went to the door and waited. Presently a number of people went by outside. She listened until she heard their steps descending the stairs. From the transparency she looked down at them. Bris Calenda and a Freeroamer were at the head of a group of six, including Calenda's prophylactic. They headed for the rear of the warehouse. Piper touched her neck; she drew a deep breath and turned away.

She returned to the multiplier and strapped in.

An explosion reverberated throughout the bay, deep and thunderous. Piper started, then touched the gate. Comm traffic frantically demanded that all exoskeletons return to the merchanter at once.

Piper walked the machine out into the main aisle. Workers were scrambling about, most heading in the general direction of the ship. Out in the bay the multipliers were all moving for the umbilical. Another explosion thundered and Piper saw debris rain onto the floor.

She turned away from the doors and strode down the aisle. A third explosion set the walls of the quonset rippling.

Hurrying toward her, the prophylactic led Cletus and Bris Calenda. Piper smiled seeing the panicked expression on Calenda's face.

The prophylactic quickened his pace to intercept her, raising a hand to gesture her aside. Piper released stims through her system. She was linked solidly with the multiplier. She issued a series of test commands to gauge response.

He came within reach.

Piper whipped an arm out and snatched him by the neck. He looked surprised, then grabbed the metal pincers to try to pry them apart. Piper raised him off the floor and held him snugly. There was no subtle way to do this. She closed the pincer. His head lolled about, blood gushing from his mouth, and his arms dropped uselessly to his sides.

She locked the multiplier in place.

Another explosion sounded. Piper unstrapped and jumped to the floor.

Calenda was staring up at his prophylactic. Cletus watched her advance, then reached inside his robe. Piper moved too fast for him to react and gripped his arm before he could withdraw it. He tensed to resist, but Piper let go, stepped back, and slammed the palm of her hand into his face. Cletus dropped, blood spreading over his chin. Piper pulled his hand from his robe and removed the pistol from unresisting fingers.

Calenda was just then starting to move away. Piper grabbed his collar. He seized her wrist. She pulled herself into him then, bringing her knee up into his groin. He swallowed his breath sharply and went to his knees.

She dragged Calenda down the narrow space between the nearby stacks. The roof flapped under a much closer blast. Piper pressed the barrel of the pistol under his chin.

"Can we be reasonable, Co Van?" he asked weakly.

"I think we're past that, Co Calenda." She smiled. "But anything's possible."

Then she was on the floor. The stacks collapsed around her as the quonset caved in. When she looked around the mess she could not find Calenda.

Cursing, she climbed out of the debris and started back for the cargo channel. Bodies littered the floor along with mangled structural fragments.

As she neared the mass of older wreckage covering the access to the shaft she had descended a white hot energy beam lanced through the air overhead and splashed against the plating. The material boiled and rippled.

"Damn!" she hissed. She sprinted the remaining distance and started heaving away at the tangled mess. Sections of the fragments fell away. The beam fired again. Piper worked frantically and finally opened a path.

She writhed through and tumbled to the floor in the corridor. The beam cracked through the air once more and she ran for the lift door.

A sickening pop was followed immediately by the sound of rushing wind. Her hair shifted. She squeezed through the opening into the lift shaft. The sound increased. Piper scrambled up the cable. Halfway up she could feel the air moving downward.

As she reached the top the roar of escaping atmosphere was starting to ascend the scale to a howling shriek.

"Close it! Close it!"

Elen worked at a console nearby. The lift doors slid shut behind Piper.

"What in hell happened?" she demanded.

Elen looked embarrassed. "An attack. I knew nothing about it."

Piper went to the observation booth. Benajim was there, looking down on the scene.

The energy beam had punctured the bulkhead. Wreckage, cargo, people were all being swept along the whirlpool of air out the hole. The lights were failing and the entire bay flickered and flashed. Charred ruins crowded in the shadows, shifted through the momentary glimpses.

"We have to leave," Elen said.

"Absolutely," Piper agreed.

Chapter Seventeen

"I'm coming with you," Elen said.

Benajim stared at her. "But—"

"It was discussed. A decision is made. I'm a good crewhand. And when you return I can be your representative."

"We talked about this," Nois, Jary's lieutenant, said. "We decided. One of us should go with you, to represent Tabit to your people, and you to our people. Jary needs me, Tabit needs Jary."

"Which leaves me," Elen said. She smiled. "And I am not unhappy with the company I'll keep."

"We might not even get back to the C.R.," Piper said.

"Then someone else will come," Elen said.

"No time to debate this," Benajim said. "I'd be pleased to have you with us," he partly lied. He wanted her, but these conditions were hardly ideal to make such a choice. He looked at Nois. "What about my other question? The genome search—"

"We have found no record to match your DNA," Nois said. "Markers suggest you have relatives here, but you are not in our library."

Benajim tried to absorb that. *I didn't come from here...then why?*

"Move, now," Nois commanded. "And watch yourself as you pull away."

Elen led them to the vacant bay. Their boots echoed off the bare walls as they hurried to the lock. When he glanced back, Benajim saw a small knot of people, watching them. For a moment fear tightened his insides. But one of them raised an arm in salute.

"It's safe to leave," Elen said, seeing them.

Benajim went first, into the belly of *Solo.* He brushed his fingers across the gate just inside.

Company coming on board.

Welcome back. I was beginning to wonder.

Rig for escape run, full alert.

He broke off. Piper and Elen crowded in after him and the hatch closed.

With the heavy sound of the seals sliding into place, Benajim let out a relieved sigh. He was on familiar ground, home. Still, his heart raced and his nerves rode an electric edge. A step closer to safety, but not safe yet. A distant hum pervaded his awareness—*Solo* powering up, automatic systems responding to Benajim's command.

Benajim went straight to the bridge and interfaced.

I said welcome back.

Not now. Diagnostics.

Ben—

Please. Let me handle this for once. Diagnostics.

Checking. Continual monitoring, status clear, negative incursions, negative dysfunction.

Recheck, compare primary schema to current configuration, search viral restructuring.

Checking. Status clear. Configuration consistent with primary schema, negative restructure.

Scan for local traffic.

Nothing nearby. We're clear for the time being.

He withdrew. Piper was bringing Elen onto the bridge. The Freeroamer stared all around.

"Let's get situated," Benajim said. "I want to leave now."

Piper nodded and pointed Elen to a couch.

Benajim pressed his hands to his gates and flooded into *Solo's* systems.

The ship angled upward and sprung away from the surface. Benajim scanned from horizon to horizon and found no traffic.

I told you that.

Benajim turned and headed for the edge of the orbital. He rifled through comm bands until he found a few occupied; none contained any useful data. As yet it seemed that no one but Leris op Jary knew that Solo was no longer at dock.

When he reached the edge of the world he dropped down to the underside and started scanning for the merchanter.

One of my merchanters?

Not now, Sean.

Now, look—

Benajim blocked the code. It was only him and the universe for now. He picked his way through the forest of structures. He passed over a number of docks, some crammed with ships. It was a huge structure, a lot of places to hide a ship, and in the shunt he had had no sense of direction.

Far ahead a ship moved quickly away from station. Benajim locked on and trailed after it. A few moments later he knew it was the one he wanted.

The merchanter was accelerating for translight, its envelope a shimmering beacon in the distance.

Benajim changed course to pursue. He initiated *Solo's* envelope and accelerated forward.

The merchanter vanished into translight.

Solo slowed down.

Frantically, Benajim checked all his control nodes. He came up against barriers around several.

What are you doing? he demanded.

Instead of a reply more barriers appeared, cutting Benajim's access further.

He withdrew.

"What's going on?" Piper asked. "One second we're going like hell after that ship, the next—"

Benajim glared at her.

"Out," he said.

"What—?"

"Out! Off the bridge!" He jumped up and crossed to the access. "Out!" He pointed down the ramp to the common room.

"Ben—" Piper began.

Elen looked puzzled, a little fearful. Benajim looked down at the deck. "Out. Please. I need to be alone."

Piper gestured for Elen to follow her and the two walked by him. He refused to meet their eyes. Anger and humiliation mingled into nauseating uncertainty.

He turned and slapped a contact alongside the access. Heavy doors slid ponderously closed, sealing the bridge from the rest of the ship.

He went to the small projection booth.

"Sean!"

At first he thought the system had failed. Then he suspected defiance.

"Sean, damnit! Talk to me!"

The air shimmered, then, and coalesced into Merrick's wizened face.

"Now you want to talk? Come charging on board, not even a hello, nice day, how've you been, just business and don't bother me with your crap, old man. So I wait and try again, a friendly welcome aboard, and I get the cold shoulder. Well I don't have to tolerate that kind of attitude, not from you or anybody!"

"Who's in control here, you or me?"

"Right now, me! It's in the program parameters. I have to assume something's wrong if communications are closed off, and in that instance I have options, one of which is cutting you out of the control nodes and running it myself until I get some damn answers!"

The ship was alive. Benajim had known that, after a fashion, the "brain" of *Solo* mimicked Sean's persona, wove him throughout the AI aspects of its perceptual functions. Alive, for all practical purposes. Conscious. But Benajim had never fully appreciated just what that meant, never understood how close to true Life *Solo* came.

Now, though, he felt cheated. In a sense the ship was more authentic than he. *Solo,* in its limited way, knew itself. The limits were even questionable. It possessed speed, the ability to clearly and absolutely access all its components, and the certainty of its contents. Perhaps it was finite in its capacities, but it knew, and that fact seemed to Benajim an infinite advantage over his own paucity of self-knowledge.

Benajim felt himself shaking. "I want some answers myself."

"Then why didn't you ask?"

"Because I'm angry! Because I don't trust myself to be civil to you right now!"

"Civil! So not talking to me at all is any better?"

Benajim jabbed a finger toward the forward monitors. "That merchanter is one of your ships that we found trading with one of the Freeroamer factions!"

"I know what ship it is and I know who's running this route. I also know where its going. At least, I have a pretty good idea. But did you ask?"

Benajim slammed his fists down on the edge of the plate. Merrick's eyes widened in surprise. "You lied to me, Sean!"

"About what?"

"About who I am!"

The face scowled. "No I didn't."

"You said I was from Tabit! They have no record of me, none!"

"I didn't say you lived there—"

"You didn't tell me about the mark!" He gestured at his own face. "You didn't tell me I was your tool!"

"You couldn't figure that out for yourself? Again, you didn't ask."

"That's lying by omission!"

"Oh, don't give me that wounded heart garbage! Lying by omission, of all the twisted piles of inchoate psychological over sensitivity that was ever created—"

"I have a right to know—"

"You have a right to know whatever you can find out! That's how that works, that's how it always has worked!"

"Not good enough," Benajim said quietly. "I have a head full of questions and no answers."

"So does everyone."

"Not everyone knows where to find those answers."

"You think you do?"

"I'm looking at my source."

The floating head laughed sharply and vanished.

"Sean!" He spun around and went back to the command couch. "I'm getting pretty damn tired of your cryptic shit."

He touched the gate.

The Flow shifted and shimmered, an incoherent flux. Datanodes scattered into new configurations; command nodes changed surface codings as he watched. The entire system was being altered. He had no idea where to start.

I can't relearn all this, Sean!

Code sparked behind a collection of reshaped nodes. Benajim moved toward it. He felt sluggish, as if the medium had become thicker, less viscous. He reached the edge of the collection. The nodes were faceted, darkly-mirrored objects, unlike the smooth-edged aspects he was used to in *Solo's* Flow. The effect of impermeability chilled him. All through the fabric of the Flow similar changes were taking place. He was being shut out.

The spark of code he had seen—thought he recognized—moved away. In the roil and tumble of the reorganizing Flow it left a clear, smooth track. Benajim pushed after it.

The track was a solid steel-white line, a curiously non-Flow manifestation. Benajim touched it—

—and could not let go. He started moving along it, gaining speed until the Flow around him distorted at the edges of his perception, details streaked and smeared before they disappeared behind him.

Ahead a pinpoint of darkness grew into a disk then became a sphere and finally, inverted, a cone, and enveloped his perception. Benajim plunged into it.

The sensation of motion ceased. He was surrounded by still darkness, uncontoured, limitless. Drifting, he could not tell if he was asleep or awake. Perhaps it did not matter. He imagined that this was the view from inside his soul—undefined, empty of details, pastless. Without history there was no referent.

A star appeared. Then another, then a cluster. The darkness became salted with them and he rolled gently in the space created. He thought he recognized a few constellations, but it was impossible to be sure.

A ship approached. At first it was just a point of oddly-shaped light. As it grew nearer Benajim knew it was *Solo*.

It filled his vision, then slid beneath him and stopped. The topside hatch opened and someone peered out at him.

"Sean?"

The old man waved him closer. Benajim fell toward him and Sean grabbed his arm. The grip was firm, real. He was pulled aboard.

It was the same ship. The bulkheads, the decks, the panels and gates, the strips of light—everything was inside-out even though nothing had changed.

"What is this?" he asked.

Sean gestured for him to follow. He led the way to the bridge. Sean pointed to the co-pilot's couch.

"Time to take a journey," Sean said.

"Where?"

"We'll see when we get there." Sean grinned at him and touched his gate.

Solo dropped into orbit around Miron.

Not the Miron with which Benajim was familiar, but a younger one. The only thing in orbit besides them was a gangly array of struts and modules, the beginnings of a transit station. Below Benajim found no trace of Miron City.

Sean maneuvered *Solo* into dock at the station. A score more ships huddled under the boom of the debarkation section, an unlovely collection of odd-sized, oft-refitted, scarred hulks. One showed ribs through an open wound and the brilliant sparks of torches as repair work progressed.

Sean led him through narrow circuits. They pulled themselves along by handholds in the absence of gravity. People moved by on their way to tasks, each one with a tight expression of concern and hope. Sean swam "up" a ladder, through an open lock, into a broad environmental module.

As Benajim entered after him he saw that the chamber was filled with people. They floated in place or clung to the walls. A man hovered in the center, speaking.

"—any provisions have got to be contingent on what comes after. We can't weld together a constitution that can't change with circumstance. That's been done before and when things changed radically enough the damn constitution was thrown out. Every time."

"And what about seti influence?" someone asked.

"What about it?" The speaker turned, went full circle until he flexed his upper body in the opposite direction and slowed his spin.

"Don't you think we need something that'll keep our identity whole? I mean, there's no telling what we might become with unrestricted interaction with setis."

"Do I hear the reasonable voice of bigotry among us?" the speaker asked. A few people laughed. "How would you do that? We're fighting a war now because we tried to limit interaction with what we couldn't understand."

"We're fighting a war because the Pan wanted to shut down our colonies!" someone else objected.

"They wanted to limit expansion, restrict our trade possibilities—" someone else added.

"Absolutely!" Sean barked. His voice was loud, abrasive. "All because we don't know what the damn seti will do to us. Pure-bred humans have to be careful. We might turn into something like a Cursian! Metamorphose into a Distanti!" More people laughed.

"All I'm saying," the first objector yelled, "is that we have to protect what is essentially human! Otherwise we'll be swallowed up in the Reaches!"

Several people nodded, muttered agreement.

"Depends on what identity is, doesn't it?" Sean threw out.

"We're not talking metaphysics here, Merrick! We know damn well who we are, but what about our children and theirs?"

"Seems to me you're taking care of that question by cutting all the ties to the Pan. That's where our history is. Without that we're starting from scratch. We get the chance here to make ourselves into whatever we want or lose anything we might ever have."

"Exactly! So any constitution we agree on has to include a statement of what it means to be human!"

"And a statement allowing us to resume relations with the Pan at some future date."

The chamber filled with angry argument. Fists were brandished, insults exchanged. For a second Benajim thought they would all fly from their holds on the walls and join in the center in a jumbled brawl. Sean touched his shoulder and gestured for him to follow.

They left the chamber and continued on "up" the same ladder to another, smaller module.

Within, Benajim was startled to find gravity. He nearly toppled headlong to the deck, but Sean caught him and balanced him. He was surprised at the strength in the old man's arms.

The four people at the single table in the center of the chamber looked at him, amused.

"About time you got here, Sean," one woman said.

"Had to pause in the peanut gallery to see what the stir is, Jedora," he replied, sitting down.

Benajim looked about for another chair, saw none. He leaned back against the wall.

"And what is it?" a man asked.

"Same shit. Everybody's worried that the seti will swallow us up."

"They might," the man said.

Sean grunted. "Then you don't understand the seti, Sutter."

"Nor do you fully appreciate the nature of what we're constructing," the second woman said. "The data continuum will virtually guarantee uniqueness."

"I agree with Cara," the other man said. "Without this construct all the worries about dissolution of identity and absorption into some seti empire would be likely."

"I'm still not sure I care for the idea," Sutter said. "There's no exclusivity in this construct. Anyone with the interface implants can participate in the continuum?"

"Of course," Cara said, frowning.

Sutter shook his head. "There ought to be some limiting factor, something to assure decisions can be made by those who can—"

"You're thinking with your ambitions again, Sutter," Sean said. "You're worried power will be diluted."

Sutter frowned. "Exactly."

"Well, that's the idea," the other man said. "Full participatory democracy."

"Yes, but our databases!" Sutter snapped. "Damnit, Ellis, are you blind to what this will do to business?"

Ellis frowned. "No, I'm not. It must work to limit the possibility of the kind of corporate imperialism the Pan is dying from."

"But isn't that a question of identity?" Sutter went on. "I mean, a state is recognized through its institutions. If they're changing constantly, with nothing permanent—"

"Nobody is proposing an end to private holdings," Cara said. "What we're proposing is an end to dynasticism. The institutions by which we'll be known will be those manifest in our interactions. The data continuum will be the only permanent feature and this assures it will reflect the state of popular thought at any given time."

Sean grinned. "What's wrong, Sutter? Worried that you won't live past your death?" He laughed. "That's the whole idea. Identity is yours as long as you're alive. After that, it's all over."

"Sutter," Cara said, "we have to put aside personal ambitions in this. We'll all be dead some day. What will be left? We don't know. Nor do we have a right to predetermine it. The framework of the constitution we have so far is designed to make sure no one can have that much influence. No individual can be allowed to exert that kind of power after death."

"Except in the disposal of estate and remains," Sean said.

"I have problems even with that," Cara said. "But I don't think there's any way to ethically qualify it. Absolute control of identity and all that accrues to it while alive, including a statement of disposal in the instance of death, absolutely no control afterward."

"And what about the direction and identity of the state?" Sutter asked.

"The continuum will decide. It will be whatever it is at any given moment."

"And when we reestablish relations with the Pan? We may be unrecognizable to them."

Ellis cleared his throat. "I don't think we should even consider reestablishing contact. The philosophies governing the Pan are completely at odds with what we're trying to do here. It may not be possible or desirable for any contact to take place."

"Except for individuals, I agree," Sean said.

"No," Jedora said.

Sean looked at her sharply. "What do you mean, 'no', Jedora?"

"Even individuals must be prevented from contact with the Pan."

Sean scowled. "Right there you're interfering with the right of primary designation. What if I damn well want to contact them?"

"You shouldn't," Jedora said. "Contact is contact, be it a state issue or an individual decision."

"This is beside the point," Ellis said. "The Pan will see to it such contact isn't possible."

"No, wait a minute," Sean said, leaning forward. "It's not beside the point. We just got done arguing with Sutter that no institution ought to exert power over individuals after the death of the constituents of that institution. You're suggesting we place a barrier on individual action which will require the establishment of exactly that kind of an institution. Furthermore, we're trying to establish a polity wherein the choices of an individual are paramount, especially in matters of freedom of travel. We're fighting a goddamn war because the Pan told us we couldn't go where we wanted to and now you're suggesting we set the same limit!"

"I'm circumventing a potential threat to everything we're discussing here," Jedora said. "The Pan is our greatest enemy. I know you're bringing trade goods across the border, Sean. I also know that without them we wouldn't have a chance. But it's got to stop once this war is over."

"If you stick this in the constitution, I'll boycott it. I'll start a revolution out here just to prove a point. No limits! The Pan as threat will end once they quit the war. It would cost them too much to pursue it. They want insularity, fine, let 'em have it. But that's not what we're supposed to be about."

"Let's compromise," Cara said. "Sometimes necessity dictates policy more forcefully than we like to admit."

"I'm curious," Sutter said. "Why are you so adamant about this, Sean?"

"A number of reasons. But one ought to be clear to everyone here. We're all merchants, we know how it works. Limit access to something and a black market grows where a legitimate market is forbidden. If it's black market, it's hidden. There would then be no control through Cara's data continuum to guarantee its corporate mortality."

"And you think with open access the same thing wouldn't happen?" Jedora asked. "The Pan obviously won't give a damn about our laws. Dynasties would form on the other side of the border."

"That's a chance we have to take," Sean said. "We're going to have to deal with the Pan again someday. Why handicap ourselves by birthing a black market with its own agenda?"

"Why should we ever have to deal with them?" Jedora demanded.

"Because they're human," Ellis said. "I agree with Sean. It makes sense not to cut ourselves off completely. But—" he added quickly as Jedora opened her mouth. "But I think it would be wise to give our own polity a chance to establish itself before we go back."

Sean sat back in his seat. "I think I don't have a problem with that. But it can't be in the constitution."

"Why not leave it in the jurisdiction of the courts and the discretionary committee we've already agreed to establish?" Cara suggested.

Jedora stared at Sean, her eyes narrowed. "I think this is a mistake. What happens, under the conditions of individual primacy you're suggesting, Sean, if it is the will of a co that personal holdings be given to the Pan upon his or her death? Including information."

Sean shrugged. "If it's part and parcel of an open trade relationship, so what? I think you underestimate the intelligence of our populace already. Would anyone do that? Not now."

"I agree with Jedora," Sutter said. "But I also understand Sean's objections. For the time being, I second Cara's motion to include this in the powers of the discretionary committee."

"Agreed," Ellis added.

"I still," Jedora said, "want to know why Sean is so adamant about this."

"You'll just have to stick around and see," he said.

"I will agree to this," Jedora said, "under one condition. That any and all proposed contact at any time with the Pan be subject to the approval of the discretionary committee."

"Oh, why not be a bit more plebiscitarian? Subject to approval of the continuum, with recommendations from the committee."

Sutter groaned. Ellis and Cara chuckled.

"All right," Jedora said. "Based on that confusing mass of probable contradictions, I may get my way after all. Agreed."

"Great!" Sean slapped the arms of his chair and stood. "Well, I've got cargo to unload. Let me know when you've got a draft of this thing."

He turned and winked at Benajim, then left the chamber.

Benajim started to follow, but hesitated.

"Sean's obsessed with this identity thing," Sutter said.

"Aren't we all?" Cara said. "The continuum will pretty well guarantee we won't lose our identity."

"Won't we?" Jedora mused. "I wonder. We're cutting ourselves off from most of humankind. When it comes times to renew our substance, where will we go? The seti? In time we may not be human."

"We'll always be human," Ellis said. "We just won't be the same. But Sutter's got a point. I wonder if Sean thinks no law will apply to him."

"No law applies to him now," Jedora said. "In time that will have to change. We can't have coes doing whatever they want, especially if what they want endangers the polity. I think the discretionary committee will be the place where we can best solve that problem."

Cara frowned. "That committee is primarily advisory. We're not actually giving it powers."

Jedora smiled. "Of course we are. It's an institution. And I think Sean's analysis of institutions is quite correct. It will have the power one day. It's inevitable."

A tap on Benajim's arm brought his attention around. Sean leaned through the hatch and with a nod of his head gestured for Benajim to follow.

He sailed down a long corridor after the old man. The corridor widened while he fell, changed its shape from a cylinder to a rectangle, and gravity gradually manifested. He settled to the deck and hurried to catch up with Sean. More people appeared, less scruffy, faces eager now instead of anxious.

They boarded a shunt.

"Dock ninety-one," Sean said.

They reached the dock and boarded *Solo*.

Sean took her out of dock. In the link Benajim looked back at the transit station. It was the huge, square block he knew. Already time had caught up with his present.

Sean flew out of the Miron System and made for the Pan border.

Though the voyage took a fraction of the time it ought, Benajim still had opportunity to glimpse—on the periphery of his senses—the Commonwealth Republic in its various aspects. Worlds settled, cities growing, stations expanding, ships weaving it all together, and in the midst of and encompassing all, the Flow, what had come from Cara Lestanza's data continuum. It bound the C.R. together and rippled with the life energies of the people. More than the Charter, Benajim recognized the real manifestation of their political ideals in the Flow.

They crossed the border.

Ahead lay a ship, drifting. As they drew closer Benajim wanted to look away. Something about the ship...a flash from behind it distracted his thoughts. A smaller ship rose above it and fired into it. The beam splashed against the hull. Again. Once more and the hull opened up. More of the smaller vessels closed upon it, vultures to a kill.

Benajim felt Sean's touch within the Flow, pointing to something even further away. Another ship, a merchanter. One of Sean's...

No, one of Carson Reiner's. By now she was using Sean's fleets as though they were her own. Her people crewed them, they sailed at her command, doing her business.

The drifting, assaulted ship was not one of Sean's. It was an independent, but still a C.R. ship. The smaller ships were Pan vessels.

The Merrick ship did nothing. It continued on toward the border. Other Pan vessels hovered between the independent and the merchanter, watching. They did not attack the Merrick ship.

Sean moved in, firing at the Pan ships. In his first pass he ruptured two of them. The others moved then, closing to engage

Solo. Benajim found himself targeting them, releasing the energies of *Solo's* batteries, killing them. Sean maneuvered among them, tight, confusing patterns that brought Benajim into the best position to fire and score.

Three of them ran.

He turned back to the crippled ship. Another ship neared, but it, too, was a C.R. independent. Sean brought them in close.

Benajim did not want to board it. He was frightened of that ship and did not know why. But suddenly he was aboard, moving through twisted corridors right behind the team from the other independent.

Bodies floated, blood frozen into crystals that sparkled in the handlamps of the searchers.

One compartment still maintained environmental integrity. They had to bring a portable lock in and fit it against the bulkhead. It punched through and they cycled into the chamber.

There were two people inside. Both had been burned. Their clothes were gone. They hung in the air, twitching from pain that rippled through their bodies.

One was a woman; the other was Benajim.

He knew. The face was gone, charred, ripped, bone protruding below the eyes. But he opened those eyes and looked at his rescuers and Benajim knew it was himself.

He squeezed his eyes closed and tried to scream.

He was back on board *Solo.*

The rescuers salvaged what they could and headed back to the C.R.

The bridge of *Solo* dissolved and in its place a familiar room appeared. The enormous bed with its constellation of monitors and life support apparatus bulked against one wall. Within the nestling embrace of the equipment Sean looked small, diminished, yet somehow not frail. Force of will alone seemed to animate his face, inform his eyes.

Across from him a large screen displayed a man Benajim did not know. He spoke to Sean, ignoring Benajim's presence.

"There's no mind left," he said. "His neural net has been overloaded, then overheated, burning sections of his brain. Also, sixty-three percent of his body was burnt, half his bones were broken. There's not even enough left to get a decent ID imprimatur to find out who he is. The logs we recovered from his ship suggest Tabit as the last port-of-call, but so much was lost. What do you want us to do with him, Sean?"

"They brought him back to me," Sean said tiredly. "I don't know why, probably to make me feel ashamed that one of my ships ignored the attack, refused help. Can you rebuild him?"

The man on the screen look shocked. "You're joking. He shouldn't even be alive. The radiation damage to his system affected even his DNA, I don't think there's enough for regrowth. But even so we're looking at a new individual, not the same person."

"Hmm. What about through donor tissue?"

"That would be the only way..."

"Do it. Use mine."

"But, Sean—"

"It wouldn't be terribly difficult for me to cut funding to Doppler. You technically don't exist as it is."

The man swallowed, his mouth turned down. "Threats aren't necessary. I just don't see the facility. When we're done you'll have a nice brand-spanking new body with no identity."

"I'll worry about that. Use my gene plasma, my reserve organs. Rebuild him. Keep me posted."

Sean touched a switch and the screen went blank. He looked over at Benajim. "Questions?"

"The Pan ships gave your ship safe passage."

"Uh huh. And that was never part of the arrangements I'd made with my trade sources. Whoever Reiner has found to deal with set that up. One of the consequences of the way things are. Well, now you have answers. What are you going to do with them?"

"I don't know." He looked at Sean. "My mind...it's partly yours, isn't it?"

"Not in any memorative sense, no. There's some genetic heritage because of the grafted gene plasma."

"But I have a mind because of you."

Sean frowned. "You are yourself."

"But I don't know who that is!"

"That's part of it. There wasn't anything left, Ben. You shouldn't even have been alive. You were a lump of living tissue when I turned you over to Doppler. That's all."

"My life began when you took me in to be your personal aide."

"So now you know as much as I do."

Benajim nodded. "Thank you."

Abruptly he was outside *Solo*, drawing swiftly away until the ship was a speck amid the stars. The stars diminished, swallowed up into a pocket of blackness like a huge sack.

He lurched back from the console and fell into the couch. He blinked at the monitors. *Solo* was moving, falling through space at translight. Benajim's body felt tight, weary, every muscle worked to the edge of failure.

Shakily, he stood. He cleared his throat and looked at the projection panel. Empty.

Images competed in his mind. Answers. He was unsure he believed them all—Sean had lied to him before—but there was a plausibility to them that he had lacked till now. He felt...

substantiated.

Sean was flying the ship. Good. He knew where to go.

And if he did not, who did?

Benajim went to the heavy doors and touched the contact. They rolled back.

Piper and Elen stood there. He recognized concern, anger, puzzlement in their faces, especially puzzlement in Elen's. It was gratifying to know they cared.

"Ben?" Piper said.

"I'm...sorry," he said. He closed his eyes. "Things haven't been...I'm not really in control around here, you see..."

"Ben," Piper repeated.

"I'd like to explain," he said. "I've been...you deserve better, but I didn't know how."

"How what?" Elen asked.

"To trust..."

He laughed and fell forward into her arms.

"Ben?"

He opened his eyes.

"Ben?" Piper's voice again.

"Yes?"

"We've dropped out of translight."

He blinked, thought about that. "Where are we?"

"In the vicinity of Tau Ceti."

"How long have I been—?"

"Almost three days. You've been in and out."

"Oh. Why did we stop here?"

"I'm not sure how, but this ship..."

He looked at her. She seemed troubled, preoccupied. "What?"

"This ship found the *Wicca*."

Chapter Eighteen

They gathered in the same makeshift conference room near the cargo
bays where Tamyn had interrogated Trace Alek at Pron, just after
the fight with the *Jarom*—how long ago? A hundred days? More?
Half their stores were gone, she knew. If this took much longer
they would have to start foraging and that opened them to new
problems. Stoan, Traville, Thijs, Innes, Ratha, Benajim, Piper, and
Leris op Elen. Joclen sat now where Tamyn had then, trying to
preside over this conference. Everyone went through the details of
what had happened. Reduced to retelling, *Wicca's* escape from Sol
System seemed simultaneously too easy and hopelessly improbable.
An Akaren should be able to bring life to such dry detail, but Joclen
did not feel capable.

Benajim Cyanus and Piper Van described what had happened,
with clarifications and emendations from Leris op Elen, in Tabit.
The bulk of the information seemed useless, but Cyanus especially
told it well. Joclen listened, sifted, tried to find something that would
point in a direction. Impossible, especially with the boiling hatred
she felt toward Cyanus that kept distracting her.

She wanted to hurt him. The urge surprised her, pulled her
fingers into fists, occasionally deafened her to what was being said as
her mind filled with an image of beating him. What prevented her
doing just that was being in command. She held Tamyn's place;
Joclen could not be irrational in the shipmaster's absence. The responsibility persisted against a growing whim to indulge. Indulge
bitterness, impatience, frustration, the desire to act that rejected reason and judgement. The conflict ground at her conscience, abraded
her spirit, and left her emotions raw and tender.

"Pilot?"

Joclen blinked and looked at Stoan. Everyone was looking at
her, waiting. She tried to recall the last detail that had been discussed.

"Recommendations?" she asked.

"The most practical course," Piper said slowly, "would be to
return to Miron with what we have."

Joclen stared at her.

Benajim shook his head. "Spoken like a true prophylactic. What about Tamyn?"

"I said that would be the most practical action, not the most desirable." Piper looked around at the others. "I wondered how many, if any, here wanted to be practical?"

"Practical none but one who isn't," Stoan said. He grinned, then scowled and blinked. "I agree," Stoan said. "That would be practical. Perhaps even the best choice. But choices luxury ran credit beyond acceptance. Hah! I said that off, didn't I?"

Joclen felt her anger expanding to include everyone in the room. She glared at Stoan, who returned her gaze evenly.

"Consider," he said, "if we attempt to rescue Shipmaster Glass and are taken as she was, what becomes of everything we've come here to do?"

"Of all the people I'd expect..." Joclen began.

"Expectations lamentations provocations!" He slapped the table. "Of all the people you don't know I'm the least one you'd suspect of unsentimental opinions!"

"We have an alternative, though," Benajim said quickly.

"Yes," Stoan said, nodding quickly, eagerly. "We do."

"I'm all ears," Joclen said tightly.

"Well," Benajim said, grinning, "we do have two ships here."

"It's possible to send one back to Miron," Stoan said, "and the other to find Tamyn."

Everyone gave their attention to Joclen. She realized after a few seconds that a decision was expected and she had to make it. Too much, too quick. The sensible thing...but she wanted to be the one to bring Tamyn back, so which ship? Was it reasonable to trust Cyanus to return to Miron? All this had begun because of his friend, someone Joclen had held in high regard, but who had cavalierly used whoever he needed to for whatever he wanted.

That left him to find and rescue Tamyn. She trusted him less with that mission.

"We all go home," she said finally, "or none of us do."

Stoan grunted, then laughed and shrugged. "Hell," he muttered.

Not sensible, part of her protested. She saw the same accusation in Benajim's expression, but he kept silent. He had realized that Joclen was barely tolerating his presence. He was uncertain about the sentiments of the others, but since Joclen was now in command he guessed that they would follow her lead until Tamyn was back. Joclen wondered if he also had guessed that she had wanted to fire on the *Solo* when it came into range. That would have been senseless, but consistent with her feelings.

She toyed with the notion of explaining herself to Benajim and discarded it. Let him wonder.

Besides, she thought suddenly, Benajim may be the only one who could get inside the Directorate. The *Solo*, after all, was a Pan vessel. The idea soured her mood further.

Damnit, they were merchants, not military tacticians!

But Benajim...

"I want recommendations," she said. "The commission we came here for is fulfilled. Now our obligation is to get Tamyn back. I want proposals."

She stood, gave them all a last, hopefully confident look, and left the chamber.

What would you do, Tam? she thought as she headed for the bridge.

Benajim detected no change in Stoan's expression as the Alcyoni listened to his proposal. He knew Stoan was seti and that it was foolish to think he could read the transmorph's facial signals. But Benajim still expected to see changes, if only minute movements of muscle in response. After the manic displays he had witnessed on Stoan's face, there should have been something. Instead, he found nothing. Stoan did not react.

Stoan's cabin was stark: a desk, a polycom terminal, three chairs. One wall was curtained with heavy midnight blue material and Benajim ached to know what lay behind it. A single lamp on the desk gave off the only illumination, a harsh yellow-orange light. Stoan sat behind his desk, hands folded before him, unblinking black eyes aimed at Benajim.

Benajim finished and waved a hand. "There. That's it. I think it's our best chance."

Stoan remained motionless for almost a minute. "Why did you bring this to me first? Why not take it to Pilot Bramus?"

"Because I'm not sure how she'll react. I want your support."

"Why is it humans have so little confidence in their ideas that they enlist others for validation?" He waved his left hand casually.

"If an idea is sound, it is just as sound expressed by one as by a hundred."

Benajim smiled. "It hasn't anything to do with ideas. It has to do with personalities."

Stoan grinned nastily. "Pilot Bramus distrusts you."

"You noticed."

"Even if you had the best proposal she isn't likely to accept it coming from you."

Benajim narrowed his eyes. "You're playing with me. You damn well understand humans. How long have you been on this ship?"

"Tamyn Glass hired me almost ten thousand days ago."

"Do you distrust me?"

"Absolutely. You're a complete unknown. However, you have an excellent idea. At least, it has the virtue of audacity."

"Audacity?" Benajim smiled.

"The Alcyone in many ways are a martial people, Co Cyanus. We once were part of the Vohec and the Vohec provided mercenaries for many others cultures. Planning, strategy, tactics—these are all qualities of thought we understand and appreciate, or so we tell others and ourselves. Sometimes they are insufficient for success. An unplannable element is then necessary. Audacity is as good a name for that as any." He jumped onto the desk and dropped down right in front of Benajim. He leaned close and put a hand on Benajim's chest. "I distrust you because I don't know you. You're a random quality, completely unquantifiable at present. Fascinating company, a ravelling experience, but a die with infinite faces, for a game I insist you win. Threats, hah! I don't see them measured. But I promise you, Tamyn's not a game. This outcome needs to be a forgone conclusion, or something else is."

Stoan turned and stared at the curtains, hands clasped lightly behind his back.

"Tamyn gave me an opportunity to reclaim myself," he said, slowly and carefully. "That is a gift difficult to give, impossible to repay, and the greatest shame to deny." He was motionless and silent for a long time. Then: "I'll urge Pilot Bramus to accept your proposal. If you fail and live, avoid me. I would take deep pleasure removing you from yourself."

Shifting streaks of azure and teal and saffron filled the main screen. Benajim had turned all the lights low, so the spectral glow flickered through the bridge.

On another screen data scrolled by. Benajim still did not know how *Solo* had found the *Wicca*. The clipper was still in close orbit near one of the three gas giants in the Tau Ceti System. But among the other things he did not know, that seemed a minor annoyance.

He was supposed to be running scans on any Pan traffic he could access, searching for a hole through which he could enter. Instead he was letting *Solo* do that for him. The ship had shown marvelous alacrity in doing the unexpected up to this point, let it surprise him again. But he expected the surprise now, which diminished its shock value.

So while the ship scanned and sorted, Benajim made lists. He had half of a third screen filled below the heading "What I Know About Myself."

Half a screen.

It was a paltry list. Much harder to fill than had he chosen to list all he did not know. Still, he had a list of things he definitely knew, which he decided was a substantial achievement.

I am a thief
I am a killer
I lie when it suits my purpose
I am a fair pilot
I have a strong will to survive
I care little for wealth
Or power
I am very curious
I have nothing that is my own
I am Sean Merrick's—slave?
creation?
burden?
clone?
heir?
son?
See all of the above...

After a time staring at it, Benajim deleted the last block starting with "I am Sean Merrick's—" and replaced it with "I owe my life to Sean Merrick."

Usually when people said that, it meant something less literal.

The other terminal beeped and he looked at the screen. A blue square flashed in the upper lefthand corner. Benajim touched the gate below it briefly. The square disappeared, replaced by blocks of langish script.

"Possibilities," he murmured, "possibilities..."

A smile slowly took over his face. He filed his self-examination for now. *Solo* had found a way in. He called Piper and Elen.

"Ambassadors?" Joclen looked at him dubiously.

They were gathered now on the bridge of the *Wicca*. The bridge crew was present, as well as Innes, Thijs, and Clif. It seemed much longer than sixty days since they had left Miron. They had been drifting too long, avoiding detection.

"Assuming we can infiltrate that level of security," Benajim said, smiling. He glanced at Shreve, who stood behind Joclen, his forehead creased thoughtfully.

"That's doable," Shreve said.

"But—" Joclen began, then stopped.

"Elen gave me the idea," Benajim said. He looked at her and smiled. She smiled in return and he felt better at once.

"I'm listening," Joclen said.

Elen turned to Joclen. "There are always ambassadors going to Earth, to fish for favors from the Chairman. The traffic to and from is constant. Sometimes they stumble over each other from the same system, they send so many. It's the customary way to petition the government."

"How do you know?" Ratha asked. "If Tabit is cut off as you described—"

"We watch, we listen," Elen shrugged. "The manifests from the ships we take tell us a great deal. Even before the Circumvention this had become the way business is done in the Pan Humana."

"So," Benajim took up, "who would notice one group of ambassadors out of so many? Especially if we make sure the proper data is in the system."

Joclen seemed to regard him with barely concealed distaste. "Who would go?"

"Well," Benajim said, "I'd need Elen to access Directorate dataspheres; Piper won't stay behind—"

"My job," Piper said. "Sorry."

"—and I think I'd need at least two more. Maybe someone with engineering skills, someone with military skills?" He looked at Stoan.

"Flattered," Stoan said, "but I wouldn't pass. Nor would Shreve. Traville and Innes."

"Does Cyanus have to go?" Joclen asked.

Benajim scowled, anger rising quickly. "Why—"

"Because," Joclen snapped, standing and stepping close to him, "I don't damn well trust you. I don't know who you are or what you have in mind. I'd just as soon lock you up and haul you back to the C.R. for disposal." She was shaking, her eyes narrow. "Give me a good reason why you should be the one to do this."

He considered saying something placating, to calm her down and efface himself and establish a clear position of her control over him. The lie was there, ready to use. Easy.

"Because," he said, "none of you can." He suppressed the urge to grin. "You're just going to have to trust me, Co Bramus. Much as that might eat you up, that's the option you've got. Unless you think you can get the C.R. to declare war on the Pan and come rescue Tamyn."

Joclen's body tensed, her right shoulder pulled back. Suddenly Piper was beside her, and smoothly edged between them. Joclen staggered back a step.

"Stoan?" Joclen asked.

"Yes?"

"What do you think?"

"I think—hah!—that for the time being Co Cyanus has accurately assessed the situation. For myself I do trust him."

Joclen frowned and looked at him. "Why?"

"He has to do this to be who he wants to be. It's too important to him. If he fails it will be inability, not betrayal." Stoan looked questioningly at Benajim. "Or do I state that too strongly?"

Benajim grunted. "Just let me know your decision." He turned and left the bridge.

Benajim rifled through the dataspheres of the local government agencies on Homestead, the settlement in the Tau Ceti System. *Solo* enabled him to do so easily. He had stopped questioning where the ship had acquired these capacities. The projection had told him flatly that Sean had never purged the system (like someone had threatened to do) and apparently the Pan had never significantly altered the major datasphere configurations, only the access codes, which were no real barrier to a good locksmith.

There was a set protocol for petitioning the Seat on Earth and a proper way to approach the Chairman. As with any bureaucracy, it was based on persistent repetition. Benajim scanned datanodes containing the particulars of past diplomatic missions and after a little statistical arithmetic arrived at the formula. A request for audience with the Chairman had to be submitted at least eight times in a three hundred day period. Up to this point no response could be expected. Then came an official communiqué inviting the submission of a synopsis of the matter the mission wished to put before the Chairman. The synopsis went out. A follow-up on the status of the synopsis was filed fifty days later. If a reply came to the first query, it was a request for resubmission. Usually, though, that came after the second query fifty days after the first. The synopsis went out again and came back within thirty days with explicit notes for revision from a lesser court official. Revisions made, the synopsis went out once more, and came back again with more revisions requested, this time suggested by someone closer to the Chairman. Submission and revision occurred still a third time. At this point a firm answer could be expected. If it was deemed appropriate for presentation to the Chairman— by some process of determination Benajim could not discover— a formal invitation to the mission was granted. By this time nearly five hundred days had passed. It seemed to Benajim that whatever might have been urgent would have solved itself in this time, but the number of missions that went out—at least from Homestead, an old and well established world—indicated that they constantly had one or two ready to leave and could change the subject of presentation at any time. Presumably once the ambassadors arrived on Earth and received their audience, they could talk about anything they wanted to. In this way, he found, permission to petition the Chairman for a given issue was granted nearly four to five hundred days after the issue had originally been presented. It seemed as efficient as any other centralized system of government.

As soon as he realized that a given mission need not be connected with a given petition, Benajim set about placing himself and his team in the queue.

Elen recommended an outlying colony, far from the centers of power. After researching it, Benajim chose Nine Rivers, a farm world for the most part, one that sent very few diplomatic missions to Earth. He was able to obtain quite a lot of information about it from the library system on Homestead.

"How do we keep in contact?" Joclen asked.

"We don't," Benajim answered. "You wait for us to come out."

"Not acceptable."

Benajim shrugged. "Too bad. On the other hand I guess it's not too late to try to start a war."

"That's not even a little funny."

"No, it's not. With only a few of us going in, as it is I'd be a little concerned about that possibility. They already know about Tamyn, I'm sure, so if a fully-mounted rescue attempt is made then war is what you might be looking at. Our best chance for all concerned is to keep it small and limited. I don't want a trace back to you if we fail."

"I'm touched by your concern."

Benajim glared at her. "You know if it were you we were going after I might just go back to the C.R. and leave you. But Shipmaster Glass is another matter. She turned out to be exactly what Sean said she was—a friend." He drew closer to her. "Now instead of fighting me at every step why don't you help?"

"Help do what? You're taking this all into your own hands! What is there for me to do?"

"Stay out of trouble till we get back."

Joclen walked away unhappy. Benajim watched her go and wondered if she intended to natter at him till he left. All the preparations had been punctuated with episodes like that, small brushfire exchanges that left them both scathed and baffled. He found himself ceasing to care. There was no room for the self-doubt Joclen's attacks seemed designed to promote. Indeed, he realized, there was no design to her attacks. She ached with fear and anger and he embodied both for her. Benajim shook off the ill-ease and did what he had to do. Perhaps later, when it was all over, he could heal the breach between them. If he was successful.

He dismissed that thought. There was no room for self-doubt...

Elen did not like washing off her body art without replacing it. Benajim was entranced by what he saw as she studied herself in a mirror. The bodypaints smeared during sex and they played with it, making new patterns on each other. He had glimpsed her just out of the shower washed clean and watched her reapply it, always altering it slightly, sometimes creating a new design somewhere that was just between them. He had let her do a few small designs on his body—nothing that showed outside his utilities—and accepted it as a part of her and therefore part of them.

She turned and scowled at the reflected image. Her optil caught light and glinted redly, adding a sinister aspect to her face.

"I look like anybody else now," she said.

Benajim laughed. "No, you don't. You look like you and to me you're different from everybody."

"Still..."

"It's only a temporary inconvenience."

She turned to him. "She hates you. Joclen Bramus. I hope this Tamyn we're going to all the trouble for is different."

"Joclen doesn't hate me, she...Tamyn is family to her. She's frightened. But, yes, Tamyn is worth all this trouble, and more." He watched her silently, thoughtful for a time. "You could refuse to accompany me on this."

She shook her head at once. "No. It's necessary."

He decided not to ask what she meant. He believed he knew and did not want that belief contradicted in any way.

They left the *Wicca* still hidden in the upper atmosphere of the gas giant and sailed out to intercept a convoy heading for Sol. Benajim introduced Traville and Innes to *Solo* so they could use the gates. The three of them monitored dataflow in the convoy, wary of traps and alarms. Shreve had done most of the difficult work of infiltrating the Directorate dataspheres and planting the necessary information. If he had done it right, a ambassadorial mission was now expected to rendezvous with the convoy. The delegates were to transfer aboard the passenger liner *DeSmet* for the final leg of the Solward transit. The convoy at least ought to have the appropriate authorizations. Shreve had said little to Benajim about what he had had to do to accomplish this, but the cybermorph had seemed confident everything was in place.

What happened once they arrived on Earth was less certain. Benajim relied on Elen to handle that part. For now he was concerned only with boarding the *DeSmet*.

This convoy was much larger than the one Benajim had slipped into before Tabit. It strung out against the stars for thousands of kilometers, a necklace of ships, all various degrees of huge. Small tender craft flitted in and out of the train here and there, transferring people and cargo, luggage and mail among the ships.

He requested recognition from the AI that managed the convoy. After a brief pause, recognition was granted and a guidon was established to lead them to the *DeSmet*. As *Solo* entered the security shell of the convoy a constant barrage of interrogatives probed for confirmations. Benajim watched anxiously as the ship absorbed and responded to them all, matching codes, lying skillfully, and securing them safe conduct.

The *DeSmet* was a long, rather flattened ship, bloated just forward of center. *Solo* dropped below it, moved toward the docks. A shuttle separated from the giant liner's belly and came toward them.

This is where I say good-bye for now, the ship said to Benajim. *It wouldn't be wise for this ship to enter Sol System. I'll monitor comm traffic and meet you outside the system when you need me.*

Wish us luck.

Luck hell. Pay attention. If you get caught it's your own damn fault.

Thanks.

The shuttle linked to *Solo*'s belly and the "legation" boarded. As they were taken toward the *DeSmet*, *Solo* quickly withdrew from the convoy.

Motiles met them in the lock area. Their baggage was carried off to their rooms and another check was done into who they were and why they were on board. Piper studied the machines, the chamber, the consoles, and wondered if any humans were on board to run the ship. There was an antiseptic feel to the entire place, even the procedures. She waited tensely while the process of verification dragged on through most of an hour.

Finally they were led to a shunt.

"Is everything here this slow?" Innes asked as they stepped into the cubicle. The seats were comfortably cushioned.

Elen frowned. "Slow?"

Benajim smiled.

"I suggest we keep comments circumspect," Piper said.

Traville nodded.

Piper wanted to secure their apartments, if possible. She did not know if everything was recorded here, or if privacy had any substance. She did not want to test it uselessly.

On the other hand, she thought wryly, there's no way out now.

The shunt let them out in a plain corridor lined with doors on both sides. A small motile asked them to follow and it led them to two apartments.

While the rooms were spacious they seemed empty. The furnishings were part of the walls or floors. There was no polycom, only an information terminal that operated solely from a keyboard and offered a video menu.

Piper went from room to room checking for listening devices.

"They don't believe in edges here, do they?" Innes commented, surveying the room.

"Nothing sharp, at least," Traville said. "They must think people will hurt themselves."

Elen went to the terminal and scrolled through the menus. "Ah." Everyone crowded around. She had called up a map of the ship.

A long section buried in the middle accommodated all the people. There was nothing indicated like a bridge or crew quarters, only large surrounding areas marked Maintenance and Stowage and Restricted. The private cabins occupied six levels wrapped around a section containing restaurants, recreation facilities, stores. At the center of this was the Promenade.

"I imagine that's where everyone mingles," Benajim said, tapping the Promenade area on the screen.

"Should we?" Piper asked.

"It wouldn't be a bad idea to learn how these people talk and act," Traville said. "They're human but we really don't know a thing about them."

"Not safe," Piper said without conviction.

"Necessary," Benajim said. "I'm going to get some sleep. Then we should go find out about our hosts."

The promenade spread out beneath a dome that showed stars. Benajim was impressed by the display, by how real it looked. Shops, nightclutches, theatres, restaurants crowded the edges of the long mall, interspersed with private halls where parties were in full attendance. Groups of people moved continuously around, breaking off here and there to enter one place or another, mostly the parties, others emerging to join the flow of opulent humanity. A series of fountains ran down the center. They depicted the terraforming of some world; water danced from the poles of each slightly altered globe, caught the starlight and lampglow, and sent shimmering reflections to shatter across those who strolled nearby.

Benajim had them all purchase new clothes. He put it on the account of the Nine Rivers Embassy. The tailor was thrilled. When they emerged from his shop they were not distinguished by the plainness of their dress, but fit in with the bright, exotic fashions of the Promenade.

Invitations to parties came immediately. Pages stopped them and extended welcomes to this party or that. Benajim watched the ever-changing repertoire of passengers and costumes and party-goers as they circuited the Promenade.

After half a dozen parties, they began to notice a pattern. Guests were ascending the parties, like students graduating from one level to the next. Each one they were invited to was a little more sophisticated than the last, with a more select group of attendees. Invitations began to come on the recommendations of someone who had been at the last party or two who had already moved up the social scale. Recognition obtained a degree of control. After a couple of days the many circuits brought them into the company of people clearly in higher positions of power.

There was food at every party; several offered a variety of inebriating substances, a few were orgies, and others seemed to be centered around a kind of audio-visual hypnosis that induced group illusions.

On the third day a young woman Benajim remembered from one of the latter parties drifted out of an archway near the last fountain, the one depicting the completed terraformed globe with white clouds, blue water, and green continents. She fell into step among them—out of the corner of his eye Benajim saw Piper move closer.

"Representative Nooneus extends greetings," she said. "He'd be pleased if you'd attend his small celebration."

"What's he celebrating?" Benajim asked.

"His birthday."

Benajim nodded and motioned for her to lead. They entered through the archway from which she had emerged.

People grouped in small clusters, islands scattered across the widening hall. Robots moved deftly among them with refreshments. A tonal cycle played just below the level where it would be intrusive.

Benajim drifted in and out of several conversations. It became clear that this party, much more than any other he had attended, was a gathering of the powerful.

"Not the very powerful," he explained to Elen and Piper as they sampled some of the hors doeuvres—the flavor was vaguely cinnamon, vaguely peppermint, vaguely brandy. "No single person here could be said to be a power, at least not anyone I've met so far. But they're all players, and the accumulated power represented here is enormous." He pointed to a tall, thin woman in an elegant black gown. "Her, for instance. She's primary manager of a bank on Homestead that oversees the value of credit on one of the three continents. She's speaking with a man who owns a distributorship of agricultural robots and another man who is on the board of an import firm on Pollux. The woman listening to them is on the advisory committee of the governor of Pollux."

"Interesting," Elen said. "I just left a group that included the judge advocate of Faron, the secretary to the transportation overseer of Millenium, the CEO of a manufactory on Neighbors, two of her aides, and the mayor of Smithgrant, a city on Homestead."

"Quite a collection," Piper said.

"Uh huh," Benajim agreed. "But where's our host?"

"Haven't seen him," Piper said.

"Do we leave?" Elen asked.

"No," Benajim said. "I'm curious why a Representative to the Forum would want us at his party. We stay a little while longer. Where's Traville and Innes?"

Piper thumbed over her shoulder. The two were engaged in conversation with a trio of startlingly robed people.

"Who are they?" Benajim asked.

"Hierophants from Newcall. I think they're trying to convert Traville and Innes."

"Hm. Let's circulate more and see if we can find Representative Nooneus."

They worked through the clusters again. Benajim never stayed long enough in any group to attract unwanted questions. He was picking up a lot of information about the Pan, but close inspection would still show his ignorance. He met Elen near the back of the hall.

"No Representative Nooneus," she said.

"No. Disappointing. Well, another drink and onward?"

"I'm getting tired," she said, touching his neck lightly.

"Back to our apartments then?"

She smiled. "It would be pleasant—"

"Excuse me." The woman who had originally invited them was beside them. "Representative Nooneus would like to meet you."

Benajim glanced at Elen, who shrugged. "We'd be delighted," he said. He looked around for Piper, did not see her.

The woman led them through a curtain nearby. In the dimmer light Benajim made out a very old man on plush cushions. He sucked a dark red liquid through a tube and drew on a slowly burning reed that filled the chamber with aromatic tang. A tray of sweetmeats stood half empty at his left and a portable monitor displayed the party on his right. He looked at Benajim through heavy, slitted eyes and smiled indulgently.

"Representative," Benajim bowed slightly. "We're honored. This is my colleague, Elen Leris, and I am—"

"Sean Merrick," the old man drawled. "By god, I thought you were dead."

Chapter Nineteen

Benajim started. "Beg pardon?"

"Sean! It's me, damn you, Bool Nooneus! Don't tell me you've forgotten? Damn." The old man laughed, coughed, sucked on his tube, and ate a sweetmeat. "Sit, sit. When I saw you wandering the promenade I couldn't believe it. You don't look a day older than the day I met you. Doesn't make sense, not even through the haze of this," he waved the tube, "mindbender the meds have me on."

Benajim looked anxiously at Elen, then sat down.

"My name is Benajim Cyanus, Representative. You must have me mistaken for someone else."

Nooneus waved a beefy hand. "Nonsense. If you want to pass as someone else, that's fine by me. But we're screened here, Sean, nobody's listening in on us. You can talk freely. I didn't think you'd have the nerve to come back after all these years. I was sure you'd die out there in your damned Distals. Staked a hell of a wager on it, too, so if you're here incognito, you best damn well keep it that way! I'll be damned if I let that ass Cambion take the pot." He grinned at Elen. "If you're partnering with this liar, let me warn you. He's not the sort pretty women should trust." He turned his eyes on Benajim. "Or ugly women, for that matter."

Benajim licked his lips, watching the old man with a terrible fascination. Through the unnerving impact of his words came the much more disturbing sensation of recognition. Nooneus was familiar. Déjà vu surrounded him like an aura.

"Excuse me," he said, "but why do you think I'm Sean Merrick?"

Nooneus laughed heavily. His face darkened and he drew on his smoking brand, coughed, and chuckled. "My god, you were always one for a joke. Why? Ask me why I've lived so damn long that everyone who could've helped me enjoy advanced age is dead. Ask me why I'm cursed with a memory so good that I continue to be worthwhile as a representative of my constituency even though much younger people have collapsed under the weight of the information necessary to be effective. Ask me why, because of that memory, I can't enjoy the simple pleasure of misremembering

someone so that someone else can pass as an old friend misplaced
for a moment, and allow me the deceit of vagueness so that for a
short time I can pretend—really believe—that one of them escaped death. Ask me why I have to watch everything I ever did
believe in—socially, politically, philosophically, privately—crumble
or turn into a lie." He grunted. "The lies are kinder in a way. I can
pretend that they'll turn round again and become what I remembered." He sucked absently for a few seconds on his liquid, then
nodded as if hearing some internal comment. "And ask me—as
long as you're bothering to ask an old man you probably think is
nearly insane by now—why I tolerate all these fools and fabrica-
tors out there, each one of whom thinks he or she is using me to
further their schemes and believes that I'm ultimately dispensable,
that when they finish gleaning what they can from me they can
wipe their hands on me and drop me like a soiled rag."

He smiled then with a warmth Benajim would not have believe
possible in a face with such a collection of wrinkles and folds and
bulges of fat and absence of muscle.

"But," Nooneus said gently, "don't ask me why I think you're
Sean Merrick. Illusions come infrequently anymore. When I find
one that persists with such fidelity I don't want to probe it. I want to
enjoy it. If it fades before I'm through enjoying it, then I'll answer
you. If it doesn't—then you have an answer." He nodded and
grunted affirmatively, pleased with himself. "What name did you
say you were using? Benajim Cyanus? Interesting. Very well. You
always had a wardrobe of personas to choose from when you had
work to do. This is one I never met before. What are you supposed
to be and why are you going to Earth?"

"I'm the ambassador from Nine Rivers—"

"You're off on the accent. Won't fool anyone who knows the
place, but there are plenty of parochial asses in the City of Homo
who won't know the difference. This was done hastily, Sean."

"—and I'm going to Earth to find someone."

Elen gave him a sharp look.

"Mmm. Well, if I can help, you know I will. I owe you
more than I have time to repay. I didn't think I'd get a chance,
frankly." He gestured to Elen. "Your companion is from Tabit,
I'd guess. She has the look. Don't be startled, Elen Leris—or is
it Leris op Elen?—I've been to Tabit. Not everyone believes in

the Circumvention. Asinine idea! You're still playing for high stakes, Sean—er, Benajim—even after all these years. By the look of you it must be worthwhile."

"I've misplaced a friend. She's on Earth, last I heard."

"Might be hard to find. Friend of yours, no doubt she got on Earth illegally, and if you've misplaced her then that means she's been arrested—or killed. There are ways to find out."

"How is it," Elen asked hesitantly, "that you two know each other?"

Nooneus smiled again and nodded to her. "Since Sean is being 'in character' I'll answer you. I wouldn't want him to have to admit that he's been seen through. Pride is one of his vanities, both his strong point and weakness."

He dragged on his reed, swallowed more of his drink, ate another sweetmeat—offered them to his guests—and cleared his throat.

"Back before the Wars," he said, "I was a section leader in Armada Security. Not as impressive a post as it sounds; it was on Neighbors, an agroworld, and not particularly important in the political scheme of things. Not as important as it was to become later, after I'd already left and become other things. All I had to do was keep track of imports, exports, strangers coming and going, and file the appropriate reports at the appropriate time. I look back now and I'm amused at how utterly nonessential that job was. I was filling in a blank in a file, occupying an empty space on a form. Bureaucracies are built of people acting like files, forms, and fixtures.

"Well, there was already trouble with the Distals. I didn't know what the problem was at the time, but I pieced it together later. I don't know if you know this—it's history, after all, which seems interesting only to those who aren't involved in its making or those who've finished their part in making it—but at one time there was only one shipyard in the Pan. Kronus Yard, in the heart of Sol System, and it was a monopoly. The Chairman had to issue licenses for yards that built starships and for a long time Kronus was it. Then—I believe it was under the third Chairman of the Interstellar Era, Capra, William Capra—two more were licensed and the monopoly was broken. Both Mufrid and Tabit became major shipyards. Both had already possessed the manufacturing capacity to build in-system ships, shuttles, support craft, tenders, anything that didn't have an envelope generator. Capra changed that. It took a while for the major concerns to incorporate them into the basically monopolistic structure of the Pan hegemony, but they did, and when this all happened the three shipyards had been quite stable braces in the infrastructure of Pan economics. The Distals wanted a licensed shipyard.

"Not such a big thing, you might say, but think about it. For the better part of a century three places controlled the number and quality of starships available. They never produced more than the orders placed and there was a waiting list. The Distals owned practically none of their own starships and so relied on the Inner Pan for interstellar transport. The monopolies controlled the economic growth of the Distals.

"Don't ever let anyone tell you differently, the Distal Wars were fought over that central fact of Pan life. Of course, the economy of the entire Pan was massively controlled. But frontier worlds, frontier needs, have a way of disaffecting people with the status quo. The Distals had been a source of disquietude since their settlement. Now they wanted their own shipyard. Couldn't be allowed, of course; they'd go any damn where they wanted to, god only knew where, and over-colonize, over-produce, and over-export. The delicate balance within the Pan would be threatened. Then, of course, there were the seti. No one in the Inner Pan understood, liked, or wanted to understand or like, anything about the aliens. Nonhuman—that said it all. Different. They were out there, by god, and the gates were breached. If the Distals had their own shipyards then we'd never get them closed.

"So the Inner Pan wasn't trading with the Distals. Nothing was being shipped. Legation after legation kept petitioning Erin Tai Chin's government and damn near got the sanctions lifted, but war broke out on Earth itself. Revolution. Ah, but that's another story. This one concerns a man who arrived one day at Neighbors with a purchase order and shipping bill for fifteen million tons of grain.

"I'd already received orders to check and recheck all exports to make sure, if possible, nothing was headed for the Distals. Damn curious order that was, because until I received it I didn't know a thing about the blockades, the sanctions, all the rest of this nonsense. After all, I was security, that wasn't my job. I was a policeman, I was supposed to arrest people for crimes, infractions, disturbances on Neighbors—what did I care about their politics? This was just another order, like any other I'd received, and I was a young man then. The man who walked into my office to get security clearance...he wasn't so young, though he looked it. I put it down to my lack of experience. But he was a good actor, this man. He strode in, tossed his chits on my desk, and smiling—smiling a lot like this Benajim Cyanus here is smiling now—as if he knew something that only he and I did and the rest of the universe was left out. Except I was just as left out. It was a cocksure, presumptuous, impertinent, damned attractive smile and I just couldn't help but like this man. I didn't want to check and recheck him. He did that to you, you know, made you want to agree with him, do what he wanted. He could do it at will. Just as easily, he could cut your throat. I found that out much later, though. This day he just wanted his grain and as little hassle as possible. I did a cursory check of his ship—a tug called the *Solo*—and found what I expected. A freelance spacer, mainly odd hauling jobs and some courier work. Well, the courier part convinced me he was all right. Couriers work for the Armada from time to time, certainly for the Forum, occasionally for the Chairman herself. They were bonded, security cleared to begin with. I was relieved. I didn't have to do an in-depth, I didn't have to go up and inspect his ship, I didn't have to—well, I didn't have to do my job. He came to me pre-cleansed by the system he was about to violate.

"I cleared him.

"Then I asked him out to dinner. Damn few visitors like him ever stopped at Neighbors, and when they did they didn't usually come down-well to the surface. I began to appreciate that this annoying order based on obscure politics was about to brighten my existence by delivering to me a constant stream of visitors, all more interesting than the locals who I had decided, from my vastly advantaged viewpoint as a cipher in the bureaucratic machinery of empire, were not particularly interesting. He accepted.

"Sean Merrick got me drunk, got me in bed with a local girl, and rolled me. He took my ID and rifled my offices, used my authority to clear five more freelancers who had been waiting for his word to accept fifteen million ton shipments, then got everything offworld and out of dock before I recovered enough of my senses to figure out what had happened.

"All ninety million tons of grain went straight to the Distals—I never did find out exactly which world or worlds.

"He made a fool of me.

"What is more he planted a data trail that showed I was nowhere near at the time he did all this and that he had dealt with a minor bureaucrat in the local government. The record showed that I had not yet received those orders to check and recheck. He saved my career while turning my world upside down.

"And he made me pay for it. Over the next several years Sean came to me again and again to help him in some clandestine scheme that I felt—that I believed—I had no choice but to participate in at risk of my career. If it ever came out...and each favor I conceded, the worse the trap. Twenty-one favors. I remember each and every one of them, vividly.

"But I'll tell you a secret. After awhile I did it because I enjoyed it. It was exciting, though I'm not entirely sure whether the excitement was from the constant threat of being caught and my career ending—and possibly my life—or from the nature of each escapade. I couldn't stop. I was addicted to the energy Sean brought me with each new favor. It made living through the bureaucratic pandemonium of Forum service better, worthwhile. Did it bother me that I was often working against myself, doing one thing in the Forum and another with Sean? No. It's all such a game anyway. What troubled me was that, the day the Distal Wars ended, I never saw him again. I was much too conservative in myself to do any of these things on my own. I needed the excuse, the seduction, the dare. Without Sean I could not do it anymore.

"However. I began to notice that my activities within normal channels became gradually more radical. After years of acting on both sides of several issues, of dealing with supporters and enemies as an ally to both, of being forced to see aspects of debates that filling exclusively one role would never have allowed, I found that I could no longer look at anything as a simple matter of this against that. It affected everything I did as a politician. I made enemies that I knew would otherwise have been staunchest allies. I made allies where otherwise would have been ghosts, shadows. My life was never the same after Sean Merrick got through with me."

He drank again, sighed heavily. "So now that you're back, what can I do for you this time?"

Nooneus was kept alive by a complex medical system built into the platform upon which he got around. The cushions, the drinking tube, everything floated on a compact agrav generator. In brighter light his skin was almost grey, his eyes reddish brown, and his teeth some dark in-between color that caused him to smile thinly to hide them. It was easy to believe the man was nearly two centuries old.

The convoy split up at the perimeter of Sol System and ships were shunted off to various bases. The liner went directly to Mars-Earth Transit. Nooneus traveled with a huge entourage; no one questioned the last-minute addition of five more and they walked through unscrutinized. Motiles tended the baggage. They filed through vaulted halls.

"Hasn't changed much since you left, has it?" Nooneus chided Benajim. "The colors are different. I recall that this hall was light blue and chrome back before the War. This austere pearly hue makes it look too much like some religious antiquarian's vision of an afterlife. Hm. No imagination anymore."

Benajim saw Elen examining everything she could. He drew close to her and whispered, "Anything familiar?"

She nodded expressionlessly and walked on. The place did look much the same as some of the sections of Tabit Orbital. But there were no crowds, the walls were clean of graffiti, and all the lights worked. It felt like a museum piece, idealized, closer to original intent. The people present paid only cursory attention to anyone. Benajim imagined he could see the walls each carried that kept everyone separated.

"The intermix," Innes commented quietly, "of machinery and human is really minimal. I haven't seen a public access interface yet."

"In the docks, though," Traville added, "there weren't any humans. All machinery."

Nooneus drifted up to them, smiling. "It'll be a day or two before our petition to the Chairman is accepted. He won't keep me waiting long—we play bridge, he says I'm the best partner he's ever had, and the CEO of Pan Machina is already there and she's an absolute genius to play against—anyway, after you get settled in your apartments here I want to see you all. Privately."

As Nooneus floated off, Benajim felt uneasy.

"What can that be about?" Piper wondered.

"Maybe it's time to part company," Traville said.

"Can't," Benajim said. "Not here, not yet. We might as well take this as far as we can."

"Why take the chance?" Traville complained.

"Because it's better to go through the front door, especially by invitation."

Piper frowned at him.

"Problem?" he asked her.

She shook her head. "No. No problem." She glanced at Traville and Innes. "We do it his way for the time being."

Innes shrugged, but Traville did not look happy.

The apartments were spacious and connected. The motiles deposited their baggage and left. After a quick inspection of the accommodations, they went to Nooneus's apartments.

They were larger still. A pool filled half of it, with a fountain at the far end designed like an abstract of a star cluster, rainbow streams of water arcing out from each spiked point. Nooneus's staff lounged about or swam. No one but Nooneus was dressed and he watched the young people with an air of melancholy and nostalgic joy that, for a moment at least, made him seem younger.

"Ah," he said, grinning, as Benajim and the others entered. He waved them to follow and floated off.

They followed him to another large room which was dominated by an enormous polycom console.

"My own personal unit," Nooneus said. "Information and access to information are what I base my entire office on. Something Merrick taught me—never ignore anything, especially if an order or edict is attached to it. He didn't tell me then that information itself becomes addictive. The more you know the more you wish to know. My colleagues would disagree, but that just makes my job easier." He chuckled dryly. "But they're all waiting for me to die anyway."

The polycom was twice the size of anything in the C.R. and lacked an interface gate.

"What's this?" Innes asked, pointing to an optical array in the center of the board.

Elen stepped closer. "An optil." She smiled at Benajim. "We have a link after all."

Nooneus floated up to the console, gently displacing Elen and Innes. "I need to do some things first, before I can let you play." His fat fingers dropped to the keyboard and began to work quickly. Three screens cleared; two went on stand-by, glowing green, and the center began filling with code. Innes kept her eyes on it. Suddenly it went blank. "Ah," Nooneus sighed, sat back, and waited. A complex pattern flashed on briefly, to be immediately replaced by a menu. "There we are. I've been considering for two days now how to access these. They are quite old and quite classified." He looked at Benajim. "Tricks you taught me long ago. If it's there it can be gotten."

Benajim bent to read to the menu. Names, followed by system names, followed by codes. Nooneus scrolled down the list and stopped. Merrick, Sean B. Sol System. 919AS5928K.

"Shall I access it for you?" Nooneus asked. He did so anyway. The screen cleared again and copy scrolled up. "All these are dead files. Agents and operatives either terminated or missing or retired. If you'll notice this notation here," he pointed in the corner of the displayed page, "you were presumed killed. Tsk. I doubt they'll want to know that they are wrong."

He touched another contact and a holo appeared.

Benajim stared.

"That's not..." Piper breathed.

"Not quite," Traville said.

Benajim felt them looking from the image to him. The edge of his vision blurred, small black scintilla threatened to occlude everything. By will he forced himself to remain conscious. The image cleared.

No, it was not him. Not exactly. The individual differences were subtle, but cumulatively resulted in a marked divergence. Eyebrows were thicker, the line between them deeper. The nose was not as straight, probably from being broken more than once. There was a compression to the lips that lent this image a crueler aspect, but one Benajim could see developing in himself. The jaw line was not as sharp, but the muscles in the neck were more pronounced.

Nevertheless the resemblances ultimately overwhelmed...

"We have the most remarkable gerontological technicians these days," Nooneus said. "I'd almost believe the trip to Peace worthwhile, seeing you."

"Peace...?" he heard himself ask. He could not stop staring at his twin, older brother, father—

"Ah, maybe you've been gone too long," Nooneus said. "Peace, where all old spacers go to die. Among others. The traveler's graveyard. One last snatch at youthful illusion before time finally claims you. Of course old spacers are not the majority of residents now. Old politicians like myself have assumed that unenviable position." He reached for the keyboard.

"Don't," Benajim said.

Nooneus raised his eyebrows, smiled sympathetically, and took his hand away.

Benajim swallowed.

"I may one day be obliged to go to Peace anyway," Nooneus said. "Retirement is becoming less and less a choice. Besides, I have it on reliable data that Peace is very much a place where the minds of its residents' grow smaller in direct proportion to the increase in Armada Security's data. I would be a prime candidate for such sifting." He chuckled. "But they can't do it to me yet. Not while I make such a perfect bridge partner to the Chairman." He laughed louder, coughed, drew on his tube.

Benajim's mouth was dry. Hearing that part of his genetics came from Merrick only deepened the impact of seeing this evidence of consanguinity. This was worse than looking at a mirror. He could have accepted being an exact duplicate of Sean— surgery would account for that. But this... it was like looking at himself having taken a different path through life, all memory intact.

He looked at Elen. She stood still, staring at...what? Her optil was visibly, dimly glittering.

"Ben?"

He blinked. Piper touched his arm.

"Yes?"

"Tam..."

"Oh." He swallowed, looked again at the holo, then turned away, toward Nooneus. "Can you access Armada datanodes through here?"

"Some." He reached for the keyboard, paused to give Benajim a questioning look, then, when Benajim nodded, closed the file. Sean's image vanished. He typed for several seconds. "Depends finally on how secure they are. A lot is ignored, there's just no time to follow up every inquiry."

The shape of a winged dragon over a twelve point star appeared on the screen.

"What do you need?" Nooneus asked.

Traville looked at Benajim, who frowned and noticed that everyone was very quiet and tentative now.

"Your companions," Nooneus said, "are wondering what this is going to cost. Nothing is free. Do you trust me or am I manipulating you for some other purpose?"

Benajim pursed his lips. "Are you?"

"Both are true. You can trust me because I am using you. Not a step further here," he waved at the polycom, "until we come to some terms."

Piper grinned. "That could be a manipulation, too."

"True," Nooneus admitted. "I enjoy manipulating people, it's one of the few pleasures I have anymore that truly satisfies me. But I don't have a great deal of time left to do meaningful things, so multiple manipulations become more expensive than they're usually worth. I want something in return for whatever help I give you."

"If we refuse?" Piper asked.

Nooneus shrugged. "Then I can blackmail you. I'm certain the Armada would be more than interested in the fact that Sean Merrick has returned from the dead—or the Distals, which to most in the Pan Humana is the same thing."

Traville paced, clenching and unclenching his hands. Innes had put on soothing music that now pooled gently about the apartment. Still, Traville's nervous energy set everyone on edge.

"We didn't have much choice," Piper said. "It was an accident encountering him and he did get us through station security."

"That's not a recommendation to trust him," Traville said.

"No, but it certainly goes a long way toward validating what he says. He wants a trade. Help for help."

"Unequal conditions, though," Traville countered. "He can still throw us to the Armada at any moment. Not comfortable."

"So? Not a good reason to refuse him, either."

"He could easily set a trap. We could walk right into detention."

"On the other hand," Innes said, "he might get us what we ask for."

Traville glared at Benajim. "All because Sean Merrick here should be dead and isn't."

Benajim frowned. "But I'm not Sean Merrick."

"Is that so? Who are you then? The answer to that is just as volatile as the other."

Piper sighed. "So what do you suggest? Do you have a plan or is all this just excess frustration?"

"We could try to get into the shuttle locks and steal one, get back to the *Wicca* and try another way."

Innes grunted. "We could commandeer the entire station, demand they give us a starship and control of Sol System."

Traville's eyes flared hotly.

Elen laughed quietly, shaking her head.

"What's funny?" Benajim asked.

She regarded him affectionately. "The fact is, you are Sean Merrick. If you wish to be."

"What do you mean?"

"Nooneus has no one on his staff with an optil," she said. "I was surprised that his polycom did. I took a look through his systems. While I was inside, I changed the status on Merrick's file from 'presumed killed' to 'deactivated'. Whenever you wish we can reactivate it and you will be Sean Merrick. At least to all the security systems in the Pan Humana."

One by one, starting with Piper, they all began laughing. Benajim, stunned, was the last to join in. Uneasily, though. He did not care for the idea of stepping into yet another part of Merrick's identity. He felt trapped by the manipulations of a ghost, who had once been his friend.

He sighed finally. "Hell, why not?"

Two days later they were all descending to Earth as part of Bool Nooneus's entourage.

Joclen decided to move *Wicca*. Shreve had been dipping liberally into the Homestead dataspheres for several days. Joclen did not believe in luck. It was time to leave Tau Ceti.

She did not like the idea of the *Solo* wandering around in Pan space on its own, but there was nothing she could do about it.

The ship contacted her from time to time to let her know that it knew where *Wicca* was, which in itself disturbed her. Moving from Tau Ceti was as much to shake off the feeling of being watched.

She moved randomly from one system to the next. Usually they did not enter the system, but paused outside, hidden in whatever cover they found—an Oort Cloud around Faron, the tangled wreckage of an ancient perimeter station near Aquas, a broad field of charged particles that formed a diffuse ring around Mufrid. Each place Shreve opened up the local dataspheres and collected information. Each place they stayed until the irritating signal came in from the *Solo,* letting them know once again that it knew where they were. Seventy-six days out of Miron and Joclen felt no nearer to completing the run...

Fifteen days into this scattered odyssey, since Benajim and his party had left, Ratha found something.

"It's a Commonwealth data envelope," he said. "But it's operating on a Pan frequency and following a guidon from a Pan system."

"A ship?"

"Has to be."

Joclen touched her gate, flowed into the sensor array.

Far away the data envelope was a bright flower. The violet thread of the guidon stretched away to vanish in the distance.

Shreve—

On it.

As she watched, layers of the envelope peeled away, briefly brightening as the Pan configurations filtered out to reveal the denser, more complex envelope of a C.R. ship. Below this the shape of that ship was visible.

Merchanter...

Looks like one of Merrick Enterprises.

Close in. I want to know what it's doing here. Full defensive posture.

Joclen withdrew and watched the ship grow in the holo as Wicca drew nearer.

"Shreve is masking our envelope as a Pan ship," Ratha said. "So far they've only acknowledged our presence."

"Request that they stand down and prepare to receive an inspection party."

Ratha gave her a startled look. She nodded in reply and turned her attention back to the ship in the holo. They were close enough now to see the markings on its hull.

"Permission denied," Ratha said.

"Weapons coming on line," Stoan said.

"Fire!" Joclen shouted.

Wicca's beams cut into the merchanter's hull. Atmosphere erupted briefly in flame.

"Shreve was already in their dataspheres," Stoan said.

"Again!"

Another barrage tore into the bigger ship.

"In another few seconds," Stoan said tightly, "Shreve will have their engines shut down."

Joclen looked at him, for a moment angry with him for interrupting her. Then she looked at the image in the holosphere. The Merrick ship was badly damaged, the hull crinkled and blackened where *Wicca's* beams had struck, debris streaming out into space. Joclen drew a deep breath and for a second she thought she would be sick. The nausea passed quickly and she straightened in her couch.

"Signal again," she said. "Request permission to board again."

Stoan continued to stare at her for a time. She frowned at him and finally he turned away.

They found a small crew on board, eight people to run the huge ship. The holds were filled with goods clearly not from the C.R. or any of the Seti Reaches. Most of the cargo consisted of manufactured items, textiles, raw materials, a fairly complete manifest that might be expected on board any long haul merchanter.

One hold, however, carried something else. People in hibernation, sleeping, a hundred of them. Thijs found subdermal beacons below the collarbone of each one. When they revived some of them and asked where they were from, none could answer. Crej'Nevan found them to be mindblocked.

Shreve discovered them on the manifest. They were bound for a system called Nescis and a distributor named Gerard.

Joclen ordered the crew placed in hibernation and had Shreve program the ship to return to the C.R. She wanted to destroy it, but Stoan advised her against it. This way would be better, she had to agree. An embarrassment to sail right into the midst of everything else that had gone wrong for Carson Reiner since this had begun.

As well as the destination, Shreve had traced the ship back to where it had taken on the cargo of humans. A world called Peace in the Gamma Virginis System.

Istanbul was a scarred city. Entire districts had been razed during upheavals that had wracked the city during the Distal Wars. The revolution had been put down. Parks covered the ground where once ancient houses and streets had been. From the palace gardens Benajim counted fifteen parks. Work was being done on five others. Between them the old quarters of the city stood, braced and repaired, spared destruction by the collapse of the rebellion.

The Chairman's palace mounted high on the Galata. Over the last few centuries it had become a city in itself, absorbing the Dolmabahce Palace, the Palace of Culture, and most of the Beyoglu district. The Galata Bridge had been destroyed during the rebellions; its jagged remains still jutted from the far side of the Golden Horn, cruelly ripped apart and left as a reminder. Only the Ataturk Bridge connected Istanbul Proper to the Palace District, though a heavy ferry traffic constantly moved between them. From the vantage of the gardens you could look past Istanbul and its still-standing mosques to the Sea of Marmarra. Huge ships came and went, flyers peppered the sky.

Earth. Benajim could not quite take it in.

Bool Nooneus went off to play bridge with the Chairman and left Benajim and his party to themselves. The first thing Benajim did was to access a map of the palace.

There were many sections labeled "Restricted" or "Authorized Access Only", including a couple in what otherwise seemed to be medcenters.

"Well, we're not going to find her through casual inquiry," he said. "Let's reactivate Sean's status and see what that gives us."

Elen nodded and set to work.

"You're sure about this?" Piper asked.

"No," Benajim said. "But—"

"Reactivated," Elen announced.

Benajim sat down and punched in his—Sean's—access code. 'Approved' flashed onto the screen, followed by 'Proceed.' Benajim requested a list of all arrests made directly by Armada security in the past thirty days.

"This can't be right," Piper said. "After all this time, why would the system recognize him?"

"It's just a filing system," Innes said. "No real oversight unless somebody tells it to. The volume of data involved..."

Piper leaned over Benajim's shoulder.

"That's too much," Piper said as the list scrolled on and on.

"Wait, wait," Benajim said. "Where was Tamyn captured?"

"Northwest of Cuttack," Traville said, "near the Brahmani River."

Benajim pared the list of arrests down. There were twenty-two. Fifteen were named, the others were coded classified.

"So many?" Piper mused.

Benajim went down the list, requesting status. All but two had been released within the last ten days. When he requested information on the remaining two the screen blanked for a moment, then flashed and interrogative for his clearance code.

"My, my," Benajim said, smiling. He typed in a request for the case officer's name and status.

COMMANDER MOSS FISHER, ADMINISTRATOR ARMADA SECURITY.

"Well, we know who has them," Innes said.

"Where would he keep them?" Benajim wondered.

"Why not just ask?" Elen suggested. "You have clearance."

"I don't want Commander Fisher, whoever he is, notified that someone else is perusing his cases. Ah!"

He requested information on the security coded medcenters. After a few tries he found one consigned directly to Commander Moss Fisher.

Benajim stepped out of the lift into the roof gardens of the palace. It was more a forest than a garden. Small pavilions rose out of the ground here and there that gave access below. He found the edge, mounted the steps to the walkway, and stared out.

He returned to the path and wound his way through the lush foliage. The scents were entrancing, the colors, the shapes of leaves...

He followed the trail he had memorized to another one of the pavilions and descended the lift. He was a little anxious without Piper. He had come to depend on her presence, but this time he had persuaded her that he ought to go alone, that two of them, especially one without any kind of identity within Pan dataspheres other than a quickly appropriated ambassadorial status, would be too risky.

The lift let him out ten floors down. He stepped into a wide, austere corridor. Twenty paces on he came to a door that did not open for him.

"Secure area," a voice informed him. "State code and status for access."

"Merrick, 919AS55928K, status classified."

"Acknowledged. Proceed."

The doors opened.

Benajim blinked, heart racing, and walked through.

He entered a wide anteroom. A terminal at the far end stood sentinel at another door. As he approached it, a tag extruded from a slot in the terminal.

"Your ID, Commander Merrick," the voice said. "Wear at all times when within secure areas."

"Thank you." He pressed the tag to his left breast. The door opened and he entered. His heart was beginning to race, but he was fascinated. Using Merrick's name to be somewhere he ought not be provided a dual goad to his adrenal gland. He consciously tried to slow his breathing and remain calm. He walked into the medcenter.

The corridors in the medical ward were basically white. Bulletin boards displayed names and codes at each intersection. Rows of closed doors stretched down each one and he saw few people, but those he encountered studiously ignored him. He walked through boldly, as if he belonged there and had business somewhere else. No one stopped him. His ID tag, he was certain, was scanned at each junction.

After several confusing turns he began to panic a little. Then he walked out into a broader circuit and saw a large desk with a man behind it surrounded by monitors. He licked his lips and strode up to him. The man looked up with an annoyed expression that almost immediately turned to caution, almost fear.

"Yes, sir?"

"What's your task here?"

"Uh...data coordination, general access—"

"Good. Do you have a listing for someone named Glass? Tamyn Glass specifically."

The man hesitated, frowned, then touched a keyboard. He looked up at the tag on Benajim's shirt, then back at the screen.

"Are you connected to Commander Fisher?"

"I'm connected with no one. This is not Fisher's level."

Eyes widened, a few more commands.

"Yes, sir, we have a Tamyn Glass listed in the criminal security wing. She's under Commander Fisher's direct supervision, though, and I have to inform him—"

"You inform no one. Check my classification if you like."

The young man swallowed, read the numbers on Benajim's tag, then nodded. He typed on his keyboard and waited.

"Uh-yes, sir, Commander Merrick. I didn't realize—"

"You weren't supposed to. Where is Glass?"

"Wing G, corridor nine. You go down there—" he pointed to Benajim's left "—turn right, then left immediately. At the end of that corridor is Wing G."

"Is Commander Fisher there now?"

"Y-yes, sir."

Benajim nodded and walked away. He kept his face straight only by extreme effort until he rounded the first corner. Though frightened, he was nevertheless enjoying himself immensely.

He found Wing G.

As he entered the lobby he saw several people. He straightened, looked into an open door—med equipment—then walked past them.

A gurney was coming from another hall into the lobby. A short man with no hair stood talking to a pair who looked like bureaucrats, expensively dressed and not at all as spartanly utilitarian as the others in this section. The man turned to the gurney. Benajim slowed, stopped, backed into the corridor a short way.

The man fell into step with the gurney and said, "You'll enjoy this trip, Glass. You're going to lose your mind on it. Most of it, anyway. Don't worry, you won't miss it much." He patted her hand and stepped away.

The gurney went by Benajim.

Tamyn lay on it. Their eyes met briefly. She looked awful. Her eyes were hollow, with dark rings, and her face was thinner. He wondered if she had been beaten. He gave her a curious look, then walked on by.

He stepped into the lobby again, went to a bulletin board.

The bald man was speaking with the two officials again.

"—Peace will be fully capable of handling the overspill by the time I'm done with it," he said. "All I need is to prove to your colleagues the efficacy of my proposal and the funding should come automatically."

He looked over at Benajim incuriously. Benajim tapped the bulletin board as if he had found what he wanted and walked away, down the corridor after Tamyn.

There was nothing he could do.

But at least he knew she was alive.

Benajim found Bool Nooneus sitting near a pool outside his apartments, watching ducks attack the bread strips he lazily tore from a loaf and tossed to the water. In the glare of late morning light Nooneus looked pale and brittle. Benajim winced inwardly and abruptly realized that he saw Sean in the old man. Sean had been less able to use his body, restricted though Nooneus was, but their faces held something similar that linked them in Benajim's mind. They knew...something. Sean had never bothered to explain, Nooneus probably could not make it clear to someone from the C.R., but Benajim actually hungered after it, because in both men he had seen a certainty that encompassed error and made it irrelevant. In his most coherent, confident moments Benajim believed himself a mass of inadequacies, a feeling neither Sean nor Bool evinced even in those unguarded moments when they thought themselves completely alone. Benajim wanted that kind of surety.

He stepped from the lip of the apartment onto grass and crushed a leaf. Nooneus looked around at him and smiled.

"Sean."

"I wish you'd quit calling me that," he said with a smile.

Nooneus shrugged. "Old habits. They have lives of their own. You look like you want something."

Benajim laughed and sat down on the grass at the side of the pond. A duck looked at him and quacked indignantly before returning to the bread it was slaughtering.

"Am I that transparent to you?"

"No. For instance, I don't know what it is you want."

"That makes two of us. You've been most indulgent to us. I don't know what you want."

Nooneus tore three more strips of bread and flicked them out to the water. He sighed and seemed to retreat slightly into his chair, blinking and vaguely shaking his head.

"It's sad," he said. "All things ultimately reduce to scales. Balance is necessary, but advantage is always pursued. When the scales finally equal, no one but those not playing the game are content. I enjoy playing out the fiction that among friends such considerations need not arise. I always discover the fiction is that one has friends."

Nooneus chuckled dryly, pulled his pipe to his mouth and drew on it. He shrugged dreamily.

"I've been playing politics for so long that I don't know any other life. And I'm not to be pitied for that. I love it! And you're responsible for that."

"Me?"

"When you used me and compromised me all those years ago I had to work like hell to keep my position. When I succeeded and found that I had weathered the storm and recovered lost ground, I sat back and took stock of everything and discovered that I had absolutely enjoyed every minute of it. Especially when I had manipulated those determined to crucify me to the point of controlling them. I loved it. I couldn't wait to charge right back into the confusion. You did that. You introduced me to my fetish, Sean Merrick, and I have nothing but gratitude." He leaned marginally toward Benajim, grinning. "But I've been waiting for the opportunity to return the favor."

"Mmm. So...?"

"What I want in return for what you want—"

"You have no idea yet. How do you know the scales will balance?"

"I don't. In fact, I don't expect them to. I trust you will get more out of this than I, but I only want one thing. If I get it then I'll consider us balanced. As long as you never tell me how much it cost."

"I think I can arrange to keep that from you. What do you want?"

Abruptly—Benajim was startled by the change—Bool's features lost all softness, all gentleness. In a moment he acquired the demeanor of a predator, hungry and amoral and absolutely committed to the kill.

"There's a man I want eliminated. I don't care how it's done, you don't necessarily have to kill him—in fact, it would be preferable that you don't, so he'll know and live with his failure. He rather insensitively disposed of a friend of mine, someone who had done me considerable good in the past and was in a position to do considerably more."

"Does he have a name?"

"Oh, a name, a rank, a position. Commander Moss Fisher, the new head of covert operations for Armada Security. He had the former head put to death on a charge of negligence. Idiotic charge, idiotic sentence, but these things happen in a bureaucracy this large and unwieldy. I must admit the man was a bit careless. He let outsiders actually set down on Earth. But he had been feeding me information for years on matters here in the Galata. The balances are far out of scale now. Fisher's not likely to take my friend's place in that respect, although I have no doubt he will be hideously efficient in every other."

"Covert operations. What was the code name...?"

"Firebrake."

Benajim nodded, watching the ducks and trying to control his elation. He looked around, startled, when Nooneus let his chair drift close and the old man reached out and grabbed Benajim's arm. His grip was stronger than Benajim expected.

"I want Fisher toppled. There are a number of other reasons than the one I just gave. He's also an inordinately ambitious man who has boasted more than once that he considers himself qualified to be Chairman. The Pan is an impressive place, volatile and flexible, but not so much that it could survive the Chairmanship of a Moss Fisher."

Benajim and Nooneus regarded each other intently. Finally Nooneus let go and floated back. He tore more bread and cast the bits to the water. He smiled as the ducks crowded each other, competing for morsels.

"Bool, you may be the luckiest politician in the Pan."

"Oh, I know that. I know that." He seemed harmless and benevolent again. "Now: what precisely can I do for you, Sean?"

Chapter Twenty

Ryan's house lay thirty kilometers out of town across undulating grasslands. The horizon line was marked by distance—blued mountains that still rose precipitously to meet clouds that underlay an azure sky. The house was a sprawling affair of add-ons surrounded by a wide deck. He set the transport down in the shade of a covered slab and left her on the deck while he fetched tea.

"Nobody cares too much for Del," he said as she sipped the cold drink. The breeze off the plain to the west ruffled their hair and set the fern-like plants Ryan kept in bulbous pots to swaying. "He's a natural-born busybody. That's why Interface uses him. That way they don't have to waste staff on spy work. Most of us could care less. We don't care much for doctors anyway, so Del is less of an irritant."

Ryan sat across from her with his own glass and looked out over the grassland. Insects hummed and buzzed, lofted by the breeze.

"Have you remembered your name yet?" he asked suddenly.

She drank, studying him over the rim of her glass. Her eyes stayed on the glass as she carefully set it down, drawn to it. "Tam...I think. Something like that. Tam."

He nodded slowly.

"You don't seem surprised I can't remember anything."

He shrugged. "Everybody comes out a little different. Treatment's not always easy, although they claim otherwise. Doctors! They've been telling us it won't hurt a bit for ages. Ouch, you son-of-a..." He laughed.

"What treatment?"

"Eh? Oh, you'll remember that, too. The treatment you received at Interface."

She pulled air through her teeth. "My mind is all messed up, Co Jones. I'd appreciate you telling me how it got that way if you know."

He looked at her oddly, then winced and said nothing.

"I don't mean to sound harsh," she said, "but under the circumstances—"

"Under the circumstances I think you'd best take the advice of someone who's been through it and seen a thousand others come out of it. You'll remember. Gradually. But you will. Trust me when I say it's best you remember on your own, without help."

"I know something about amnesia. It generally only affects parts of memory, those that deal directly with a trauma. Otherwise we couldn't carry on this conversation."

"I'm surprised we are anyway. Your accent's strange."

"Funny, I thought it was you." She raised her glass to her mouth.

Ryan laughed, then shook his head. "Believe me, what happens at Interface is very personal and very traumatic."

She slammed her glass down. Cold liquid spilled over her hand. "But I should know what this is as an abstraction!" She went to the railing. "Judging from what I've seen and heard, the way people react, nothing about this place is unusual, so I ought to know what it is! But I don't! You said 'welcome to Peace' almost as if you thought I knew what you were talking about. Peace doesn't mean anything to me!" She turned to him. Quieter, she said, "I don't think I belong here."

Ryan scratched his beard thoughtfully. "I'm no psychologist, but you do have a point, I guess. Sounds logical, anyway, but then that must mean some of your memory is coming back. Seems to me, though, that I knew where I was when I came out." Then his hands came up and he waved them negatively. "No, I'm not going to mess with it." He stood. "Too much I don't understand."

"Wait—"

"Now," he went on, stepping away, "you stay here as long as you like. I personally think it's best for newcomers to have some privacy, I don't care what Interface or Del Robello might say. This way all your remembering is done in peace. I know it was important to me to be left alone when I started remembering. So, I have plenty of room here. Just pick a bedroom and settle in."

He smiled quickly and left her standing on the deck, her hands half raised to implore. He disappeared within his house. After a time, she turned to stare out at the unfamiliar yellow grass and the too-blue sky. The light was too white for a G type star, almost harsh. It was completely unfamiliar, devoid of the tell-tale signs of places she had been to before, leaving her only the fascination she usually felt upon arriving somewhere new...

Usually? she wondered.

Her attempt to get Ryan Jones to explain things had been a
gamble at best. She did know something about amnesia—how she
knew was a mystery—and if this world, the Interface, everything
she had seen so far was an intimate part of the trauma causing hers,
then she would not know anything about it. Not until her memory
returned. But she felt certain that when—if—her memory returned
she still would know nothing about Peace.

Images flashed through her mind, like remnants of too many
dreams all shoved together. Broken glass, she thought, and frowned.
Glass. She rolled the word around in her mouth, played with its
shape for a few minutes. It failed to resolve—and it very much felt
like it wanted to resolve—so, frustrated, she shrugged and turned
from the railing.

"All my remembering done in peace," she muttered and grunted.
"All my remembering done *on* Peace...wherever Peace is."

She crossed the wooden deck to the wide doors and stepped
inside. A great room dominated this section of the house. Tall windows all around let in the brilliant sunlight. In the center rose a large,
round fireplace, its coppery metal flue funneling up through the bare
rafters. Heavy couches surrounded it. Throw rugs were scattered at
whim on the tiled floor. A double door split the wall opposite the
windows in half. Covering the wall to the right of the door books
filled a ceiling-high case. On the left of the door was a bulky unit that
looked like a biomed, but she was not sure. It was somehow different than it ought to be. To the left of the this stood a big cabinet,
inlaid rose-colored wood, alabaster slivers representing a star cluster
she did not recognize. A liquor cabinet stood beside this.

She walked by the books and glanced at a few titles and recognized none of them. Another wide doorway led onto another section of the deck.

About eighty meters away ran a stream. She stood at the railing
watching the sun shatter on the cascading water and her mind went
pleasantly blank. Beyond were the mountains.

The deck wrapped completely around the house. She found
five more doors, one of which stood open. Inside she found a bed,
a thick pad on an adjustable frame with a control panel that could be
swung out of the way. A small dresser stood against the far wall.
She stepped around the bed and studied her reflection in the mirror.

The face. She knew the face. It was agonizingly familiar, but it had no name. Tentatively she began mouthing "glass" again. A teasing familiarity goaded her. She raised her hand to absently stroke her lower lip—and pulled her finger away to study it. No, it did not feel right, but...she rubbed her thumb over her fingertips; they felt hard, calloused. The skin was brown, pleasingly roiled in delicate patterns—and totally unfamiliar. She looked at her face again. A line deepened between her dark eyebrows.

I know you...

Brown skin, darker than it should have been.

"Tam...?" Her mouth felt good saying it. She blinked, smiled. "Tamyn." She grinned. Yes, that was correct. Maybe Ryan was right and it was only a matter of time. "Tamyn." She leaned on the dresser and brought her eyes close to the reflection. "My name is Tamyn."

The next morning she went down to the stream, stripped off her coverall, and waded out into the water. Tamyn clenched her teeth at its initial icy bite and kept going. The pebbly surface under her feet stabbed at her soles. When she reached waist-deep water she drew a deep breath and dived under.

Sunlight sank in constantly shifting curtains before her. Above, at the surface, the light scattered, diamonds and gold. She swam against the current, forcing her muscles to move her along until they burned pleasantly, then threatened to cramp. She broke surface, and let herself float, and found she had come only eight or nine meters upstream. The current took her below where she had entered. She filled her lungs and swam again.

It felt good to push against an obstacle, better to push and succeed. After four tries she managed to swim twenty meters against the water. Laughing, she drifted on her back for a while, then stood and walked to shore. She moved a few large stones from the ground and fell, stretching out in the warm sun.

The red glow of sunlight through her closed eyelids darkened. Tamyn opened her eyes and saw Ryan looking down at her.

"Good morning, Co Jones," she said.

"Morning. You know, you ought not to do that."

She sat up and turned to face him. "Do what?"

"Too much water and sun aren't good for you. Things deteriorate faster, get harder to put back together."

"I don't know what you're talking about."

"The geriatrics. All your reconstruction. It's not invulnerable. You abuse it they might not be able to fix it."

"Geriatrics…"

Ryan shook his head. "Did you remember anything yet?"

"My name. Tamyn." She smiled. "Only the first one so far."

"Hm. Good. The rest'll come. I'm cooking breakfast." He turned and walked back to the house.

Tamyn snatched up her coverall and followed. The heavy odors of bacon and syrup filled the kitchen.

"This doesn't make sense," she said as she stepped back into her clothes.

"What's that?" Ryan asked from the stove. He broke eggs over a skillet; they sizzled as they struck the hot metal.

"You said I'd damage the geriatrics."

"That's right."

"That implies I'm old."

He looked at her with raised eyebrows.

"I'm fifty-two."

Ryan frowned.

Tamyn went on. "If I were old enough for reconstructive surgery, I wouldn't have been able to swim so long against the current. I'd be a mass of pain and probably injured right now."

He nodded slowly, turned over an egg.

"So what's going on?"

He did not look happy. "Well, I guess I figured you wrong. Some of us on Peace are here for other reasons than retirement."

"Retirement?"

"Not by choice," he snapped. He dished up pancakes and eggs onto a plate, then added strips of bacon. "Here. Eat this while it's hot. There's juice and coffee over there." He nodded toward the small table by the window.

Tamyn took the plate and went over to the table. Movement brought her gaze up to the window.

"You have a visitor," she said.

Ryan looked at the shape coming over the low hill. "Damn," he breathed. "A meddlesome ass from Interface."

He went out onto the deck. Tamyn followed. The transport reached the house and settled to the ground, its whine dying. It was newer than Ryan's, better maintained, dark blue with a white stripe along the side.

"Uh huh," Ryan grumbled. "Interface."

A man stepped from the transport and waved at Ryan. He came up the steps to the deck, walking briskly and smiling. He was young, blondish hair, a slim build covered in a pale blue jumpsuit.

"Hello, Ryan," he said.

"Morning, Len."

Len looked at the house. "This is the first time I've been out here. You're a little hard to find."

"With reason," Ryan said darkly.

Len looked at him quizzically, then glanced at Tamyn. "Good morning. I hope I'm not interrupting anything."

"Just breakfast," Ryan said. "Since you're here, would you like some?"

Len nodded. "I can smell it from here."

Ryan grunted and turned. "Well, come on in, then."

"I'm Tamyn."

"Len Venel. I'm with the Interface."

"So Ryan said."

"All right," Ryan said loudly. "No professional crap until we've eaten."

Len smiled and Tamyn laughed.

Ryan prepared another plate and set it before Len, then sat down himself. He carved his eggs and scooped a forkful into his mouth.

"Cold," he announced and continued eating.

Len said, "It's delicious. Thank you." He looked at Tamyn. "Just Tamyn?"

"For now. I haven't figured the rest out yet."

"Hmm. You came out yesterday?"

"In the morning," Ryan said. "As if you didn't know."

"Contrary to what Ryan thinks, I'm just the administrator, which means I usually hear things last. This time not until I heard Del Robello grousing about what you did to him."

Ryan looked up, frowning. "Grousing to who?"

"Michel."

Ryan narrowed his eyes, then grunted and continued eating.

Len gave Tamyn an apologetic shrug. "We're supposed to all know what goes on here, but we've had staff cuts, new regulations, and a higher admission rate than before, so details slip through once in a while—"

"Like entire residents," Ryan said.

"That hasn't happened before," Len said defensively.

"No?" Ryan gestured with his fork. "What about that fellow, Smannen? You didn't know he was here for three days. Now that he's disappeared I bet you don't know when or where he went."

Len looked uncomfortable. He pushed the remnants of his food around the plate.

Ryan shook his head, stabbed another forkful. "I bet you still don't know where Alma is."

Len cleared his throat and looked at Tamyn. "I'm not here to discuss our shortcomings, Ryan."

"Hah! Damn right."

"You haven't remembered your last name yet? How about where you're from?"

Tamyn shook her head. "Why? I thought not remembering was the whole point."

"That's just a side effect to some of the blocks," Len explained. "The idea is to help you adjust. Nothing's supposed to be erased or occluded, just suppressed, so you don't think about it constantly."

Tamyn shuddered. Blocks? Something nagged at her about the word. It repelled her.

"To what end?" she asked.

"Well, to make it easier for you to cope with retirement. The idea of Peace is just that. Live out your life in Peace. You should remember everything if you try hard enough, but the way we've modified your synaptic responses you won't suffer a continual onslaught of painful memory."

"I'm not retired, though."

"Oh?"

"I'm only fifty-two. Why would I retire with a good seventy, eighty years of optimum health ahead of me"?"

Len blinked at her. Ryan looked up. Len took out a small handpad and stylus and jotted some notes.

"If," Len said, "you could remember where you're from it would help. I don't recognize your accent, but the Pan is a big place, I can't know them all." He put away the pad and stood. "It's been nice meeting you. Ryan, if she hasn't started remembering in three days bring her to Interface and let me have a look, okay?"

Ryan nodded, still staring at Tamyn.

"I have to get back," Len said. "I'll have to tell Lyrda that she did a marvelous job on you. You're lovely."

Tamyn watched him leave. She heard the transport whine to life and move away.

"Who's Lyrda?" she asked.

"Their resident cosmetic surgeon and geriatrics specialist."

Tamyn shot him a startled look.

"Where the hell," Ryan asked slowly, "do you think you are? Nobody lives to a hundred and thirty, much less at 'optimum health'!"

"Why are you angry?"

Ryan stood, knocking the chair back. He snatched up the plates and went to the sink.

"And that damn accent," he added, turning on the water.

When it was clear he intended to say no more, Tamyn went into the great room. She was growing weary of all the disorientation. What did Ryan mean, no one lived to a hundred and thirty? Merrick was nearly two hundred—

She blinked, startled. She closed her eyes. There was a face connected with that name, old, lined, grinning. It changed as she grasped to hold it. For a moment it was younger—much younger—with a full head of thick blondish hair, pale eyes, but the same smirk. Merrick. Sean Merrick.

He's dead though, she thought. I buried him.

A mausoleum flashed through her mind, accompanied by a voice reciting names and dates. Is that my heritage?

No, I'm an orphan...

Tamyn opened her eyes.

"—didn't mean to be harsh, but you touched a sore spot."

She looked to her right. Ryan stood there, thumbs hooked in the waist of his pants, his eyes lowered, evasive.

"You certainly don't look fifty-two, though," he said.

"I'm fifty-two," she said. "My name is Tamyn...something." She shook her head, irritated, and looked outside. "Who tampered with my mind?"

"Everybody here gets adjusted—"

"It's obscene!"

"Well, I wouldn't—"

"That's who you are! Why would you let anyone change that?" His face reddened. "So you don't think about what you haven't got anymore. It's hard enough—" He growled and strode off. She heard a door slam.

Tamyn pressed her hands to her head. My mind...my memories...who did this to me?

Len parked in the underground garage and took the lift up to the administrative level. This new resident, Tamyn, disturbed him. Obviously she was another one like Smannen. Damn Ryan for bringing that up. Len wished he could forget, but...

He reached his office and touched the comm.

"Central, is Lyrda in her office?"

The machine replied, "Yes, she is. Do you wish to talk?"

"In my office. Please ask her to come down, would you? And send some coffee around."

"Yes, Dr. Venel."

He sat down at his desk and called up his files. Now that he had a name and a description, perhaps he could match her up. From memory he started constructing a portrait on the screen. When he finished he set the machine to searching.

He was still rummaging when Lyrda Stanson came in.

"Knock, knock?"

Len looked up. "Oh. Lyrda, come in, please."

Behind her a tray trundled in with the coffee service. Len removed it and sent the tray out, then closed the door.

"Is this business?" Lyrda asked, smiling.

Len smiled back. Lyrda had a pleasant round face, large brown eyes, and thick black hair. "Unfortunately, business. I need to ask you about one of your better reconstruction jobs. A woman named Tamyn."

"Tamyn who?"

Len shrugged. "She doesn't remember, I can't find her in the file."

He turned the screen so she could see the portrait.

Lyrda shook her head. "Not one of mine. But we've been busy as hell, I've got thirty new ones freshly delivered. One might have slipped my notice."

"I doubt that. This one is...memorable. This doesn't do her justice—she's intense, makes a solid impression. I don't think I could forget her if I tried. I wonder what she used to do."

"No. Not one of mine. Probably one of Fisher's."

Len looked significantly at the ceiling, then at Lyrda.

Lyrda made an impatient gesture. "We're none of us going to be employed here much longer, you know that. What difference does it make what we say out loud?"

"Well...where our next place of employment is. I'd rather not work in Ghagaol."

"With your talents? You'll probably run a resort for the hand-chosen elite." She looked at the screen again and frowned. "This is getting worse instead of better. Five of the last group were under sixty, in perfect health. I traced three of them to former positions in Armada security."

"And before that we had six former inmates from Ghagaol." Len scowled. "Peace was never—"

The door opened. Moss Fisher stepped in, smiling.

Len glared at him. "It's considered polite to announce yourself first."

"I'm not polite," Fisher said. "Peace was never what? I didn't mean to interrupt."

"Peace—" Len hesitated. Fisher waited with a bland, mildly interested expression, too pleasant to be casual. But that was paranoid thinking and Len had no patience for that. "Peace was never intended to be a prison."

"No? Maybe not, but I'd say old age is its own prison, so what difference the accommodations?"

"Or the company?" Lyrda added sardonically.

Len sighed. "You know, Commander, one day you'll be old yourself."

"Mm. By then it won't matter." He glanced at the screen. "Ah. You found her. Good. Where is she?"

Len considered withholding that information, but it seemed pointless—Fisher would find out by other means.

"She's staying with Ryan Jones," he said. "He has a place about fifty, sixty klicks from town. Nice place."

"Have you spoken with her?"

Len nodded.

"Has she remembered anything?"

Len gave him a narrow look. "Her first name, that's it."

"Excellent. I'm not happy, though, with the sloppy way she slipped out of town, untraced. That has to change."

"As I said—"

"Peace is not a prison, of course, but some people ought to be treated like they're in prison regardless."

Len was startled. "You're suggesting Tamyn's a criminal? I doubt that."

"Oh? Your professional judgement?"

"As a matter of fact—"

"Dr. Venel, your expertise is in the psychologies of your patients. You understand how a particular psyche develops the way it does, how it arrives where it is when you get it. My expertise lies in what those psyches do with themselves after they've developed. There's overlap, certainly, but I'm sure you'll admit that my area of interest is substantively different than yours." He looked at the portrait again. "I want directions to Jones's place. And I want better track kept of the people under your charge, Doctor."

Len bristled. "If I knew they were under my charge before they're released into the general population—"

"Point taken," Fisher interrupted. "This one was a special case. She's shown me the holes in your operation. Now we can plug them. Good day, Doctor."

He wheeled around and strode out of the office.

Lyrda nodded slowly. "I've never found anyone I so wanted to disassemble before."

Len sank back in his chair. It was all out of his control now. Since Armada security had arrived they had, piece by piece, whittled away at his authority. Ever since Smannen and Alma, he thought.

Smannen had been obviously political. Half the staff had known who he was when he arrived. Opposition leader on Homestead, the only real authority that might challenge the ruling clique. Popular. He had disappeared while on a tour through the system orbitals. A few months later he had arrived on Peace with an Armada escort, for processing and admission to the population. Len and a few others had protested. More Armada security arrived. They were ordered to proceed, and did so, with the few intractable dissenters dismissed and sent elsewhere.

One time only, Len remembered telling himself, just one time, no more. Smannen had started remembering within a few weeks. Alma had been one of the resident firebrands, like Ryan used to be, and had begun kicking up a fuss when Smannen started remembering.

Len never found out what had become of them. He had called on them at their homes one day and found nothing but vandalized apartments. All his inquiries had been systematically referred elsewhere until finally they were not accepted at all.

Still, Fisher was moving secretively. He did not have blanket approval for his program. Things were being manipulated too personally, and too slowly, and the charade that Peace was still what it had been designed to be—retirement, a decent place to live out a dwindling handful of years, a place for those injured or displaced to find some solace and...peace—was assiduously maintained. Fisher was not yet invulnerable. Perhaps what he was doing with this new one, Tamyn, would give him that status.

But what options did that leave? Len could only issue another interrogative, another scrap of pleading to be lost in the system, ignored, and, possibly, filed for later evidence of his disloyalty.

He found himself in complete agreement with Lyrda's sentiments. It would be interesting to disassemble Fisher, just to see what made him work.

She woke in the middle of the night and sat up in bed. It was an uncomfortable thing, this solid pad. She wanted a suspensor field. Then she wondered if there was such a thing or if her mind were playing tricks on her again.

She had not seen Ryan the rest of the day. He kept to his room. Tired, Tamyn had gone to bed early.

Nacreous light filled the windows. She went to the door and stepped out onto the deck.

And caught her breath.

Stars crowded the sky. One in particular was much brighter than the others, a yellow-white jewel. So this is a binary system, she thought. An ache worked through her breast, to her arms, and she reached up as if to hold them. The strains of ancient music drifted through her mind. She knew above all else that she wanted to be there, that she belonged there.

"I'm a spacefarer," she hissed.

Jagged bits of dreams surfaced. Faces mostly, so familiar, but there were no names. A death. Someone she did not know, though she could not say how she knew that. And a ship...

Music played from the house. Tamyn followed the deck around to the great room. The doors were open and she stepped inside. A fire burned low in the fireplace. Music flowed from the player tucked in the bookcase.

Ryan lay on the floor by the fireplace. Tamyn crossed the floor and rounded the couches until she saw his face. He was locked in rigor, eyes bulged, foam drooling down his beard. Only his fingers moved, clenching and opening spasmodically.

Tamyn dropped to her knees and grabbed his head. Blood coated his lips. She ran into the kitchen and grabbed a steel ladle, then returned. Her hand was not large enough to reach around his jaw, so she took the ladle in her teeth and, with both thumbs, pressed against his jaw hinges. His mouth opened and more blood trickled out. His tongue had been bitten, but it was intact. She lowered her head carefully and dropped the ladle across his mouth. When she took her thumbs away his teeth snapped loudly against it.

She opened his shirt and checked his heart. Strong beat, but too fast. No fever. She checked his pants. No release of fluids.

"Ryan, why didn't you say anything?"

She went to his bulky biomed. There was a bottle of cholisetrum on top, but it was in pill form. She opened doors until she found a niche full of medicines. One was a charge of duoanaproxine and a hypodermic gun. She loaded the charge in and pumped it into Ryan's arm. The gun "poufed" loudly and left a reddish patch like a rash.

Five minutes went by. The ladle wobbled in his mouth. Cautiously, Tamyn removed it and his mouth remained open. His eyes fluttered. Tamyn let go a loud sigh and fetched a pillow for him.

About ten minutes later he said, weakly, "Thank you," then passed into a heavy sleep.

"Now I guess I know why you're here," she said. She went back to the biomed and tried to access its programs.

Her fingers felt odd on the keyboard. She looked at them again and again; they were not right, but she did not know what would be right. She tried to ignore them and continued searching.

All Ryan's records were sealed with a blunt "Access Denied".
So she tried for general information.

She found a menu for an encyclopedia. Desultorily, she scrolled down the list of entries to see if anything caught her attention. She accessed the listing for "Pan Humana" and skimmed through the text.

"—representing the furthest extent of human expansion in interstellar space—"

Tamyn frowned. That was wrong, but she did not know why. Annoyed at another missing memory, she closed it out and went through the rest of Ryan's menus. She opened a file labeled "Peace".

"Peace is hell," it read. "I came here to heal and found a prison. I don't know where I am, where this is, though I can make a guess based on the positions of certain stars—got to be Porrima, Gamma Virginis. But a guess won't get me out.

"Interface is a sham. They're supposed to be doctors and all they do is patronize you until you die. I've watched them die here and it's horrible. Young people. They look young, anyway. Just all of a sudden go to bed one day, complaining of pains and weariness, and they never wake up. You go in to them to help and find a shrunken, desolate corpse—not old, but not what you'd expect a young body to look like—and you realize that it's a failure of the masks. It was their time. Maybe a hundred and ten, hundred and fifteen. Interface takes them in one end—they arrive—erases the painful memories, makes them look young, and lets them out the other. You befriend them, grow to care, and before long they die. The doctors do nothing. Peace is a graveyard and I'm the caretaker.

"I've built a house far out from the town around Interface. I go in only when I need things or the loneliness eats at me like a sore tooth. I have everything I need out here. Almost. The stars are brighter here than in town. Still, they shimmer too much, so I suspect an environmental blister around the whole area. I've found others like me now. We've grown used to the isolation, so we only meet occasionally.

"We have all been betrayed. None of us belong here. I don't want to die here. More than that, I don't want to watch anyone else die. There've been so many."

It ended then. Disturbed, Tamyn closed it down and tried to find an entry on Ryan's medical condition. Nothing. Perhaps it was all in the clunky biomed. She shut off the terminal and went to the big boxy device. It was nothing like any biomed she had ever seen, except one in a museum—

Where? She chased the memory. Eyes closed, she turned down the hallway in her mind, reached out to the sign. Eight years old, careering among the enclosed cases with others, exploring. On...Dawnrise...home...born there, anyway...twenty or so light years from Miron...

"Don't smudge the glass, Tam."

Tall man, beard...father? No, but might as well have been. Kind eyes, large, powerful hands, gentle...periodically enraged...retired spacer, could not function within the Flow, the entire network burned during the War...Gordon...Glass...don't smudge the glass...

"Tamyn Glass," she mouthed and here eyes snapped open. "I'm Tamyn Glass."

It was a small triumph. She looked at Ryan still asleep on the floor. No, let him sleep, she thought, and went to a couch and sat down. The blocks were not permanent, then. Memories, when they came to her, came in clumps, slipped loose of their bonds to drift through her consciousness. Gordon Glass had been the man who had raised her after her parents had given her up...Gordon had been unable to pursue his chosen profession. He was a pilot, by all accounts a damn good one, but he had been caught in an accident during the War and the leads of his interface had burned out. He could link imperfectly at best, not nearly well enough to pilot a starship, and in the shaky postwar structure good medical service was at a premium. By the time the technological base caught up with the needs of everyone Gordon had been irretrievably sunk into a depression that would eventually kill him. But he had infected Tamyn with the desire to sojourn.

She looked at her fingertips, rubbed them. Not right, but she did not know what would be right. Time. Give it time.

She let her hands fall to her stomach. Gently she probed. Muscle. Hard, shaped from long hours of high g exercise. She felt along her thighs and found the same thing. No pain, nothing frail, not a sign of geriatric reconstruction. She was in good health.

"My name is Tamyn Glass and I'm fifty-two years old. I do not belong here." She looked out the windows. "So where do I belong?"

A few hours later, Ryan woke up. He complained loudly of aching all over, protesting that he was not an old man, he could damn well take care of himself, and no, he did not want more sleep. Nevertheless, he permitted Tamyn to help him to bed, where he sprawled across his mattress and passed into deep sleep almost at once.

Tamyn dropped back onto the couch in the great room and let herself sleep. She dreamt of stars again, only now they were not so confused. Some she recognized, though the names refused to come clear.

Her eyes snapped open. For an instant she was disoriented, but she remained still, listening. The room was rosy with dawn light. Someone was moving around, too quietly for Ryan, almost too quietly for her to hear. A cool breeze stroked her face; one of the nearby doors to the deck was open.

Slowly, she raised herself on her elbows until she could peek over the edge of the couch. A man stood before Ryan's polycom, studying the menu. He was stocky and powerful, pale grey hair so short that for a moment she thought he was bald. His stance was authoritative, somehow...military.

Silently, she rolled off the couch. Gracefully, she crawled to a couch nearer the intruder. He showed no sign of having heard her. He was intent on the menu. Muscles tense, she stood and walked toward him, measuring him.

He spun around, bringing a pistol up toward her face. Their eyes locked for an instant. Tamyn went cold all at once and the sense of recognition almost took her breath away. His eyes lowered—she was still naked—and widened slightly. He smiled and began to let the pistol down.

In a fluid motion, she kicked his arm. The weapon arced away. She stepped quickly inside his reach and jammed an elbow into his solar plexus, then again across his jaw. He sprawled to the floor. Tamyn swept the pistol up and crouched before him as he raised his head, shook it, and gaped at her.

"Sit," she ordered. "On your hands, spread your legs. Wider. That's good."

"That's only a stunner," he said, his voice thick and a little sluggish.

She aimed it directly at his face, about a meter away. "At this range, then, a direct shot will blind you. At least. Understand?" He nodded. "I know you," she said. "I don't know how, but I do. Name?"

"Moss Fisher."

"You're from Interface?"

His eyes flickered briefly and he nodded. "Forum liaison, Department of Health."

Tamyn frowned. That was a lie, but she did not know what the truth could be. Not yet. "What were you looking for?"

"You, I think, if you're Tamyn Glass."

"Am I?"

He raised his eyebrows.

"I'll take that as yes. How'd you find me? Del Robello?"

"Of course."

"Do you always inspect the furniture before you announce yourself?"

"You didn't announce yourself, either."

"I'm an invited guest. Or isn't hospitality one of the remaining virtues in the Pan?"

She tightened her grip on the pistol. Remembrance flashed through her, but she did not have time now.

"I'm only doing my job. I'm not here to steal anything, if that's what you're worried about. May we stop this silly game and let me stand?"

"You may leave."

"But—"

"No more talk. Leave. Now."

"May I have my pistol back?"

She shook her head once, emphatically.

Fisher stood slowly and went to the door. He looked back, seemed about to say something more, then changed his mind and left.

Tamyn watched from the deck as he walked quite a distance, over the nearest low hill. Seconds later she heard the whine of a transport.

Tamyn let out her breath and fought the shakes. Images spun through her mind now, all revolving around Fisher's face. She should have killed him, she thought, for something...she would not kill without knowing why. He laughed at her in her mind and she knew he had something to do with her blocks.

She pressed her fingers to her temples. "Stand still!" she commanded the cascade of images. "Stand still!"

Chapter Twenty One

Ryan stared out the kitchen windows while Tamyn told him about Fisher. He did not interrupt her, just let her talk, his hand bringing the coffee cup to his mouth every so often.

He was scruffy and rumpled. His bright hair shot out at odd angles and his eyes supported deep bags. His hand trembled slightly. Tamyn finished talking and watched him. He continued staring wordlessly out the window. Occasionally his eyes narrowed.

"Why didn't you tell me you had seizures?" she asked.

His eyes flicked in her direction. "None of your business."

"Even if you die? You're fortunate I know something about biomed. I'm not taken with the notion of having your death on my conscience, even if it is your idea of privacy."

"You don't think a person has a right to decide when to die?"

"Of course I do. But you state it in your will and you let people know. Dying by accident when it could be prevented is murder."

Ryan gave her a puzzled look. "Put it in your will—what are you talking about?"

"Your primary designation..."

Ryan shook his head and pushed up from the table. "You got some strange ideas. Is that why you're in here? Were you trying to convince people that suicide should be legal?"

"It's not?"

Ryan laughed sharply. "I wish the hell it was!" He went to the coffeepot and filled his cup, turned. His eyes were fierce. "God, I wish it was. I wouldn't be here now, living—existing—ah, hell with it." He looked away from her. His eyes glistened.

Tamyn ran her fingertip over her lower lip, then frowned at the sensation. It was wrong, but she did not know how; it annoyed her that she could not break the habit.

"I don't belong here," she said.

"None of us do," Ryan said. "But here we are. Peace. Retirement. Which is a joke for me. Even by your standards it's unreasonable. I'm only sixty."

"Why are you here, then?"

He shook his head. "Maybe later. I have to talk to some people about this Fisher."

"Do you know who he is?"

"Never heard of him. But he's a type. I've been waiting for someone like him to show up. I hoped he wouldn't, but..."

Tamyn looked out over the plains, toward the mountains. "This whole place is wrong," she said.

"Peace is seventy, eighty years old."

"Not to me. I've never heard of it before."

"Oh?"

She scowled, annoyed. "My name is Tamyn...Glass. I'm a shipmaster..."

"You mean a commander."

"No, shipmaster."

Ryan shook his head. "That designation hasn't been used in fifty years, not since all spacing was absorbed by the military."

"What military?"

"The Armada."

"That doesn't mean anything to me."

Ryan grunted. "I wish everyone could make that claim."

"I mean when you say 'Armada' you say it as if I should just know what it is. I don't. There's nothing, no echo, no faint recognition, nothing. It's just a word for something I have no experience with."

Ryan sat down again. "Chairman Burnam II."

Tamyn blinked at him, shrugged.

"The Pan Humana."

"Familiar, but..."

"What's your home world?"

"Dawnrise...I think."

Ryan frowned. "Parents?"

"Didn't have any."

Ryan's eyebrows went up. "You just sprang, full grown, from the head of Zeus I suppose?"

"No, I'm an orphan. I think."

"Mm. Well, that's something."

"This isn't getting anywhere. My memories are blocked very thoroughly. I still don't know where I am or why. I would appreciate some answers."

"The...blocks...aren't supposed to last this long. I mean, sure, I said three days, but you should start remembering some things before that. More than you are. That means either they did a sloppy job or..."

"Or this is intentional, which I think is more likely. What are the blocks for?"

Ryan shrugged. "Peace of mind."

"And that's all they leave you with? A piece?"

Ryan chuckled. But then he sobered, shaking his head. "When you live in space you live for it. When they take that away from you and stick you on the ground, it destroys part of you. So they play with your memories, damp the pain so you can live with it. I'm told the same applies to other kinds of people, but I don't know about that."

"They've done more than just damp a little pain with me."

Ryan nodded. "I think so, too. Fisher's visit confirmed that."

"So what do I do?"

He held up his hands in a helpless gesture. "Nothing much you can do. Wait and see when the rest of the blocks fade."

"Is that how you passed the time when you arrived?"

"At first. The reorientation takes the urgency out of everything. You feel lost, dizzy. I hated it, but even the hate was blunted. When I came out of it I came out pissed. I started working with newcomers, trying to ease them into their new lives a bit more humanely than Interface does it. Interface got upset about that and started interfering. They even took me back for another reorientation session."

"You went through this twice?"

Ryan nodded. "Second time I bounced back a lot faster. I was angrier. I vented it by building this house. They let me have just about any kind of material I wanted, even offered to loan me some of the robots from Interface maintenance to do the work. I refused that and did it all myself. Well, most of it. I found a few others like me, not really retirees, younger than the rest. Angry. All angry. I stayed away from town for over a year. Gradually I started going back in, meeting some of the newcomers, doing things differently than before. Interface didn't bother me then, as long as I was just being helpful to the program."

He sighed sadly. "They were right, too. A lot of those people were old—really old—and they didn't have the reserves left to waste on anger and resentment. I hadn't helped any of them, except to an earlier death."

"What about the ones like you, though?"

"I watched for them, found a few more every year. People put here for other reasons. Most of them keep to themselves. They're so full of hatred over what's happened to them they can't trust anymore, can't stand being around others. Bitter, lonely, furious—but it's all they've got and they don't want to share it. Occasionally Interface goes looking for them and administers some euphorics or something, brings them back for another attempt at reorientation."

"And you think I'm one of those?"

"Maybe. Everyone says crazy things when they first start coming out of it. You're...odd."

"Thanks."

"You're certainly welcome."

For a moment they grinned at each other. Then Tamyn asked, "So how did you end up here?"

Ryan lost his smile, seemed to chew his words for a few seconds, finally shook his head and left the table. Tamyn felt ashamed for a moment, having ruined the pleasant feelings with a prying question. Then she became angry. She stood and started to follow Ryan, then stopped. More prying would not help answer this particular question.

She blew out a breath of exasperation and left the house. The breeze took a strand of hair and tickled her face. She brushed at it absently. I have to pull things together, she thought. She looked toward the line of mountains.

She picked one as a marker and started walking.

Len Venel stepped out of the shadows as the transport motors died. The sound echoed distantly throughout the chilly garage. He found himself nervously rubbing his palms against his hips. It was comical in a way—not since university had he been so uncomfortable confronting anyone, it was almost a new feeling.

Moss Fisher stepped out of the Interface transport. His face was somber, thoughtful. He seemed completely absorbed and nearly collided with Len before he looked up.

"Doctor."

"Commander." Len resisted the urge to lick his dry lips. It baffled and irritated him that this man affected him this way. He looked past Fisher to the transport. "Field trips without an escort? I've asked you not to do that."

"So you have, Doctor." Fisher moved to go around Len.

Len stepped sideways, blocking the man. It gave him a thrill to see the startled, cautioning expression on Fisher's face. *So I can make you react, Len* thought. The realization did little to bolster his confidence.

"Is there something I can do for you, Doctor?"

"Yes, Commander." Len hooked his hands behind his back. "Another squad of your security people arrived this morning."

"Yes?"

"I'd like to remind you that this is a hospital and research center, not a prison. I've already spoken to my superior Commissioner Foster about your intrusions and he assured me the charter under which we operate is still in force."

Fisher almost smiled. "Meaning?"

"Meaning that first you're supposed to clear all additional personnel with me as director of the institute and second you're supposed to abide by my directives. We've already spoken about this— this prison mentality you're trying to introduce here. I thought we'd agreed—"

"You agreed, Doctor. With yourself. If you press Commissioner Foster you will find that my authority supersedes his. Which means, frankly, I'll do what I please. I asked for your cooperation, as director of this institute. Till now you've at least stayed out of my way. If you wish to retain your position I suggest you continue to do so."

"Commander, this is not a prison! These are old people—"

"I'm not in the least interested in your residents."

Len drew himself up. He felt his control slipping. "I know that. That's my concern. It was bad enough when the Armada opened their own project here, but at least you had the courtesy to keep it on the other side of the barrier. I can't see the same things happen here!"

Fisher narrowed his eyes for a moment, then grinned. "I assure you there's a qualitative difference between what's happening there and what I intend for here. Is that all?"

Len realized that he had lost whatever authority he had brought to this confrontation. In fact, he thought, it's not even a confrontation; I'm throwing a tantrum and he's being tolerant. He felt himself redden.

"No," Len said. "I insist, if nothing else matters, that you keep your damn slave trading elsewhere."

Fisher's grin faltered and Len felt a brief resurgence of power.

"Your mercenary emissary is waiting in your office," Len continued. "Next time he shows up I'm not letting the shuttle land."

Fisher looked unhappy. He gave Len a last shallow smile and pushed past him, to the lift.

"Oh, Doctor."

Len turned. Fisher stood in the lift door.

"Interesting choice of arenas," Fisher said, waving around at the garage. "Perhaps a leaning toward more subterranean tendencies?"

"Not at all, Commander. It's the only place you don't have under surveillance."

For a few moments, Fisher looked genuinely surprised. Then he laughed softly and stepped into the lift.

Len stared at the door. He was losing. In fairness to himself he had to admit that probably no one could win this one.

For the first few kilometers Tamyn concentrated on finding a rhythm, settling her body in for a long trek, and enjoying the feel of exertion. She felt light and for the first time thought that the gravity here was less than she was accustomed to.

The grass did not impede her very much. It parted like diaphanous curtains. She tore off a stalk and examined it. The leaf was symmetrical flat surfaces on either side of a central spine, much like a knife blade. Clear fluid leaked minutely from the tear. It had a faintly sweet odor.

She tossed it aside and looked out over the fields. A memory tugged at the back of her mind, something familiar that would not come to the surface. She was sure she had never been here before, but the vista around her reminded her of something. The grass should be taller, a different color, the sounds aren't right, or the smells, and there should be roads...

Annoyed, she located her mountain peak again and strode on. Her memory had once been excellent. She knew that, though she could not remember how. She reviewed everything that had happened since Ryan picked her up in the town around Interface. It was all clear, sharp, the days separate and distinct. Seven days. And the only familiar things had been Fisher and these grasslands. Everything else was locked behind barriers set in place ostensibly to help her. The idea was repulsive. The reality infuriated her.

These are parts of me, she thought, taken away...I need to find the pieces and parts...

The ground sloped down gently. For several meters she lost sight of the mountains, then came up out of the well and saw them again. They were the wrong color. She expected them to be bluish-grey, not striking purple.

They tampered with my mind, she thought, and felt a wave of anger. She curled her hands into fists. Who had tampered? Fisher. If not him directly, then he gave the orders.

She forgot her rage for a moment as the memory—the certainty—fixed her attention. Fisher. Commander Fisher. Commander Moss Fisher. Him she knew.

Each fragment of memory was precious. She recounted them now, checking each one off. Perhaps a constantly-repeated inventory would flush more to the surface. Tamyn Glass, Shipmaster, Dawnrise, Moss Fisher...too disparate, too small. Not even enough to provide an idea of what part of her life had been damped. Clearly she remembered some things. She could converse, swim, fight, she knew basic biomedical procedures. Without the interconnective bits, much of it minutiae surrounding larger memories—like her name, her birth world, the fact that she was an orphan—there was no cohesion.

This is the true purpose of the Akaren, she thought.

Akaren...?

A philosophy, an ethic, an order, something she believed in, was committed to. Again, not enough. Pieces and parts, fragments, potsherds in the dirt. Where's the rest of me?

Go to the mountain, she thought. Then: *Mres cosa nem savro...*

"One may hope in certainty..."

She glanced over her shoulder. Ryan's house was a small interruption amid the even grassland. She thought she should go back in case he had another seizure. No, she decided, he would be very careful after one. For now he would be fine.

The landscape continued on as far as she could see in the gradual sloping and dipping, nothing extreme, nothing severe. Clearly it was a made place. Only the mountains were "natural" in their severity and grandeur. Everything else was softened, reworked to be as gentle as possible. Walking was easy. Even in the grass, now as high as her waist, there were no surprise holes, no rocks to twist ankles, no other plants. It was restful...and boring.

She made for a rise to her right. From the top she looked down on the stream that continued on toward Ryan's house. In the sandy strip that bordered it she saw a bush that broke the monotony of grass. She smiled and continued walking along the shore of the stream.

"It's not the destination," she said aloud, "it's the journey."

Toward midday she stripped off her shirt and tied it around her waist. Her muscles were beginning to burn pleasantly with the exertion.

The stream was wider here, almost a small river. The water slapped and bubbled playfully and drowned out the silence. The plant life was becoming more varied the further she went. A few insects buzzed by her. It was beginning to feel more like a world.

Thin clouds formed above the mountains and drifted toward her in some unfelt wind. She watched them trace a path up, up, and then curve downward. Tamyn stopped and observed them for a time. They coiled round to form little whirlpools, drawing in other wisps, then dissipating before acquiring any size or force. Something stopped their progress upward, and the currents were shaped by a barrier high overhead.

Tamyn continued on. She no longer used the mountains for guidons, following the stream instead. It was curving gradually away from the distant cliffs, which had not changed size significantly in the four or five hours since she had begun. She was not likely to reach them in a day or two, maybe not even a week.

She drank from the river. The water was cold and comfortable going down. She knew somehow that it could not harm her, that her body, or something about it, would eliminate any harmful phages. She sat down at the water's edge and looked skyward. Fatigue was a pleasant numbness throughout her body. Her anger, she noticed, pleased, was dissipated. It would return later, but for now she was free of it.

A distant high keening interrupted her reverie. Tamyn stood and looked east. Sunlight glinted off three specks on the horizon. She crouched and slipped into the water. It's chill bit into for a few seconds. She waded out to where it covered her shoulders. When she looked up again the specks had resolved into three large carriers. The carriers did not pass directly over the river, but flew parallel to it a few hundred meters to the south. They were big, heavy equipment transports, all white with blue stripes, identifying them as Interface craft. Their passing smothered all other sounds. Tamyn watched them speed off toward the mountains.

She walked out of the river, eyes tracking the diminishing carriers until the formation vanished against the distant mountains.

It should be night, she thought, then I could recover all the parts...

Mres cosa nem savro...

She looked back the way she had come. Only endless sky and grassy plains. She continued on toward the mountains.

She realized she had probably made a mistake when the sky behind her began to grow noticeably darker. As benign as this place seemed to be, she had entered areas that were not as carefully tended as those closer to the town. There was no way to know if she was safe out here at night.

There was no way she could cover the same ground back to Ryan's house before nightfall. Tamyn shrugged and started looking for a suitable place to make camp.

A sound she thought was a large insect resolved into the asthmatic whine of Ryan's transport. Tamyn scampered up a rise and saw the old machine heading slightly south of her. She started waving her arms. After a time, Ryan turned toward her. He settled the noisy transport down about fifteen meters from her and jumped out.

"What are you doing out here?" she asked.

"Looking for you obviously," he said harshly. He came up to her.

"You look like hell," she said.

His hair was matted and his eyes looked bruised. His skin was pale. He shrugged and motioned for her to come back to the transport.

"What was the idea coming out here like this?" he demanded.

"I needed to think."

"Mm."

The back of his transport contained a couple of sleeping rolls, a backpack, and canisters. Ryan got in and started it up. Tamyn stared at him, waiting for an explanation.

"You coming?" he asked.

"Where are we going?"

"Probably where you were." He pointed toward the mountains. Tamyn shrugged and got in beside him.

"What's going on?" she asked.

"I got a warning from Interface. Things are changing. You wasted my time by being gone, it took me a while to figure out what you did. You're lucky I found you."

Ryan flew on in silence, the muscle in his jaw working occasionally. Tamyn said nothing, unwilling to interrupt his thoughts. She glanced back at the baggage. If the canisters contained provisions, he had brought enough for a lengthy stay away from his house.

Ryan pushed the transport until it shuddered under the strain. The ground whipped by in a blur, made murkier by twilight. His hands flexed on the controls. The landscape grew hillier. Clumps of rock became more frequent, as if the sculptors had done only the minimum necessary to make it habitable. The territory closer to the mountains was incomplete, neither wholly artificial nor natural.

Another stream, wider than the other, came into view, and Ryan turned up it, slowed, and followed its twisty path. After a few kilometers he settled down on the beach and powered down.

He led the way up the embankment. Tamyn came up beside him and saw a shambling structure nestled against a spur of rock from the mountains. A transport that appeared even older and more abused than Ryan's lay nearby.

Ryan moved cautiously out of the grass, toward the house. Tamyn strained her hearing to detect the whine of other carriers, but all she picked up was the winds across the crags high above.

The main entrance was shaded by a tattered awning that stretched the length of the house. As Ryan neared it he slowed. Tamyn scanned the surrounding area, a tingle of caution heightening her senses.

Near the transport the ground was smoother, stalks of nearby grass broken. Tamyn frowned. Carriers, she thought, and looked skyward.

Ryan pushed open the front door.

Within the living room furniture had been shoved around, a chair was overturned, and a glass lay on the floor near the spill of its contents.

"Welles!" Ryan called. He went through the house, shouting the name.

Tamyn stayed at the threshold, attention divided between the interior and the exterior. Ryan stomped back into the living room.

"They couldn't have left long ago," Tamyn said.

He shook his head. "Long enough. I'm too late."

"What's going on?"

"I got a call from Conol, another hermit like me. He said Interface had sent notice yesterday that everyone was to come back to town, no exceptions. Some of us just won't. Conol's one."

"And Welles is another?"

"So they came and took him. Conol said they've been gathering everyone in for a few days now. No reasons, no answers to questions, just—" He blinked angrily and stared around.

"You received a call?"

"Yeah. It was filed in my comm."

"Those carriers that we saw..."

"Interface field meds, portable biomed units, ambulances, call them what you want. Jailers." He glared at her. "And your Moss Fisher shows up at the same time. I don't know who he is, but he's no doctor. He's military, probably security." He stepped toward her. "Makes me wonder just what it is that's buried in those supposedly blocked memories of yours."

"The blocks are real."

"Mm. If I thought they weren't I'd break every bone in your body."

"I'm not your enemy."

"Maybe not."

"Isn't it possible this is routine?"

"No, it isn't. Welles has been out here longer than me, about ten years now. They've never done this before, they always sent someone out the way Len Venel came out to see you." He gestured at the room. "Does this look like Welles went voluntarily, like this was routine?"

Tamyn shook her head. "So what do we do?"

"'We'? I don't know about that. I intend going up into the mountains and waiting it out."

"What about this other friend, Conol?"

"He tried to get away, I'm sure. There's a place we can meet."

"Then let's go meet him."

Ryan regarded her narrowly. Tamyn read his mistrust and bristled. She stepped close to him, leaned into his face.

"I'm not your enemy. Whoever did this probably did it because of me, possibly for some unrelated reason, but either way I'm not your enemy."

"You could get us all caught."

Tamyn blinked, moved back. "True. But if I'm being traced then they would've picked me up in the open, when they flew overhead."

Ryan nodded slowly, grudgingly. "All right, let's go."

He flew north, hugging the contours of the mountains. Spurs jutted out, but most of the cliffs looked sheered, as if huge claws had scooped away at them to form a wall rimming the entire environmental blister. Above the ridge of rock and the peaks that remained Tamyn saw murky clouds form and bubble, roil against the unseen barrier, and dissipate, growing ominous in the coming twilight.

Ryan set down at another house. This one was built out from the cliff face, half hidden by boulders. It was small, very private-looking. There was no transport, but Tamyn clearly saw the signs that transports had been on the ground and left. Ryan ran into the house and came out quickly.

"He's already gone," he said as he lifted off.

He flew another kilometer north, then turned in at a high wall of stone that shot out from the cliff. It curved inward, forming a corridor. At the apex, where it blended into the mountain itself, was a small cave entrance. The transport barely fit, but once inside the cave opened out.

Ryan set down and switched off. He rummaged in the back and produced a lamp, which he flicked on. Two more vehicles were already present, deserted.

The cave was like a steeple, soaring to a peak high above in the darkness. Sounds echoed and amplified and Tamyn felt chill after the comfortable heat outside.

"Does this lead anywhere?"

Ryan pulled canisters from the transport. "Probably not. A cave system was exposed when the mountains were dug out. For all I know the digging created them."

She pulled a bedroll and a backpack out of the transport.

Ryan hoisted the other pack onto his shoulders, grabbed a pair of canisters in one hand, and led off with the lamp.

The cave floor sloped up for several meters beyond the parked transports. The walls narrowed till there was room for only two people side by side. Then it dropped sharply and sloped down, turning to the left. The lamp struck highlights in the walls. Green glinted, layered with strands of silver and gold and patches of red, suspended in the overall slate grey.

The passage turned right. Ahead Tamyn made out warm light from a fire. They stepped from the narrow tunnel into a bubble.

Three people stood around a campfire. One aimed a rifle. Ryan raised the canisters in salute. Shadows flashed and flickered on the walls.

"Ryan," one, a woman, said with audible relief.

Tamyn moved cautiously behind Ryan, eyeing the man with the rifle. He was tall and slender, almost gaunt, and stared at her from deepset, dark eyes.

"Anna," Ryan said. "Conol, Pit. This is Tamyn. She's been staying with me the last week or so."

"Newcomer?" the one with the rifle—Pit—asked quietly.

"Uh huh. She still hasn't fully remembered." He set his load down and Tamyn did the same.

Conol squatted by the fire. He was thickset, hair thin and auburn and swept straight back from a low, deeply-etched forehead. Anna seemed a powerful woman, heavy thighs, broad shoulders, but she moved carefully.

"Do you mind aiming that elsewhere?" Tamyn said to Pit.

"You vouch for her, Ryan?" Pit asked.

"Of course. Do you think I'd've brought her here if I didn't trust her?"

Pit lowered the weapon.

"What the hell happened?" Ryan asked.

"We all received official notification to report back to Interface," Conol said. His voice was thick with anger. "Welles let us all know that it was not optional; they were setting down at his place as he spoke with me. They're rounding everyone up. No excuse, no explanation, just an order. We managed to get out before they arrived."

"They caught Garris as he was leaving," Anna said. "We saw. They drugged him and carried him into the ambulance."

Ryan scowled, the firelight throwing demonic severity across his features. "What the hell is going on?"

"Word has it Armada security is involved," Pit said.

"Armada?" Ryan looked questioningly at Tamyn. "We were visited by some Armada pol. Yesterday."

"Early this morning," Tamyn corrected. She looked at Ryan. "You're guess was right. Commander Moss Fisher."

"Why?" Pit demanded, glaring at Tamyn.

"Checking up on me," Tamyn said.

"She hasn't remembered much yet. They really buried her."

"Where are you from?" Anna asked.

Tamyn shook her head.

"Not here," Ryan said and laughed harshly. "She says she's a shipmaster."

"You mean a commander," Conol said.

"No," Tamyn said. "Shipmaster."

Conol frowned. "But we haven't—"

"Exactly," Ryan said. "So whoever she is and wherever she's from, Armada's mighty curious."

"And you brought her here," Pit said.

"What else was I supposed to do? She's in trouble, she needs help."

"And now everybody's been rounded up," Pit pointed out. "People who've been living out of town for a decade suddenly have to go back to Interface."

Tamyn pursed her lips and looked from one of them to the next. They were angry and frightened and Pit clearly resented her presence. In the orange light they looked like fading images of formerly substantial people. Ryan alone looked vital, even though he was haggard and worn from his seizure.

"I'm sorry if my being here has brought this on," she said, "but I'm not here willingly, either. You can blame me for your problems if you want, but that's not going to change anything."

Conol shrugged. "Hey, at least something's changing." He laughed. "A little excitement."

Pit gave him a humorless expression. "Armada isn't just a little excitement. Armada's real trouble." He looked at Tamyn. "Who's to say she isn't a plant?"

Ryan barked harshly. Conol smiled and Anna looked amused at Pit.

"A plant for what?" Ryan asked. "Any of us plotting the overthrow of the Chairman? Are we about to tunnel our way out of the planet and make a break for open space?" He laughed again and leaned back on his elbows. "I swear, Pit, you are an imaginative fool. Peace is such a security risk, all us geriatric dependents, that the Armada has to sequester us for fear of our discontent."

"You can be as sarcastic as you want, Jones," Pit said, "but the fact remains that you have no business being here and I certainly don't belong on Peace. If the Armada pols are interested in your guest, she doesn't belong here either. So ask yourself, as long as you're asking sarcastic questions, just what the Armada would want Peace for?"

Tamyn sighed heavily and everyone looked at her. "It ought to be obvious. All of you feel like prisoners, from what I've been able to tell. I feel like I'm in prison."

Anna frowned. "Prison? But—the Pan already has Ghagaol, in Procyon. Why would they need another prison?"

"Ghagaol," Pit said slowly, "is a penal colony. Psychopaths, sociopaths, the chronically malcontent all go there."

"So?" Anna said obstinately, glaring at Pit.

Tamyn looked into the fire. "So Peace is for a different sort of criminal."

Pit nodded. "Politicians, artists, thinkers—activists."

"If a politician creates a place for his enemies," Ryan said, "he's got to consider the possibility that he might end up there one day. Why not make it as pleasant as possible?"

"But," Anna pressed, "Peace is for us."

Conol grunted. Ryan shook his head. "Are you here willingly?"

"No, but—"

"But since you're here and you have to be you don't want anyone taking it away from you."

Anna frowned. "True, it doesn't make any sense. It's not ours. But at least we had the illusion."

Tamyn watched them all lapse into a delicate silence. The sounds of the fire filled the bubble, accompanying the ghostly shadows thrown up on the walls. She felt uncomfortable here. She was not one of them and, despite her own argument, she felt responsible for the upheavals now rippling through their lives.

Ryan sniffed loudly and pushed himself up.

"I've got more provisions in my transport," he said, getting to his feet.

"I'll help you," Conol said, rising ponderously.

Tamyn spotted the stack of gear against the wall behind Anna, near another exit from the bubble.

"How far back does this go?" she asked.

Anna glanced over her shoulder at the black maw. "I don't know. We've never explored past here."

Tamyn grabbed a lamp from the pile of Ryan's provisions and headed up the narrow passage.

The walls scintillated here the same way, with streaks of green, gold, silver, and red. The rough floor tended upward, though it was difficult to be certain. Tamyn moved carefully. The cold worked at her. She aimed her lamp up and saw that the walls met above as if two slabs had been tilted against one another.

The passage split. One went clearly upward, the other seemed level. She went left, upward.

After half an hour of picking her way through the crags she saw light ahead. The passage became rounder, more like a tube. Rock slid under her tread, but she kept her balance. She switched the lamp off finally when she came then into bluer light. She looked right and saw an alcove open to the sky. She made her way into the open air and looked up.

The evening sky was a rich dark blue. Stars glittered. The flue in which she stood shot up perhaps two hundred meters. She could see no other passage except the one from which she had emerged.

She sat down and stared up at the sky. Her mind empty, distracted, she found her way into a shallow peace, at ease for the moment and balanced among all the puzzles and contradictions that defined her existence. For the moment it was easy to believe that all this illusion could be dissipated when she willed it. But she was too committed to the textures and foundations of reality to believe for long that her will alone was all that mattered. Other realities occluded the pureness of ordering her own universe. That she did not know those other realities made them no less real, and that only strengthened her basic adherence to her own solidity. To be so affected by other realities she herself had to be real—to them as much as to herself. In a way that was a comfort.

Rocks pattered. Tamyn snapped to her feet and flicked the lamp on.

Pit stood in the throat of the passage. He blinked in the sudden harsh light. His own lamp hung at his belt, dark.

"You're a quiet one," Tamyn said.

"And you're not so old."

"Didn't say I was." Tamyn lowered the light. Pit came out of the tunnel. "You followed me to tell me how you won't tolerate me hurting your friends."

Pit raised his eyebrows. "That, yes. And to find out who you are."

"My name is all I remember."

"And rank."

"Yes, that too. Nothing else."

"Honestly?"

"Why would I lie?"

Pit leaned back against the rock. "I used to be in charge of one of the facilities on Ghagaol. People started showing up who didn't belong there."

"Politicians, artists, thinkers?"

"The same. Others who just had unpopular opinions or who were unpopular to the wrong people. The kind of disfavoritism history tells us we ought to have been through with centuries ago. But Chairman Burnam II is...medieval...byzantine...this can't last, the Pan isn't structured to tolerate it long, but before it's stopped a lot of people will be irrevocably damaged. I am. They've played with my brain so much I can't imagine I'm the same as I was."

"What did you do?"

"I wrote a letter. I protested. That month there was a prison revolt. Not in my facility, but that didn't matter. Both the administrator of the rebellious facility and I were removed, put through readjustment, and sentenced here. Anna likes to think Peace is what it's supposed to be, a retirement community, but it's been used to be rid of certain troublesome individuals from time to time. I have the feeling that it's about to become exclusively that sort of place."

"And I'm one of the new inmates?"

"Or a spy."

"I can't prove a negative. You'll have to take my word for it or take measures to protect your friends."

"Doesn't matter. You've already done what damage you could. The freedom we had is gone."

"I didn't intend that."

"Again, it doesn't matter. A reasonable hypothesis is that someone wants to keep a close watch on you and it can't be done out here in the perimeter. So we all have to give up living in our own homes, conducting our daily lives with what self determination we have left, just so you don't have anywhere to run and hide from whoever it is who's interested in you."

Tamyn nodded. "That is reasonable. You don't believe it?"

"Partly."

"What's your unreasonable hypothesis?"

"That you're here to determine if there is a potential problem among us loose cannon. That we're all about to be herded into a tight little group where we can be controlled until we die. And then Peace can be turned exclusively into the luxury penal colony we were discussing back in the cave."

"Now that's byzantine. And rather silly."

"It'd be in character for our Chairman."

Tamyn stepped closer to him. He stiffened, placed his hands against the rock face.

"You want to do something," Tamyn said. "You want to act. Why don't you?"

"I don't know enough. You could be a threat, then again not. If I make the wrong judgement..."

"So you stay in the cave where it's safe and wait for someone else to do something."

Pit frowned deeply. Tamyn smiled and shook her head.

A hum grew. Tamyn turned off her lamp and looked overhead. A shadow crossed the circle of night sky.

"Carriers," Pit whispered. He hurried back into the tunnel.

Tamyn watched him disappear inside. A few moments later she saw the glow of his lamp. She looked up. The carrier had moved on.

She shined her lamp on the rocks around her. There was ample purchase for a climb. She hooked the lamp on her belt and started up the chimney.

Halfway up she was breathing heavily. The hum of the carrier came again. They were scanning the mountains. Probably, she decided, they're looking for me. She continued her climb. She used the lamp in short bursts to gauge her progress. When she made the lip she crawled onto the relatively level shelf and looked out.

Searchlights bathed sections of the mountain from three slowing moving carriers. They were several hundred meters away. She risked a brief look with her lamp and found the shelf blended with a saddle between two truncated peaks to her right.

She crawled along silently, willing her breath to quiet, until she was on solid ground. She sprinted to an outcrop of rock and rested.

A carrier moved by. The shadow of the outcrop leapt into relief before her as the searchlight crept past. In darkness she walked straight out, in the direction the shadows had pointed, and found a cleft in the vaulting wall. She shined her lamp and found a narrow path upward.

She wanted to get far from the cave. Perhaps she was being tracked. Perhaps she wore a tracer. If she could keep them from being caught with her—

A carrier rose before her, blocking the top end of the path. A searchlight speared down onto her, blinding her. She turned and scurried back.

Something kicked her squarely in the back. She lost feeling in her legs and arms. She did not feel the impact against the rocks as she sprawled downward.

Chapter Twenty Two

The planet was a grey and brown waste and Porrima Transit was a small station. Three long booms stretched from a central hub. *Solo* was directed to the one that berthed Armada ships. Benajim slid into dock between a pair of sleek armed cruisers. There were four such ships.

"Retirement communities must be dangerous places," Benajim said sarcastically. He grunted and pushed up from his couch. "All right," he said. "Any questions?"

"I'd feel better if I knew where *Wicca* was," Traville said.

"That's not a question." Benajim touched fingers to a gate briefly. Then: "On the move. Right now *Solo* can't find her. Anything else?"

Innes nudged Traville with an elbow. "No questions," she said. "If we don't know the procedure now we never will. As soon as we receive your signal, tie the ship into the station datasphere. Then wait for the next thing to happen."

Benajim nodded. "It shouldn't take long after that."

Traville fidgeted.

"You'd rather be with us when we find Tamyn," Benajim said. "Not advisable. If anything goes wrong—"

Traville held up a hand. "Don't say it. I'll be fine." He turned away and went to his couch.

Innes shrugged and gave Benajim nod.

Benajim joined Piper and Elen in the lock. "Ready?"

Both of them nodded.

"Don't be too enthusiastic," Benajim said.

Piper scowled briefly.

Benajim closed his eyes before opening the lock. Once they stepped onto the station they were committed, beyond the safety of *Solo*. He had felt the same anxiety during the shuttle trip out of Sol System to rendezvous with *Solo*. The signal had been sent, but there had been no way to know the ship had received it or could respond in time. But *Solo* had been there, waiting for them.

He opened his eyes and touched the contact. The hatch cycled open.

Six grey-uniformed troops waited in the debarkation chamber. Benajim handed over the sheaf of chits Nooneus had provided him and waited while the officer fed them into his reader. Two officers watched from behind the desk, two on the incoming side, two on the other side. All wore sidearms. The desk formed a barrier that cut the already small chamber in half. Low, harsh light made shadows of eyes. Benajim spotted three automated defensive units mounted in the ceiling.

"Very good, Commander Merrick," the officer said, sliding the sheaf across the desk to Benajim. "Everything seems in order. Welcome to Porrima Oversight. Lt. Commander Nillix is waiting in his quarters to meet you."

Benajim glanced at Piper and Elen.

"This way, Commander," one of the stationside guards gestured.

"Thank you."

The two soldiers flanked them and guided the way out of debarkation, into the corridor beyond.

Instead of the broad circuits of a transit station, the tight corridors felt more like those on a small ship. They passed by rows of numbered doors.

"I hope leave comes regularly," Benajim commented.

The soldier to his left laughed dryly. "Regularly. Too seldom, but regularly."

Benajim laughed and nodded knowingly.

"I've got leave coming next month," the soldier went on. "I had been scheduled for this rotation, but all this coming and going fouled me up."

"Sorry," Benajim offered.

The soldier nodded and shrugged. "Maybe you're the last one, eh? Maybe my next leave won't be fouled."

"Not if I can help it," Benajim said.

They rounded a corner, went by half a dozen more doors, and stopped. The soldier speaking to Benajim knocked on the door.

"Come."

The door slid open and the soldier stepped ceremoniously aside and bowed slightly. Benajim, Piper, and Elen stepped through.

Nillix was a heavy man who seemed too large for the office he occupied. The ceiling was low and the room felt small. Nillix rose from behind an L-shaped desk that supported a monitor and terminal. Mounted on the wall behind him was a plaque with three medallions that caught the dull light and glinted yellowly. Nillix smiled and extended his hand toward Benajim.

"Commander," he said. "A pleasure. A pleasure."

Benajim shook hands. "These are my aides, Piper Van and Elen Leris."

Nillix bowed to both and gave Elen a curious look.

"Well," he said then, "how may I help you?"

"A shuttle down would be sufficient." He flashed a grin. "Our task is purely routine, filling in blanks, nothing complicated."

"Mmm. That may be a problem."

"Oh?"

"Yes. I already have orders concerning traffic to the surface." He went to his terminal and tapped a few keys, read what came up on the monitor, and nodded. "Yes, there. Armada Security has interdicted any further traffic unless specifically authorized by the officer on site."

"Ah. Well, I'm sure there's been a misunderstanding, Lt. Commander. I'm hardly what you would call a security risk. I'm just an assessor—"

"Oh, I'm sure something can be arranged. May I see your authorizations?" He extended a hand for the sheaf of documents. Benajim passed them over and waited while Nillix scanned them. He frowned deeply at one point and his eyes flicked up to Benajim. Then he read on. Finally he extracted them and handed them back. "There should be no problem, Commander. I'll list you as guests of Dr. Len Venel, who is the present chief administrator for the Interface. The Armada security agent on site is Commander Moss Fisher himself. As long as you two don't cross paths..." He smiled knowingly.

"Of course," Benajim said. "I perfectly understand."

Nillix began entering data through his terminal. "Either way I go I'm going to irritate someone. I'd rather not annoy Representative Nooneus or General Ashfor." He glanced up. "Or the other people you work for." He looked slightly nervous and shrugged. "Commander Fisher can be difficult, but under the circumstances he wouldn't have a lot to complain about. You'll be working directly with the research staff, am I correct?"

"Correct."

"Good." He worked silently for several seconds more. "There. Tomorrow at, say, ten hundred? I'll have you on your way down." He smiled.

Benajim blinked, dismayed. He felt he was missing something here, that more was happening than he was aware of, but he smiled in return and stood. "Thank you, Lt. Commander Nillix. I'll note your accommodation to my superiors."

"I appreciate that, Commander. I'll get you an escort to your quarters. Would you do me honor of having dinner with me this evening?"

"Of course."

"I'll send someone around for you, then. Till later...?"

A sergeant arrived to escort them to Nillix's cabin. His personal rooms were larger than his office, but still cramped. The walls pressed close, lending the dinner an air of conspiracy as they ate.

"How long have you been commandant here?" Benajim asked as Nillix poured brandy.

"Five years," Nillix said.

"Interesting work?"

"Not particularly." He sat down and opened a small silver box. He removed a large bluish-white tablet. "Sens. Would you care for some?"

Elen frowned and shook her head. Piper looked at her curiously, then also shook her head.

"No, thank you," Benajim said. He sipped his brandy.

Nillix shrugged and placed the tablet on his tongue. He closed his eyes for a few seconds, then smiled. He shut the box and sighed, then chased the sens with a swallow of brandy.

"Forgive me," Nillix said, "for not being more direct with you earlier. My position makes me vulnerable to opportunists. In private I can be a bit more open, as long as I know with whom I'm dealing."

"I understand your reticence."

"Do you? I wonder. I'm in charge of the security of this system, Commander. What I'm keeping it secure from I have no idea. People arrive here and never leave. It's not a prison, not like Ghagaol, but once you've become a resident of Peace you know you'll be here till you die. The people who come here, though, don't want to die. They have no choice anymore. They're told to come here. So am I keeping them in? They have no ships of their own to take them off surface. Am I keeping others out who might rescue them? There's very little independent shipping that isn't automated and almost everyone in residence here has no family. But this is my job and I normally do nothing to jeopardize it."

Benajim folded his arms and did not interrupt. Nillix was looking past him. There was a faint tinge of fear in his face which added years in place of displaced dignity.

"I wonder when I'm going to be required to take up residence in Peace. I'm sixty-eight. With any luck and a good physician I've got at least another twenty years. But I watch the ones who come and they seem to be getting younger."

"What was your last post?" Benajim asked.

"I was commander of a light enforcer, the *Sparta*. Good ship, I was very pleased with her. Five years ago I was assigned here. I protested. I'm a ship officer, all my experience is mobile. They'd already slated my replacement, I was given no option. Now I suspect my options will be pruned again, between you and Commander Fisher."

"I'm an assessor, here to inspect the work being done—"

Nillix chuckled. "You arrive in a personal ship with two aides and a letter of introduction from both Representative Bool Nooneus and General Cres Ashfor, both strongly suggesting that whatever other orders I've received, your orders are to be given priority— suggesting, strongly, carefully avoiding anything that might be construed later as direct instructions on their parts, leaving me to hold the responsibility for whatever blows up—and you expect me to believe you're just an assessor?"

"Since," Benajim said carefully, "we're not in detention, I gather you've decided to take their suggestions?"

"Yes and no. I'm throwing you into the arena to see who walks out alive. I'm not sure about you, so I'll tell you frankly that I expect to be compensated for my risk if you do achieve whatever it is you're here to achieve. If Fisher survives, well then I'm more likely not going to survive. At least not as a career officer."

"You'll live. Fisher wouldn't kill you."

"He won't have to. I have no illusions how responsibility is parceled out in security matters. The most visible officer takes the most, whether deserved or not. If you fail, Commander, any trouble that falls out as a result will fall on me. I may be commandant for a short time afterward, but I suspect my retirement will be sooner than I like. So I have to wonder if you can know how I feel, Commander.

"You're young, you have fifty or sixty years of career ahead of you. You probably don't even think of it ending. If you do then you have some vague notion of dying in uniform, death coming as a big surprise, catching you in the midst of some worthwhile action. Not lying in a gerontology unit watching it slowly ebb away. You are a most unsettling sight, Commander. I wasn't happy when Fisher showed up. I already knew him by reputation. He's the sort who makes certain he survives by sacrificing everyone around him. What he's doing on Peace is a puzzle to me. He's changed things, even before he acquired his present position. There are ships that enter and leave this system that I'm ordered to ignore. Where are they from, where do they go? I can't even ask. They don't dock here, so I'm spared having the problem shoved in my face. But it still puzzles me. You, though—you're the latest component of the Moss Fisher puzzle. Now that you've shown up I know what the future is."

"Why is that?"

"Nooneus and Ashfor—Fisher is their natural enemy. They've sent a weapon—you—and to tell you truthfully I hope they've aimed well. If not, then Fisher will succeed and nothing will matter anymore."

"You're being extremely frank with me. I could be something altogether different than you think."

"Maybe. But I think I'm right. And my frankness is the only logical course I can see through this, given what Fisher is doing down there."

"Oh? And what is he doing?"

"He's preparing a grave for his enemies."

As soon as the shuttle left the station and began its long slide down to the surface, Benajim began to feel better. He was excited, his nerves alive with anticipation, but he was less afraid. There was no backing out now. He was committed.

And he loved it.

It was an odd revelation at this moment, and as he watched the monitors displaying the telemetry of the descent he relished it. He had been enjoying himself enormously the past weeks. All of this had the taste of familiarity, of old muscles freshly used. Odd, comforting and disturbing all at once.

The surface expanded on the monitors, took on detail, changed, small things became large—and all the while Benajim was deep inside himself exploring this new realization.

Music played through his memory—Bach, he recognized, one of the Brandenburgs, the First, he thought—and he laughed lightly. Piper and Elen frowned at him.

"Won't be long now," he said.

Nillix had stuck them on board a scheduled shuttle, along with standard cargo items and personal mail. They might slip in under Fisher's guard. Nillix had told them Fisher had brought along only eight of his own people and two squads of regulars. That and the Armada authorization to utilize resident personnel gave him a potential complement of about sixty.

There were six resident specialists, including the director, and fifteen nurses, plus scores of motiles. It still seemed insufficient to Benajim for a resident population of over twenty-two hundred dependents. Sean had had a dozen specialists and twice as many nurses, an unlimited budget, and all the automated monitoring available in the C.R. and he was just one man.

The Brandenburg played on his mind, the memory perfect. He could not recall where he had heard it the first time, but it had never left him, and now the faceted flawlessness of it disturbed him. It was such an old thing, yet endlessly fascinating, always new if you just took the trouble to find the newness. Had Sean introduced him to it or was it something locked into his genes, derived from the old man?

You are me!

No, he thought, I'm something else. Maybe I'm not me, but I'm not you, either.

The ancient melody danced on through his mind.

Len read over the transcript again and pursed his lips. He glanced vaguely at the corners of his office, closed down the reader, and left. He knocked on Lyrda's door.

"Yes?"

"Len."

The door opened and she stepped out. They walked together down the corridor, toward the balcony overlooking the central hall of the complex. The benches, plants, the quiet pattering of the fountain—it was more a set piece, like something belonging to a museum, than a functioning hospital. Too empty.

"We have company coming down," he said.

"Again?"

"An assessor named Merrick."

Lyrda scowled. "Whatever for? The last one pruned us down to nothing."

"The last one pruned us down for Fisher. This one may be here to prune Fisher. His authorization comes from Representative Bool Nooneus and General Cres Ashfor."

"I don't..."

Len smiled at her. "Neither of them cares much for Armada security. Nooneus is old enough to worry daily about coming here."

"Mm."

"I'm thinking maybe this is our chance. I'm thinking that Fisher doesn't have all the authority he needs to act with impunity. I'm thinking—"

"We're caught in the middle of a political war and you're thinking of choosing sides. Nobody wins that kind of war."

"No, but we might come out of it without Fisher."

She was silent for a time. Then: "You know Fisher has re-opened the sealed research sections."

"I know. I haven't been able to find out what he's doing in there, though."

"Perin's been trying to tap the datalogs."

"I hope he's being careful, then."

"He hasn't managed to get in yet, just found an increase in dataflow. Do you have any idea what they used to do down there?"

Len shook his head. "Back to my point..."

"Which is?"

"If this Merrick is here to check on Fisher—"

"Then we ought to cooperate with him to a fault?"

"Something like that."

"You don't think appealing to Fisher's good side would win us just as many benefits?"

"Fisher doesn't have any good sides."

"I'll meet him then. When is he due?"

"In the morning."

"Short notice."

"Lt. Commander Nillix cleared him without consulting Fisher. Whatever's going on, I suspect it has to be on short notice."

At the end of a long umbilical stood a woman in a pale blue smock. Her eyebrows bobbed when she saw them.

"Commander Merrick?"

Benajim nodded, smiling.

"I'm Dr Lyrda Stanson, assistant administrator and chief physiologist. Welcome to Peace."

"We expected a Dr Len Venel...?"

"He's in conference at present, so the job fell to me. He apologizes and says that he'll be happy to meet with you later."

Benajim introduced Piper and Elen, then looked around the debarkation area. Drab grey polycrete flooring contrasted with brightly-colored walls. Motiles stacked cargo and canisters on skids off to their right.

"I'll show you to your rooms," Lyrda said. "Are you familiar with our work, Commander?"

"I'm a digit pusher," Benajim said.

She laughed. She pointed toward a wide doorway. "Peace is a full service retirement community. It was modeled after concepts developed by Rafael Buckner over a century ago, utilizing advanced applications of geriatric conditioning and total gerontological oversight."

They entered a broad corridor dominated by pleasant pastel shades of blue and lavender. The wall on the right was transparent and looked out over a village of red-roofed villas along winding streets. In the distance yellowish fields were visible.

"The Interface is the point of entry where most of the initial orientation and physical work is done," Lyrda went on. "Here the chronologically advanced undergo a series of therapies and interventions to alleviate the more severe aspects of their condition. At the same time psychological reconditioning is applied to aid them in orienting to their new environment and capacity. We then release them into the community at large," she waved out the window just as they reached the end of the corridor, "and maintain continual monitoring for the duration of their stay."

They entered a broad plaza. Dark green carpet alternated with patterned tile. Three fountains marked the apices of a large triangle, within which were benches, small trees, and columns with what looked like data terminal screens. A motile came from another door, crossed the plaza quickly, and disappeared down the opposite corridor.

"This is the common area of the Interface. Patients and staff can mingle here, access to the community is through that row of doors, sometimes we have special events—lectures, music, science demonstrations, art fairs."

"Where is everyone?" Elen asked.

Lyrda flashed her an embarrassed grin. "Slow part of the day."

"Dr Stanson," Benajim said, "you have a staff here of about twenty-one people. Is that average? I understood that at one time you had closer to a thousand."

"That's been a long time, when more basic research was conducted here," she said. "We presently support a population of just over twenty-two hundred residents. Twenty-one personnel is more than adequate."

She took them around the complex. The structure was based on four enormous turrets; a dome stretched between them which contained the common. One turret contained the warehouses, another the maintenance shops and the access to the shuttle field a kilometer east, the third the residential quarters, and the fourth the offices and laboratories. A fully equipped hospital sprawled below the common.

Lyrda showed them their apartments, all interconnected, and then took them to the offices. The grey floors and white walls were brighter and less pleasant at the same time. Dark grey doors bore small nameplates. Many were blank.

"Here," Lyrda punched a code into a door and entered. "The terminal is linked to the central database, just like the one in your rooms. You can find us all here at one time or another during the day."

"When can we meet Dr Venel?" Benajim asked.

"He knows you're here, but..."

She seemed pensive. Benajim gave her a reassuring smile. "No hurry."

She relaxed and smiled. "Things have been a little chaotic lately."

"Well, then, why don't we start by showing us how your data is organized?"

It was late afternoon before Dr Venel showed up in the office to meet them. He was younger than Benajim expected.

"My apologies for not meeting you when you arrived," he said. "Who, uh"—?"

"Dr Stanson was kind enough to show us around," Benajim said. "I'm Commander Merrick. These are my assistants, Piper Van and Elen Leris."

Dr Venel nodded to each in turn and sat down. "Well, then, what can I help you with? I don't have a lot of time right now, but I can at least get some idea what you're here to assess. What can I tell you about Peace?"

"You can start with telling us about your work here."

Dr Venel laughed self-consciously. "I'm sort of picking up where my predecessors left off," he said, grinning. "A lot of gerontological research used to be done here. Budgetary restraints have closed most of the cutting edge research down, but I've been working my way through the bureaucratic swamp and getting things reactivated. There's still a lot of potential here."

"Potential for what, Doctor? If you don't mind my saying so, this looks like a place for forgotten people."

Len Venel frowned uncertainly. "Well...yes, it does have that function. Unfortunately. It's a side effect, though, not its primary purpose." He checked the time. "Could we have breakfast in the morning and talk more then? I have an appointment—"

"Certainly, certainly. We need to get some rest anyway."

As Dr Venel reached the door, Benajim said, "Doctor, about Moss Fisher."

Dr Venel frowned. "Yes...?"

"Where is he?"

"I don't know. He comes and goes as he pleases. He's a security officer..."

"I'm aware of who he is, Doctor. I just wondered if you knew his present whereabouts."

"I...think he's away from the institute. I could check...?"

"No, that's fine. We'll have a chance to meet tomorrow. Thank you, Dr Venel."

Dr Venel nodded uncertainly and left.

"What do you make of him?" Piper asked.

Benajim shrugged. "He seems...sincere."

"Sincere about what, though? I've been going over some of their old records. I thought Nooneus was exaggerating, but this really is just a place to die."

"That might be comforting in way," Benajim said. "To know where you'll be when you die, where you'll be buried."

Piper pursed her lips.

"But," Benajim added, "it is morose."

Elen tapped into the secured comm channels late that night. "Many sentinels in the system. I hope this won't take very long."

"Shouldn't take more than a minute or two," Benajim said, watching her work. "Uplink to the station and through to *Solo.*"

Elen entered instructions through the keyboard. The system lacked an optil interface. A moment later the screen cleared and a cursor pulsed.

"Linked," Elen said.

"Let me." Benajim sat before the screen and set his fingers to the keys.

He pursed his lips and entered a different code, then typed: SEAN MERRICK TO SEAN MERRICK. ARE YOU THERE?

He waited tensely for several seconds. Nothing appeared on the screen. "Damn," he breathed and retyped it.

OF COURSE, I AM, appeared.

Benajim stared at the words. A thrill of fear sparked along his spine.

THIS IS BENAJIM.

I KNOW. THIS CHANNEL IS OPEN?

YES.

GOOD. STAND BY.

Benajim, Piper, and Elen waited, watching the screen. The time stretched and he began to wonder if something had gone wrong. Then:

IN. CLOSE DOWN. I'LL BE HERE IF YOU NEED ME.

Benajim stiffened.

WHAT ABOUT TAMYN? he typed.

The screen remained blank.

SOLO.

SHE'S ON FILE, BUT NOT IN THE FACILITY. NOW CLOSE DOWN. SOME OF THE PROPHYLACTICS ARE PRETTY GOOD. LET ME LEAVE YOU WITH SOMETHING, THOUGH.

The screen cleared and a schematic of the hospital section appeared. A sealed section highlighted in red and the word RESTRICTED glowed. Benajim made a copy and closed the terminal down.

Len Venel met them in the cafeteria on the roof of the apartment turret. The transparency that capped the structure gave a view across gently swelling grasslands. Clouds scudded in the distance.

Venel looked harried. He smiled as he sat down and gave a quick, clipped order to the robot servitor, which rolled away.

"Sorry I'm late," he said.

"You're a busy man, I'm sure," Benajim said.

"Normally not this busy. We're undergoing an organizational change that I'm not particularly keen on."

"Oh?" Piper prompted.

He looked at them and his smile faded. "Why is the Armada so interested in us all of a sudden?"

Benajim blinked. "I beg your pardon?"

"You're from the Department of Assessment, which is attached to the Armada. You're a Commander. I already have an Armada officer here raising different...difficulties. I just wondered why, after being neglected and ignored for so long, we're so popular now."

"I'm sure I have no idea."

"Mm. Well, if you don't want to discuss it I understand."

Benajim leaned toward him. "That you even bring it up says you're either angry, inexperienced, or a fool."

Len Venel glared at him briefly, then laughed. "Probably all three." The motile returned with a tray bearing a cup of coffee and toast. It placed them before Venel and scurried off. "I doubt I'll be director for much longer, so make use of me while I'm here. I have the feeling the next director will be a medical officer from the Armada."

"When did Fisher arrive?"

"Six days ago with eight of his 'aides'. I have another meeting with him in an hour. Unfortunately, it's supposed to be private, or I'd invite you along—"

Benajim raised a hand. "It's fine, Doctor. I understand. I am curious about something."

"Mmm?"

"You have a sealed area in the hospital. What's in there?"

"I don't know. It was sealed when I took over and even *my* access is denied. Rumor has it there was some research in aging reversal going on in there and it got out of control, but it's been under ban for almost forty years."

"Contaminated section?" Elen asked, shocked. "Why don't you purge it?"

"I'd love to, but I can't get the authorization." He shrugged. "Well, what other details can I help you with? I don't have a lot to do today. After my meeting I'm all yours."

"There's no hurry. Tell me about your work here, Doctor. Dr Stanson explained a little, of course, but I'm sure she was hardly exhaustive. What do you try to accomplish?"

Venel's eyes shone. "Well, our primary function is a comfortable old age for our residents. Most have between five and fifteen years left to live. For one reason or another it's become impractical for them to continue in the greater community, so we provide a matrix wherein they can finish their lives with a degree of dignity and in some comfort."

"How many suicides do you have?"

Venel frowned. "We don't—last year we had two. We do our best to avoid those."

"Avoid them?" Piper said. "How do you...?"

"Well, the matrix I referred to is a total sensory makeover. We have a process for blocking and rerouting neuronal pathways, adding or subtracting memories. At its finest we can provide a resident the illusion of youth and vigor and they feel in complete control of their lives. This is part of what makes us so special here, because it's much more than just sitting around waiting for the inevitable system failure that will result in death."

Benajim suppressed a shudder. Piper had gone white. "You tamper with the conscious substrate?"

"To an extent. Initially the process is overwhelming, blocking out everything. Gradually memory returns and we can gauge the degree to which it's safest for the resident and control it. Almost everyone here knows who they are and where they came from, but that knowledge can be limited more or less to allow them the comfort—"

"It's fairly obvious, Doctor," Piper blurted, "what the Armada finds interesting here."

Venel frowned at them.

Benajim waved a hand to indicate the facility. "This is a marvelous prison you have here, Dr Venel."

Piper watched Benajim pace the apartment the rest of the morning. He had a distant, almost obsessed look in his eyes and when spoken to required everything to be repeated.

Here's where my job falls apart, she thought. How do you protect someone from their own torments?

Elen concentrated on the data coming across the terminal. Piper envied her ability to concentrate. But every now and then the Freeroamer looked up at Benajim and Piper was continually amazed at how much sadness only one eye could convey.

Joclen withdrew from the Flow and turned toward the holo. The planet looked desolate. In many ways it reminded her of Miron.

Eighty-two days out, she thought...

"Inventory?" she asked.

"Small transit station," Stoan said, "several ships docks, a few geosynchronous satellites, not much at all. Looks almost like a backwater, but what does that mean in a vacuum?"

Joclen glanced at Stoan irritably. "Anything else?"

"Hah! Yes, else!" He turned and stared into the holo. "The *Solo* is here. Docked, snug between the other ships at the transit station. Brass! That one is nervy."

Joclen leaned forward. "Can we contact him without being picked up?"

"I think so," Ratha said. "Are you sure you want to?"

"No, but we can always run."

Ratha touched his gates.

"It never mounts, it retracts," Stoan said. "Hah!"

Benajim stood at a balcony above the common and watched patients herded in by armed guards. None of the residents seemed particularly frail and most were loud and belligerent. Moss Fisher was among them, issuing brief orders and conferring with his aides. Venel burst from a corridor among them.

"Just what do you think you're doing, Commander?" he demanded.

"What you should have done long ago, Doctor," Fisher said, then turned away and continued speaking to a guard.

"Damnit, you do not run this facility!" Venel said.

Fisher regarded Venel wordlessly, till Benajim thought he would strike the doctor. Abruptly he said, "Come with me," and walked out of the common.

Benajim descended a stair to the main level. He eased open the door and peered down the corridor. Fisher and Venel strode quickly away, turned the corner. Benajim looked around, then hurried after them.

He stopped short of the next turn, hearing voices. He edged to the corner and listened.

"—don't care what your theories are about personal dignity! They're spread all over the compound!"

"This is not a 'compound', Commander! I don't run a prison here!"

"You don't run much of a hospital, either! I'm gathering them all up—according to Interface protocol—and placing them in residences in the township, where they are supposed to be! My subject could be any damn where instead of where she's supposed to be, thanks to your liberal ideas! This is sloppy, Doctor, and irresponsible! What would happen if any of these independent souls of yours suffered an incapacitating injury? Tell me! Wouldn't that be a matter of some concern to your conscience to have them fifty kilometers away—or more!—and dying because you decided it was more important to let them stay where they wanted to rather than administering to their medical needs? Answer me that!"

"These people have dignity. They didn't have any choice about coming here, the least we can do is give them the option—"

"Nonsense. Things are about to be run differently. You've violated your charter, Doctor. You are derelict."

"You are not the final authority in this."

"Since Peace is now under security jurisdiction, I am final authority. You will do nothing without my approval."

The silence stretched out. Venel almost whispered, "These are human beings. You can't disrupt their lives like this."

"Their lives? Doctor Venel, I see where you've gone wrong with this. Their lives are nearly over. What difference does it make where they spend their last few days, weeks, or months? I don't give a damn. I have work to do and they, being strewn all over the place, are impeding my progress. I can disrupt their lives. I can disrupt a lot more than that. If you give a damn at all about them you better find a way to help me facilitate my goals and stop moralizing like a fresh student."

"What do you want me to do?"

"Stay out of my way. I'm only interested in one resident, the one you carelessly let slip away from here shortly after her release from adjustment."

"No one told me she was a special subject."

"You weren't supposed to know! If this place were run more efficiently it would never have come to this! You have greatly inconvenienced me, Dr Venel!"

Benajim moved back from the intersection, then walked quickly away. His heart hammered.

As he reached the door a man stepped through. He wore a patch over one eye and frowned at Benajim.

"Oh, excuse me," he said. "I'm looking for Commander Fisher."

"Haven't seen him," Benajim said. "Sorry."

The man gave him an odd look. Benajim shrugged and eased by him, through the door.

Chapter Twenty Three

Benajim looked up at the polite knock on the office door.

"Yes?"

As Moss Fisher stepped in, Benajim controlled an impulse to stand. Instead, he made himself lean back in his chair and laced his fingers over his stomach.

"Commander Merrick?"

"Yes."

"I thought it was time we met," Fisher said. "May I sit?"

"Of course."

"I am Commander Fisher, Armada Security. I'm sorry I wasn't able to greet you your first day here, but I was occupied."

Benajim made a gesture of dismissal. "No problem, Commander. Dr Venel and his staff have more than compensated."

"Ah. So, you're having no problems finding your way around? You have everything you need?"

"It seems so."

"Excellent. I was wondering if you wouldn't mind letting me inspect your ID and assignment chits. Frankly, I wasn't informed of your coming." He smiled briefly. "Nothing unusual, I haven't been able to put all the appropriate machinery in place yet to function smoothly."

Benajim fished the disks from his pocket and passed them across the desk. Fisher studied them vaguely for a few seconds, then pocketed them.

"Anything you need," he said, standing. "I'm just four doors down on the right."

"Thank you, Commander."

Fisher left.

Piper stepped in from the adjoining office. "What was that?"

"A challenge, a threat, a probe," Benajim said. He shrugged and looked back at his terminal. "I've been studying this neural block method they have. It's fascinating. Have you looked this over?"

"No. I've been going over the schematics for the complex. It may be useful to know where all the openings lead when we find Tamyn."

"Hmm. This method, though...they can place a false memory that overlays the actual. It damps down the intensity of memory, filters it."

"How else do you make people happy with losing the life they love?"

"But it's fully reversible."

"Do you know where they've got Tamyn yet?"

"In the hospital, I'm sure, in the security section. I haven't been able to find the entry codes or anything on the security measures."

"Neither can I. Elen's in the primary computer room trying to find a way into secure files. What about *Solo?*"

"No response to queries," Benajim said. "He's buried in the system somewhere and won't talk to me right now."

"Why?"

"I have no idea. Better let Elen know that Fisher has deigned to spare us time from his busy schedule."

Piper nodded and left. Benajim leaned toward the screen, the intricacies of the neuronal process absorbing him completely.

Benajim found Venel in his office.

"May I speak to you?"

Venel gave his terminal a wistful look, then shrugged and nodded. "Certainly. Come in."

"I've been going over the details of this process you use and some of the case histories." He sat down across from Venel. "I'm fascinated, Doctor. If I understand it correctly, you use an enzyme-electrolysis site block. How do you tag specific memories and track them?"

"Signature imprint. Memories have their own...form, I suppose you could say, a combination of identifying features like a retinal pattern, only subtler. We have a master plate of the electrochemical geography of the brain and induce REM sleep to key specific memories. The related neuronal flare has a unique signature. Now, we can't locate a memory like, oh, what did you say to the server at the restaurant you ate at eleven years and twelve days ago. It's not that specific. But that year will have a unique signature, the memories conglomerate on a finite number of neurons, and so on. We can suppress the entire year. If you had particularly interesting month with in or even a week, it stands out and we can suppress that. But it's a total suppression."

"How?"

"We duplicate the overall configuration of that memorative formation and introduce inhibitors tailored to block reception of those specific neuronal transfers."

"How thorough is the block?"

"That varies from person to person. We can block everything if we want to risk irreversible brain damage. Most of our residents have trouble remembering their names, where they are, where they came from, but that only lasts a day or so while the brain finds a way around the blocks. Many memories share the same pathways, even with a different signature, and those uninhibited memories have to reroute. It's amazing, really, how fast an adjustment can be made."

"Do you ever have to do it again?"

"A booster? Certainly, depending on the psychological state of the patient. A lot of residents manage to adjust as long as the initial impact of being here isn't massive. The blocks are basically to blunt the blow until they can adapt."

"Can you maintain a memory block indefinitely?"

"Yes." Venel frowned.

"And it's reversible."

"Yes."

Benajim rubbed his chin thoughtfully. "What if someone came to you with major memorative impairment to begin with. Can you reverse this condition using a similar method?"

Venel's eyes widened excitedly. "I wanted to attempt that, to find out. I was not given approval and I don't have the budget to go ahead on my own. In fact, I've done theoretical work on exactly that. I built models and ran simulations. I think it's possible."

"It would seem logical that when Peace was established such a method would have been part of the initial research."

"I haven't found anything in the archives to indicate so."

"Of course, there's the sealed section."

Venel shook his head. "Why suppress that kind of data?"

"Maybe they didn't. Maybe that was just part of something else suppressed." Benajim cocked his head to one side. "You don't believe the uncontrolled environment story then?"

"No. It's too easy to purge an environment and there's no reason to block data access." He looked wary suddenly, realizing he had said too much to an Armada officer.

Benajim laughed. "Thank you, Doctor. I have the information I need."

He left the office and headed to the common. What Venel had told him matched with his own ideas. The signature he talked about was very similar to the personal identity configuration that manifested in the Flow during link. Clearly both applications emerged from a common root. In the Pan, though, the link manifested in the optil and only as a specialty very few possessed, while in the C.R. neuronal blockage was a radical procedure that wiped the memory clean.

Maybe. Benajim leaned on the rail of the balcony and looked down into the common. Small groups of residents clustered here and there, sitting on the benches, talking quietly. The honored aged. In the C.R. they would have been the center of groups of younger coes eager to learn, traveling free on starships from place to place, welcome anywhere, a resource carefully cultivated. Only one each of each mind, only one each of a set of experiences unique to that mind. Death took them forever out of reach, a lost gem. Here they were shoveled into a place where specialists took pains to damp their memories and see that they died out of sight of the rest of the universe.

But not all. Sean beat death, it seemed. His encoding was him, through *Solo*...

Where, he wondered, were the millions of other ancient citizens of the Pan? Here on Peace a token population, something, perhaps, the Forum or the Chairman could point to and claim absolution for the sin of negligence. Ultimately, though, it was only an example of what this culture thought important, and everyone had to conform or be discarded. Entire systems were treated so.

How had they diverged so much? They were all human, the C.R. sprang from the head of the Pan, yet...

Perhaps they were not very different. Carson Reiner and her associates, he thought, would fit in quite well here. There was, after all, only one difference—the individual seemed unimportant here. And by extension entire groups lost worth. A chain reaction of neglect catalyzed by a narrow perception. What would happen, he wondered, if a large segment of this disaffected population were dumped into the C.R.? Perhaps it was time to bring the exiles home. Perhaps that was part of what Sean had in mind. And what's in my mind? he wondered.

"Inward to deeper vistas," Stoan muttered and grinned quickly. He clapped his hands. "Another vessel. C.R., big, and hidden from the transit station by the planet and by a careful rerouting of the satellite signals."

"Like we're doing?" Joclen asked.

"Just!" He touched his gates again. "Shuttles back and forth to the surface. A few, like cargohaulers." He glanced at the holo. "I wonder what's at the market?"

Joclen looked at Ratha. "Let Innes and Traville know where we're going." She turned to her console. "Let's go have a look at this other ship."

"Wait," Ratha said. "*Solo* is channeling data. I think you better look at this."

Joclen touched her gate and linked with the dataflow Ratha was receiving.

The moment the elevator door opened to the corridor leading to the secured area two armed guards filled it. Benajim glanced at Piper, then turned to the guards.

"Is Commander Fisher here?" Benajim asked.

"ID," one of the guards said.

"I'm afraid Commander Fisher has my ID. He invited us down, in fact. I'm Commander Merrick. Is he here?"

"Wait." One of them stepped away and put something up to his throat. A moment later he said, "Come with me."

Benajim and Piper walked a step behind and to the left of the guard. The nursing station was fully staffed, five blue-smocked people intent on various tasks. Motiles drifted up and down the corridors, a few with no obvious task but with fittings that looked like defense.

They turned down the corridor leading to the sealed area. Benajim's heartbeat quickened. The corridor continued on into a section that looked no different than any other part of the hospital.

Moss Fisher was walking toward him, smiling.

"Commander Merrick," he said. "I am sorry, I should have returned your identity to you yesterday."

As Benajim stepped over the threshold of the newly activated area, Fisher extended his hand and gave the sheaf of disks to him.

"Thank you," Benajim said, sliding them into his pocket. "I was unaware this area was open."

"It wasn't. I required it, though. This way I can conduct my operations without interfering with normal hospital routine. Would you care to see?"

"Well..."

"You have the clearance, I checked."

Benajim nodded. Fisher gestured and the guard left.

"In fact," Fisher continued as Benajim and Piper fell into step alongside him, "I'm rather dismayed that you're in Assessment. You have clearance all the way to General Ashfor and the Chairman's Aide."

"Assessment isn't my only area," Benajim said. "I'm usually called in only when something delicate needs to be looked into."

Fisher looked at him, surprised. "Like me?"

"Well. You must admit your rise to directorship of Operation Firebrake was sudden—"

"Oh, I don't think so."

"—and so soon afterward you're conducting a new program on Peace. You're holding things rather close. Too close to comfort certain individuals."

"So they send you in to ask questions?"

"And look at things."

"Mm. I've never heard of you before."

Benajim stopped and looked directly at Fisher. "There are many people you've never heard of before, Commander. You'd be surprised."

"No doubt." Fisher laughed quietly. "So who do I have to speak well of to assuage their fears and get you off my back?"

Benajim laughed. "Why don't you just let me know what you're doing here. I'm fairly confident that you wouldn't engage in anything impolitic so soon after promotion. Your career doesn't indicate that sort of recklessness."

"I've been reckless before."

"Only in well-calculated degrees."

"I'm impressed, Commander. You've done quite a study on me."

"My duty, Commander."

They regarded each other in a dense silence. Benajim watched Fisher to see if his gambit had worked. He did not know how much of Merrick's file was still accessible—not enough apparently to inform Fisher that Sean Merrick ought to be ancient or, as he in fact was, dead—but what had been there convinced Fisher. There was no doubt, though, that they were enemies. Benajim hoped Fisher would decide that this one was a useful enemy.

Fisher nodded politely and gestured for Benajim to proceed him. Piper stayed a step behind Fisher.

The corridor joined another that circled round a central area. At regular intervals windows looked down into operating theatres crammed with beds and equipment. Most were unoccupied, though the monitors showed life. Benajim stopped at one that was occupied. He stared down at the person strapped to the table, leads running from her shaved scalp, the equipment around her lively with information.

"This is my present subject," Fisher said. "And a more interesting subject I could not have asked for."

"Who is she?"

"She says her name is Tamyn Glass and she claims to be from across the boundary, from among the seti. She might as well have told me she'd come back from the other side of the Styx, returned from the dead."

"What are you doing to her?"

"I'm giving her a new mind."

"The basic research done here," Fisher said, warming to the topic as they walked away from the theater, "involved altering the internal landscape of the mind. Most of the relics who live here have had their memories altered to some extent just so they don't commit mass suicide. In this section, the research was being done to extend that ability to a complete remapping of the identity. It astonishes me no one looked into this before."

"How long has it been sealed?"

"Forty-eight years."

"Is this the only research done here?"

"Oh, no. There was quite a lot of gerontological research being done and limited cloning work. I gather, from what little else I've looked into, that they hoped to produce a series of rejuvenation therapies."

"Fascinating."

"Yes, well, transplants are still the most reliable countermeasure to old age."

"Assuming you have sufficient supply. Cloning could easily provide that."

"Mm. It's my understanding that cloning was tried once before, long ago, but for some reason was abandoned. I'm inclined to think it has certain unforeseeable consequences making it impractical. But we've come a long way since the days of legend, no? Maybe it's time."

Fisher gestured toward a door. Benajim proceeded him through and found himself in a large chamber filled with polycom terminals.

"A library," Fisher said. "Genome. Genotype, chromosomal pattern, DNA matrix, everything on file from every citizen of the Pan for the last three centuries. Entire family histories. A research resource as complete as any I've seen, all for looking into inherited traits, family tendencies, environmental conditions and results...impressive, no? There was a piece of work being done here!"

"Why was this closed down?"

Fisher raised his eyebrows skeptically. "Really, Commander, I'm surprised at you. Think what you're saying."

Benajim smiled grimly. "Ah. Who needs rejuvenated old when we're constantly making new?"

Fisher's face compressed into a wide grin and then—startling Benajim—a laugh.

"I wouldn't have put it quite that way," Fisher said, nodding, "but that's good, that's good."

Fisher led Benajim out into the corridor again. Med personnel moved about. They passed an open area containing consoles, polycoms, and people concentrating on a variety of tasks, oblivious to the visitors.

"Here," Fisher said, "I can devise a portfolio of methods for restructuring personality."

Benajim nodded, feigning interest. He studied the layout, entrances and exits, looked for security devices, counted personnel.

"All those people I saw being brought in the last day or so," he said. "What was that about?"

"Yes. Well, the policy of this facility has been shabby. Live and let live. There were three or four hundred hermits living on the fringes of the habitat. We gathered them all in. I don't like loose details. We've set them up in residences in town."

Benajim counted about twelve staff. None of them spoke to him or even acknowledged Fisher's presence. There were other chambers where simpler "memorative assonance" could be performed, the damping procedure all residents received. They stopped before Tamyn's chamber again.

"She is fascinating," Fisher whispered. "Her mind is permeated with a conductive mesh of some kind, that lies along the neuronal branches, connects with the major trunks, but doesn't interfere with normal synaptic function. It has given me some problems with memory dissolution. I initially tried to just erase her memory, but it seems to be stored differently than in an unmodified brain."

"So what now?"

"I'm investigating removing the mesh. The problem is, though, it seems to run along her entire nervous system."

"You could kill her," Benajim said, hoping that he kept his voice even, unconcerned.

Fisher nodded. "Mmm. Could, could." He shrugged. "Then we start over with a new subject."

"You have another one of her?"

Fisher nodded and turned to him. "You."

"I'm not sure I understand, Commander."

"He does, though," someone said.

Benajim turned. The man with the eyepatch approached, a pair of guards beside him.

"We never met," he said. "But Co Van knows me. Allow me to introduce myself, Co Merrick—actually, I mean, Co Cyanus. My name is Bris Calenda."

Len knocked on Merrick's office door. It opened and Elen Leris peered at him from her one natural eye. The artificial one picked up the overhead light and glinted eerily.

"Is Commander Merrick in?" he asked.

"No. He's down in the hospital at Commander Fisher's invitation."

"Oh? How long ago?"

"Commander Fisher called him an hour ago." She leaned against the doorway and crossed her arms.

Len ran a hand through his hair and looked up and down the corridor. "Uh, may I come in?"

"Is there a problem?"

"I—"

"Len!"

Ryan Jones was coming toward him. Len cursed silently.

"Ryan, I don't have time right now—"

"You'll make time," Ryan said. He stopped and looked at Elen. "Tabit, right? You're a Freeroamer."

Elen straightened suddenly.

Ryan chuckled. "Don't mind me, I won't say anything. I'm one of the inmates. And I don't think Len will say anything."

"No, I—" He looked from Elen to Ryan. "Is that true?"

"Both of you come in," Elen said. "Who knows who else might happen along."

Len waved Ryan through the door first and followed.

"Now—" Elen began.

"Wait a minute," Ryan cut her off. He rounded on Len. "I got a hell of a complaint. What's the purpose of hauling all us in like cattle? And what happened to Tamyn?"

"What do you mean?"

"Tamyn Glass?" Elen asked.

"Do you know her?" Ryan asked.

"I've never met her, but—"

"I didn't issue the orders, Ryan," Len said. "Now, please, I think there's a problem—"

"Damn right!" Ryan said. "We were stunned and dragged back asleep. When I came to I found everybody but Tamyn. Now I want to know—"

"Ryan, shut up," Len said. He turned to Elen. "I just received a message in my office on my terminal. I have no idea who sent it, but—Fisher has just ordered a full security alert, not a minute ago. I expect his people to show up here to arrest you."

"That's what I thought you were," Elen said. "I received the same message." She waved at the monitor on the desk behind her. "Doctor Venel, you're about to lose your facility."

Len stared at her, stunned.

"What would you be willing to do to try to prevent that?" she asked.

"I'm not sure I follow you."

"She's asking you to be a hell raiser," Ryan said. "You better make a quick decision if we're under a security alert."

"I need access to the primary dataspheres," Elen said. She looked at Ryan. "We'll probably find Tamyn Glass along the way, Co Ryan."

Len chewed his lip for a few seconds. I've spent most of my career making careful moves to assure the best possible situation, he thought.

"Come with me," he said. "You, too, Ryan."

"Wouldn't miss it," Ryan said.

Benajim looked toward the door when it opened. Bris Calenda stepped into the room and Benajim felt his pulse increase. He swallowed dryly and squeezed his hands into fists. The restraints that held him into the medunit were solid.

Technicians worked on him steadily, shaving his scalp, running tests, placing probes on his body. They paid no attention to Calenda.

"I've been wanting to talk to you for a long time, Co Cyanus," Calenda said. He sat down beside him. "Now you know how Sean felt."

Benajim glared at him.

"Commander Fisher is going to open you up for me," Calenda said. "We're going to have a look inside your head and see just what's there that Sean Merrick thought was so important." He glanced at the technicians. "It shouldn't take much longer. This part is pretty straightforward."

"What are you doing here?"

"I work for Carson Reiner, perhaps Piper told you. I'm her field representative. We've developed an arrangement with Commander Fisher. Of course, you very nearly ruined it. You and Shipmaster Glass and that dead bastard Merrick."

Benajim shook his head. "I don't understand."

"That's disappointing. I expected you to be more intelligent. Well, it's fairly simple." Calenda placed his hands behind his back. "The border was bound to open eventually. The way things were going, though, it would have been a chaos of interaction. No controls, no order, no way to predict anything. Co Reiner appreciated—correctly, I think—that this could mean the end of the Commonwealth. Steps had to be taken to assure a reasonable, gradual reintroduction of the C.R. to the Pan. Well, when she discovered that Sean Merrick had been running a trade route to Tabit all along, it was too good to pass by."

"You sound like a propagandist for Carson Reiner. She blackmailed Sean."

Calenda laughed. "That cut both ways. He intended to do the same to her. Well, to be brief, Sean Merrick failed and Carson Reiner succeeded. First we established ourselves on Tabit and then we contacted Commander Fisher. He was most willing to make an arrangement with us. Through us he can accede to the Chairmanship. Through him Carson Reiner can protect and stabilize the C.R. They'll be very useful to each other."

"But Reiner's dismantling the C.R. to do it. Why?"

"Nonsense. The C.R. was dismantling itself. You don't honestly believe it could go on the way it was. How many Merrick Enterprise dissolutions could it survive? No, this was best. Not only will she offer stability to the Commonwealth, but she'll avert a war with the Pan. With Fisher as an ally, once he acquires the Chair, the interaction can proceed reasonably. Unregulated interaction could only result in conflict."

"So what are you doing for Fisher in the meantime?"

"Oh, helping him with a small problem he has. Peace will become a solution eventually. He's also busily forging alliances and acquiring political support in the outlying systems. We provide transport for a particular kind of trade route—and some of the goods."

"Trade?"

"Just on the other side of the environmental blister is a prison. It's far too crowded, but we're taking care of that. The procedures developed here enable him to erase the memories of the prisoners. From there we transport them where they're most needed or wanted."

Benajim shuddered. "Transplants...?"

Calenda nodded. "And labor. Entertainment—"

"Slaves."

Calenda shrugged. "If you wish. They don't know any better, though, and they are serving useful purposes—some of them for the first time in their lives." He leaned on the edge of the bed and brought his face close to Benajim. "Now I'm going to go and leave you to Commander Fisher. He's fascinated by us. I'm fascinated by you. I'll be very interested in going over what all is in your head."

"I'm really sorry Piper didn't kill you."

"She came close." He tapped his patch. "I miss my prophylactic, too. But at least I get to watch the same thing happen to her." He laughed lightly. "Good-bye, Co Cyanus."

The next person through that door, Piper thought, staring at the featureless white panel, is going to regret it—briefly.

She had purged her system of toxins as best she could and now there was an elevated level of boosters, adrenal-analogues, and endorphins, kept just below peak. Piper did not know how long she could stay like this. Her entire metabolism was in overdrive and before long she had to do something with the increase, or collapse under the strain. It had been nearly two hours since Fisher had her put in here.

Bris Calenda. Damn, she berated herself, I should have made sure. But every time she ran the scene at Transit Freeroamer Orbital through she could find no point at which she might have been more thorough. At least the prophylactic was gone.

Small comfort now.

The door whirred as the locks retracted. Piper stared at it, let her implants edge her levels up slightly more, and braced herself for a lunge.

The door slid open.

No one came through. Piper waited a moment then moved forward.

The door slammed shut.

And opened again. Piper backed up. As she watched, the door snapped open and closed twice more. The light in her cell flickered.

She stepped close to the door and waited. It opened again and she lunged through.

She hit the floor and rolled, coming to her feet with her back to the opposite wall. Her cell door closed.

The corridor was filled with arrhythmic thumping. Piper looked up and down its length and saw all the doors opening and closing at random. The lights flickered again.

Next she heard running feet. She pressed her back against the wall.

A pair of guards and three technicians came quickly around the bend of the corridor, their faces all masks of confusion and fear.

At first they did not see her. They were almost on her before one of the technicians blinked at her and started to point a finger.

"Mistake," she mumbled and rushed them.

She broke the pointing technician's wrist, swept her leg across the legs of the one beside him sending that one sprawling. One of the guards was raising a pistol. Piper spun around and came in under his arm, drove her fist into his groin.

The other guard tried to grab her. She grasped his wrists and dropped to her knees, pulling. He tumbled over her back onto the floor, sitting. She twisted his head around sharply—cracking cartilage and a clear snap of bone.

She stood. One technician was running away. The first guard leaned against the wall, vomiting. Piper kicked his buttocks, driving him into the wall. He fell face down in his bile and lay still.

The remaining technicians were huddled together a short distance away, watching her. One cradled his wrist and sobbed softly.

The lights winked out. A few seconds later they came on again and all the doors continued to open and close sporadically.

"Calenda," Piper whispered. She grinned at the technicians. "Time, I think, to shut bedlam down."

She sprinted off down the corridor, her muscles warm and her senses humming with power and a delicious tension.

Chapter Twenty Four

Tamyn floated within a slowly changing cell, a shifting collage of geometries, disorienting yet familiar. Suspended like a baby in a womb, her hand drifted toward her mouth, thumb following the shape of her lips. Something was missing, though, but when she opened her eyes the dim, mutating geometries distracted her completely.

After a timeless, aimless contemplation, a brilliant fluoresce lightened everything around her. She stared at the fabric of her cell, amazed. The patterns remained unchanged but she knew that the light meant they soon would change.

Tamyn reached out to touch the surface of the cell. Her hand plunged through the material as if it were fog. She pulled back, startled. This was even more familiar.

She tried to turn around, to see what lay behind her. She could not tell if she succeeded—everywhere was the same. Now she knew she had to escape this comfortable place. It saddened her a little; it had been a long, long time since she had felt this safe. When…? A face appeared before her. A man, thick, unkempt beard, narrow blue eyes, thinning grey-brown hair. Gordon. Father. No, stepfather. Still, this was Pater. A big man with endless hugs and smiles who was always pleased to see her. He was only happy for her, never for himself. Not unhappy, either, but in a state of waiting. There was something wrong with his hands, she recalled. He was always rubbing his fingertips, worrying at them, always going to see someone about them. But he made things with his hands, he ran machines that turned out myriad shapes—parts, bits of other machines, all shiny and precise and necessary. Many coes came to him to have these things made. He was good at this, working with his hands, yet there was something wrong with them. It nagged and ached at her that she could not remember what.

They lived in a rambling collection of modules on the edge of a sprawling spaceport. Tamyn could not recall a time when the sound of shuttles lifting off did not fill the background of her days. She lived amid the service shops, omnirecs, manufactories, supply houses, warehouses, flops, and hangars of the port.

Gordon maintained his machine shop in their home. The ships
came and went and she grew up dreaming of starships and space.
Gordon showed her his art and she learned it eagerly.

The tips of his fingers were black and pitted. She remembered.
Chill went through her. She raised her own hands and studied
the fingertips. Dull grey metal capped the end of each finger and
she sighed in relief. Gordon's interface had been burned out in an
accident he would never talk about. He could not link with the
datasphere, become part of the Flow. On the frontier where they
lived it had not been as much a handicap as it might have been on a
more settled world like Miron, but he had been a starship pilot and
he could not do that anymore. The facilities to repair the damage
had not been available in the Distals for years after the War. When
the technology finally reestablished itself Gordon simply could not
bring himself to trust it.

But her own links were intact.

The light pulsed again. There was a familiarity to that, too, now.
She fixed her attention on the cell around her and illuminated the
seams. Dull green light glowed along the connections, along the
pathways. A few seemed twisted, on the verge of snapping. She set
them back the way they should be, then sought the major pathways.
There and there. She moved down them. Somewhere ahead—or
behind, above, below—lay the perimeter of the network. It might
be a long journey, but she had to find the point of intrusion, from
where the yellow light emerged into the cell. It was a tangled array,
this place she recognized, but the tangles began to make more sense.

When the yellow light came again she was prepared. She saw it
funnel down a few pathways that led back to the source. She followed it. There, in the center of several minor branchings, glistened
a pinpoint intrusion.

The pathway was not the easily traversed sort with which she
was familiar in the Flow. Everything here, it seemed, was different by degrees, archaic and difficult. She pushed her way down
the narrow, confining trunk. The signals racing toward her now
were visibly coded and she let them slide over her while changing
key components. They would reach the intrusion point changed,
ineffective.

Finally she came to a place where the trunk widened out. A
sphere rotated slowly around her, comprised of thousands of

bright pinpoints. From within this diatom she could go anywhere in the system.

A beam shot across the sphere. It entered a node on the opposite side, then emerged again, entered a different one. When she followed it she found a bright blue ball of energy waiting at the end of a short pathway. It blocked the pathway, rippling sinuously, seeming alive. Frightened, she tried to retreat, but the pathway had been blocked.

The ball rolled toward her. It stopped a membrane's width away from her. Her move now, it seemed to suggest. She reached a tenuous finger toward it, barely touching its surface.

TAM?

She pulled back, shocked. A vague memory floated loose, came to her attention.

SEAN?

The ball writhed in mirth. Despite herself she felt suddenly glad she had found it.

DAMN, it said, I'VE BEEN WANDERING THIS SYSTEM FOR AN ETERNITY AND DIDN'T THINK ANYBODY ELSE WOULD EVER LINK!

WHO ARE YOU?

WHO AM I? BUT—

It backed away, its surface quiet now, the blue darker, somber. After a time, it rolled toward her again. The pathway was unblocked and it shoved her back into the diatom.

It became a streak once more and shot in and out of scores of nodes, finally coming back to rest beside her.

THAT ONE, it said. One of the nodes glowed brightly.

WHAT IS IT?

ACCESS IT AND FIND OUT.

Uncertainly, she plunged into it.

FILE NAME: GLASS, TAMYN F.

She rifled through the datanode. Yes, she was all here. All that needed to be done was replace it where it belonged. She began shunting the data.

When she was finished she ran an internal diagnostic. Yes, it was all there. The intrusive code now had no effect. The blocks that had been placed on memory nodes were gone.

Tamyn remembered herself.

And she remembered Sean.

WHAT ARE YOU DOING HERE?

COME TO GET YOU OUT, AMONG OTHER THINGS. I HAD BUSINESS HERE THAT NEEDED TENDING TO PERSONALLY. I'VE DONE THAT, NOW I'M MAKING SURE YOU'RE SAFE.

There was something different about this encoding. It was more forceful, more decidedly Sean than the one she had left on Earth.

The blue ball rippled.

TRUE, it said, BUT THEN I'M NOT THE ONE YOU HAD. I'M SOLO.

YOU ALMOST HAVE THE SUBSTANCE OF A LIVING CODE.

ALMOST. NOT QUITE. CLOSE ENOUGH. YOU NEED THE BRAIN ITSELF FOR PERFECT MIMICRY OVER TIME, BUT MY TECHNICAL PEOPLE GOT PRETTY CLOSE. CLOSE ENOUGH TO KEEP UP THE SHAM INDEFINITELY WITH MY CORPSE IN THEIR POSSESSION.

WE BURIED YOU, SEAN. YOU'RE ON EARTH, IN YOUR FAMILY CRYPT.

THANK YOU. FOR WHAT IT'S WORTH, YOU HAVE THE GRATITUDE OF SEAN MERRICK. BEFORE HE DIED HE PLACED A RETAINER FOR COMPLETE LEGAL SER-VICE WITH YOUR LAWYER. YOU'LL NEED IT. THERE WILL BE OTHER ITEMS IN THE WILL WHEN YOU RE-TURN WITH THE CONFIRMATION.

I'M NOT SURE I HAVE CONFIRMATION.

NOBODY WILL QUESTION YOU AFTER YOUR COURT.

IF I HAVE THAT.

YOU WILL. THE AKAREN WON'T STAND FOR THE KIND OF MANIPULATING REINER AND HER COL-LEAGUES ARE TRYING. YOU'VE PULLED THE PIN, TAM. WITHOUT SEAN'S BODY IN THEIR POSSESSION THEY CAN'T MAINTAIN THE SHAM.

SHE MAY SUCCEED ANYWAY. WHERE AM I?

HERE.

Another datanode sparkled and she touched it.

It flooded back in on her, then, everything that had occurred in the last few weeks. Tamyn shuddered.

HOW DO I GET OUT OF HERE?

LET'S GO TURN SOME MACHINES OFF, SHALL WE?

Her eyes snapped open without any transition from sleep to wakefulness. It was a cold, almost painful experience. But she sat up and began unhooking the surface patches.

A nurse stared at her with wide, frightened eyes.

"You don't have to help," Tamyn said, "but don't get in the way." The lights flickered briefly. Tamyn could hear people running in the corridor outside. She pulled the last of the contacts from her neck and slid off the table. Her scalp felt tight, odd, and she ran her hand over it. Her hair was gone and some kind of antiseptic stain had been slathered on her, staining her fingers orange.

She whirled on the nurse. "You were going to cut me open, weren't you?"

The nurse seemed to switch on then and made a break for the exit. Tamyn caught her in three quick steps and hammerlocked her arm.

For a few seconds, the nurse struggled. Tamyn kept her free hand pressed into the woman's back, holding her against the wall. Tamyn searched the nearby equipment for something to use, but very little of it looked familiar enough for her to be sure.

The nurse tried to kick backward.

"Damn," Tamyn hissed as she reached up, grabbed a handful of hair, and slammed the nurse's forehead into the wall twice. The nurse slumped to the floor.

Tamyn turned the unconscious woman over, then did a quick search of the room. She found a thin single-piece that she slipped on. Alongside the examination table, a tray held a variety of devices, one of which looked like an injector. She grabbed it in lieu of any other weapon.

A bulky polycom squatted against one wall, but she saw no interface gates, and had no idea how to access it safely. She sighed and went to the door.

She hesitated. She had no idea where she was within the complex. The possibilities were good that she would be back in custody within minutes.

But—

She touched the contact. The door slid open.

Three guards turned toward her simultaneously.

Then Piper Van appeared.

Tamyn watched, transfixed, at the blur Piper became among them. Tamyn heard the blows strike, saw the bodies jerk and fall, but could not make out an individual move.

Piper faced Tamyn then. Sweat slicked her face, darkened her clothes in patches. She looked feverish and enraged.

The lights winked again.

"What's doing that?" Tamyn demanded.

Piper looked around, puzzled for a second, then seemed to calm down slightly.

"I think—I think Elen's in the system," she said.

"Who?"

Piper frowned at her, stepped closer. "Shipmaster Glass?"

"Yes!"

"Oh. You look...different."

"Thank you. Who else is here?"

"Benajim. Somewhere. Near here."

She rushed by Tamyn then, suddenly a blur of energy again. Tamyn felt her pass. The lights went out, came on several seconds later.

"Ryan..."

Tamyn started down the corridor in Piper's wake.

"Now we'll see what all is in there."

Benajim was not sure who said this. Fisher, perhaps. It did not sound like Bris Calenda. Whoever, identity was lost in the next second. He closed his eyes and watched the inside of his skull ripple with chaos.

He was terrified and fascinated. Everything he was or might be, dredged up and laid out like an archaeological dig. Sift through the dirt, brush away the obscuring grime, wash the fragments till their true nature glistened, clean and clear. He wanted to know. He believed what Sean—*Solo*—had told him about how he had been found, what had gone into rebuilding him, but he stubbornly refused to accept that nothing was left of who he had been before. Now perhaps he would find out. The probes eased into his mind, pulled apart the curtains, pushed light into the dark places.

He spiraled down into himself, toward a barrier that kept everything that he was since Sean Merrick separate from all that he had been before. It rose up to shatter against him as he plunged through.

And all around him rushed the empty regions, abandoned caverns where, by the echo returned from his screaming passage, he knew he had once been.

Len watched Elen work and felt helpless.

"Stop pacing," Ryan said. "What's wrong? Second thoughts?"

Len jabbed a finger at Elen. "I don't know who she is, where she's from. For all I know I've just broken several security regulations—in fact, I know I have." He looked at Ryan. "Why are you so calm?"

"I'm a resident here. I'm never getting out. What've I got to lose?"

The room was crammed with unopened crates. Technically, no one was supposed to enter the central computer room. Everything in the complex was more easily done from the satellite terminals. Len had never been in here.

Several monitors above the main polycom showed images of the panic Elen was creating. She had disrupted most of the automated operations throughout the complex. Doors opened and closed at random, the lights flashed, comms did not work, the lifts were all malfunctioning. Down in the secured section the ventilation system was turning on and off. Fisher's people rushed about in a panic. Several tried to override central's hold on the systems to restore order, but Elen fended it off.

"Hey, look!" Ryan pointed at a monitor.

Tamyn Glass and Piper Van sprinted down a corridor.

"They're nearing a lift connected to the common," Len said loudly.

Elen raised a hand to indicate she heard. She stared at the polycom, a faint ruby light attaching her false eye to a receptacle on the console.

"A shuttle is coming down," she said.

"Damn," Len said.

Ryan patted him on the shoulder. "You stay here and help her. I'll go meet the shuttle."

"Alone?" Len reached for Ryan's arm.

"No, I got some friends here that'll go with me." He grinned. "Don't you trust me?"

"I—what the hell can you do?"

Ryan shrugged. "More than I'm doing here." He laughed and patted Len's shoulder.

He left the room.

Joclen withdrew and slammed her fist on the edge of her console. "Damn!"

In the holo the merchanter was receding rapidly. It left a shuttle coming upwell, now with no ship but *Wicca* to receive it.

"Not worth the venom," Stoan said. He pointed at the shuttle. "That, though!"

Joclen nodded. "Down to the bay, Stoan. I want you there when we grab it."

"The Armada ships are leaving dock," Ratha said.

"Now what?" She shook her head. "Any of them moving toward us?"

"No. It looks like two are moving to intercept the merchanter."

"Then don't worry about them yet. Keep an eye. Stoan, we take the shuttle."

She touched her gate again, eased into the skin of the ship, and moved toward the shuttle. Shreve reached out to cut it off from the ground.

Wicca took hold of the small boat and pulled it to the bay.

Piper stabbed at the contact on the lift. The air had stopped moving again. She twisted around, scanning the corridor. Tamyn held a pistol ready. Piper had one tucked in her pants, but had yet to use it. She slammed her hand against the contact again.

"Come on!"

"Do you even know where we're going?" Tamyn asked.

"I'm getting you to the upper levels first, then I'm going after Benajim."

"Maybe we ought to—"

The lift door opened. A man stood in the car, gaping at them until Piper clipped him just beneath the ear. He fell forward into her arms. She laid him almost gently on the floor.

"In," Piper ordered. Tamyn hesitated, then entered the lift. Piper joined her and stabbed a button.

The door remained open.

"Elen!" Piper stood and stepped into the corridor.

A short way down the hall, Bris Calenda emerged from a room. He glanced left, then right, froze when he saw her.

Piper smiled, raised her pistol.

Tamyn pulled her arm down. "Benajim," she hissed.

Calenda turned and ran. Piper dropped the pistol and sprinted after him.

She came alongside him and grabbed his collar. She stepped across his path and pushed at the same time. He skipped over her leg and crashed against the wall.

Piper turned him over. He blinked up at her, dazed, from his one eye.

"You should get that fixed," she said, tapping his patch. "One eye is terrible for coordination." She hauled him to his feet. "Where's Cyanus?"

The lift door remained open. Tamyn waited nearby, crouched against the wall opposite, watching. She wanted to take time to sort her thoughts, get a better hold of her bearings, but she was too anxious, too alert to every sound, every possible threat. Sounds came from odd directions, punctuating the silence. She heard running occasionally, but no one else ran by.

The lights went down again.

When they came on someone stood alongside her.

She jumped away, tried to bring the pistol up. Fisher was quicker this time and charged into her. They went down on the floor, his weight forcing the air from her lungs, and his fingers locking around her wrist. She tried to wriggle into a more advantageous position, but he brought his leg up into her pelvis. The pain radiated instantly, blurring her vision for a moment. The pistol fell from her hand and he got to his feet.

"I'm still bruised from our little conversation of the other day," he said. "I hate that."

He swung the barrel of the pistol, grazing her scalp.

Fisher grabbed her neck and held her.

"I suppose this Benajim Cyanus came to get you out of here," he said close to her ear. "Well, he won't now. He's empty. We opened him up and found no one home. Fascinating. But what I want to know is how he managed to get Sean Merrick's ID to use. That really interests me."

"I don't know," Tamyn said.

"I don't expect you to. I may never find out now. You'll never know if I do or don't."

She felt the pistol rest against her head. She squeezed her eyes shut.

"This isn't a stunner," he said. "At this range—"

The pressure of the barrel left suddenly. Tamyn heard scuffling, the clatter of metal and plastic on the floor.

"We are not amused!"

She twisted around.

Stoan held Fisher off the floor, one hand on his belt, the other on Fisher's throat. Fisher stared at the Alcyoni with wide, frightened eyes.

Thijs knelt beside Tamyn. Beyond her, she saw Clif and Steg. Her vision blurred. She wiped at the tears, but more came. The change was too swift, too great, from death to home.

It would take a good part of the voyage back to straighten out all the details. Tamyn stared out the windows at the town below, the red-tiled roofs at once friendly and terrifying. She shivered.

Stoan had flown down in a commandeered cargohauler. The Merrick Enterprises merchanter had been blocked from leaving the system by the Armada ships. *Wicca* stayed away from the transit station, but, through the link with the *Solo*, Tamyn had spoken to Joclen. Soon enough they would be on their way.

"Tamyn?"

She turned away from the window. Len, Ryan, Stoan, and Innes stood nearby. The Armada commander, Nillix, joined them.

"I don't know what's wrong with Commander Merrick," Len said, glancing at Nillix. "I've never seen anything like it. Usually traumatic amnesia is a simple matter of unmasking the blocks, but in his case..."

"That's what was done to him," Tamyn said. "Don't worry, Doctor. You weren't responsible." She looked at Nillix. "Thank you for your help, Commander."

"Yes, well...I've received a communiqué from Representative Nooneus. A new Armada team is on its way to take Fisher into custody." He glanced at Len. "At least, what's left of him. It seems the staff here provided him with some blocks. Right now he doesn't quite know where he is or who he is." He cleared his throat. "Representative Nooneus is also interested in some sort of communication with your government. Probably through Tabit."

"Elen can deal with that," Piper said.

Tamyn nodded. "Where is she?"

"With Benajim," Ryan said. "Tamyn, I want to ask—"

"You're more than welcome to come with us," she said.

"Oh." He grinned. "Really? Thank you."

"Or any of your companions from the town," she added. "If the borders are going to come down I can't think of better representatives than sojourners and spacefarers."

Nillix cleared his throat again. "My instructions pertained to cooperating fully with Commander Merrick or his associates. The data he managed to release to us and to General Ashfor and Representative Nooneus was enough to shut down Commander Fisher's operations. However, I'm not sure how to deal with this situation. Commander Merrick is no longer functioning and I'm not sure what status I ought to accord to you, Shipmaster Glass."

"You ought to leave soon," Len said to Tamyn. "Before too many questions get too complicated."

"That would probably be best," Tamyn agreed. "Commander Nillix, if you could continue being indecisive, we'll gladly remove ourselves from your presence. Formal letters to the government of Tabit and to the Board of Regents will be sufficient to start things moving and relieve you of the responsibility."

"Those documents are on their way," Nillix said. "We can transmit them to you as soon as we receive them."

"Excellent. In the meantime, let us see about getting our people out of here."

"Of course." Nillix nodded to everyone and left.

"Thijs?" Tamyn asked. "What about Benajim?"

"I don't know. I don't see any reason the past two thousand days should be gone. He wasn't stripped down. There should be some memory left. It's possible his prior mindwipe has complicated this. Maybe, in time..."

Tamyn recognized the helplessness in his voice and face. "All right, then. Stoan, see to getting everyone upwell. Can Piper pilot the *Solo?*"

"She says yes," Stoan said. "We can only see if she can."

"Fine. She can at least dock with *Wicca*. See to it."

He nodded and left.

"I'm going to go talk to the others," Ryan said.

"I have to prepare Benajim," Thijs said.

Len remained.

"Anything I can help you with, Doctor?" Tamyn asked.

"Nothing. And everything. I thought you people were stories, myths. I didn't think such a lie was possible, that you were all dead."

"Space is wide, Co Venel. Plenty of room to hide the truth."

"I hope we get to know each other, now that the truth is out."

"Is it? You know. This Representative Nooneus knows. A few others. Perhaps these overtures to dialogue will amount to something. But it hasn't been in anyone's interest since the War to talk." She shrugged. "Still. You may hope in certainty."

Leris op Elen refused to leave Benajim. She traveled with him up-well. Tamyn watched the woman and ached sympathetically. She seemed so young and there was so much for her to do, it was unfair to have this to deal with as well.

Joclen met them at the lock. Tamyn was shocked at the tension in her face, relieved to see the joy slowly come into Joclen's eyes. Tamyn wrapped her arms around the younger woman. They held each other for several moments, as if to prove to each other that it was no dream.

Crej'Nevan waited near the hatch. "Tam. Thijs has informed me what has happened. I offer to be matrix for Cyanus."

Elen looked at the seti, her natural eye wide.

"Get him settled," Tamyn said. "Leris op Elen? I need to talk to you." She saw the Freeroamer grip Benajim's unresponsive hand. "Later. After we're underway."

Tamyn busied herself getting the ship ready. Piper docked the *Solo* to *Wicca* for the voyage home and came on board. More communiqués' arrived from Bool Nooneus. Details mounted, but Tamyn fell into her routines smoothly and Wicca was quickly underway.

In one of the medunits Benajim lay staring at nothing. Elen sat beside him. Tamyn found them this way when she entered. Thijs and Crej'Nevan were already there.

"Elen," Tamyn said. "You know Thijs, my med. Has he explained to you what Crej'Nevan is offering?"

Elen looked at the Stralith and shook her head.

"The Stralith," Thijs said, "possess an ability to share dreams. They can give them in their absence. It's a healing process for many. Co Cyanus has no memories, no dreams. Perhaps Crej may help."

"Share dreams..." Elen repeated.

"Crej can simply give them, stimulating the brain the way a newborn infant's brain is constantly worked by surges to expand it and exercise it. But Crej can also take memories from others and pass them along. We can all give what we remember of Benajim to Crej and then to Benajim."

Elen nodded, her natural eye wet and red.

Epilogue

Huddled in the corner of her chambers, Crej'Nevan enveloped Benajim in the embrace of tentacles, wrapping him securely, almost lovingly. His eyes were closed now and his head lay back, as if reclining in the arms of a lover or a mother. Elen knelt before the Stralith, trembling slightly from fear, from worry, and anger, and touched the extended tentacle of the seti. From this touch the Stralith drew her memories and her dreams so that Benajim might—might—heal. They all would do this. Tamyn, Piper, Joclen, even Stoan offered to give what he had. They all had known Benajim and it was that which they could return now, through Crej'Nevan.

What would he wake to find? Tamyn wondered.

Perhaps a better world than before?

In less than fifteen days they would cross back into the C.R. Nothing was certain.

Elen touched the seti.

Nothing at all was certain but hope.

Mark W. Tiedemann

Born in St. Louis, Missouri, in 1954, I grew up during the heyday of America's space race. A fan of science fiction since I can remember, I began a minor literary career by writing and drawing comic books (based largely on favorite movies and tv shows). At 13, I made my first foray into publishing by writing half a dozen short stories and submitting them to the magazines I'd been reading—*If, Analog, Magazine of Fantasy & Science Fiction, Galaxy*, and *Venture*. After a number of polite but succinct rejections, I turned toward other endeavors, and soon took up a camera, leading to a career in photography.

In 1980, I met Donna. She read my stories and novels and began encouraging me to try publishing again. So began the challenge to write and publish, which has resulted in over 40 short stories and 7 novels, with more to come. Along the way, I spent a season at the Clarion Science Fiction & Fantasy Writers Workshop, held at Michigan State University, in 1988. Under the guidance of instructors Tim Powers, Lisa Goldstein, Samuel R. Delany, Kim Stanley Robinson, Kate Wilhelm, and the late Damon Knight, I brought my writing to a level of craft and professionalism that quickly led to my initial sales and publications.

In June 2001, Meisha Merlin Publishing brought out *Compass Reach*, the first volume in my ongoing **Secantis Sequence**. The book quickly garnered critical praise and was shortlisted for the prestigious Philip K. Dick Award. The **Secantis Sequence** is an experiment in depth and detail, a collage approach at constructing a complex, realistic universe in which to set stories. Each volume is intended to be read on its own, but the scope of the world under examination is enriched with each new book. To date, *Metal Of Night* and *Peace And Memory* complete the initial phase. Next will be *Ghost Transit and Other Tales From the Secant*, a collection of the short stories set in the **Secant**, scheduled for summer of 2004.

Besides writing, I'm an amateur musician, and I still produce visual art, both in photography and other media. My interests range across a wide spectrum including history, science, philosophy, film, fine cooking and wine.

For more information, please check out my website at **www.marktiedemann.com**

Come check out our web site for details on these Meisha Merlin authors!

Kevin J. Anderson

Robert Asprin

Robin Wayne Bailey

Edo van Belkom

Janet Berliner

Storm Constantine

John F. Conn

Diane Duane

Sylvia Engdahl

Phyllis Eisenstein

Rain Graves

Jim Grimsley

George Guthridge

Keith Hartman

Beth Hilgartner

P. C. Hodgell

Tanya Huff

Janet Kagan

Caitlin R. Kiernan

Lee Killough

Jacqueline Lichtenberg

Jean Lorrah

George R. R. Martin

Lee Martindale

Jack McDevitt

Mark McLaughlin

Sharon Lee & Steve Miller

James A. Moore

John Morressy

Adam Niswander

Andre Norton

Jody Lynn Nye

Selina Rosen

Kristine Kathryn Rusch

Pamela Sargent

Michael Scott

William Mark Simmons

S. P. Somtow

Allen Steele

Mark Tiedemann

Freda Warrington

David Niall Wilson

www.MeishaMerlin.com

Compass Reach
1-892065-39-8
$16.00

Compass Reach
The first volume of the Secantis Sequence
Philip K. Dick Award nominee

Fargo owes nothing to the Pan Humana. He turned his back on them long ago, when he was stripped of his identity, his class, his position, and all the other ties to human civilization enjoyed by its billions upon billions of citizens. Fargo joined the ranks of the Freeriders. To themselves, Freeriders are interstellar gypsies, the disinvested and therefore the truly free. To most of the rest of society, to the Invested, they are parasites, freeloaders, bums.

But now Fargo finds himself caught up in events that are dragging him back into the folds of human culture and forcing him to choose sides in a struggle to determine the future of humanity in the galaxy. The aliens have come to make treaties, to interact with a paranoid humanity, to bridge the gaps that separate them. They do not understand the resistance they encounter and enlist aid where they can. Among those they pick, Fargo is their most unlikely choice. He is also their most dangerous choice.

To the humans opposed to embracing the new future offered, Fargo is representative of everything they reject, a threat to everything they hold important and fear to lose. He is an outsider, unwanted, unwelcome, in many ways a barbarian, yet indispensable to both sides.

For himself, Fargo has his own reasons for going all the way to Sol, to Earth, into the heart of power.

Fargo has touched an alien mind.

Metal of Night
1-892065-65-7
$16.00

From the introduction to *Metal of Night*
by Jack McDevitt

But none of this touches on what, from my perspective, is the most unusual aspect of *Metal of Night*. Some years ago I was sitting on a panel during which we were discussing how to make villains believable.

I've never liked villains. Not because they twirl mustaches and serve to keep the action rolling when the author can't think of a better way to throw obstacles into the path of his hero. The problem with villains is that, with rare exceptions, they are boring. They're hard to make believable because once you do, they become human and the reader discovers affinities for them, and then they're not villains anymore. There's nobody duller than a homicidal maniac.

Every standard military SF novel has a homicidal maniac stashed somewhere. Usually at the top of the enemy force. He glories in conquest, in torture, in pure malice. He is the focus for the hero's efforts, and we know that, in the final pages, the climactic confrontation will surely come. And we know also who will win.

There's no such character to be found in *Metal of Night*. I'm not suggesting these are noble people. What they are is *ordinary*, which makes them compelling. They've been hardened and damaged by ongoing conflict. People they love have died, sometimes in exceptionally brutal ways. But they hang on, most of them. They do what people have always done, stay out of harm's way while forces no one understands roll over them. They react as one would expect, sometimes out of fear, sometimes out of desperation, but always we recognize why they behave as they do.

This is all by way of saying that both the conflict and the characters are fully realized.